We Were 'posed to Get Married

Emmy's Story, Part 1

By
Kenneth Lee McGee

This is for Sheila.
Without the support of my loving wife, this book
would not exist.

I would like to thank Denise and Stephanie for their support and for sharing their knowledge and opinions. Without their help, this book would not have been possible. I would also like to thank Liz and Sue for reading my books. Yes, this is a series. I will forever be indebted to the people of WriteOn Joliet without whose knowledge I would have never learned the skills necessary to become the writer I am today. Thank you Tom and Colleen.

I want to thank the people from my church who have graciously allowed me to include fragments of their lives as inspirations.

A special thanks to Sue Midlock for creating the cover. http://suesart.wixsite.com/rosewoodseries

I want to thank my wife Sheila for letting me bounce ideas off of her. I would like to thank her for her suggestions. Some of which I have used. Some were off the wall and made me laugh.

Prologue

The wooden stairs squeaked as four-year-old Emmy Colasanti, blue eyes sparkling, scrambled up to the second-floor apartment where she lived. She turned the doorknob, pushed hard on the slightly warped door and jabbered excitedly, "Mommy! Mommy! I know who I want to marry when I get older."

"Oh, and who are you planning to marry, Emmy?" Mom asked as she broke some spaghetti in pieces and dropped them in the boiling water.

"I'm gonna marry Tony from downstairs." Emmy pulled the purple ribbon from her hair, letting her ponytail fall free. "He kissed me, so we are going to get married."

Mom smiled. "Okay, but you need to ask your father when he comes home. He might have something to say about that." She thought about the family who moved in last week. *I don't even know their names.*

Emmy scurried to the room she shared with her six-year-old sister, Diane, grabbed her favorite doll and hugged her.

"Doll Kitty, I'm in love with Tony downstairs, but I won't forget about you. We are going to get married when I grow up."

She hurried back downstairs to play with her three-year-old friend. Dressed in his navy blue jersey with the number fifty-two printed on the front, Tony appeared to be twice her size in spite of being three months younger than Emmy. They ran outside to the small backyard and started playing with his football again. They chased each other around the brown grass and dirt.

Soon his grandmother hollered, "Anthony Peter Bertucci, e 'ora di mangiare."

"Sto arrivando," he responded.

Emmy turned to look at Tony's grandmother. Other than his name, she could not make out exactly what Tony's grandmother said to him.

"I gotta go eat." Tony waved at Emmy as he hustled inside.

A few days later, Emmy sang merrily as she skipped down the squeaky stairs to play with Tony. She reached up to feel the purple ribbon in her hair as she knocked on the door. No one answered her knock. She knocked again, just a bit harder and waited. Still no answer.

"Tony! Where are you?" She knocked even harder. "We're 'posed to play football today."

No one came to the door.

She stomped her foot and banged her small fist on the door as tears began to fill her eyes.

"Tony, open the door!"

But still no one came to the door. Emmy didn't understand why, and cried as she trudged slowly up the stairs and into the kitchen.

"What's wrong, baby?"

"I can't find Tony." Tears ran down Emmy's cheeks as she held up her arms wanting to be hugged. "We're 'posed to play, but I can't find him. What if he doesn't want to marry me anymore?"

Mom wiped her brow and fanned herself to fight the stifling heat, and then continued to iron her husband's work shirt.

Mom did not remember the significance of the day for very long.

As Emmy grew older, the memory faded of the summer of 1984 and the boy she promised to marry.

Chapter One

"It's such a beautiful spring day today. Who would like to go for a walk with me?" Grandpa Colasanti asked. *I'll go nuts if I have to spend another hour in this cramped apartment listening to those people upstairs arguing.*

"I wanna go! I wanna go!" Emmy waved her hand.

"Okay, you can come with me, baby girl. Diane, are you interested in going for a walk?" Grandpa asked.

"No, I'm watching my show," Diane said as she concentrated on the TV.

"I guess it will just be the two of us, Emmy. Where would you like to go?"

"We can walk around the neighborhood, but I can't cross the busy streets. Daddy told me to never cross them."

Grandpa knew exactly which ones Emmy meant. He put on his jacket and covered his wiry gray hair with his baseball cap. Emmy zipped up her windbreaker, and then held Grandpa's hand as they left the apartment.

"How old are you now? Are you three?" he teased as they reached the sidewalk.

"Grandpa!" Emmy put her hands on her hips and rolled her eyes. "I'm going to be seven on my birthday. I'm *not* a baby anymore."

"Oh, that's right. I forgot." He grinned while scratching his chin, and then looked both ways. "Let's go this way, Emmy." He shielded his eyes from the sun.

She looked up and smiled. "I like to walk, but Mommy and Daddy are usually too busy."

"Walking keeps me from feeling old," Grandpa said. "It makes me feel like I'm not even eighty."

Emmy ran around a large tree next to the sidewalk. She jumped up and tried to grab a leaf. "Do you know what kind of tree this is?"

"That's a maple tree."

"How can you tell?"

Grandpa pulled a leaf off of the tree. "By the shape of the

9

leaves."

"I know why trees have leaves in the summer, but not in the winter," Emmy said.

"Why is that, Emmy?" Grandpa waved at a neighbor using an electric trimmer on his evergreen bush. The neighbor ignored Grandpa's wave.

"It's because trees kinda go to sleep in the winter, and when they wake up in the spring, they grow new leaves."

"You are so smart." He patted the top of her head as he heard the siren from a squad car.

"I hear sirens all the time. Daddy said it's because the neighborhood on the other side of the cemetery is a rough part of the city and different kinds of people fight with each other."

"That's true. The whole city has changed and not for the better. When I was younger people helped each other. Now no one will even talk to you."

"I heard Daddy tell Mommy that we might move again this summer. He said we might buy a big house." She spread her arms as far as she could to indicate the huge size of the house.

Grandpa chuckled as he thought, *It's about time you buy another house, Raymond. You and Patricia have been renting for the better part of thirty years. Such a colossal waste of money.*

"Look, Grandpa! There's a big spider." Emmy leaned to get a closer look.

"Don't touch it, Emily." Grandpa waited while Emmy squatted down on her knees. *Diane would scream if she saw a spider.*

"It went into the crack in the sidewalk," Emmy said as she stood up a moment later.

"Let's keep walking," Grandpa said.

"I know my address, and I can even write it out," Emmy informed Grandpa proudly. "The teacher taught us in first grade, but I really knew how to do it in kindergarten."

Grandpa watched a small jet fly overhead. "Where do you live, sweetie?"

"I live at 17254 East Fourth Street in apartment one in South Hampshire, Illinois."

"That's very good. People who live here shorten it to SoHam."

"Why?"

"Because it's shorter and easier to say. Do you know the name of your neighborhood?"

Emmy looked up at her grandfather. "Raynor Park. I think I've always lived in Raynor Park."

Grandpa knew that Raymond and Patricia had probably lived in ten other neighborhoods through the years before the girls were born.

"Why is it called that, Grandpa?" Emmy dropped to her knees to smell a purple flower.

"Well, this used to be a very fancy area where the rich families lived, and a man named Raynor opened the first bank in the city. I guess they named it for him."

Emmy took the time to smell each of the half dozen flowers in the manicured flowerbed before running to catch up with Grandpa. She jumped over a broken section of sidewalk.

"Why?"

"Well, I guess they liked to live here because they could build real big houses, and this area was away from the river." Grandpa stepped off of the sidewalk to let an elderly couple slowly shuffle past. He thought back to his childhood. "Years ago there used to be much larger homes on this street and especially the block over."

Emmy looked at the two one-story houses to her right. "You mean even bigger than these?"

"Oh, yes. Much bigger. My grandfather told me that, in the beginning, East Fifth Street was the most desirable address in the city. Several of the wealthiest families built homes in the 1600 block—including the Colwell family. They still live here, but now their house might be the only one left."

"Do you and Grandma have a lot of money? Is that why you live in a big house?"

"Our house isn't as big as the ones that used to be here." He closed his eyes and recalled a day when his grandmother brought him to that very street. He pictured the large houses that once lined both sides of the wide street.

"Where are they now? What happened to them?" Emmy asked and then raced ahead.

"Over the years most of the large houses were torn down and replaced by smaller ones."

"I know where the river is, Grandpa." She skipped across a side street without him.

"Emily, you stop right there!" Grandpa hollered. "Did you look both ways?"

"Yes, I did. There usually aren't any cars on this street."

"Well, I want you to hold my hand when we cross any of the streets, okay?"

"All right. I'm sorry." Emmy bit her lip. She didn't like it when Grandpa yelled at her. She was used to Mom and Dad yelling, but not Grandpa or Grandma.

Grandpa crossed the street and took her hand. "Do you know the name of the river?"

"I know it, but I can't say it right. It's a weird name."

"It's called the Kinmundy River and a long time ago, back in the 1850s, a group of people built log cabins on the high bluffs." Grandpa waved to another elderly couple, who were working on the flowerbeds in their yard. He smiled when they waved back. "That's where SoHam first started. They chose that area because they could see up and down the river." *You aren't even listening.* Grandpa grinned as Emmy ran ahead, jumped up and slapped a tree branch.

"I read a story about Indians in school. Did Indians live here, Grandpa? Did you have to fight the Indians when you were younger?"

Grandpa ducked under the branch as he caught up to her. "At one time they did, but there aren't any left. They left before I was born." Grandpa laughed. "You must think I'm awfully old, Emmy."

"Are there more than a hundred people in SoHam?"
Grandpa nodded.
"More than a thousand?" Emmy raised her hands in the air.
"Oh, yeah. Much more than that."

12

"Are there more than a gazillion people?"

He laughed and said, "There are over 150,000 people in the city now."

They kept walking and eventually reached Raynor Street—a four-lane street lined on both sides with small businesses..

Emmy shouted to be heard over the sounds of the traffic. "This is one of the busy streets that I can't cross. I don't think you should cross it, either, Grandpa. There are too many cars and trucks."

"We won't cross it, Emmy. We can go this way." He pointed to his right while looking across the street. "We never used to have so many strip malls. There used to be a farm just over there, Emmy."

"What happened to it?"

"The people who lived there probably died, and it was sold." He pointed at a large church. "I helped build that when I was younger."

Emmy ran ahead a short distance and then stopped in front of one of the stores. "Daddy brought me here for ice cream last year."

"Would you like to stop, Emmy?" Grandpa made sure his wallet was in his pocket.

Emmy grinned while bouncing up and down on her toes.

Grandpa opened the door, and they walked up to the counter.

"Can I have a cone with sprinkles, please?" Emmy held her hands together hopefully.

"You can have whatever you want, sweetheart." Grandpa chuckled as he read the sign on the wall. *Robbins Old Fashioned Ice Cream Parlor. Home of two flavors. Three when strawberries are in season.*

The smiling lady behind the counter smoothed down her long reddish-blonde hair and asked, "Hi! What can I get for you today?"

Grandpa noticed her name tag. "My granddaughter would like a vanilla cone with sprinkles, Colleen," he said, "and I'd like a chocolate cone. No sprinkles."

"Coming right up!"

Grandpa helped boost Emmy onto one of the tall stools at the counter along the windows overlooking Raynor Street.

"Grandpa, I'm not a baby. I can get up here without any help."

"I know you can, sweetie. Sometimes I forget how big a girl you are now."

"It's okay. I still love you."

They watched the traffic as they took their time eating their cones.

Emmy licked her fingers when she finished. "Thank you, Grandpa."

"You're welcome, Emmy. Are you ready to finish our walk?"

She jumped down and pushed open the door for Grandpa. She held Grandpa's hand as they continued to walk around Raynor Park.

"This neighborhood has always reminded me of an island," he said as they turned right down another side street and away from busy Raynor Street.

"I know what an island is. It's land that's surrounded on all sides by water." Emmy tilted her head as she thought. "There isn't any water around here, Grandpa, except the river, and that's far away."

"I think the busy streets are kinda like rivers. They isolate Raynor Park," Grandpa said and then explained what *isolate* meant.

Emmy ran ahead, and then turned and faced Grandpa. "There's a park on this street."

"Would you like to stop there?"

"Can we please? I like to swing, and they have a big slide, but I don't ever see any other kids playing there. I wish they would."

Grandpa looked around. "I think most of the people who live here are older, Emmy. Their kids are all grown up." He realized he hadn't seen a single child anywhere on their walk.

"I'm gonna show you how high I can swing. Just watch."

14

Emmy dashed ahead.

By the time Grandpa passed through the mature trees surrounding the park, Emmy was already in a swing.

"Watch me, Grandpa."

He noticed that of the four swings, two were broken. *I bet the city hasn't painted these old swings and slides for thirty years. They're gonna rust away to nothing.*

Grandpa stood on the grass behind Emmy and waited patiently as she kicked her legs and swung as high as possible. *At least the legs are set in concrete. They won't tip over.*

Emmy loved the feel of the breeze on her face as she swung higher and faster.

A few minutes later Grandpa felt a couple of raindrops. "We should get back now, sweetie."

"Okay, Grandpa." Emmy jumped out of the swing as Grandpa cringed. She landed on her feet and pointed. "If you look through there, you can see my school. It's called Robert T. Colwell. Diane goes there, too." Emmy made sure Grandpa could see the red brick school.

"So your father is talking about buying a house, huh?"

"I heard him tell Mommy, and she yelled at him. She said he should stop going to Miller's Bar."

They headed back to the apartment and arrived just before the sky emptied.

Chapter Two

During the summer of 1987, Emmy's parents purchased a home. The clapboard-sided, gray house stood at 16301 East Fifth Street, only a block away from where they currently lived. The Realtor called the place a fixer-upper with good reason. The two-bedroom, one-bath house needed work both inside and out, but matched their price range.

One Sunday afternoon Emmy sat on the old-fashioned radiator by the picture window in the living room waiting for Grandma and Grandpa Colasanti to arrive.

"They're here!" Emmy hollered as Grandpa parked the car in the street.

Emmy ran out the front door and flew down the cracked concrete steps to greet them while Diane waited inside. Joseph Colasanti walked around the car, opened the passenger door and helped his wife Mary.

"Hi, Grandma! Hi, Grandpa!" Emmy bounced on her toes and waved as she waited on the sidewalk.

Grandma held onto Grandpa's arm to keep her balance as she stepped over the curb and onto the grass. She smiled at Emmy. "I'm all right now, Joseph. I think Emmy wants a hug." Grandma smoothed out her dark blue dress which made her seem as wide as she was tall.

Grandpa nearly stumbled as Emmy wrapped her arms around his legs and held on.

"Hey, take it easy, Emmy. You almost knocked me over," he said as he took his first look at the house.

Emmy let go and grabbed his hand. "Come on in, Grandpa."

He looked back at Mary. "Are you all right?"

"Go! I'll be there in a minute."

Diane opened the door as Grandpa came up the steps. Emmy hurried back to Grandma's side.

Grandpa patted Diane's back. "How's my big girl today?"

"I'm fine," she answered and then wrinkled her nose. *Oooh, Grandpa, you need a shower. You smell old.*

16

Diane stood in the doorway and watched as Grandma gingerly avoided the cracks in the sidewalk. Grandma stopped and looked at her two granddaughters. *You girls are looking more and more like sisters the older you get. You have your mother's nose and cheekbones and your father's dark complexion.*

Both girls had long, dark hair, though Diane's hair was straight and she had brown eyes instead of blue like Emmy.

Diane rolled her eyes. *What is taking you so long?*

Grandma reached up to the bun in her gray hair as a gust of wind rustled the overgrown bushes along the front of the house.

"Sometime today, Grandma," Diane muttered.

Grandma finally stepped inside, and Emmy tried to stretch her arms around her rotund grandmother. "I'm so happy to see you, Grandma."

"I'm glad to see you, too, sweetheart. I need to talk to your mother. Where is she?"

Just then Patricia Colasanti walked out of her bedroom. "Hello, please have a seat." She pointed to the couch.

"Thank you, Patricia. I need to sit down. My knees are hurting more than usual." Grandma Colasanti brushed the dusty couch with her hand and then sat down.

Mom sat in her recliner facing her mother-in-law. "I'm sorry you aren't feeling well."

Grandpa remained standing. "I want to see the house."

Emmy took his hand. "Come on, Grandpa, let me show you my room. It's in the back." Emmy held Grandpa's hand as she led him through the living and dining rooms.

Grandpa paused and noticed. *These walls could use a fresh coat of paint and the carpet needs replacing.* When he entered the kitchen, he stopped, looked around the room and shook his head. *I would gut this entire kitchen and start over.*

"This is our room," Emmy said as she beamed at Grandpa. "We have a dresser and a bed and behind that door is a huge closet. I can even walk into it."

To Emmy, it might have appeared huge, but Grandpa remained unimpressed as he noted the faded, old-fashioned looking floral print wallpaper.

17

"I'm glad you like your new room, Emmy. You should show it to your grandma."

Emmy ran out of the room, nearly tripping on a curled up part of the threadbare, room-sized carpet, to find Grandma Mary.

Grandpa walked through the kitchen, glancing with disgust at the metal cabinets and white appliances. "I hope that old stove doesn't burn down the house. Though, on second thought..." He muttered, shook his head, and walked out onto the covered back porch. He saw his son in the backyard and walked down the rickety wooden stairs to join him.

"You want a beer, Dad? I got some in the garage."

"No thanks, I'm good."

Father and son stared at each other for a moment. The family resemblance apparent in their lined faces and wiry, gray hair. Raymond stood two inches taller than his father and outweighed him by fifty pounds. Most of it in his beer belly.

"Well, what do you think?" Raymond asked after taking another sip of his beer.

Grandpa Colasanti noticed a few broken boards in the five-foot-high white fence. "You want the truth?"

"Yeah! Tell me the truth. I want to know what you think."

"I hope you're handy with tools. You're going to need to do a lot of work around here."

"I know that. I couldn't afford anything better. At least the neighborhood is decent."

Grandpa looked at the houses on either side. "You've got the smallest house on the block."

"I'd rather have a small house in a good neighborhood than one of those huge places in some parts of the city."

"That's not what you said when you bought that large house all those years ago," Grandpa said.

"I was younger back then. I assumed my salary would grow, and we could afford the house. I realize now it was a mistake to have such as large mortgage payment. I've learned my lesson. We can make the payments on this place even if Patricia doesn't work full-time."

"You should have sold the place before the bank

repossessed it."

"I tried to sell it, but the market sucked. No one would offer enough money," Raymond said.

"I told you that Jim and I would help you out. You could have found a better house."

"And I told you that I don't want any money from you or my father-in-law," Raymond replied as his anger grew.

"Did you pay off St. Bart's yet?" Grandpa asked. "I offered to..."

"I know you did, and my answer is still the same. I pay my own bills."

"You wouldn't have had such a large bill if you hadn't lost your job back then, but that's water under the bridge," Grandpa said as he watched Emmy showing Grandma the back porch. *She's doing fine now.*

Raymond turned and saw Emmy. "Emily! Don't jump off the porch again. I warned you what would happen the last time."

"I was just showing Grandma the backyard. I wasn't really going to jump down," Emmy explained.

Raymond looked at the back of the house. "I'm fifty years old, and I know how to fix this place up. We won't stay here forever. I'll sell it and buy something bigger."

"Have Patricia's parents seen this place yet?"

"Yeah, the Sanduskys stopped over yesterday. He offered to lend a hand if I need help. He volunteered to help paint the garage and fix those stairs." He crushed his Budweiser can as he pointed first to the garage, and then the porch. "Patricia's mother didn't act as upset as you and Mom. She suggested a few ideas, but they didn't make us feel like we're living in a dump like you are."

"I'm just trying to be honest."

"Give me a year or two, and I'll have the place fixed up as nice as that big house a couple doors down."

One morning after breakfast, Mom informed Emmy and Diane, "Today we are going to walk over to your school. When school starts, I am going to start working again, and I won't always be home in the morning to see you off. I want to make sure you know how to get there from our new house."

"Mom! We know how to get there," Diane whined. "It's the same one I have always gone to."

"Yes, but you have to take a different street to get there."

Diane rolled her eyes at her mother and muttered, "I'm not a baby."

"I need to show Emmy the way, so you're coming along."

They walked out the front door and turned left at the sidewalk. As they neared the corner of Fifth Street and Clement, Emmy stopped and peered through the black wrought iron fence at the large red brick house with white shutters that occupied the oversized lot. "That house looks like a mansion."

"Come on, Emmy! Let's get this over with," Diane pleaded.

"I'm coming. Do you know who lives here?" Emmy kept her head turned and her eyes fixed on the house and another building she thought might be a huge garage. She tripped on a raised part of the cracked sidewalk and fell to her knees.

"Emily, watch where you are going," Mom scolded.

"It's okay, Mommy," she answered. "I didn't rip my pants."

"Clumsy kid," Diane muttered. "You're always skinning your knees."

The buildings on the corner lot were older than all of the others on the block, but even Emmy could tell they were in better shape than the house where she lived. The manicured yard and well-maintained flowerbeds gave the property more curb appeal than any other house in the area.

They continued walking until they were across the street from the school.

"Do you know how to get here, Emmy?" Mom asked.

"I won't get lost."

They took a different way home.

"Emmy, this is the alley in back of our house."

Emmy nodded her head, but Diane responded sarcastically. "Geez, Mom. We know that. We play in the alley sometimes. We hide behind the fences and the garages."

"You shouldn't let your sister play in the alley," Mom said. "She might get hurt."

When school started in the late summer, Emmy and Diane cut through the gravel alley to save time getting to Robert T. Colwell Elementary School three blocks away. Both girls carried a book bag on their shoulder.

On the Tuesday after Labor Day as she and Diane were walking along the alley to school, Emmy noticed a boy come out of the large house on the corner. Emmy turned her head to look back at him, and then reached out to hold Diane's hand.

"What are you doing, Emmy?" Diane pushed Emmy's hand away, as she saw one of her friends walk past the alley on the sidewalk along Clement Street. "Hey, Glenda, wait for me." Diane took off running leaving Emmy behind.

Emmy froze for a moment as the boy approached. "Diane! Why did you leave me here by myself." Emmy watched the older boy as he came closer and closer. She thought about running away, but her feet wouldn't move.

The boy caught up to Emmy, stood alongside and said, "My name is Kenneth Travis Robert Colwell, but everyone calls me Kenny. Mom calls me Kenneth Travis Robert if she's mad at me. I'm ten and in fifth grade," he said with a smile. "What's your name? How old are you?"

"Emmy," she answered shyly. "Emmy Colasanti. I'm seven and in second grade."

"Pleased to meet you, m'lady." He shook her little hand. "You just moved into the gray house, right?"

"Yes." She tried not to stare at his funny looking ears sticking out from under his close-cropped hair.

"Was that your sister with you?"

Emmy nodded but didn't say anything.

"Do you have any brothers? There aren't many kids in this neighborhood, so I was hoping you might have a brother."

"It's just me and Diane."

"Oh, too bad. I was looking for someone who likes to play football."

Emmy's eyes lit up. "I have a football, and I play catch with Daddy sometimes. I could play with you."

"Yeah, maybe we could try that sometime even if you're a

21

girl," Kenny teased. "I could carry that bag for you if it's too heavy. I wouldn't mind."

Emmy smiled at him and handed him the book bag.

"This is really heavy for a little girl like you, but I can handle it all right."

He didn't frighten her as much now.

The next morning Emmy told Diane about her new friend. "His name's Kenny and he's ten. He carried my bag for me yesterday."

That got Diane's attention. "You mean the boy from the big house with the funny looking ears?"

"Yeah, why?"

"Nothing."

When Emmy and Diane left for school, they saw Kenny waiting for them in the alley. Diane rushed up to him as Emmy trailed behind.

"Hi, are you Diane?" Kenny asked.

Diane grinned. "Yes, I'm Emily's big sister. I hear you are ten."

"I thought her name was Emmy?"

"I'm Diane Lynn Colasanti, and she's Emily Olivia, but everyone calls her Emmy except for Grandma Isabel." Diane smiled at Kenny and then sighed. "Oh, my bag is so heavy. Would you carry it for me, please?"

He looked at Diane, and then smiled at Emmy, who caught up.

"Maybe I should carry Emmy's bag."

"She doesn't have anything in it except for her lunch. I have these heavy books."

Kenny took a deep breath. "All right. Just today though."

Diane walked beside Kenny and made Emmy follow along behind.

"Emmy told me she can play football. Can you play, Diane?" Kenny asked.

Diane shook her head. "No, I don't like football. Daddy plays catch with her because he wanted her to be a boy."

"I was hoping to find some boys to play football."

Diane knew she had to impress him somehow and quickly thought of something. "I've kissed a boy before. Emmy's just a baby."

Kenny stopped walking. "Have you really?"

"Yes, I kissed Josh Adamson. He's in sixth grade."

"But you can't play football, huh?" Kenny looked at both girls for a moment. He decided he would carry Diane's bag today, but from now on, he would carry Emmy's.

After that, Emmy walked to school with Kenny every day. He often carried her bag, and they became good friends despite their age difference. Many times as they walked to school, he would sing a song to her, and sometimes she would sing along. After school she would play with Kenny in his large backyard. The lot the Colwell home occupied was three times as large as any other homesite on the block. They had plenty of room in the backyard to play her favorite sport—football.

Near the end of September, Emmy sat reading a book in class when a new student took a seat in the empty desk next to her. She smiled at him, but they didn't talk. Several days passed, and Emmy realized the new boy didn't say much or fit in with the other kids. He stayed by himself at recess, much like Emmy, so she decided to be brave. As he perched on the front edge of a bench, watching the other kids playing, Emmy plopped down next to him.

"My name is Emmy. What's yours?"

"Barry Newton," he shyly replied.

"I have a football. Wanna play catch?" Emmy asked.

"Okay. Nobody else will play with me. Why do you want to?"

"Nobody likes to play with me, either, so I think we should be friends, and we will both have someone to play with. The girls won't play catch, and the boys won't let me play with them because I'm a girl."

"I'll be your friend if you will be mine, Emmy," Barry replied hopefully.

"Okay, I'll be your friend."

They stood a few feet away from each other, and Emmy threw her football to him. It bounced off his hands and knocked off his glasses.

Emmy ran over, "Are you all right?"

"I'm okay. I guess I'm not very good at playing catch. I don't think I've ever played that game before."

Emmy tilted her head, looking at him curiously, and asked, "Doesn't your dad ever play catch with you? Daddy plays catch with me all the time."

"My dad doesn't play games with me."

"Hold your hands out, and I'll throw you the football again," Emmy said.

This time Barry caught it. He smiled and tossed the ball back to Emmy.

"Do you have any brothers and sisters? I have one sister, Diane, and she's older than me." Emmy tossed the ball to Barry.

The football bounced off of his hands. "I don't have any brothers or sisters. It's usually just my mom and me." He picked up the ball and tossed it toward Emmy. "My dad works all week long, and I only get to see him on the weekends once in a while." Barry remained quiet for a moment before he asked, "Do you have a mom and dad, Emmy?"

"Sure I do. Doesn't everyone have a mom and dad?"

"My mom and dad used to yell at each other. Now they don't because Dad doesn't live with us."

"Mommy yells at Daddy all the time. He yells back sometimes, but, usually, he goes to Miller's Bar. He took me there a couple times. I sat on this big counter and drank a glass of milk and ate peanuts. I didn't like it because of the smoke, and the men would yell at each other."

"Maybe your dad will find a new place to live."

"Why? He lives with us."

Just before dinnertime that day, Emmy dashed from her bedroom at the sound of voices coming from the dining room. "Grandpa is here!" She slid on the linoleum kitchen floor, grabbed the corner of the counter and stopped abruptly at the sight of the two men.

24

Grandpa Colasanti stabbed his son in the chest with a finger as he said sternly, "I've told you a hundred times to drop the matter, Raymond. It's my money, and I will do what I think is right with it."

"I could have used that money to open my own business," Raymond said.

"Yeah? What kind of business?"

Raymond shrugged. "I don't know. An auto repair garage or a liquor store."

"Hmmmph! That would have been a great idea."

"All right," Raymond said. "Maybe not a liquor store, but I could have come up with something."

"Yeah, well, Bill Robertson had a good plan, and that technology market is going to be huge. I gave you a chance to get in on the ground floor, but you're too stubborn."

"I don't want to take a chance on wasting what little money I have."

"You could get a job that pays more, you know?"

"I'm happy with the electric company, and I got my job without any help from you."

Grandpa laughed. "A janitor. That's such a prestigious position. You should have stayed in school and gotten your diploma. You're smart enough. Just lazy."

"I'm a custodial engineer, and I have two men working under me," Raymond explained.

"If you would stay away from the beer and wine, maybe you would still be working for me."

"I don't want to work for you, and I'll drink as much as I want."

"You've made that abundantly clear."

"Get off my back," Raymond said and then walked away.

Emmy didn't understand why they were fighting and tried to stay out of the way. She feared that her father and grandfather would get so upset with each other that she would not be allowed to see her grandfather and grandmother. Or worse yet, her father would move away like Barry's father.

25

Chapter Three

Emmy burst into the tiny kitchen, narrowly avoiding her mom and ran straight to the calendar tacked on the pantry door.

"In two more days it will be my birthday!"

Mom looked up from the pot of oatmeal she was stirring just long enough to glance at the red circle around July eighth. "You're right, baby. Is there anything special you would like for dinner that night?"

Emmy thought about it. "Could I have French toast, please?"

"French toast! Why on earth would you want that for dinner?"

"Because I like it! Grandma made it for me last week, and I loved it. Oh, please?"

A half smile formed on Mom's lips as she shook her head at Emmy's exuberance. "I'll have to make something else for your father, but you can have French toast."

Two days later Emmy sat on the couch and carefully opened her birthday present from Grandma Colasanti. "Grandma, I love it. It's perfect." She smiled and opened her eyes wide. "What is it?"

"It's a music box, Emily."

"Does it really play music?"

"Yes, it does. It's very old. My grandfather made it in Italy. Here." Grandma handed Emmy a small key. "You have to wind it up with this," Grandma said. "It plays Claire de Lune. Don't ever lose it, because it's a magic key."

Enraptured, Emmy gasped, "It is?"

Grandma nodded. "The key opens a secret compartment. I'll show you."

Emmy watched closely as Grandma inserted the key and turned it. The drawer slid out without a sound.

"That is so cool, Grandma. Let me try." Emmy closed the compartment, listened for the click, and then opened it.

"You can use this secret compartment for your most

26

precious mementos, and they will be safe forever."

"Thank you, Grandma. I'll be sure I don't ever lose the key." Emmy hugged her grandmother and kissed her cheek.

When Emmy left the room, Mom turned to Grandma Colasanti. "Why didn't you give the music box to Diane? She's the oldest."

"I thought about it," Grandma said, "but Diane would toss it aside and probably break it. Emmy, on the other hand, will treasure it the way I have."

Emmy sat on her bed and listened to the entire song. Then she placed her music box in her drawer of the dresser she shared with Diane. She placed the key on a string and hid it under a loose board in the corner of the room.

It was the last present she ever received from her Grandma Colasanti, who passed away before Christmas. Grandpa Colasanti died two months later. Emmy understood enough to know that she would never see either of them again. A week after her grandfather's funeral Emmy sat on the living room couch with her father.

"Daddy, do you miss Grandma and Grandpa?" Emmy asked. "I miss them, but Diane said they were really old and that's what happens to old people."

Dad turned down the volume on the TV. "Everyone dies eventually, sweetie. Grandma and Grandpa lived a full life."

"Are they in heaven now?"

"Of course. They were good Catholics and went to mass several times a year," Dad said. "Now they aren't sick anymore, and one of these years we will see them again. You just have to keep them in your memory."

"I will always take good care of my music box, and I'll think of them every time I play it." Emmy jumped down and hurried to her bedroom. She took her music box out, wound it up and listened to the song.

Dad turned the TV back up. He watched and episode of *Seinfeld* without another thought of his parents.

Another school year ended, and Emmy dreamed about owning a purple bicycle. She knew how to ride a bike because her friend, Kenny, taught her how to ride a month after they met. In early July, Mom surprised Emmy. Mom led Emmy into the cluttered garage.

"Look what I found at the garage sale down the street. It's nearly your tenth birthday, and it only cost five dollars. I thought you might like to have a bike of your own." Mom gave Emmy's shoulders a squeeze. "Now you won't have to use Diane's old bike. What do you think?"

"Thanks, Mom. It's okay that it's green and not purple," she said as she ran her hand along the bike leaning against the wall. "Do you think Daddy could paint it purple for me?"

"We can ask, honey. I'll talk to him at dinner." Mom smiled. *I don't think I've ever seen a purple bike.*

Later, Dad laid out his biking rules in between bites of spaghetti. "You can ride anywhere in the neighborhood, but if I catch you crossing any busy streets, I'll take your bike away."

Emmy listened intently nodding her head. "I promise, Daddy."

"I'll see if I can find some purple paint," he said as he reached for his can of beer, "but I won't make any promises."

"Oh, thank you, Daddy!" Emmy gushed.

Diane rolled her eyes. "Why would anyone want a purple bike?"

Emmy agreed to abide by her father's rules, and rode her bike all through the Raynor Park neighborhood. She found out where Barry Newton lived, and they rode their bikes together.

While riding bikes one warm summer afternoon, Barry suggested, "Let's go to Darby's Dogs 'cause I'm hungry." He took off on his bike. "I'm going to get there first."

Emmy followed Barry to the corner where they waited. "I can't cross this street because I promised Daddy I wouldn't."

"Oh, come on. We'll cross with the light. It will be okay. I've done it before lots of times." Barry pushed his glasses up as he watched the traffic signal.

Emmy shook her head. "I'm not supposed to, Barry. Look at all the cars and trucks whizzing past."

"I'm going. Are you coming or not?" Barry asked.

Emmy wasn't sure what to do, but when the light turned green, and Barry took off, she followed. As she crossed the street, she heard a car honk its horn.

"That wasn't so hard, was it?" Barry asked, as he jumped off his bike and leaned it against the side of the building.

"That's not the point. I promised Daddy I wouldn't cross this street, and now I've broken that promise."

"So big deal. Just don't tell him. How's he ever gonna know."

"I'm not gonna lie to him if he ever asks."

They went inside, ordered hot dogs and pop with the money that Barry saved from his allowance and sat outside to eat.

Emmy asked, "Do you have any money left for some more pop? I'm still thirsty."

"There's a water fountain over there. Give me your cup, and I'll fill it up for you."

Barry filled Emmy's cup with water, but as he carried it to her, he tripped on the sidewalk and spilled the water all over Emmy's shorts and shirt.

"Barry! Look what you did. I'm soaked."

"I'm sorry, Emmy. I didn't mean to do it."

"Oh, it's all right. It's only water. I probably won't melt."

"If you do melt, can I have your bike?" Barry teased her.

At dinner that night Emmy took her usual seat closest to the bedroom door. Mom passed around the bowl of pasta. A couple of minutes later, Dad asked, "Emily Olivia, have you been obeying my rules about not crossing the busy streets?"

Emmy's heart beat faster. She nearly choked on a piece of ravioli. She knew something was up because her father used her full name.

"I just happened to be driving along Campbell Avenue when I saw two kids on bikes crossing right in front of me. I honked at them. Then I realized who they were. Do you know anything about this?"

29

She was tempted to lie to him but confessed.

"I'm sorry, Daddy, but I went to the hot dog stand today with Barry. He wanted to go and…" She started to blame Barry but then continued, "I decided to go with him."

"I'm very pleased that you told the truth, Emmy. You do understand that I still need to punish you, though."

Emmy lowered her eyes. "I know."

Dad looked at Emmy and made his decision. "I think that I will take your bike away for one week. That will make more of an impression on you than a paddling which is what your mother suggested."

"A whole week?" Emmy sighed.

"Yes, you have to promise me that you will leave your bike in the garage and not ride it for one week."

"I promise, Daddy," Emmy answered as her lip quivered.

After dinner Emmy hugged her father and went to her room.

"I should have never listened to you, Barry. I'm so mad at you," Emmy muttered as she plopped onto the bed and stared at the ceiling.

Emmy stayed upset at Barry for getting her in trouble and didn't see him for a week. For seven days she tried not to think about her bike. She walked everywhere instead.

"Emmy, have you kept your promise to me?" her father asked.

"Yes, Daddy. I have not touched my bike all week. I haven't even gone in the garage to look at it. Does this mean I can ride it again?"

"Yes, Emmy."

"Thank you, Daddy. I promise I won't disobey you again."

Emmy sprinted out to the garage and opened the side door. She flipped on the light, and against the wall, leaned her bike. At least she thought it was her bike. Instead of her rusty old green bike, though, she saw a freshly painted purple bike. Emmy walked out of the garage with a hand over her mouth. Seeing Mom and Dad on the porch, she ran to them.

"Oh, Daddy! You painted my bike purple for me," Emmy exclaimed jumping up and down. "Thank you! Thank you!"

"You're welcome, sweetie," Dad said as he blinked his eyes rapidly.

Mom shrugged her shoulders. *What a waste of money to buy purple paint. We're never going to use it for anything else.* Mom hollered, "Make sure you stay in the neighborhood now, or else I will take it away for good."

Since Emmy regained permission to ride her bike again, she rode to Barry's house. She saw him outside playing in the yard. Emmy jumped off her bike, marched up to him and punched him in the stomach.

"Ow! Emmy, why did you do that?"

"That's for getting me in trouble last week. Remember when we went to Darby's?"

"Yeah," Barry replied.

"Well, my dad saw us, and I got in trouble. He took my bike away for a whole week."

"I'm sorry. I didn't know you were serious when you told me about not crossing the street. Is that a new bike?"

"No, it's the same bike, but Daddy painted it for me. Doesn't it look super?"

"It's okay. At least it's not pink."

"Let's go for a bike ride, but this time we gotta stay in the neighborhood."

Chapter Four

"Hey, Emmy, wait up."

She turned around and saw Barry and a couple of other boys.

"Why are you walking to school by yourself this morning?" Barry asked.

"Maybe because we're heading to Adolph Tockstein Junior High, and Kenny and Diane are at Roosevelt High now."

"I know that." Barry noticed Emmy was wearing her usual jeans, sweatshirt and scuffed sneakers. "You don't have to be a smart aleck."

"Sorry, Barry."

"Hey, shrimp, are you gonna play football with us after school today?" one of the other boys asked. "We need someone like you. Someone real short and light weight."

Emmy stood slightly under four and a half feet tall and weighed less than seventy pounds which made her one of the smallest girls in the seventh grade.

"I can't. My mother is making me take piano lessons."

The guys laughed. "Why? Doesn't she know you'd rather play football?"

"She's making me take lessons so I *can't* play football. She's afraid I'll get hurt or something."

Emmy pushed the walk button, and they waited at the corner for the traffic light to change. Emmy exchanged glances at the two older boys who were in eighth grade.

"You know you're kinda cute... for a kid," the guys teased her.

"And you guys are kinda ugly. You remind me of cavemen."

They crossed the street and left Raynor Park. The junior high was three blocks ahead.

The taller of the boys pulled on her ponytail. "Can you play anything on the piano, Emmy?"

"Stop that, you creep." Emmy smacked his arm. "Of course I can play some songs."

"I've heard Emmy singing with Kenny Colwell, and she actually sounds pretty good," Barry said.

"Yeah, so what? Hey, Emmy, are you gonna wear a dress for Picture Day?"

Emmy wrinkled her nose at the thought of wearing a dress.

"Do you even own a dress?"

"I suppose Mom will make me. She always does." She kicked a pop can toward the street. *I wonder if the kids at school know the dresses I wear are Diane's hand-me-downs. Some of the other girls are such snobs about the fancy designer clothes they wear.*

"Well, if you change your mind about the piano lesson, we're gonna meet at the park after school. Maybe we can talk Barry into playing."

"Fat chance of that," the taller boy said. "He's too much of a nerd. He's always afraid we're gonna hurt him or break his stupid glasses."

"Hey! Leave Barry alone," Emmy yelled. "It's not his fault he isn't very good at sports. None of you guys know how to do anything on a computer like Barry can."

"Yeah, well, who wants to work on a stupid computer, anyway?"

In the fall of her first year at Roosevelt High, Diane convinced her parents to allow her to go to a school-sponsored dance with Glenda Matuzak. The girls selected two boys to double date with them. Glenda chose her date because of his access to his parents' 1990 Nissan Maxima. Diane decided that Glenda's date's best friend satisfied her requirements. He knew how to kiss.

A few days later, Diane walked into the kitchen. "Are we having leftover spaghetti for dinner again? I'm tired of it." She was still mad about being grounded for staying out past midnight after the dance.

Mom slammed the refrigerator door closed. "Hey! I just got home from work. I don't feel like spending an hour cooking something right now. If you're hungry, warm up the spaghetti. I

33

need to change clothes."

"I'll warm up the spaghetti, Mom," Emmy said.

"I'll get it started." Mom pulled a pot from the cabinet and set it on the stove. "Make sure you stir it, Emmy. I'll be right back."

Ten minutes later they were sitting at the kitchen table. Diane frowned and leaned on her elbow as she picked at the spaghetti. After playing football with Kenny and some other guys after school, Emmy was hungry. She ate the leftover spaghetti without complaint.

Mom watched Diane. "That's all I'm making for dinner, so either eat that or go hungry. I have to meet my friends at seven."

"More bingo?" Diane asked sarcastically.

"Yes, and I don't know when your father is coming home. You have to keep an eye on Emmy tonight. Don't go anywhere and leave her by herself. Don't drag her down to Darby's and leave her there, either. Mr. Darby is not her babysitter."

Diane raised her eyebrows. *Oh, maybe Mom forgot I'm supposed to be grounded until Sunday.* She kept herself from smiling and frowned. "Mom, I had to watch Emmy all summer long. I'm tired of it."

"Diane, you have to keep an eye on Emmy because otherwise she will be home by herself, or else hanging out with that Colwell boy."

"She's twelve and going to be a teenager on her next birthday," Diane complained.

"She just turned twelve," Mom said as she glared at Diane.

"She likes to stay home by herself, Mom. She feels in the way if she comes with me."

Mom gripped her fork tighter.

"None of my other friends have to bring their little sister, or brother, along. Why do I have to be punished? Is it because you don't trust me? Huh, is that why?

Mom pointed a finger at Diane. "That's not true. I trust you, but I don't completely trust any boy you might be with."

"You don't want me to have any fun, so you make Emmy come along and spy on me for you."

34

"It's not my fault I have to work so many hours. If your father would stop spending so much time at Miller's Bar, maybe I could be home to watch Emmy."

After quietly listening to the conversation, Emmy spoke up, "I'm old enough to come home after school and take care of myself."

"I don't want you to be alone," Mom said.

"I can always hang out with Kenny. He doesn't mind. His parents are usually home. They even make him do his homework before he does anything else."

"I hate doing homework," Diane interrupted. "Teachers give us homework just so we can't have any fun. I can't wait until I'm out of school."

"Well, I like to make sure I get mine done so I can get good grades," Emmy said. "I might want to go to college someday."

"Why are his parents always home? Don't they have to work?" Mom glanced at the clock as she shoved the spaghetti into her mouth.

"Mr. Colwell has an office in the house. Kenny said he does some financial consulting now."

"Did he retire from that big firm?"

"I guess so. I never asked, and his mom does charity work or something. Kenny said she's on a bunch of committees."

"Probably a bunch of gossiping old women," Mom said.

Diane grinned. *You mean just like you, Mom.*

"I don't want you to be pestering the Colwells. I'm sure they must get tired of you..." Mom stopped in mid-sentence.

Diane pushed her plate of spaghetti away and stomped her feet. "It really ruins my social life to have her hanging out with me after school. It's an absolute kiss of death if I have to drag her along on a date."

"You are still too young to go on dates by yourself, so that is why I want you to take Emmy along."

"The Colwells don't mind me spending time with Kenny. I get my homework done. Then Kenny and I play his CDs. He likes to play his guitar and sing, and sometimes I play along on their piano."

35

"He's too old for you," Mom stated between bites of spaghetti.

"He's only three years older than me. That's not any different than Diane's friends. She always hangs out with older guys," Emmy replied.

"That doesn't mean you are allowed to." Mom finished her dinner, stood up and put the plate in the sink.

From the moment they met, Diane thought Kenny liked Emmy better and felt envious.

"Do you know she played football with the guys after school again?"

"Thanks, Diane!" Emmy glared at Diane with a look that said, "You're gonna pay for this."

"How many times have I told you not to play football anymore, Emily?" Mom scolded. "You're gonna get hurt."

Emmy explained, "We didn't play tackle, just two-hand touch."

"Yeah, and I bet the guys liked touching you." Diane grinned.

"That's enough!" Mom yelled. "No more football! I don't want you giving those boys a chance to touch you."

"They don't touch me like you're thinking, Diane." Emmy barely refrained from punching her sister.

"Maybe I should play football with you. I could meet some cute guys that way," Diane teased. "I wouldn't mind how they touched me."

"That's enough! I'm going to have a talk with your father if he ever gets home from that bar." Mom stomped out of the room.

Emmy and Diane sat in silence for a moment.

Emmy whispered, "That's all you ever think about. I bet you and Glenda flirt with every guy at school."

"No, just the cute older guys," Diane smirked.

Emmy stuck her tongue out at Diane.

Diane stood up and dumped her spaghetti in the garbage. "It's a waste of time going out with freshmen or sophomores. They can't even drive."

On January 20, 1993, Diane turned fifteen and received permission from her parents to go on solo dates on Friday and Saturday. Now she didn't have to sneak around to see her boyfriends. Her parents imposed a midnight curfew and one other rule: her parents must meet the boy taking her out. She went out with a different guy every weekend, so she never got too serious about any certain boy. Then in March, Diane started spending time with Owen Porter, a neighborhood boy up the street.

Mom glanced up from her kitchen chair as Diane rushed past. "Hold on! Where are you going?"

"I'm going over to Owen's. We might go to a show."

"Is Owen that boy with the funny haircut?" Mom asked. "The one who's always wearing that long black coat even when it's warm out?"

"It's stylish," Diane said.

"It's stupid. One side of his head is almost shaved and the other is long. It's like his barber screwed up," Mom said and then laughed.

"He's a trendsetter, Mom."

"You have to be home by midnight," Mom said.

"I'll try. Don't wait up." Diane grabbed her coat and raced out the door.

Diane hurried down the alley to the Porter house. She banged on the back door and listened to the sound of loud music from somewhere upstairs. She waited for half a minute and then banged on the door again. "Open the stinking door, Owen. It's freezing out here." She shifted from foot to foot, stamping her feet against the cold. The door opened, and Diane rushed into the warmth. "About time you let me in."

"Sorry, I didn't hear you." Owen smiled and kissed her cheek.

She rolled her eyes. "You knew I was coming over."

He shrugged and then grinned.

"Owen, why do I have to walk over here to your house?" Diane took off her coat and gloves and hung them on an empty hook. "Why can't you pick me up like you do for your other dates? It's freezing."

Owen shut the back door. "I've told you before, Diane. Your father doesn't like me," he said remembering the day Mr. Colasanti caught him coming out of his garage with his power saw. Owen ran for his life and now avoided going anywhere near the Colasanti house.

"Are we gonna go somewhere, or just stay here?"

"Let's go up to my room, and then maybe we can go out."

The friendship between Emmy and Kenny Colwell grew even stronger. Though now in his second year of high school, she saw him several times a week. Kenny and Emmy shared a very special interest—music.

"Hey, Emmy, you'll never believe what I'm doing on Wednesday," Kenny said on Saturday.

"What?" Emmy waited as Kenny opened the door to Darby's.

"I'm gonna play my guitar at church for the teen service."

"Why? I've never seen anyone play a guitar at St. John's. Course, I haven't been there for a while."

"The youth pastor thought it would be a good idea to add a guitar. The lady who plays the piano doesn't want to keep doing it. Wanna go with me?"

"I doubt that Mom would let me go on a school night. Maybe I could sometime in the summer if you're still doing it."

"I'm sure I will. You know how much I like to play my guitar and sing."

As their first year of high school neared the end, Diane and Glenda enjoyed an increasing popularity with the upperclassmen. Word spread throughout the school of both girls' willingness to make sure their dates had a good time.

Chapter Five

"Are you ready for school to start tomorrow, Em?" Kenny handed Emmy a cold Coke and sat next to her on a wooden bench in his back yard.

"Thanks." She smiled, popped the tab of the Coke and took a drink. "I guess so, but I'm a little nervous. Are you gonna walk with me?"

"I suppose I could do that for your first day of high school. Roosevelt High can be a bit intimidating. I'll meet you in the alley in the morning." Kenny took a long drink of his Coke.

"I see you got a haircut. Did your father make you?" Emmy ran a finger through his hair.

"He strongly suggested I get it cut." Kenny ran his hand through his now only shoulder length hair and brushed against Emmy's hand. "I figured I should get it cut for school. Some of the teachers are rather strict about hair length."

She pulled her hand away. "I like it. Don't cut it any shorter or else your ears will stick out."

"You're so funny, Em."

Emmy rushed to the alley the next morning; she didn't want Kenny to leave without her.

"Hi, Em, are you ready for this?" Kenny smiled and waved as he saw her running toward him.

"I'm kinda scared, but at the same time, I'm really looking forward to high school." She looked up at him and smiled, but then she bit her lip. *I have this whole year to be in school with you.*

They walked out of the alley and turned onto Clement Street.

He looked at her hair. "Did you do those braids or did your mother?"

"Mom made Diane do them. Do you like how they look? I think they make me look younger."

"I really like it when you have your hair done like that," he said. *It really does make you look younger, though.* He grabbed one of the braids. "At least your mom didn't make you wear your hair in pigtails."

Emmy turned and grabbed his arm. "Diane and I had to talk her out of that. She originally wanted me to. God! That would have been so embarrassing."

Kenny remembered a time when Emmy wore pigtails to school, and the older boys teased her.

"Kenny, I know you probably don't want to be seen with a freshman since you're a senior, but I promise not to get in the way."

"Emmy, you can walk to school with me any day you want. In fact, most days I plan to drive to school. When I do, you can have a ride. You are my friend, and I would never be ashamed of that."

"Are you sure? I don't want your friends to think you hang around with junior high kids, 'cause I know I still look like one."

"I don't care if you look like a first grader, Emmy."

"Diane gets a ride from her friends, but they won't let me go with them."

"She can be rather obnoxious at times," Kenny said, thinking about Emmy's popular, and very pretty, older sister. *I'm glad I decided to be friends with Emmy all those years ago. Diane is not the kind of girl I want to become involved with.* "Do you remember where all your classes are?"

"I'm pretty sure I can find them. You drew me a map of the school, and I have it in my backpack. If I get lost, I'll ask one of the teachers."

"You won't get lost."

As they got closer to the school, Emmy's heart sped up. The three-story school, built with locally quarried limestone in 1930, covered an entire city block and could be very intimidating to new students.

She stopped and grabbed his arm as he took another step. "Kenny, I think the school looks like a castle."

He turned, took a step back to her and then glanced over his shoulder at the building. "I've always kinda thought it did. It's got a crenelated roofline."

"A what?"

Kenny explained the meaning of the unfamiliar word.

Emmy looked up and laughed. "I can picture knights on horseback attacking the school, and archers firing arrows at them from the roof."

"I know. I can picture that, too. Like in a Robin Hood movie or something." He laughed. "Come on, Em. Let's get inside before we're attacked by knights."

Emmy smiled at Kenny with admiration. Her heart raced as he held her hand while they hurried across the busy street in front of Roosevelt High. *I don't care if you still tease me a little. I'm so glad I can see you everyday.*

Diane knew about Owen Porter's many girlfriends and suffered no illusions that he could ever be faithful to one girl. She willingly overlooked that character flaw because of how important it made her feel to be his part-time girlfriend.

Walking down the alley one afternoon, Owen lit a cigarette and blew smoke in Diane's face.

"Stop that!" Diane pushed him away. "Are you ever going to give up that disgusting habit?"

"No, I like smoking." He tried to blow a smoke ring, but the breeze blew the smoke away.

Diane shook her head. "What would you do if I threatened to break up with you unless you quit smoking and drinking?"

"I'd say 'it's been good to know ya.'"

Diane turned on her heels. "You're an ass! Don't bother calling me again." She held up her hand and extended a finger for emphasis.

Owen didn't see her finger as he kept walking home.

I'm not going to become involved with someone with the same addictions as Grandpa. Diane thought about her maternal grandfather who had died from lung cancer. She did an about face and ran toward him. "Hey! Wait for me. I didn't mean it."

Rory Porter, Owen's younger brother, was the same age as Diane, but frequent suspensions forced him to repeat his sophomore year of high school. Rory didn't care much about school, which concerned his mother. Mrs. Porter discovered, through Diane, that Emmy never received anything lower than an A on her report cards. Mrs. Porter asked Diane to bring Emmy to the house soon.

When Diane stopped over to see Owen one day after school, she brought Emmy along.

Mrs. Porter asked, "Emmy, could I talk to you about Rory?"

"Sure, Mrs. Porter. What did he do now?" Emmy watched as Rory zipped up his black leather jacket, ran a hand through his slicked back dark hair and left the house without a word.

"Since he flunked most of his classes last year, would you consider tutoring him if I pay you? I asked Diane, but she isn't interested at all." Mrs. Porter blew a few strands of her gray hair off of her face and sighed in frustration. "I'm afraid he will never graduate and get his diploma if he doesn't get help soon. He is too lazy to study, and I am at the end of my patience with him. How much would you want? I can't afford to pay much, but I'm desperate."

Emmy thought about it and answered, "How about the same as when I babysit? I normally charge three dollars an hour."

"Three dollars an hour isn't much. Tell you what—I'll give you three dollars an hour now, and if he graduates, I'll give you a bonus."

"Okay, Mrs. Porter. I'll try to help him if I can. We are taking some of the same classes."

After school a few days later, Emmy walked up the sidewalk to the Porter house to tutor Rory because, like his brother, Rory refused to set foot in the Colasanti house. Emmy noticed two girls laughing as they left the two-story house when she arrived for her tutoring session with Rory.

"Who were those girls?" Emmy asked as Amy Porter let her inside.

"Bimbos," Amy said as she adjusted the ring in her eyebrow. "I'm not sure if Mom knows how often Owen and Rory bring girls home." Amy pointed up the stairs. "They have girls up to their rooms all the time. I heard Owen bragging to Rory the other day about those two. It's like they're having a contest to see who can have the most girlfriends."

"What do they do in his room?" Emmy asked as she glanced around and noticed the sagging cushions on the couch, the smell of stale cigarette smoke and the beer cans on the floor.

Amy looked down at Emmy as if she were a child. "Are you serious? You really have to ask?"

"I know they aren't studying for school."

Amy explained more to Emmy. "Now do you understand why I think they're jerks?"

Even at two years younger, Amy knew more about boys than Emmy.

"I understand now, but Rory has never tried that with me," Emmy said.

"Only because he thinks you're way too young. He used to hit on Diane all the time, but she shot him down." Amy laughed as she used her hand as a pistol.

Emmy replied, "Diane told me that she thinks Rory is too immature for her because she likes older men—like her new boyfriend. His name is Craig something, and Diane claims he's twenty-one."

"She's dating a twenty-one-year-old? Do your parents know?" Amy asked.

"I think so," Emmy said as she shrugged. "Where's Rory? We're supposed to study."

"He left to hang out with friends," Amy said.

Emmy sighed. "He knew I was coming over. I talked to him at school."

"What can I tell ya?" Amy said. "You can hang out with me if you want."

"Thanks, but I have homework. Tell Rory I was here."

Because of Diane's mature appearance, Craig Garrett believed her when she lied to him about her age. He took Diane at her word when she proclaimed to be eighteen. She even showed him her fake ID.

43

"Diane, why don't you find a different boy to go out with? Craig isn't all that ambitious for a nineteen-year-old." Mom nagged again after Diane returned from a date.

"Can we talk about something else for a change?" Diane looked away.

Mom continued, "He doesn't go to college, and I don't think he will ever have a decent job."

"He works full-time for Thompson Manufacturing in their warehouse on the south side of town. He probably makes more money that Dad."

"What about Wayne Sanders? He's a nice young man."

"Not a chance in hell." Diane shook her head emphatically. "Mom, I'm old enough to make my own decisions about who I date. I like Craig, and I think he's ambitious enough. He's working over forty hours a week, and he doesn't waste his money. More importantly, I am in love with him."

"Hah! You can't be in love. You're only sixteen. That's just your... never mind. You need to date other boys, too. I'm not trying to tell you not to go out with Craig at all, but go out with other boys once in a while. Then you will know if you *love* him or not."

"I don't need to date other boys anymore. I have dated enough of them to know who I like and who I don't. Besides, you always forget that you were only seventeen when you got married. I'll be seventeen in a few months. Maybe Craig and I will get married. Then I won't have to live here." Diane thought about the apartment Craig shared in a seedy, rundown building with a friend from high school. *But he will have to find a new place.*

"Times were different then, and you are not going to make the same mistake I did," Mom added without revealing the reason she married at such a young age.

One night Diane came to bed after midnight and shook Emmy's shoulder. "Wake up, Emmy."

"Leave me alone. I'm tired." Emmy turned away from Diane.

"Do you promise to keep a secret if I tell you?"

Emmy, still half asleep, replied, "I guess so. What time is

it? Why did you wake me up?"

"I have something important to tell you, that's why. Now listen. Tonight I went all the way with Craig," Diane announced nervously.

"All the way where?" Emmy asked groggily.

Diane shrugged her shoulders and then poked Emmy's side. "Never mind. Go back to sleep, Em. I'll tell you in the morning."

In the morning, Diane woke Emmy up again and asked eagerly. "Do you remember what I told you last night?"

"I remember that you woke me up to tell me you went somewhere," Emmy replied as she stretched her arms above her head, trying to wake up.

"I went all the way with Craig last night. We did it."

Emmy's eyes opened as she remembered what Diane told her about sex and understood that going all the way meant something very special. "Get out! Did you really?"

Diane nodded. "Don't tell anyone, Emmy, because it is our secret."

"I promise. Tell me how it happened. Why did you do it, anyway? Did Craig get you drunk? You know it's wrong to do that, don't you, Diane? Will you get pregnant?" Emmy asked all at once.

"If you stop asking so many questions, I will tell you." Diane rolled her eyes. "Craig loves me, and he needed me to show him how much I love him."

"Why? Can't you just tell him that you love him?"

"Because... because he needed to know, that's why." Diane looked at Emmy like she didn't understand anything.

"Are you sure you won't have a baby?" Emmy asked.

"No, because we used protection."

"I'm not going to do that until I'm married," Emmy told Diane with determination. "I'm not gonna let a boy use me like that."

One day after school, Emmy walked into her bedroom to find Diane and Craig in bed together. Emmy didn't utter a sound as she left the room. She ran out of the house and sprinted down the

45

alley.

"Oh, crap!" Diane swore.

"Do you think Emmy will tell your folks?" Craig asked.

"Is that all you can think about? Emmy has to sleep in this bed, too."

"I knew I shouldn't have come over here. From now on you have to come to the apartment."

Emmy raced over to the Colwell house and pounded on the back door. No one answered, so she returned home and waited in the backyard for Craig to leave. When he did, Emmy glared at him.

"I'm sorry for surprising you like that." Craig gloated.

"If you get her pregnant, Daddy will kill you," Emmy warned. She went back inside and met Diane in the kitchen. "Did you forget that I live here, too. I saw you and Craig in bed together." She pushed Diane.

"Yeah, I know. I didn't know you would get home so early. Are you gonna tell Mom?"

"No, I won't tell. Your secret is still safe."

Diane sighed with relief. "Thanks. Mom would probably ground both of us if she found out."

"Why would she ground me? I'm not the one doing something wrong."

Diane put her hands on Emmy's shoulders. "Because that's the way she is. She doesn't love either of us, so we have to stick together. You will be better off if you don't say a word to anyone."

"I won't rat you out," Emmy said as she bit her lip.

Emmy caught a ride home after school with Kenny a week later. He smiled at her as she got in his 1993 red Honda Civic. "How was your day?"

"All right. Nothing special going on."

He waited for her to continue, but she didn't. "What's wrong?"

She stared out the window and then turned to Kenny. "I don't know what to do about Barry. We used to be such good friends, and now he hardly ever talks to me. They moved into a house just down the street, but I don't see him as much as I used to when he lived a few blocks away."

"Do you still want to be friends?"

"Well, yeah. We've been friends almost as long as the two of us."

"Just friends, right?" Kenny grinned as they sat at a red light.

"I've never thought of him as more than a friend." Emmy poked Kenny in the side, and then felt her face turn red. "We don't have any classes together, and sometimes his acne is pretty bad. But that doesn't matter."

As he pulled into the alley and parked outside the carriage house, Kenny suggested, "Sometimes as kids grow up... even kids who have been really good friends... they develop different interests and don't have the same friendship as before. Like with some of your girlfriends. They are interested in different things now, and you aren't close like in junior high and grade school. The same thing with Barry. If you wait for Barry to come to you, you might never be friends with him again. Why don't you go over to talk to him? Make the first move if you really want to be his friend."

"Thanks, Kenny, I appreciate the advice." Emmy smiled at him. "See ya. Thanks for the ride."

A few days later Emmy stopped by the Newton house after school. She walked up to the front door and rang the bell. Mrs. Newton answered the door.

"Is Barry home, Mrs. Newton? I'd really like to talk to him."

"I'm sorry, honey, I don't think he's home from school yet, but let me check."

"Thanks, Mrs. Newton."

Mrs. Newton called up the stairs, "Barry! Barry! Little Emmy is here and wants to talk to you." Barry didn't answer. "I'm sorry, Emmy. Do you want to leave a message for him? Should I have him call you when he comes home?"

"If he wants to call me, that would be all right."

As she left, Emmy caught a glimpse of Barry in the

window upstairs before he ducked out of sight.

She stared at the window for a moment and muttered. "Are you too afraid to even talk to me, and you're making your mother cover for you?" Emmy kicked at a crack in the sidewalk. *Little Emmy! Isn't anybody ever going to understand that I'm not a baby anymore? I'm going to Darby's by myself.*

"Good afternoon, Emmy. What can I get for you this beautiful fall day?" asked Mr. Darby. He checked the clock and realized school was out for the day.

"Could I have a medium Coke, please?" Emmy asked as she leaned against the stainless steel counter.

"Is that all?"

"Yes, that's all I can afford today." Emmy pulled out her last dollar from her backpack. "Can I ask you something, Mr. Darby?"

"Of course. What's on your mind?"

"How old do I have to be to work here?"

"You need to be sixteen. I know you're not sixteen."

"I was afraid of that. I'm earning some money by babysitting, but I want to earn more so I can go to college."

"Tell you what. If you still need a job when you turn sixteen, you come and see me." Mr Darby handed Emmy her Coke and an order of fries.

"I didn't order fries, Mr. Darby."

"I know, but they will just be tossed out, so you might as well eat them."

"Thanks, Mr. Darby."

"No problem, sweetheart."

Danny Darby shook his head at his father. "I just made those fries."

"Yeah, well, do a better job next time. They were too... too... salty or something."

Mr. Darby had a reputation for treating his employees and customers rather gruffly at times, but he had a soft spot in his heart for Emmy. He knew her parents and the rough times Emmy faced at home.

Emmy sat in a booth and finished her homework as she ate

48

her fries and drank her Coke. She put her books in her backpack and tossed her trash. She saw Mr. Darby and smiled. "Bye, Mr. Darby. Thanks again for the fries."

He waved. "Did you get your homework done?"

Emmy grinned. "Yes, can I go play now?"

"Yeah, get out of here."

She put her backpack on over her second-hand army jacket and walked home. She turned into the alley and kicked at an empty beer bottle with disgust. She paused for a moment as she heard Kenny playing the drums in the room above his parents' garage. The *garage* was a large two-story brick carriage house built over a hundred years ago. It was the only one left out of several that used to be on her street.

Emmy recalled the first time Kenny showed her the upper part of the carriage house when they were much younger. She had been leery of the steep stairs and the creepy upper room. Back then junk, accumulated over the years and covered in layers of dust, filled the room practically to its capacity. Cobwebs gave the room a very spooky appearance.

Emmy listened to her friend practicing for a moment. She walked over to the service door and turned the knob—it opened. She summoned up enough courage to walk in and climb the stairs to the second floor. Kenny was wearing headphones and pounding on his drum kit. Catching sight of Emmy, he stopped playing, took off the headphones and turned down the stereo.

"Hey, Emmy, what's up? Welcome to my humble abode, m'lady," Kenny announced with a bow and flourish.

She laughed at his use of *m'lady*. She curtsied and replied, "My lord. What a change. You've really cleaned the place up."

"Yeah, I wanted to teach myself to play the drums, and Mom suggested I use this space. She didn't want to hear me banging on the drums in the house. Dad helped me get rid of the junk, and we sold a bunch of stuff to an antique dealer."

"What a difference from the first time I saw this place." Emmy looked around. "I must have been eight or so, and this place scared me."

"Yeah. It took us over a week to clear everything out and

clean up. Let me take you on a grand tour of my castle. Step this way please. This is the kitchen." He pointed to the fridge and a counter and cabinets. "This is the bedroom." He turned around and pointed to a dusty old couch. "And over here is the grand ballroom."

"Quite the castle you have here, m'lord." Emmy smiled as Kenny pointed to the large open area in front of the band equipment. "I'm impressed. It's huge. I didn't realize you had this much room up here."

"I found some old carpet remnants, and I'm using them for right now. These old wooden planks are kinda rough. One of these days I would like to redo the whole place. I'd like to turn it into an apartment. Dad told me that years ago the groom lived up here. But after they got rid of the horses, they tore out the small apartment. Most of it, anyway." Kenny walked over to the wall and slapped it with his hand. "These brick walls are over a foot thick. So I can make a lot of noise up here without disturbing the neighbors."

"I noticed that as I walked in the alley. I could barely hear you playing the drums."

"Wanna sing along with me?" Kenny asked abruptly. He had been practicing while listening to songs on his stereo.

She bit her lip and didn't answer.

Kenny asked her again, "Well, you wanna sing or not? Have you been singing at all lately?"

"I sing in the shower sometimes when I'm by myself."

Kenny's eyes opened wide, and then he grinned. "Are you sometimes not alone in the shower?"

"That's not what I meant," Emmy stammered.

He smiled at her discomfort. "I'm only teasing you, Em. Let me hear you sing along to this song, if you please." He handed her a microphone.

He played the drums as Emmy sang along to "Storms." She sang timidly at first, but gained confidence as the song went along.

"Not bad, not bad at all." Kenny gave her a high-five.

"It sounds weird to hear my voice through the speakers."

"You still have a beautiful singing voice, Emmy. You should come with me to church sometime. I still play the guitar and sing for the teens. You could sing with me."

"That might be fun. Maybe I will sometime," Emmy replied without conviction. She sat on the old couch.

"You said that a couple of years ago, but you never came with me." He plugged in a guitar and started playing. He played several guitar riffs and then stopped.

"That sounds amazing. How long have you been playing that guitar? It's a new one, right?"

"I've had this Gibson for almost two years now. It's a lot better than the first one I had."

"Do you still have that old acoustic guitar?"

"Yeah, it's in the house. That's usually what I use at church. It's a Martin, by the way."

"I remember when you first got that. You were so excited when you learned how to play a whole song."

"Do you remember when I told you about starting a band?"

"Yeah, you must have been just starting high school."

Kenny said, "Well, I *am* going to start a band, and I'm gonna make a career out of music. We are going to use nicknames for the guys in the band like a couple of the guys in U2. I even have a name for the band, but it's a secret. I'll tell you later."

"What nickname are you going to use?"

"I don't know if I should tell you because you might make fun of me."

"I won't make fun of you. I promise."

"Well, okay," he whispered the name in her ear. "It's Gra."

"Gra?" Emmy repeated it quietly.

"It's what I used to call my Grandpa when I was a kid."

"That is so sweet. You must have really loved your grandpa a lot to use that for your nickname." Emmy looked at Kenny with wide eyes.

"I don't know if that will really work out, but I wanna try it. There are going to be four people in the band, maybe five, and everybody will know how to sing. Oh, and we all have to get along as friends, too. That's very important."

Chapter Six

Everyday after school for the next few weeks, Emmy stopped by the carriage house to practice singing while Kenny played his guitar.

"You are already so good, and you are getting better with every practice," Emmy said.

"Thanks, Em. You have such a beautiful voice, and you're getting better on the keyboard."

"I guess maybe my piano lessons weren't a total waste."

"You are the band's first official fan, Emmy, and I will see that you always have tickets to see us, even after we become famous rock stars, okay?"

She laughed. "Soon there are going to be thousands of fans, and you will forget about little ol' me."

"Never happen, Em, honey." Kenny held her shoulders and looked into her sparkling blue eyes. She looked up at him, and he kissed her forehead. "You're my sweet girl. I'm starvin'. C'mon, I'm hungry enough to eat a horse. Let's go over to Darby's. My treat."

"Yeah, I'm in with that."

After a month of auditions, the right personnel came together. The guys decided to use the name Kenny picked out, and so the band, Fridays At Five, entered into existence. The members were, in addition to Kenny: Jeff Rawlings, who played bass and guitar; Jeremy Lenhart, who played all kinds of keyboards and could also play guitar; and Dave Persching, who played guitar and drums. Jeff, Jeremy and Dave were all professional musicians in their early twenties and had been in other bands, but were blown away by Kenny's talent. They worked part-time jobs but only to make some cash. Kenny and Dave switched off playing the drums at first, but within a week Dave volunteered to take over the position of full-time drummer. The guys believed the band would be better off with Kenny being the front man. All the members of the band could sing, and they harmonized well together. Emmy came to every practice and sang along on some of the songs. She sang some songs by herself and gained confidence in her ability.

One day Kenny surprised Emmy, "I wrote a song specially for you and about you, Em."

"You did? Can I hear it? What's it called?"

Kenny sang while he played the song on his guitar for her. The soft ballad described Emmy perfectly without ever using her name.

"That's really beautiful, Kenny. I like the line 'her blue eyes sparkle in the sun.' Is it really about me?"

"Yes, Emmy, and it's called 'Sweet Girl.'"

A few weeks later the band found a better place to rehearse—a warehouse owned by Jeff Rawlings' father. Jeff convinced his father to let the band practice in the empty loft at the south end of the otherwise open, two-story, 55,000 square foot building. The band could leave their gear set up and didn't have to worry about the neighbors complaining about the loud music.

"Mom, we need to talk to you," Emmy said as she led Kenny into the living room after school one day. "It's important."

"What is it, Emmy? You're not getting married, are you?"

"Mom! Don't be silly. I'm way too young to get married." Emmy rolled her eyes. "This is about the band."

"Have a seat and tell me what's so important."

Emmy pulled Kenny to the couch. "You know how the band has been practicing in the carriage house, right?"

Mom nodded her head.

"You tell her the rest, Kenny." Emmy bit her lip.

"Well, Mrs. Colasanti, Jeff's father has this warehouse with an empty loft, and he offered to let us use it for a permanent rehearsal space."

"Where is it?"

"It's in Gordon Hill, and it's about a mile from here."

"That's a long way from here." Mom knew what Emmy was going to ask.

Kenny continued, "We're still gonna practice right after school and on Saturdays because that fits everyone's schedule."

"Mom, I want to keep practicing with the guys," Emmy

blurted out.

"I could tell, Emmy. I'd like to know more about this warehouse."

"Right now it's empty because the last company that used it went bankrupt," Kenny explained.

"Is it secure?" Mom asked. "There must be a lot of ways to get into it."

"There are some loading docks, but they're all locked up. There is a side door that requires a code. There is a small office area up front, but that's always locked. It's pretty secure."

"I'm assuming you will drive Emmy over there after school and bring her home."

"Of course, Mrs. Colasanti." Kenny nodded.

Mom said, "I will talk to your father about this."

"Can you ask him tonight, please?" Emmy put her hands together and stood on tiptoes.

"All right, Emmy." Mom turned on her heels. *I've got a bad feeling about this.*

As they sat in their recliners watching TV that evening, Patricia had a conversation with her husband about the warehouse.

"I think I know which building he means." Raymond popped the cap off a bottle of beer.

"I know where Gordon Hill is, but is that area safe?"

"For the most part. It's not like the south side of the river. I wouldn't let her go over there no matter what."

"So, what do you think?" Patricia asked.

Raymond drained half the bottle before answering, "I'll check it out, and, if I think it's safe, we could let her try it for a week. I don't want her schoolwork to suffer."

"Do you think Kenny Colwell's interest in Emily is unhealthy for a child of her age?" Patricia turned down the volume on the TV.

Raymond frowned and grabbed the remote. "What do you mean? They've been friends since we moved here."

"I mean, he is older, and she's getting to the age where sex might become something she is curious about."

"Just because you and Diane were interested in sex at that

54

age, doesn't mean Emmy is." He paused and lowered his voice, "Is she?"

"I hope not."

"Have you ever talked to her about sex?"

"No, but I'm sure Diane has."

"That's just great!" He swore as he pounded the arm of his recliner. "I don't want to think about that possibility. Emmy is still a tomboy, and I don't think Kenny would want to cause a problem by... you know." It embarrassed him even thinking about his younger daughter becoming sexually active. "Will you get me another beer?"

"Get it yourself. Your legs aren't broke, and I'm not your servant even though you treat me like one."

"For crying out loud, woman. I'm gonna go over to Miller's Bar." He slammed his footrest back and stood up.

"Go ahead. While you're there you can think about what your baby girl might be doing with her future rock star."

He froze in place. "Fine. I'll stay here. Emily, come here," he shouted.

Emmy came bounding out of her bedroom. "Did you guys decide? Can I still practice with the band?" She hopped back and forth as she waited for their decision.

"I'll go with you on Saturday to check it out," Dad said.

Mr. Colasanti went to the warehouse with Emmy. He checked out the building, met the other guys in the band and inspected the building. He even listened to the band for a time.

"Did you decide?" Emmy asked as she rode home with her father.

"We will try it for a week." Dad wagged a finger at her as he listed the rules and expectations.

"I won't let my grades slip. I promise."

"I don't know much about music, but they sound pretty good. Loud, but good."

"They are really good, Daddy," Emmy said.

"One other thing."

"What, Daddy?"

55

He looked at her and smiled. "You have a voice like an angel, sweetie."

Because of all the time they spent together, Emmy started to see her friend Kenny through different eyes. She clutched a pillow to her chest as she lay in bed one night. *I think I'm developing a crush on Kenny, but I'm too afraid to tell anyone.* She rolled over, put her feet in the air and kicked them back and forth. *I can't tell Diane because she will just make fun of me.*

The older guys in the band became very protective of her because they could sense how she felt about her friend.

In January, Kenny graduated from Roosevelt High—one semester early.

"I'm sorry I didn't tell you about this at the beginning of the year, Em. I know you are disappointed," Kenny said as they hung out in the carriage house one afternoon.

"It's all right. I'll get over it. How were you able to graduate early?" Emmy asked as she sat on the drum throne and played a simple rhythm on the drums.

"I've got all the credits I need. You probably don't remember the summer courses I took. The bad news is my parents want me to spend one year at Paul Frank Junior College. I want to start touring full-time with the band."

"What are you gonna do? Are you gonna do what your parents want? Diane would never do that."

"Yeah, they've been very supportive of my goals. The least I can do is wait for a year. I enrolled for the spring semester, so I can get this over as soon as I can." Kenny plugged in a guitar and turned on an amp.

Emmy smacked a crash cymbal and then said, "I'd like to finish high school early since you won't be there."

"You have other friends." He tuned his guitar and began jamming. Emmy played along on the drums. "Emmy, since I won't have time to pick you up before we practice..."

"It's okay, Kenny. I know you guys don't want a high school kid in the band. Especially not a girl."

"I wish you were older, because you really add to the sound of the band. Not only with your voice, but you know enough about playing keyboards to play them. Jeremy could teach you even more."

"I always hated taking piano lessons. I know Mom made me take them, so I wouldn't be playing football all the time."

"If you were playing keys, Jeremy could play guitar." Kenny said thinking how the band would sound with two guitarists. "I wish Paul Joseph had decided to join the band."

"You know my mother would never let me be a real part of the band, right? I'm surprised she and Daddy ever agreed to let me hang out with you as much as I do."

"If you were a guy, she would."

Emmy threw a drumstick at him. "Would you like me better if I wasn't a fourteen-year-old girl?"

"No way!"

The band practiced for several months because they wanted to polish their act to perfection. News of the band spread though the music community. One day, Mr. Colwell came to the band's practice with two other men. They listened to the band for about forty-five minutes. Mr. Colwell shook their hands, and they left without talking to anyone in the band.

Emmy walked down the alley to see Kenny one spring Saturday. They tossed a football around in the backyard.

"Why are you grinning so much? Did I do something?" Emmy asked.

"I have a favor to ask of you."

"What?" Emmy ran up to Kenny and tried to take the football away.

"I want you to come to our gig Friday. It's at the Christian Youth Center on Douglas Street. Do you think you can make it?"

"For real? You guys are finally going to play? About time. I'd love to see you guys play in front of a crowd. I'll have to ask Mom if I can go."

"Tell her that my parents will be there, and they can keep

you company, Emmy. It's at the youth center, so there won't be any alcohol. We've got twenty original songs and at least that many cover songs ready. We have enough material to play for three hours."

"Why are you still grinning like a dork?" Emmy asked.

"There is one other thing, Em."

"What?"

"The guys and I want you to sing some harmony with us and do a solo, too."

"No way! I'm not going to sing in front of all those people."

"Why not? You sound really good."

"I would be too scared."

"Well, think about it, Em."

"I'll ask my parents if I can go, but no way will I sing in front of people."

Because of her young age, her parents would not let her go to the show without supervision.

"You are not going to a rock concert by yourself, Emily. I won't even think about it," Mom said.

"But I have to be there. It's Kenny's first gig," Emmy pleaded as she stomped her foot.

Diane intervened, "Mom, I could go with Emmy. I want to hear the band."

Mom thought about it for a moment. *I suppose it will be all right since Mr. and Mrs. Colwell will be there.* "All right, but your father will drive you there," Mom insisted.

Emmy shook her head. "He doesn't have to. We can ride with Kenny's parents."

Diane and Emmy walked down the alley to the Colwell house and rode with his parents to hear the band play their first show on April 21, 1995.

"Why are you wearing that stocking cap and that old army jacket? It's not that cold." Diane poked Emmy in the side while sitting in the back seat.

"Kenny told me he likes it. He said it makes me look cool... and older."

"You're a goof, Em."

After the first set, Kenny jumped down from the raised stage. He saw his parents sitting at a table off to the side of the packed dance floor and walked over.

"Did you like it?"

"You guys sounded great," Carter Robert Colwell asserted.

"Have you seen Emmy?" Kenny looked at the crowd.

"I think she's with Diane," Mr. Colwell mentioned.

"Bob, you can tell Kenny where she went," Eloise Colwell said. "They went to the restroom, Kenny. She'll be right back."

"I didn't want to embarrass her, Elly," Mr. Colwell said.

Kenny talked to some fans as he waited for Emmy.

He saw her returning and smiled. "Are you willing to sing a couple songs with us. I won't make you sing a solo if you don't want, but the guys want you to sing on a couple tunes."

She bit her lip. "Just two songs?"

"Two songs and I promise I won't embarrass you."

Halfway through the second set of the very first Fridays At Five gig, Emmy Colasanti joined the guys on stage. She looked out at the crowd of over three hundred kids. *Oh, my God! I don't know if I can do this.* She sang harmony on two songs. Kenny made her wave to the crowd. Then she rejoined Diane and Kenny's parents. Mr. Colwell had been taking pictures throughout the night, and he captured some shots of Emmy on stage with the guys.

Diane screamed and hugged her little sister. "Oh my God, Emmy! You sounded great. I never knew you could actually sing."

Emmy's eyes sparkled and danced as she faced Diane and Mr. and Mrs. Colwell. "Did it really sound good? Please tell me I didn't make the band sound totally awful."

"You sounded like an angel, Emmy. Kenny is a good judge of talent, and he would not have let you on stage if you weren't talented," Mr. Colwell assured her.

Emmy whispered to Diane, "I could feel my heart pounding, and I thought I would pee my pants when I first got up there. Then Kenny smiled at me, and I felt better."

Emmy even sang on a couple of tunes in the final set. Neither Kenny nor the other guys saw Mr. Colwell talking to the same two men who showed up for practice that one day. The guys shook hands with Mr. Colwell before they left. Mr. Colwell's face beamed as he pumped his fist.

Fridays At Five became an immediate local success. Because of the success of the first gig, the band landed a gig at Larry's Uptown Grill, a much sought after venue for local bands. Several music industry people stopped by to check out the band. After the gig, the band met with an agent, who had music industry connections, and he set them up with a band manager. The guys talked to Andrew Walker, and he agreed to take them on. Before long the band signed a recording contract with the Steward Music Group, an independent recording label based in South Hampshire. They continued to play local events for a time, and Emmy never missed a show. Kenny would bring her on stage to sing harmony with the band. Some nights she would even stay on stage and play some of the percussion instruments Dave had with him. She even learned the keyboard part to a few songs, which allowed Jeremy to play guitar. She was thrilled to be singing with her friend.

One night at an all-ages show at a small venue in Newcastle, Kenny pulled Emmy to the center of the stage.
"I want to introduce you to a very good friend of mine. She's been singing harmony for us. Her name is Emmy Colasanti, and she is the first person I ever sang with. If you holler loud enough, maybe we can convince her to sing a song for you guys. How about it?"
The crowd hooted and hollered until she agreed to sing.
"Emmy, I guess they want to hear you sing," Kenny hollered in her ear.
"You are so gonna get it later, Kenny."
He grinned. "They will love you. Just like I do."
After the song ended, Emmy received a loud ovation for her effort. Although she felt very nervous and didn't think she sounded all that great, the crowd loved her song. Emmy didn't realize it at the time, but this would not be the last time she would sing for a large crowd.

Chapter Seven

"Stand still, Emily. I need to straighten out this hem." Grandma Isabel Sandusky scolded as she stuck some pins in the hem of Diane's old dress. "How tall are you now?"

"I'm just under five one, and I'd still rather wear jeans than these hand-me-down dresses."

"You are almost fifteen. You need to act more like a young lady than a tomboy." Grandma had Emmy spin to her left on the small step stool in the dining room.

"Yes, Grandma," Emmy said as she looked out the window and sighed. "I'd rather be playing football."

"Stand still, child, or else I'll stick you with a pin," Grandma threatened.

Though she still wore Diane's old dresses, now they fit better. Grandma Sandusky taught Emmy how to alter her clothes. She learned to make do with what she had, but dreamed about getting a part-time job and earning some money to buy nicer clothes.

Now that summer arrived, Kenny's band traveled to some out-of-state gigs to broaden their fanbase. Emmy knew she couldn't travel with the band because they would be away for several days at a time.

"Emmy, you can still sing with us if we play locally," Kenny told her one afternoon in the carriage house before the guys left for Ohio.

"I know the guys are just putting up with me because I'm your friend." Emmy bunched her long, dark hair into a ponytail and used a rubberband to hold it together.

"That's not true, Em. If you weren't talented, we wouldn't let you on stage no matter what."

"I will miss you when you're gone. I don't like staying at home all day." She sat on the old couch and tucked her feet under her.

"Are your parents fighting again, Em?"

"They have never stopped fighting. Diane stays away as

61

much as she can. She's working two jobs, and I hardly ever see her. Mom gets on my case because of what Diane is doing. Like it's my fault."

"We won't be gone all summer, but this opportunity to travel is too good to pass up. I'll talk to you when I get back."

Tears filled her eyes. "You better not forget about me."

One evening, as Emmy ate leftover spaghetti for the second time that week, she commented, "I'll be fifteen next week, and you allowed Diane to date when she turned fifteen."

Mom slapped her palm on the table. "I've told you a hundred times, you are not dating until you turn sixteen. Maybe not even then."

"Why do I always have to wait to do everything?" Emmy pouted. "I never get to do anything my friends are doing."

"If your friends wanted to drive off a cliff like those women in that movie, would you want to do that, too?"

"That's not what I mean, and you know it," Emmy sassed.

Mom slammed her hands on the table and raised up from her chair. "Don't you dare take that attitude with me, young lady. You are not too old to be paddled by your father." Mom explained, "Diane matured faster than you, so that's why it doesn't seem fair to you at times."

If you only knew how mature Diane behaves with her boyfriend, you would ground her for life. But Emmy kept that thought to herself. Instead she said, "I wish I was sixteen already. Maybe Kenny would let me go with the band."

Actually, dating didn't interest Emmy, but she resented her parents treating her more strictly than Diane.

The band returned from their trip on Tuesday, and Kenny called Emmy. She grabbed the phone in the kitchen.

"We're back. Are you busy? Can you come over?"

"Who is this? The voice sounds kinda familiar, but I can't remember the name," she teased.

"And you thought I would forget about *you*. Now you can't remember me. I haven't been gone that long."

"Oh, I think I remember you now. Maybe I can come over for a little while."

She hung up and shouted to her mother, "Kenny's home, and I'm going over there to see him. I'll be back later."

"Emily Olivia, you wait one second," Mom hollered from her living room recliner.

Emmy walked into the living room. "What? I want to see Kenny."

"Is your room clean? Did you take out the garbage?"

"Yes, Mom, I did everything you asked."

"What time are you going to be home?"

"I don't know. Probably before it gets dark."

"You can stay at the Colwell home, but don't go anywhere else. I don't want you out past dark."

"All right, Mom. Can I go now?" Emmy rolled her eyes. *I'm not afraid of the dark.*

"Yes, but I'm not cooking any supper since no one will be here. If you get hungry, there is some leftover spaghetti."

Emmy stuck her finger down her throat.

"I have my bingo tonight, so I won't be home until around ten. That doesn't mean you can stay with him until that time. Do you understand?"

"Yes, I'll see you later." She ran out the door and down the alley, narrowly avoiding one of the neighbor's cars as he returned home. She ran into the carriage house and sprinted up the stairs.

"I'm here. I ran all the way, and my mother isn't going to be home until ten. She told me to come home before dark, but she won't know. I just have to get home before she does. How are you?" She sat on the old couch and tried not to sound out of breath.

"I'm doing fine, Em." He sat on one of his amps and told her about the trip. "We opened for Darius and the Hooties."

She laughed. "What is a Hootie?"

"Don't know," Kenny said.

"What else did you guys do?" She listened attentively as he told her the details.

"We caught a Collective Star show one night."

"Never heard of them."

"They were pretty good," Kenny said. *But we're better.*

Emmy noticed some cobwebs in the corner.

"Now tell me how you've been getting along with your mother."

Emmy leaned back against the couch. "Where should I start? My mother still treats me like I'm ten. Daddy doesn't say much, but he stays at the bar after work. They never let me do anything. They allowed Diane to date when she turned fifteen. It's not fair!"

Kenny listened as Emmy vented her frustrations. "Are you ready to date guys by yourself?"

"Not really, but that's not the point." She sat up straight. "I should be treated the same as Diane. Mom just wants to keep me under her control."

Kenny smiled at Emmy; she stood up and whipped a throw pillow at him.

"Emmy, you shouldn't be in too big a hurry to grow up. You don't have a boyfriend, so why get upset about it?"

"I hate it when you're right. Why can't you simply agree with me and not be so logical?"

Kenny stood up, held her shoulders and kissed her cheek. "I love the look in your eyes when you get all riled up. Come on. Let's go to Darby's, and you can complain to Mr. Darby while he makes us chili dogs."

"Is food all you ever think of?"

"No, I think about music, too."

Emmy shrugged. "You have to buy because I'm broke."

"You're not broke," he said. "You don't ever spend any money. I bet you have more money in the bank than me."

Emmy grinned. She saved every penny she earned for college. She had no clue as to the amount of money Kenny earned with the band. Kenny drove them over to Darby's. They each ordered chili dogs, fries, and pop. Kenny added a slice of chocolate cake for them to share. Emmy found an empty booth while Kenny waited for their food. He joined her, and they talked as they ate.

"What are you doing tomorrow night, Em?"

She poured ketchup over her fries. "Nothing that I can

64

think of, why?"

"Would you come to church with me? I'm going to play my guitar, and I need you to sing with me."

"Me! Why me?"

"Because you have such a beautiful voice."

"What songs are you going to sing? Are they old-fashioned church songs? Do I know any of them?" Emmy licked ketchup off of her fingers.

"They're not old songs. They're contemporary worship songs. You've heard the CDs."

"Good. I've heard a few of them."

"After we finish eating, you wanna go back to my place to practice?"

"Sure. Why not? There's no one home at my house. I can stay as long as I want."

They returned to Kenny's practice room in the carriage house, and he picked up a Martin acoustic guitar. He played the songs as Emmy listened. Then they sang together.

"Emmy, you're a natural. You are singing the right harmonies."

"Really? I don't have a clue about what I'm doing."

"Yes, you do. You know more about music than you let on."

They kept practicing, and soon Emmy knew the songs as well as Kenny.

"So, will you come with me?" he asked.

"Okay, as long as Mom lets me."

"Do you think she will object?" He put the guitar back in the case.

"Probably not. It is church, after all."

Kenny looked at the clock. "Em, it's after nine. You should get home before your mother does. I don't want you to get in trouble."

Emmy shrugged. "Okay, but she won't know what time I get home."

"Are you becoming a rebellious teenager, Em?"

She grinned. "Not really, but I'm not a little angel, either."

"You're not, huh?" Kenny tilted his head. "Care to elaborate?"

"Did I ever tell you about the time I went with Rory Porter to the football field at Roosevelt?"

"Not that I can remember. What did you do with him?" Kenny put the chord charts in a folder.

"He met a bunch of his friends there. We climbed the fence and had a party in the end zone."

Kenny's eyes opened wide as he turned to face her. "You never mentioned this."

"There were three other guys and a bunch of girls. I don't even remember their names. Oh, John Grafton was there."

"Grafton!" Kenny raised his hands over his head. "I remember him. He got arrested for stealing a car. He'll probably end up in prison soon."

"John brought some beer, and everyone was smoking..."

"What? Wait a sec! Were you drinking and smoking, too?"

"No, you know I've never smoked, and they weren't smoking cigarettes, anyway." She made a puffing motion as she pretended to hold a joint.

"Did you have a beer?"

"Just part of one."

"Unbelievable! How old were you, anyway?"

"Fourteen. I was a freshman." Emmy grinned. "I haven't told you every naughty thing I've ever done."

"Did your parents ever find out?" Kenny shook his head in disbelief.

"No way. Daddy would have grounded me for life and probably killed Rory and that Grafton guy. I didn't do anything with Rory."

Later that night, Mom sat at the kitchen table counting her bingo winnings, her good mood soaring higher with each twenty dollar bill she added to the pile. "All right! I won a hundred bucks tonight."

Emmy seized the opportunity and asked, "Mom, can I go to church with Kenny?"

Mom smiled as she hid the money in a coffee can. "Yeah, I

66

guess you can go." Mom pointed a finger at Emmy. "You better not tell your father about this money. It's my secret stash."

"I won't tell anyone." Emmy held up her hand as if swearing an oath. She grinned. *I'm glad I caught you in a good mood for a change.*

Emmy called Kenny with the news. "I can go. What time do I need to be ready?"

"We need to leave at five thirty. Service starts at six thirty."

"I'll be ready. Oh, do I have to dress up?"

"No, just wear your usual jeans and shirt."

Kenny picked Emmy up the next evening, and they headed to the church.

"What parish is it, Kenny?" Emmy asked as she scanned the facade of the brick building.

"It's not a Catholic church, Emmy." Kenny opened the rear door and pulled out his guitar case.

"Then what is it?"

"It's called Faith Bible Church. You came to Vacation Bible School one summer, remember? You won a contest for memorizing Bible verses."

"I forgot about that. It doesn't matter. A church is a church, right?"

"There are some differences."

Kenny and Emmy practiced their songs, and then waited for the service to start.

"Are you nervous, Emmy?"

"Maybe a little. I know I've been on stage in front of a lot more people than will be here tonight, but I was with the whole band. I didn't have to sing on my own."

"You don't need to be nervous. The kids will sing along. They won't even hear us if they sing loud enough."

Emmy counted over twenty teenagers in the room. A ping pong table and a pool table stood at one end of the large room. Emmy waited with Kenny at the other side of the room until the youth pastor called them to the stage. After singing a number of songs, they listened as the youth pastor spoke. After the service,

Kenny introduced Emmy to some of the kids. Some of them Emmy recognized from Roosevelt High.

"Well, did you like it?" Kenny asked as they walked out to his car.

"Yeah, I did. They made me feel right at home."

He chuckled and then said, "They're a pretty friendly group."

"Yeah, I kinda got that, and it felt like they weren't all that concerned with being popular and cool like some of the jerks I know at school."

"Did you think they would all be dorks or something?" Kenny opened the car door for her.

Emmy grinned and said, "Well, yeah, I thought they would be like you."

"You are so gonna pay for that."

Emmy reached over and unlocked his door. "Do you go to this church every week?"

"I can't always make it on Sundays, but I try. Wanna come back with me next month? I'm gonna sing again." He started the car.

"Sure. As long as Mom doesn't mind." She paused, and then asked, "Why do you go to this church?"

"I suppose it's because my family has always gone here. One of my earliest memories is coming here and listening to a guy singing and playing a guitar."

"Is that why you have always wanted to be a musician?"

"Maybe. Emmy, do you believe in God?" Kenny asked as he searched her eyes.

"Yeah, sure. Why? Doesn't everyone?"

"Since I've been going to church for my whole life, I've based a lot of my values on what they teach. When I was twelve, I got saved."

"Is that like getting confirmed? I started that, but we stopped going to mass before I finished. Daddy got into an argument with the priest because he called Daddy a drunk. I thought Daddy was gonna hit him."

Kenny thought for a moment. "Getting saved is different.

68

It's not a class you have to take, or a long process. It's a matter of confessing your sins and accepting Christ into your life. After I did that, I started reading the Bible. Dad gave me a devotional book written especially for teens by a guy named Bob Rector. It dealt with situations that teens face and gave scriptures to read."

"Do you still have it?"

"I might have it somewhere, but I kinda wore out my copy. It dealt with peer pressure and stuff. There was even a section about sex."

Emmy grinned.

"Not like a manual, you goof. He wrote about why it was important to not treat sex lightly."

"So does that mean you're not gonna have sex until you're married?"

"Well, I can't know for sure, but I think it's better if people are married."

"Diane has sex with Craig. She tried to convince me that's it's not a big deal, but I think it is."

"I feel the same way, Em."

Emmy giggled.

"What is so funny?" Kenny asked.

"Do you think you will like having sex when you get married?"

Kenny blushed. "Geez, Em. Guys are supposed to like it. You should hear how some guys talk about it. No, wait, you shouldn't hear it."

"I do know how babies are made. I'm not totally ignorant about the process."

"Can we talk about something else? You know I get embarrassed."

She poked his shoulder. "I remember how embarrassed you got when I told you about starting my..."

"Oh, look." He pointed at the sky. "I think that's the North Star."

Chapter Eight

"Hey, Em, how's school goin'?" Kenny asked as she stopped at his house one afternoon. "You're a sophomore now, huh?"

"It's all right, but I miss being able to walk with you, or share a ride." She hopped up on a stool at the black granite breakfast counter. She glanced at the gleaming stainless steel appliances with envy.

Kenny flipped a switch, and the recessed lighting came on. "Can't you catch a ride with Diane? I know she gets picked up by her friends." Kenny pulled two cold Cokes from the fridge, walked over and sat next to her.

"She won't let me ride with her. She definitely won't let me hang out with her clique of cool popular kids." Emmy grabbed two glasses from the rack in front of her, as Kenny popped the tabs on the cans.

"That's all right now, but what will you do in the winter?"

"I'll catch the city bus if I have to, but I suppose I'll walk most of the time."

"Can't your parents give you a ride?" Kenny poured too much Coke in his glass. It fizzed over the side.

"Doofus! Be careful." Emmy jumped down and tore some paper towels from the dispenser. "You can wipe up your own mess." She handed the towels to Kenny and sat down again. "They have to leave before us."

"And I suppose you haven't told them about Diane not letting you ride with her."

"No, I don't want to complain and get her in trouble. She would try to make my life miserable if I did."

Like she doesn't already do that. Kenny shook his head. "I bet Mom would give you a ride."

"She probably would, but I don't want to be a nuisance."

Kenny took a sip of his Coke and then grinned. "You're always gonna be a pain in the butt."

"At least I'm not a dork like you." She stuck out her tongue and punched his arm.

70

Kenny's mom walked into the kitchen at that moment and caught Emmy in the act. "Are you kids fighting about something?" She put her hands on her hips.

"No, I was just teasing her." Kenny put his arm around Emmy's waist and poked her side.

Emmy jumped. "Hey! Stop that."

"Mom, would you mind giving Emmy a ride to school when the weather's bad?"

"Not at all. Are you planning to walk to school all year?" Mrs. Colwell asked Emmy.

"Yeah. I don't want to be a pain like Kenny thinks."

Mrs. Colwell walked over to Emmy, put her hands on Emmy's shoulders and squeezed tenderly. "I'm sure either Carter or I would be able to give you a ride to school. You're never a pain in the butt like someone else I know."

"See! Your mother likes me better than you." Emmy grinned and smacked Kenny's arm. "Thank you, Mrs. Colwell. I appreciate the offer, but I'll walk most of the time."

"Well, if you need a ride, please call me. I won't say anything to your parents, but I can't see why your sister has to be so mean to you."

Kenny rubbed his arm. "You still love me a little, don't you, Mom?"

"Of course I do, dear, but Emmy is like the daughter I never had."

In early September, Kenny's classes at Paul Frank resumed. He arranged his schedule to allow the band to do Friday and Saturday gigs in the Midwest—no evening classes and no class after noon on Friday. Mr. Colwell purchased a new Honda Odyssey minivan for the band. They leased a trailer for their gear. The other guys still worked their part-time jobs, and the band still practiced in the late afternoons. Emmy would stop by to practice if she didn't have to babysit for Mrs. Rivera.

Kenny called Emmy on Tuesday evening. "I'm going to sing for the teen group again tomorrow. Wanna come with me?"

"Sure, are we gonna do the same songs?"

"No, I thought we could do some new tunes. Can you come over and practice?"

"I'll be right there." She was alone in the house, so she ran right over to Kenny's. She ran up the stairs and saw him sitting on the edge of the old couch strumming an acoustic guitar.

"Hey, Emmy, that was quick. How are you?" He set the guitar down.

"I'm all right. Are you having fun at Paul Frank?"

"School is... so-so, but I do like my writing class," he said. "I never realized writing could be so complicated. I always figured it was something anyone could do."

"Anyone with half a brain," she said and then giggled.

They chose the songs and spent an hour rehearsing.

After school the next day Emmy saw a to-do list on the fridge from her mother. *Why do I always get stuck doing this? I know what Diane would do with this list.* She looked at the garbage can. *It is rather disgusting.* She decided it would be best to go ahead and do what her mother requested. It took an hour. She checked the list one last time. *Okay, the dusting is done. I vacuumed the living room. The kitchen is done. My room is clean. My side at least.* Satisfied that she would be in her mother's good graces, Emmy approached her mother as soon as she returned home from work, "Is it all right if I go with Kenny to his church again tonight? I did everything on my list. You can check if you want."

"It's a school night. What time will you be back?"

"I should be home by eight thirty, I guess."

"All right. Have a good time." Mom slumped in her recliner. "This job is killing me."

Kenny and Emmy sang again for the teen group. She liked the lyrics; even the ones she didn't fully understand. After they finished singing, Emmy sat on the couch next to Kenny as the youth pastor addressed the respectfully quiet teens. Emmy paid close attention again and felt a stirring in her heart.

After the leader finished, Kenny took Emmy's hand. "I

should introduce you to Ronnie Rojas. I'm sorry I didn't have a chance the last time. He was busy talking to some of the kids. He's our teen group leader. He used to belong to a gang, but he straightened out his life. Maybe Jesus straightened out his life. Anyway, he went to college and became a youth minister. He knows about all the crap kids go through, and he doesn't put up with any BS."

They waited patiently as some of the kids surrounded Ronnie. When he finished talking to them, Kenny got his attention. "Ronnie, this is my friend, Emmy Colasanti. We're neighbors, and we've known each other forever."

Ronnie shook her hand. "It's nice to meet you, Emmy. I enjoyed listening to you."

"Thanks, Mr. Rojas. I hope I didn't sound too terrible."

"You sounded perfect, and please call me Ronnie."

"Okay... Ronnie." She noticed a tattoo of a cross on his arm.

"This isn't your first time here, is it?"

"I came last month with Kenny."

"Oh, that's right, I forgot." He smacked his forehead. "I planned to introduce myself, but then I got busy. Well, come on back whenever you can. Everyone enjoyed hearing you and Kenny sing together."

Kenny put his arm around Emmy's shoulder and smiled at her. "I've been trying to convince Emmy to sing a couple of solos. All she needs is a little more confidence."

"Kenny's right. You have a beautiful voice, and the kids really like you. Will you at least think about it?" Ronnie asked.

"Okay, I'll think about it." Emmy kept her eyes on the carpeted floor.

When Emmy finally noticed the time, she swore under her breath.

"Kenny, I should get home. I told Mom I would be back by eight thirty."

"Em, why didn't you tell me? We can leave now."

By the time Kenny dropped Emmy at her house it was after nine. Mom met her in the kitchen as Emmy came in the back door.

"You are late, young lady."

"I'm sorry, Mom. We got involved with the other kids, and I lost track of time."

"You realize this is a school night, right?"

"I said I'm sorry. What else can I do?" Emmy replied impatiently.

"For one thing, you can lose the attitude," Mom snapped. "I am your mother, and you will not take that tone of voice with me." She seethed, still angry from an argument she had with Raymond that ended with him storming out of the house.

"I didn't mean to be rude," Emmy said meekly.

"From now on, you will be home by eight on school nights. Do you understand?"

"But if I go with Kenny to his church, I won't be home until eight thirty."

"Then I guess you will not be going with him." Mom opened the fridge and pulled out a plate of leftovers. "I don't care if it is going to church. I expected you to be home at eight thirty, and you weren't."

Emmy clenched her fists and seethed inside but didn't respond.

The next day she stopped by his house and told Kenny the news. "I'm sorry I can't sing with you anymore."

Kenny shrugged his shoulders in resignation. "I guess you need to obey your mom, even if she's being totally unreasonable. I can't imagine my parents treating me like that."

"Your parents are sensible human beings. Mine aren't." Emmy sat on a stool, put her elbows on the counter and rested her chin in her hands.

"Maybe she will change her mind after a few weeks, if you behave."

"Ha! Never happen."

"Don't cop an attitude, Em. You mother won't always treat you like an infant."

"Yeah, when I turn thirty and am really old."

"You just want me to feel sorry for you," Kenny said.

74

"Maybe, but she can be really stubborn sometimes."

"Maybe I should talk to her. What do you think?"

"Don't you dare!" Emmy glared.

Emmy's mother refused to change her mind, even after Kenny apologized.

Amy Porter invited Emmy over on Friday night. While Emmy watched a *Seinfeld* rerun, Amy polished her fingernails and toenails.

"Don't you want to do your nails?"

"No, maybe some other time." Emmy cringed. "My mother might get mad if I come home with black fingernails."

"My mother freaked out when she first saw me dressed up."

"I know you hang out with those other Goth girls, but I could never do that." Emmy looked at Amy's ears. "How many piercings do you have?"

"Three in each ear. I'm gonna get more as I get older."

"Where did you have it done?"

"One of Owen's girlfriends works in a beauty salon. She did it. Mom threw a hissy fit, but what can she do, huh?" Amy pulled out one of her earrings and handed it to Emmy. "I could pierce your ears if you want."

"No, thanks." Emmy grabbed her ear lobe as she stared at the earring. "Is this supposed to be a drop of blood?"

Amy nodded and took the earring back.

Owen came home early from his job at Burger Bob's. He grinned as he stood in front of the couch. "Have I ever told you how cute you are, Emmy?"

"No. Do you think I'm cute?"

"I think you're the cutest girl I've seen all day."

Emmy stifled a laugh. *You're so full of BS, Owen.*

Amy stood up, stepped in front of her brother and put her hand on his chest. "Leave her alone, Owen. She's not interested in you."

"Maybe she is, Amy." Owen stepped to the side. "Why don't you be quiet and let Emmy decide if she's interested or not?"

Emmy felt somewhat flattered by the attention from the twenty-year-old as he sat next to her on the couch.

"Have you ever been kissed before?" He slipped his hand behind her shoulder.

"Not that it's any of your business, but Rory tried to kiss me once when we were supposed to be studying, but I turned my head at the last second so he missed. Then I punched him in the belly."

Owen laughed. "Rory sucks at kissing. I'm much better. Just ask Diane."

To prove his point, Owen leaned forward and tried to kiss Emmy. She realized his intentions, so she scooted to the other end of the couch and hugged her knees to her chest. She didn't like the fact that Owen smoked, and she could smell it on his hot breath.

Amy shook a fist at Owen. "I'm telling Mom that you tried to kiss Emmy."

"Go to bed, you little bitch," Owen snarled. "Sorry for the French."

Owen had no idea Emmy heard much worse language at her house almost every night. When her parents argued, they used every four-letter word they knew.

"Emmy, do you want to come upstairs and see my room?" Owen stood up and held out his hand.

"No, not really." Emmy remembered what Amy told her about Owen taking girls up to his room.

"Why not? Don't you like to be kissed?"

"Not by you. You smell like cigarettes, and I don't like that at all."

Owen shrugged and then laughed. "As if I would really mess around with a kid your age." He headed upstairs to his room alone.

Rory bumped into his brother as they passed on the stairs. "Watch where you're going."

"Get out of my way." Owen pushed Rory.

"Anytime, Owen!" Rory smiled. *You can't pick on me now because I'm bigger than you.*

Owen turned and hustled up the stairs.

Rory came downstairs, walked into the kitchen and grabbed

a pop from the fridge. He peeked into the living room, and Emmy saw him.

"Did you pass your math test yesterday?" Emmy asked.

Rory ignored her.

Emmy turned on the couch to face him and raised her voice. "Well, did you pass or not?"

"Yeah, I passed with a seventy-nine, no thanks to you," Rory answered and then smacked the door frame.

Emmy jumped. "What do you mean by that?" *Thanks for the gratitude.*

"I could have done better if I had cheated like I used to do."

"Then forget it. I'm not going to waste my time if you don't even try." She turned away and crossed her arms over her chest.

"Sorry, Emmy. I didn't mean to get on your case." He took a couple of steps toward her. "I appreciate the help, but I've got lots of stuff on my mind."

"Like what?" Emmy put her feet on the floor and stared at him. "You can tell me anything."

"Nothing that you should know about." He turned around and walked through the kitchen and out the back door.

Emmy cringed as he slammed the door shut.

Amy checked her toenails, pulled the cotton balls from between her toes and looked at Emmy. "You've got a crush on Rory. You should let him know."

"I do not!" Emmy insisted.

"Yeah, right," Amy said. "I saw how you looked at him."

Emmy saw Owen Porter occasionally at Burger Bob's. One afternoon, Emmy waited in line behind some guys from Roosevelt as Owen worked the counter.

"May I take your order, please?" Owen asked in a monotone.

"Yes, I'd like a double cheeseburger with a large fry and a Coke. No, wait. Make that a triple cheeseburger without pickles and an onion ring. Think you can get that right, Porter? The last time I came in here, you screwed up my order."

"I'll try to get it right this time," Owen said.

The other two jocks repeated the routine as they harassed Owen. Owen couldn't respond to their taunting because his boss stood a couple of feet away. When Emmy's turn came to place her order, Owen asked, without looking up, "May I take your order, please?"

"Yes, you may."

He looked up. "Oh, hi, Emmy. What can I get for you?"

"Could I have a small chopped salad and a medium Coke, please?"

"I'll bring it over to you when it's ready."

"Thanks, I will be over there by the window."

"I think I'll be able to find you," Owen answered sarcastically.

When Owen brought her salad over, she said quietly, "I'm never going to do what you asked, Owen."

Owen didn't remember exactly what he asked Emmy to do. "If that's what you want, fine with me. Don't bother coming over to see me anymore."

Emmy's eyes flared with anger. "I never come over to see you. You arrogant, egotistical jerk."

"Yeah, whatever." He turned, saw a cute girl waiting in line and waved at her. "I'll be right there." He forgot about his conversation with Emmy as soon as he took the next customer's order.

Emmy finished her salad and took her pop home with her. Though pleased she stood up to Owen, she became angry at herself for ever allowing him to try to kiss her. She remembered what Kenny told her about learning from her mistakes and vowed to do just that.

Chapter Nine

In mid-December Kenny finished his year at Paul Frank. He stopped to see Emmy and tell her the news. "I finished my last final. I hope I never have to take another one of those."

"Do you think you passed?" Emmy folded freshly laundered clothes on the kitchen table.

"Probably, but I'm not gonna lose any sleep over it if I didn't. Wanna help me celebrate?"

"What do you wanna do?" Emmy finished folding her laundry.

"I'm hungry. Let's go to Darby's."

"Sure. Just give me a sec to put these away."

She carried the basket into her room, and Kenny stood in the doorway.

"I haven't been in your room for years, Em." Kenny noticed the old wallpaper had either been removed or painted over. "I like this color. What do you call it?"

"Green," Emmy teased.

"I know that. I thought maybe it was a special shade."

"Diane picked it out. I don't know what it's called," she said as she opened a dresser drawer.

"Do you still have your music box?" *How do you and Diane manage to share a room this small.*

"Of course. I'll never get rid of it."

"I remember when you first showed it to me. You loved it so much."

"I always think of Grandma when I see it." She put the last of her clothes away. "I'm ready to go."

He took her to Darby's. While she grabbed a booth, Kenny brought the food back and noticed a new photograph on the wall above them.

"Hey, did you see this? I think this is from our first gig at the youth center."

Emmy snatched a couple of fries, and then looked at the photo. "I look like a little girl."

"You look very pretty, Em."

79

She blushed. "So you're all done with college, huh?"

"Yeah, this year lasted forever. I'm glad it's over. My parents are happy that I finished out the year."

Emmy bit her lip. "Now you guys will be gone all the time. I won't ever see you again."

"That's not true, Em. Yeah, we will be traveling a lot, but we will be home occasionally."

"Not often enough," Emmy's voice cracked.

Christmas morning turned into a disaster as Emmy's parents argued about money, unpaid utility bills, and a light fixture. Her father stormed out of the house. Diane fled to spend the day with Craig.

"Looks like it will be just the two of us. I can't believe your father is too lazy to fix the light fixture in our room," Mom said as she collapsed into her chair

Emmy moved to the edge of the couch. *I don't want to be stuck here.*

Mom interrupted Emmy's thought. "I get so aggravated at your sister. I caught her in a lie yesterday, and you don't make matters any easier, young lady." Mom shook her finger at Emmy. "I'm going to have another glass of eggnog."

Emmy followed her mother into the kitchen. "I'm gonna see if Kenny's home." She grabbed her coat and escaped out the back door before Mom could react.

"Oh, well, at least I'll have some peace and quiet," Mom muttered under her breath as she added some rum to her eggnog.

Emmy dashed through the alley to the Colwell's house. She knocked on the back door, and Kenny's mother let her in.

"Is Kenny here, Mrs. Colwell?" she asked.

"He's in the living room with his father, dear. Are you all right?"

Kenny heard his mother talking and walked into the kitchen.

Emmy bit her lip to keep it from quivering. "I'm okay."

Kenny knew better. "Come on, Emmy. Let's sit in the living room." He held her hand.

She whispered, "Mom and Daddy yelled at each other. Then he left. Diane escaped to go see Craig. I didn't want to stay home with just Mom because she will complain about everyone and make it be my fault somehow."

"You can stay here with us. Are you hungry?"

She realized Mom had not made any breakfast. In fact she had not eaten since Christmas Eve in the late afternoon. "I am kinda hungry."

Mrs. Colwell stood up. "We haven't eaten, either. We usually have a late brunch on Christmas Day. I was going to make pancakes with blueberries. Maybe some hash browns, sausage, bacon and eggs. Would any of that appeal to you?"

"I've never eaten pancakes with blueberries before. That sounds really good." Emmy could hear her stomach rumbling and wondered if everyone else could.

"Why don't you come to the kitchen, and we can get started."

Fifteen minutes later everyone took a seat at the kitchen table. Mr. Colwell prayed, and they began eating.

Emmy's eyes lit up as she tasted the blueberry pancakes. "These are so good, Mrs. Colwell."

"I'm glad you like them, dear. I can make more if you would like."

Emmy's heart filled with joy as she shared a Christmas breakfast with the Colwell family.

Later, Emmy mentioned, "I can help with the dishes, Mrs. Colwell. I do them at home all the time."

"That's very generous of you, dear, but Carter and I can take care of the cleanup. Why don't you and Kenny have some fun?"

Kenny set the plates on the counter next to the sink. "I got two new movies for Christmas. Wanna watch with me?"

"Okay. What did you get?" Emmy followed Kenny to the living room.

"I got *True Lies* and *Pulp Fiction*. Have you seen them?"

"No, but I've heard about them. I like Ah-nold." She sat on the couch.

"We can watch *True Lies* first since you like Ah-nold so much." Kenny popped the DVD into the player and joined her on the couch. "Can you hand me the remote, please?"

She grabbed the remote from the end table, handed it to Kenny and scooted closer to him.

"Thanks." He smiled as he looked into her blue eyes. "I'm sorry your parents were fighting, but now we can spend the afternoon together."

"I'm used to it." She bit her lip. *I'm kinda glad they did fight. It gave me a good excuse to come over.*

His parents joined them partway through the movie. Mr. Colwell sat in his recliner while Mrs. Colwell sat on the couch next to Emmy. Emmy scooted closer to Kenny.

"Do you mind if I sit this close?" she asked as her leg touched his.

"I don't mind. Do you have enough room, Mom? Em can scoot over if you need more space."

"I'm all right," Mrs. Colwell answered, but Emmy still scooted closer to Kenny.

Kenny smiled at Emmy. "It's a good thing you don't need a lot of space."

She smiled back. *I might have to sit on your lap if more people come over.*

"I remember this part." Mr. Colwell laughed. "Watch what happens..."

"Dad, Emmy hasn't seen it. Don't tell her about it."

"Sorry, Emmy. I'll be quiet now."

Ninety minutes later the movie ended.

"What a cool ending," Mr. Colwell remarked.

"I'm glad you woke up in time to see the end, Dad."

"I stayed awake for most of it."

Mrs. Colwell stood up. "I think we should go upstairs and take our afternoon nap, Carter."

"What about the next movie?"

"You can watch it later. Let's let Kenny and Emmy watch it first." She took his hand and led him upstairs.

"I like to take my naps in my recliner. Why do we have to

leave?"

"So the kids can have some privacy," Mrs. Colwell answered as they climbed the oak stairs.

"Why? It's Emmy. She's always watched TV with us."

Mrs. Colwell shook her head. "You don't get it, do you?"

"I'm clueless. Fill me in."

"She's not a little girl anymore."

Mr. Colwell stopped and looked back down the stairs. "Are you telling me?" He waved his hand.

"They are growing up, and their friendship is gonna go through some interesting changes." She pulled him up the stairs. "You can watch TV in our room if you want."

"I had no idea," he said as he scratched his jaw.

"Are you ready for *Pulp Fiction*?" Kenny asked Emmy as he switched the DVDs.

"Yeah, I'm thirsty. Do you want something?" She headed to the kitchen. "I'm gonna grab a Coke."

"I'll take one, too. Can you grab a bag of chips from the pantry, please?"

She came back with the pop and chips. "Make sure you use a coaster. I don't want your mother to get mad at you."

"I only forgot that one time." He noticed the circle on the end table.

After the movie ended, Kenny grabbed the two empty pop cans and headed to the kitchen, "So what did you think, Em?"

Emmy ate the last crumbs from the chip bag and followed. "I got lost a few times when they were doing those flashbacks, but I liked it."

Mr. and Mrs. Colwell came back downstairs.

Mr. Colwell grinned. "How was the movie? Or did you guys even watch it?"

Mrs. Colwell smacked his arm.

"What?"

"You're worse than a child at times, Carter." She looked at Kenny and Emmy. "Are you hungry? I could make something."

"Maybe later, Mom," Kenny answered.

Emmy looked at the clock. "I should go, Kenny. Mom will

get mad if I stay away all day." Emmy retrieved her coat from the hook by the back door.

"Hang on a sec. I'll walk you home."

Emmy's eyes sparkled. "You don't have to do that." *But I'd really like it if you did.*

"It's all right. I could use the fresh air."

He walked her back to her house. She paused on the back steps and faced him.

"Thanks for letting me come over." She glanced up as a few snowflakes started falling.

"You're always welcome, Em. You know that." He waited for her to dash inside, but she didn't. *Is it my imagination, or are you getting prettier as you grow up? I know we're best friends, but one of these days I'm gonna kiss you.*

"It's a little late for a white Christmas, but I love it when we get a lot of snow." She looked at Kenny and took a deep breath. *I really liked watching those movies and sitting real close to you. I thought maybe you might kiss me since your parents weren't in the room.*

Kenny reached for her hand. "If we get a lot of snow, maybe we could go to Windsor Park and go sledding. You always liked doing that when we were younger."

"Yeah! That would be fun."

Kenny leaned forward. *I wonder if she will get mad if I kiss her cheek?*

Emmy's eyes opened wide. *Is he gonna kiss me? Oh, God! What should I do?* She slipped on the wet step and placed her hands on his shoulders to regain her balance.

"Are you all right?" Kenny asked as he licked his lips.

"I slipped." She leaned her head closer to his and closed her eyes.

The mood was shattered as the back door opened, and Emmy's mother stepped onto the porch. "Are you getting cold, Kenny? Do you want to come inside? Emmy needs to get in the house."

Emmy jumped as her mother startled her. She turned around. "Mom! Why did you do that?" *You ruined everything just*

84

like you always do.

Kenny put a hand on her back to keep her steady. "I should get going. I'll call you later, Em. Merry Christmas, Mrs. Colasanti."

Emmy clenched her hands into fists, frowned at her mother, and then spun around to face Kenny. "Bye, Kenny. I had fun."

"Merry Christmas to you, too, Kenny. Please say hi to your mother for me." Mrs. Colasanti held the door open for Emmy as Kenny walked away.

"Mother, how could you?" Emmy muttered. She hung up her coat and moved past her mother. She hurried to her room, lay on the bed and stared at the ceiling. *I think I will remember this Christmas for as long as I live.*

In early February, Diane walked into the bedroom after her shift at Teens Forever. Emmy was on the bed with a picture frame in her hands.

"What are you looking at, Em?" Diane sat on the edge of the bed.

"Nothing!" Emmy attempted to shove the picture under her pillow but Diane grabbed it.

"This is you and Kenny. Why were you staring at it?"

"I wasn't staring. Give it back to me." Emmy grabbed at the picture, but Diane stood up and held it behind her back. Emmy moved onto her knees. "I'll hit you if I have to."

"Here! You can have it. Have you talked to him lately?" Diane asked as changed clothes.

"Not for a couple weeks. They've been busy." She moved onto her back and held the picture up in front of her. "I kinda feel like I don't know what's going on with the band anymore."

"You're sorta out of the loop, huh?"

"Yeah, and I miss him."

Diane jumped onto her side of the bed and landed on her back. She turned on her side and looked at Emmy. "Oh, my God! You've got a crush on him..."

"No, I don't!" Emmy shouted. "He's my friend."

"That a bunch of bull. You like him, and I don't mean as a

85

friend. Does he feel the same way?"

"I'm not sure." Emmy explained everything that happened at Christmas. "I thought he might kiss me, but he didn't. Then when he walked me home, Mom interrupted us."

"It sounds like he might feel the same way. That is so weird. You guys have been best friends since you were a baby."

"I was not a baby when we met. I was seven."

"I guess it's not impossible for friends to fall in love with each other." Diane turned onto her back.

"I'm not in love with him." Emmy kicked Diane's foot.

"We'll see about that."

One warm spring afternoon, Emmy stopped by Kenny's after school. Climbing the stairs to the second floor of the carriage house, she listened as Kenny's fingers flew over the neck of his guitar. She kicked off her shoes and laid on the couch, her legs dangling over the arm. She wore her favorite faded jeans, the ones with the hole over the knee, and an old sweatshirt. After he finished his guitar solo, Kenny finally noticed her and smiled. He stepped on the pedal to mute the sound, placed his guitar on the stand and collapsed next to her on the worn sofa.

"I'm sorry, Em. I didn't even hear you come upstairs. Have you been here long?"

"Maybe a minute."

"I thought you would be babysitting today."

"Normally, I would be, but Mrs. Rivera gave me the day off."

"I was so wrapped up in practicing that solo. How are you, by the way?"

"I'm fine. I've really been busy lately. How's the band doing? I really feel out of the loop."

"We're doing great. We have a steady gig at the Graffiti Gallery in Chicago on Fridays, and, on Saturday, we play in Newcastle at the Broken Horseshoe. That way we don't have to travel as much. We play on Wednesdays and Thursdays occasionally, too. We're also working in a local recording studio. We're gonna release "Too Bad" as a single before the CD comes out."

Emmy glanced at him and bit her lip.

"What's wrong?" he asked.

"Nothing."

"Emmy," he said slowly. "Something's up. You can tell me." He sat on the couch and motioned for her to turn around.

She sat up and swung her legs around, putting them in his lap.

He grabbed her ankles. "Are you gonna tell me what's bothering you, or am I going to have to tickle it out of you?"

"I'm not in the mood for tickling."

"I won't." He released her ankles. "What's wrong, little one?"

She sat up. "Are you sure you want to hear about my stuff? It's boring compared to your life."

"If it concerns you, then it's important to me. Tell me, Em."

"Rory Porter tried to kiss me. I didn't let him."

"That's good."

"Then another time Owen tried to kiss me. He smokes, and I could smell the cigarettes on his breath and his clothes. He asked me to... do something, but I didn't." She blushed—too embarrassed to tell Kenny that Owen asked her to come up to his room.

"Tell me you're not still sneaking around with Rory."

"No, I'm not doing that anymore."

"You should stay away from those guys." Kenny knew their reputations. "Why do you see them at all? You deserve better than those two jerks."

"I don't know any other boys in the neighborhood, except for Barry Newton, and Barry doesn't like me anymore. He won't even talk to me."

"There must be some other boys in the neighborhood, and why do you have to be thinking about boys at all? You aren't even old enough to date. I know, because I've listened to you complain about Diane before and the way your parents treat you differently."

"I don't always think about boys, but I do sometimes. Most of them are immature and not as nice as you." Emmy moved closer to him until their hips touched. She watched his eyes to gauge his reaction. *I hope you like sitting this close.*

Kenny's heart began to beat faster. *This is even better than Christmas!* "Are you all right with this?" He put his hand on her knee and touched her warm skin through the rip in her jeans watching closely for her reaction. He moved his fingers on her knee. "You know you are always welcome to hang out with me and the band. The guys miss you." He didn't add, *I miss you.* Instead he asked, "Did Owen really try to kiss you?"

"He tried, but I punched him in the belly."

Kenny shook his head at her for being so gullible and naïve. He looked down at her knee and touched a small scar.

"I remember when you got this."

"I fell at school, and you carried me inside." *I wish you would carry me like that again.*

His heart began to race. "You were so brave. You didn't even cry." He looked at her face.

She bit her lip as she looked into his eyes. *Do you know how I feel about you? Do I really know how I feel?*

He took a deep breath and held it. *Oh, Em, you are prettier than ever. I don't know how much longer I can think of you as just a friend.*

He exhaled as she moved closer to him—their faces now only inches apart. He didn't know where to put his hands.

Diane was right. I do have a crush on you. She felt her face and neck blush as she imagined his lips on hers.

He reached for her hand, and their fingers intertwined.

Your mother had better not appear out of thin air and ruin this moment. He leaned forward and kissed her.

She kept her eyes closed as she felt the brush of his lips on hers. Then they were gone. *More! Kiss me some more.* She wished with her very soul.

It was the first time he ever tried to kiss her, though he had thought about it many times. He kissed her again as he squeezed her small hand.

"Oh, Em, you taste sweeter than wild mountain honey," he whispered. "Can I kiss you again?"

Emmy kissed him back as he leaned over her. "You can

88

kiss me as much as you want." She touched his chest with her free hand and felt his beating heart.

He closed his eyes and tilted his head. "I want to keep kissing you until we can do it perfectly."

She giggled and then said, "We might have to practice a lot."

He twisted his upper body and held her in his arms. "I'm used to a lot of practicing."

She felt her heart thumping and her face turning red. She wanted him to kiss her forever, but he stopped. He sat up and moved his hands away.

"Did I do something wrong?" Emmy asked. "I can learn to kiss better."

"No, Emmy, you didn't do anything wrong. That's the problem. You did everything just right."

"Then why did you stop?" She reached out and kissed him again.

"Oh, Emmy, you are so trusting. I don't want to take advantage of you."

"I know you wouldn't do anything to hurt me. That's why I trust you."

"I'm sorry I took advantage of you when you were feeling vulnerable. I don't know what came over me. I have always thought of you as being very pretty, but I never gave in to the urge to kiss you like that before."

"I'm not sorry. I've dreamed about how it would be to kiss you for the first time."

"Was it as good as your dream?" He took her hands and squeezed them.

"Even better!" she said with a grin. "Are we gonna keep practicing?"

"I'd like that very much, but we need to be careful."

"I'm not gonna be like Diane."

"I know that, but your feelings for me might change. We are still really young."

"No they won't! You're my hero for hire, remember." She stood up and faced him, "Do you have a girlfriend that I don't know about?"

He jumped up. "You know I don't have a girlfriend." Kenny playfully swatted her backside. "I spend so much time practicing my music that I don't have any time left over for a girlfriend."

Emmy turned to face him suddenly, and he bumped into her. "Would you have time for me if I was your girlfriend?"

He held her shoulders tenderly. *We've been best friends for as long as I can remember. I can't change everything overnight.*

She bit her lip as she put her hands behind her back. "Well?"

"I can't get into anything serious right now. This takes time, Em."

"Good." She put her arms around him and pulled him close. "As long as I know you're not looking for a serious relationship with someone else, then I can wait."

He could smell strawberry shampoo as he buried his nose in her hair. He felt her tremble as he put his hands on her waist. For a moment they just held onto each other without saying a word.

"I gotta go. I have to be home for dinner. I'll be grounded for life if I'm ever late again."

She started to go down the steep stairs, but paused. "Will you go down first? I don't like these steep stairs, and I'm always afraid I might fall."

"Okay, give me a second." He climbed down and looked up at her.

Emmy smiled, knowing he cared enough to watch out for her. He walked her home and kissed her cheek. Before she ran in the house, Emmy hollered, "You're still my hero for hire, even if you like other girls."

"You're still my sweet girl, Emmy."

When Kenny got back to his room, he remembered the phrase Emmy used and scribbled it down. He thought it might make a good song title.

Every day that she could, Emmy visited Kenny after

90

school. They sat on the old couch and studied his notebook of ideas for songs. She sang along to his songs. Occasionally she offered suggestions for the lyrics.

One afternoon, Emmy decided to surprise him. She brought a blanket. Kenny didn't notice it at first because his back was turned as he practiced his guitar. Emmy placed the folded blanket on the couch. Then she touched his shoulder.

"Hey, Kenny, I'm here."

He turned on his heels to face her nearly clobbering her with the guitar.

"Whoa, sorry, Em. That was close."

"Good thing I ducked." *Are you gonna kiss me again?*

I wish I knew if you wanted me to kiss you again. The temptation virtually overwhelmed him. Instead of kissing her, he mentioned, "We are going to be on the road full-time real soon. We have a professional band manager, Andrew Walker. He just left The Swirling Teddys. We're using the Prater-Saylor Agency as our booking agent, and we already have a tour booked. I can't wait to be able to play our music for a living," he explained. He finally noticed the blanket. "What are you doing with that old blanket, Em?"

She turned and spread the blanket out on the couch. "We're going to get under the blanket and make out." She turned back toward Kenny and grinned.

Kenny's jaw dropped. Slowly his expression changed to a smile, and his brown eyes danced. *I guess you do want me to kiss you.* He placed his guitar in its case.

"So you want to practice something other than music, huh?" He took a step toward her and reached out his hands.

She stuck out her hands to keep him away. "I'm kidding! I just wanted to see the expression on your face. I put the blanket on the couch because it's so dirty and dusty."

"So you don't want to kiss me again?"

"I didn't mean it like that. You can kiss me, but I'm not gonna do what Diane would." She closed her eyes and tilted her head up.

He moved closer. "How's this for a kiss, Em?" He kissed

her cheek.

She opened her eyes and put her hands on her hips. "Hey! That's how Grandma kisses me. I want a real kiss."

"Okay, one kiss, but that's all for now." He wrapped his arms around her waist but didn't pull her too close. He kissed her lips tenderly for a few seconds.

"That's better." She moved to the couch, took off her shoes and sat down. "This is better. We have to remember to take it outside and shake it out once in a while."

She looked at Kenny with admiration. His brown hair was getting longer. It dangled over the edge of his collar, and he needed a shave. He turned on the stereo.

"Who is that?"

"It's White Heart. This is their *Highland* CD."

"I like! Turn it up."

He cranked up the music, turned off the lights, walked to the couch and sat beside Emmy. The red lights from his stereo cast an eerie glow. He had also been thinking about *the* kiss. Emmy felt her heart flutter. Then it began racing. She yearned for Kenny to kiss her again. He needed to kiss her. He reached out for her. She fell back on the couch. He lost his balance and landed on top of her. She felt his cheek brush against hers. Their noses bumped. Then their lips met.

Emmy giggled and then said, "I think we should practice more often."

"I think so, too. We just have to remember to be cautious." He moved his hands to her shoulders.

Suddenly, the room was flooded in light. Jeff turned on the light startling both Emmy and Kenny.

"What the heck?" Jeremy hollered.

"What are you guys doing in the dark?" Jeff asked.

Kenny jumped up as he saw the guys. Emmy lay on the couch with her eyes closed, and both guys saw her before she could get up.

"We weren't doing anything!" Kenny exclaimed as his face turned red.

"It sure looks like you were getting ready to," Jeff teased.

Emmy crossed her arms over her chest and bit her lip. Then she stood up, smiled at the guys and asked, "Am I your favorite groupie now?"

They laughed at her joke.

"You're too young to be a groupie, Emmy," Jeff said as he chuckled.

Kenny turned down the music, and then looked at his watch. "I'll be right back, guys. I gotta get my chores done before Mom gets home."

"Do you need my help?" Emmy asked as she followed him to the top of the stairs.

"Thanks, but it will only take a few minutes. Why don't you hang out with these two yahoos and listen to some tunes."

Emmy stayed upstairs in the carriage house with Jeff and Jeremy. They listened to the music, and she grinned impishly. "I've got a crush on Kenny."

"No! Really? Tell us something we don't know," Jeff said. "Emmy, you are going to break a lot of hearts when you get older."

"Why do you say that?"

"Duh! You are going to be so gorgeous that every guy in the world will want to be your boyfriend, and you will be true to only one of them."

Jeremy played a few chords on the keyboard. "Hey, that sounds like a song. 'I Will Be True To You.' Yeah, I think we can fit that to the tune we worked on last week. We just need to come up with the rest of the lyrics."

Emmy sat on the couch with Jeff. "Thanks for the compliment."

Jeff said, "We knew you were developing some stronger feelings for Kenny. We didn't want to say anything as long as nothing happened, but..."

Jeremy stopped playing. "You are still rather young, Emmy."

Emmy frowned. *Come on. You guys aren't that old. You're starting to sound like my father.*

"He's right." Jeff nodded. "And besides, we will be on the road full-time pretty soon. It's really not the best time to be starting a serious relationship."

"I know," she said. "Kenny and I talked a little bit about that. He's not ready for a serious relationship yet."

"It's really hard when we're gone so much." Jeff looked to Jeremy for reassurance. *Help me out here, buddy.*

"He's right, Emmy. Amanda and I have been dating for two years, so I know how difficult it is to keep things going."

Emmy's feelings were hurt, but she knew Jeff was giving her some good advice. "It's kinda good in a way. At least he won't be looking for a girlfriend on the road."

Kenny returned, and the guys practiced a couple of new songs as Emmy sat behind the drum kit and kept time on the snare.

"Hey, remember that tune we worked on last week?" Jeff played a riff on his bass.

"Yeah, we need to finish the lyrics," Kenny said.

"Jeremy thought of a title. 'I Will Be True To You.' I think it fits the few lyrics we had."

"Well, let's work on it and see what we come up with."

Within an hour the guys completed the song. Emmy even made some contributions to the lyrics.

"I wish all our songs were so easy to write. Sometimes it takes forever to come up with decent lyrics," Kenny admitted to the guys.

"I hear ya. I like the chord progression, and that guitar hook is sweet." Jeff high-fived Kenny.

They finished practicing, and Emmy told Jeff and Jeremy goodbye outside the carriage house.

What am I gonna say to her? Kenny thought as they walked along the alley. *I really don't want to lose her friendship.*

Emmy held Kenny's hand as they walked. "How long do we have before you have to leave again?"

"We'll be home part of the time until June. After that." He shrugged. "I'm not sure how often I'll be back. Why?"

"Just wondering." She jumped over a puddle of water.

Kenny grinned as he thought it was charming that she still acted like a kid at times. *I've gotta think of something to say.* His feelings for her flipped back and forth.

They turned into her back yard and walked up to the house. She stood on the bottom step of the porch and faced him.

Okay, here goes. He held her hands. "Emmy, I love you like... like my little sister, or my best friend. I don't want to jeopardize the love I feel for you by starting something that would only end in you being hurt."

"I don't care if you hurt me." Emmy's face radiated because he said he loved her.

"Emmy!" Kenny turned away until he regained his composure.

"What's wrong?"

He turned back and placed his hands on her shoulders. "You should care. We are both too young to get really serious. Your friendship is worth more to me than anything, and I don't want to jeopardize that."

"I guess I understand. I wish I was older. Then it wouldn't matter."

"Em, you're only fifteen."

"I'll be sixteen in July. I know that's still too young to get serious, but I'm not interested in any other guys."

He smiled. *That's good!*

She kissed him quickly and ran into the house.

Kenny waited outside for a moment as he tried to make a decision. *I am gonna be around until June.* He could still taste the sweetness of her lips on his. He put a foot on the bottom step, and then the next step. *We don't have to get too serious.* He paused for a second, climbed the next steps and stood before the back door. *What am I doing?* He started to knock but stopped with his hand inches from the door. *The timing is all wrong. My heart tells me to knock, but my mind says no.*

Emmy leaned against the wall just out of sight. *Oh, Kenny, don't leave. Please knock on the door. Please! Please!* She crossed her fingers.

He turned around and quietly left.

Emmy waited for ten seconds before she looked out the door. "Why did you leave, Kenny?" she whispered as a tear slid down her cheek.

95

He returned to his room above the garage. He sat at his desk and wrote another song about her. He cried as he wrote the song, because he wasn't totally honest with Emmy. He did have feelings for her and definitely not as a little sister. He read through the lyrics again. Made a few changes and then sang them out loud. *Whoa! This is really personal. I don't want Emmy to hear this just yet.* He chuckled. *I definitely don't want to share it with the band. I'll keep it locked away for now. Maybe I'll sing it to Em in a few years.*

He stared at a picture of them taken years ago as they sat on the back porch, sighed and whispered, "Oh, Emmy, if only you weren't so young."

Chapter Ten

"It's new release Tuesday on WSHO. This is a new one by local favorites, Fridays At Five. It's called 'Too Bad,' and it goes like this."

Emmy heard the tune on the local SoHam station and screamed as she pounded the dashboard of Rory's red 1993 Camaro Z28 in time to the music.

"I guess you must like this song, huh?" Rory pulled into the parking lot of Burger Bob's.

"You do know who this is, right?" She jumped out of the car. "I'm going to buy a dozen copies as soon as Mrs. Rivera pays me."

Rory walked around the car and smiled at her. "Can I have one? How about an autographed copy?"

"Maybe. If you buy today, I'll see if Kenny will autograph a copy for you."

"Deal." He put an arm around her shoulders. "Does he know you've got a crush on him?"

She didn't answer.

Fridays At Five were now on the road full-time, playing on their own at small venues and opening in larger locations for the main headliners. Often they blew away the main act. Steward Music Group released the CD single "Too Bad" on June eleventh, and it hit the charts two weeks later.

Kenny called her unexpectedly one evening. "Hey, Emmy. Are you busy? Wanna hear about what I've done with the carriage house?"

"No, don't tell me, show me. I'll be right there." Emmy hurried over. Kenny met her at the bottom of the stairs holding the CD single in his hand.

"I have a present for you though it's not your birthday yet."

"I heard it on WSHO the other day, and I screamed. Just think. You guys are on the radio."

"Yeah, and people are actually buying it."

97

They went up to his room. *Wake Up Call* by Petra blasted from the stereo. Kenny turned the volume down so they could talk without shouting.

"Wow! You've been busy, I see." Emmy spun 360 degrees. "I'm impressed. I really like what you've done."

He used some of his earnings to fix the upstairs into a livable apartment.

"I wanted a closet, so we did that. The water and waste lines were already in the garage so we extended them up here. We upgraded the electrical, put in a new furnace and get this... it's even air-conditioned now."

"Do you plan to live out here and not in the main house when you're home?"

"Probably. I have more privacy out here. Mom never comes up here. I'm going to get some cheap furniture and a microwave. Then I'll be all set."

Emmy saw the old couch in its familiar spot. "Why have you kept this dusty old thing?" she asked over her shoulder as she walked toward it.

"It has some sentimental value. I don't want to throw it away." Kenny didn't want to tell Emmy that he really kept it because that was where he first kissed her.

Emmy plopped down on the couch, and Kenny sat next to her. He kissed her cheek tenderly, but didn't try anything else.

"Did I tell you I applied at Darby's?" Emmy said though she thought, *I want you to kiss me, you dork.*

"You might have mentioned it." He wet his lips as he looked at hers.

"Mr. Darby told me he would hire me when I turn sixteen." She turned sideways and sat on her feet.

"Good. That will pay you more than babysitting for Mrs. Rivera."

Emmy sat up a little higher. "If I ask you something serious, will you tell me the truth?"

"Depends."

"Come on, Kenny, promise you'll tell me the truth."

"All right. I promise." He thought Emmy would ask him if

98

he still thought of her as a little sister.

"Do you meet lots of girls on the road?" She ran a hand through his hair.

"Yeah. A lot of our fans are girls. You know that."

"Have you slept with any of them?"

Kenny's face registered surprise, but then again, Emmy had never been shy about asking him anything.

"Yes, I have met plenty of girls on the road, and, of course, I sleep with a different one every night. Sometimes two or three."

Emmy looked hurt until Kenny told her, "I'm kidding, Em." He paused. "But I did kiss a few girls in the beginning of our tour."

"I knew it!" She poked him in the chest. "You're only in a band for the girls."

"That's not true." He protested as he grabbed her hands. "Yeah, maybe that's one of the perks, but it's not the main reason and you know that, you stinker."

"How many have you really kissed?"

"Oh, way too many to count. I lost track after reaching a hundred," he teased.

Emmy pulled her hands away. "You better be careful, or else you will catch a disease." She poked his arm. "I hope you use protection if you plan to sleep with any of the girls you meet. I know you probably have lots of offers."

"Without fail. I know better than to have unprotected sex."

"You shouldn't be having sex at all."

"Do we have to talk about this?" He leaned back and closed his eyes.

"Yes, now open your eyes and pay attention." She turned on the couch. She sat with her feet dangled over the front edge. She touched his cheek and felt his whiskers. "Did you go to confession?"

He opened his eyes. "We don't have confession at our church, Emmy."

"Then how do you get absolved?"

"You ask Jesus to forgive you for your sins. Remember when I talked to you about being saved?"

"Yeah, kinda. You don't have to talk to the priest?"

"We don't have priests. We have pastors and ministers. They even get married." He slid his hand along her leg.

"Do you still go to church every week?"

"I used to before the band started touring. I suppose I should start going again. I miss it, and I know my parents want me to go. Do you think your mom will let you go with me again, Em, or is she still mad at me?" He patted her thigh in time to the tune in his head.

"I don't think she's mad at you anymore, but she said if I wanted to go to church, I had to go to St. John's."

"If she changes her mind, I'll take you with me."

Kenny looked at her and noticed a tear in the corner of her eye. "Emmy, are you upset that I kissed someone else?"

"Of course not. You know I'm too young to make out with you," she replied, although she was disappointed. "I know that guys sometimes need to... you know..." She didn't know quite how to say what she meant, but he understood. Emmy smiled at Kenny and reminded him, "Do you remember that you were going to kiss me that day before Jeff and Jeremy caught us? I'll always remember that day because I got all embarrassed, but now it seems funny."

"It will always be special to me, and not because Jeff and Jeremy interrupted us."

Emmy laughed as she remembered how they were caught in the act. "Have you tried drugs?"

"No way. I don't want to ruin my career. I haven't tried any drugs, and I don't smoke alcohol or drink cigarettes, either... You know what I mean."

She smiled at his mistake. She intertwined her fingers with his and squeezed his hand.

"Jeff smokes, but he's trying to quit. The guys will have a beer after the show, but that's it. Andy is real strict about not having drugs around. He fired a guy we were trying out for the crew when he caught him with some pills."

"I'm kinda scared of Andy," she admitted.

"He can come across as rather intimidating." *Until you get to know him.*

100

"Do the other guys go to church?"

"That was one of the things we talked about before we even started practicing. Jeff goes to a Baptist church, and Jeremy and Dave attend a Presbyterian church. Although they admitted they are not real regular at getting there."

"What about the guys in the crew?"

Kenny told her what he knew about the rest of the crew.

"Since we are asking serious questions, I have one for you, Em. Do you have a new boyfriend?"

"No!" Her ponytail flipped back and forth as she shook her head.

"Are you still sweet and innocent?"

She giggled and then said, "If you are asking if I am still a virgin, the answer is definitely yes."

He sat up straight and let go of her hand. "Emmy! I meant, have you kissed any other boys? I never for one second thought you would... you know."

"I know. I wanted to see if you would get embarrassed by me saying that." She scooted around and sat next to him with her back against the couch.

"Well, I am kinda embarrassed. I know there is a lot of peer pressure from kids today to grow up quicker than you should."

"I'm not ready to be all grown up yet, Kenny. I just can't wait 'til I turn sixteen, though. I'm not really ready to date, let alone do something more serious. Some of the girls in school brag about how many times they've had sex with their boyfriends."

"You should stay that way until you are absolutely ready. Don't give in to pressure from some of those kids who think you have to... uh, give yourself away or whatever. Sex is better when you are in love with the person, and even better when it is saved for after marriage."

Emmy looked at Kenny but didn't say anything. *This is something I should have heard from my mother but never did.*

"Do you still see Owen or Rory?" Kenny asked to break the silence.

"I see Owen at Burger Bob's once in a while, and I still tutor Rory occasionally, but not as much as before." *Should I tell you that I went there once with Rory? Maybe later. It wasn't like a date. We kinda hang out at times.*

Kenny pulled Emmy closer and put his arm around her shoulder. They looked into each other's eyes. They talked about old times when they were kids and laughed at some of the things that happened before... as if it were a long time ago. She snuggled close and rested her head against his chest. She felt his heart pounding.

"I miss you. I'm afraid you'll forget me when you become a famous rock star."

"I'll never forget you, m'lady," Kenny used his old term of endearment for her. "You're the inspiration for the first song I ever wrote, remember? You'll always be my 'Sweet Girl.'"

He held her in his arms, and they sat quietly on the dusty old couch. The bulb in the lamp next to the couch popped and burned out, leaving them in total darkness. "I think I have another bulb around somewhere. I'll turn on another light so we can see."

She held onto him and didn't let him up.

"You don't need to, Kenny. I'm not afraid to be in the dark with you. It's kinda nice. Even a little romantic." She snuggled even closer to Kenny and turned her head toward his.

"Emmy, what are you thinking about?"

"I want you to kiss me again, Kenny. I want to kiss you so much, and I want you to hold me close."

"Emmy, is this because of what I told you about the girls on the road?"

"No, I don't care about them. I want you to kiss me so you won't forget me."

"You know that's never going to happen, Em."

"I just want to make sure," she whispered.

Emmy moved close, and her lips met his. They kissed once very quickly, and then stopped. Kenny took her hand in his, and they kissed again. *Your hands are so small compared to mine.*

Emmy moved onto his lap as they held hands. "Did you kiss those other girls like this?" She locked her lips onto his for a moment.

"I suppose, but it's different with you."

"Why is it different? Don't you like me as much as them?"

He kissed her again before answering. "Emmy, I like you so much more than those other girls."

She kissed him, and Kenny could feel Emmy leaning. She tugged on his arm. They moved around on the couch until Emmy lay on her side with her back against the back of the couch.

She whispered, "Move next to me, Kenny."

He moved next to her, and they kissed again. She tried to pull him on top of her.

"Kenny, let me move under you."

"No, Emmy. You're still too young."

He sat up and looked at Emmy. He could barely see her in the darkness of the room. Emmy sat up beside him.

"Please kiss me some more, Kenny. You can hold me if you want. I don't mind."

She took one of his hands and moved it to her side. He left it there as they kissed. They stopped kissing and held each other. She could sense his need but also his reluctance to continue.

"I don't want to be like Diane. I really don't, but I will if I must. You can have me if you want, Kenny. I know I'm probably younger than your other girls, but I will do it if you want. I want to make you happy."

Kenny kissed her again and could feel her trembling next to him.

"Emmy, my sweet Emmy. You make me so happy every time I see you. You don't have to do anything..."

"Don't you want me?" Emmy asked with a trace of relief evident in her voice.

"That's not it at all."

"I can tell you are ready."

Kenny placed both hands on her shoulders. "Emmy, please stop!"

"Are you afraid we will get caught again?" she teased. She relaxed because she knew Kenny would not take her virginity tonight.

"No, the guys are not going to come over here, and my parents would not bother us."

They both laughed as they remembered being caught. Emmy kissed him again as he held her still.

"Your kiss tastes so sweet, Kenny," she whispered.

"If you only knew how good that felt and how..."

"I think I can tell."

Kenny smacked her lightly on her thigh, "That's not what I meant, and you should be ashamed for thinking about that."

Even in the darkness of the garage, he could tell Emmy was smiling at him.

"Please, hold me for a while, Kenny. I'll behave now."

Kenny held her as they remained quiet for a moment. He moved his back against the couch, and Emmy slipped next to him with her back against him. Kenny put an arm around her and pulled her close.

"Are you warm enough, Em?"

"It's a little chilly in here. Do you have a blanket we could snuggle under?"

"Yeah, if you let me get up, I will turn on a light and find it." Emmy moved, and Kenny got up. He bumped against his desk. "Ow! That hurt."

Emmy giggled.

"That's not funny, Em. It really hurt."

Emmy jumped up and switched on a light. "Poor baby! Did you get a booboo on your knee," she teased.

"You're going to get it, Emily Colasanti." Kenny threatened her as he smiled.

"I don't mind if I get it," Emmy said and then giggled again.

Kenny put his hands on her waist. "You are being very naughty today for some reason."

Emmy grabbed two blankets and a pillow from the closet. She moved back to the couch and pulled Kenny with her. "You get back where you were. Here's the pillow and the blankets. Now lie down, and I'll get the light. I wouldn't want you to hurt yourself again in the dark. Oh, you should take off your shoes, too."

"Why? What are you going to do, Em?"

"Nothing too wicked. Take off your shoes and get under

104

the blankets."

He did as she ordered. She turned out the light and slipped under the blankets next to him.

"Put your arm around me like before and hold me close."

They talked as they lay under the blankets. Soon they were both getting sleepy, and Kenny mentioned, "Emmy, you can't spend the night with me."

"Is that right? Did you always kick those other girls out of your bed after you finished with them?"

"Emmy! How can you ask me that?"

"Well, did you?"

"They were never in bed with me, if you must know."

"Good! Are you worried that I might take advantage of you if you fall asleep?"

"I don't think I have to worry about that. You will be sound asleep soon. It's past your normal bedtime of nine o'clock."

Emmy kicked him under the blanket.

"Ow! That hurt."

She turned on her side to face him. "I meant for it to hurt. Are you going to keep teasing me all night, or are you going to hold me and talk to me?"

They both laughed and talked more about school and her family.

"My parents are fighting more than ever. Daddy has been going straight to the bar after work. Sometimes he doesn't get home until after ten. Mom screams at him, and she has stopped making him any dinner. I don't know what to do."

"Em, has your father ever... hit... your mother or you or Diane?"

"No, he's never done that. They yell and scream at each other and sometimes at me and Diane. They're not like your parents at all."

"You know you can always come over to our house if you get scared."

"You mean like I used to do when I was younger?"

"Yes," he said. "I know it's not funny, but you used to run away and hide with me in the backyard."

105

"I always felt safe with you. I used to wish your parents would adopt me."

He kissed her tenderly. "If they had, then we wouldn't be able to do what we are now."

"I like kissing you. Maybe we should practice some more."

They kept kissing until she fell asleep with his arm underneath her. He eventually dozed off.

Emmy still faced Kenny when she woke up later.

"Hi, Emmy. Are you all right?"

"What happened?"

"You fell asleep on top of my arm. I didn't want to wake you up. Can you lift up for a second?"

She did, and he pulled his numb arm out from under her.

"Can you feel it?" she asked.

He shook his arm flexing the hand to return the blood flow. "It tingles."

"What time is it?"

"I think it's almost midnight. What are your parents going to think about you being gone this late?"

"I told them I was spending the night with you."

"What?" Kenny bolted upright.

"I'm kidding. I wish I could see the look on your face."

"What time did you tell them you would be home?"

"The morning. I think they assumed we would be in the house, though."

"Emmy!"

"Okay, I didn't have to tell them anything. They're gone, so you don't have to worry about Daddy knowing how late I stayed here with you."

"Emmy, you make it sound like more than it was."

"I told you before that I'm not a perfect little angel." *Not by any means.* She bit her lip for a second. "Mom went to visit her sister, and Daddy went fishing with friends. Diane is over at Craig's, so no one will know how late I stay out. Not that they really care, anyway."

"They care."

"No they don't," she snorted.

106

"You still shouldn't spend the night."

"I know. I'm being naughty, but I will remember this night for a long time. Maybe forever."

Emmy got up and turned on a light. They held hands, and Kenny smiled at her.

"You are still my favorite groupie, Emmy. Even if we never do anything other than kiss," he teased.

"Who knows? Maybe when I am older, we might." She put a hand on her hip and smiled seductively. At least, she tried to be seductive.

"Emmy, you better go home before I forget how to behave."

"Do I have to?"

Kenny put his hands on her shoulders. She looked up at him. He sucked in his breath, and then released it slowly. "Yes, you have to go."

"Will you walk me home?"

"Of course. Do you think I would make you walk home alone this late at night?"

"You better not."

"By the way, we're going back into the studio soon. We're about finished with the CD."

"Oh, thanks for the single. I love 'Too Bad.' I think it could be a huge hit."

"So did Mr. Kesson. There are a couple other tracks on it."

"I can't wait to actually play it."

"We even have a bunch of extra songs that we're saving for the next project. I'll make sure you get a copy as soon as I can."

She moved close to Kenny and closed her eyes. Nothing happened. "Aren't you even going to kiss me after I spent the night with you?"

"Emmy! You didn't spend the night with me. Don't say that." Kenny kissed her on the cheek. "There, now go home, little girl, before I swat your behind."

Emmy turned away and wiggled her butt at him. "Go ahead if you dare."

Kenny smiled but then sighed. *God, Emmy. I wish we were*

107

both older and married. Like in that old Beach Boys tune. He climbed down the stairs and waited for several seconds. "Are you coming?"

"Yeah, I need to tie my shoes."

Emmy made it down the stairs, and Kenny walked her up the steps to her back door.

She turned to face him. "Are you gonna behave on tour now?"

He raised his hand. "I promise I will, Emmy."

Such a dork. She smiled. "Good! You better, or else I will be mad at you."

"Will you be all right by yourself, Em?"

"Yeah, I'll be fine. I'm getting used to being alone in the house." She paused and put a finger to her mouth. "On second thought, maybe you should come inside and check the house for burglars. There might be a monster under my bed. Will you check?"

"I don't think so, Em."

"Fine! Be that way. I'll be okay by myself." *I really don't like to be here alone, but I can't tell you that because you already think I'm too young.*

He waited as Emmy opened the door and turned on the kitchen light.

"It's okay. I don't see any monsters."

"Night, Emmy." He laughed and shuffled down the steps. He softly sang "Sweet Girl" as he walked home through the alley.

Chapter Eleven

"Are you sure there isn't anyone else you want to invite, Emmy? There's only six names on this list." Diane stood at the foot of their bed and shook the piece of paper at Emmy. "What about Kenny? Don't you want to invite him?"

"I would, but he's on tour and won't be home."

Emmy convinced her parents to let her have a summertime "Sweet Sixteen" party. Diane took care of all the preparations and invited Emmy's friends.

"When I turned sixteen, I organized my own party without any help from Mom and invited lots of kids," Diane said.

"I don't have as many friends as you."

"Don't you want to invite some boys?" Diane read the list of names again.

"Not really."

"So, this is going to be like a slumber party for eighth graders. How special!"

"Please don't make fun of me," Emmy whispered.

"Whatever, Em. It's your party," Diane said.

They held the party in the backyard. The sun shone, the birds sang and a breeze kept everyone cool—not that the seven teenage girls noticed. They talked about fashion, jobs and more importantly, who they were dating. Emmy felt out of the loop because she didn't have a boyfriend. She didn't tell the other girls about her crush on Kenny.

Later, Emmy thanked Diane. "I really appreciate the effort you put into this. It's been so long since I had a birthday party."

"I was happy to do it for you, Emmy. Mom gave me some money for the food and pop, but I bought the cake myself."

Diane ran into Glenda Matuzak at the mall a few days later.

"What have you been doing since graduation?" Glenda asked as they walked toward the food court.

"Staying busy. I'm working here at Teens Forever. I get a discount, so I end up spending most of my check on clothes."

"I thought you were working at Larry's Uptown Grill?"

"Yeah, I'm working there, too. I love the tips, but that place wears me out. Are you working?"

"I was, but I quit."

They ordered from the Wok Wok and looked for an empty table.

Glenda pointed. "Let's sit over there. I don't want to listen to those screaming babies."

Diane turned to look and saw two young mothers holding infants.

"Oh, my grandmother gave me a thousand dollars for a car," Diane said as she slurped her wonton soup. "Craig had a friend who was getting rid of his Chevy, so I bought it."

Glenda poured hot mustard sauce over her fried rice. "So you're still with him, huh?"

"Yeah, for the time being." Diane checked the time. "I'm on my lunch break. I need to be back in ten minutes."

"I heard the manager at that store is a jerk. Is that true?"

The mothers with the screaming babies gave up. They put the babies in their strollers and walked past Diane and Glenda.

"Oh, such cute babies," Glenda said as she smiled insincerely. *God! I'm never going to get pregnant.*

"She can be a real ass at times." Diane looked around. "Don't say anything, but most of the employees are stealing stuff just to get back at her."

"You better be careful. I got caught shoplifting last year, but I talked my way out of it."

Diane asked, "Would you be interested in being roommates? I can't afford a place on my own, but if we split the cost, we could both get out of our parents' houses."

"Sorry, but I'm leaving for southern Illinois in August. I'm going to Kaskaskia College. If I wasn't moving, I'd share a place with you. We could have our boyfriends over anytime we wanted and not have to worry about what anyone would say."

"I've got to find someone to share an apartment with me."

"Can't you move in with Craig?" Glenda asked.

"I'm not really sure I want to live with him. We end up fighting when I go over there. I would feel better in my own place.

110

I could let him come over. Then I could toss him out if I get mad."

Glenda laughed and asked, "Does your mother still kick your father out of the house like mine does?"

"Not very often. She makes him sleep on the couch some nights. Mostly, she just yells at him. I guess that's the way all married couples live." Diane checked the time. "I gotta run."

"Yeah, call me." Glenda wiped her face with a napkin just as two boys ran into the back of her chair. "Hey! Watch where you're going." *You miserable little creeps. If you were my kids, I would shoot you.*

Emmy waved at Rory Porter mowing the yard one day as she walked to the Pantry Hut. He shut off the mower, wiped his brow and walked toward her.

"Hi, Rory. How are you?"

"I'm sweating like a pig," he complained. "Mom told me I have to take care of the yard if I want to keep living here. I should move out like Owen did. Then I wouldn't have to put up with her nagging. Amy ain't here."

"That's all right. I'm on my way to the store. I got a job at Darby's."

"Yeah, so what? I applied there, but old man Darby wouldn't hire me." He shook his long sweaty hair out of his eyes. "I ain't cuttin' my hair for no stinkin' job."

Emmy smiled and said, "I turned sixteen. I'm allowed to go on dates now."

"And I'm supposed to care because?" Rory glared as he burst her happy mood.

"Sorry, I thought that maybe you would be interested. My mistake."

"Yeah. Your mistake all right." He stared at the street as a car sped past and then looked at her. "Hang on. Sorry, Emmy, I'm just pissed at my mother. I shouldn't take it out on you. Hey, Grafton's throwing a party at his place. Wanna come with me?" He remembered two other times Emmy snuck away to a party with him. "We can have some fun."

She shook her head. "No, I'm never doing that again."

"Aw! Nothing happened. I didn't even kiss you. I wanted to, but I didn't."

"I better not go. There will be beer, and you might try to take advantage of me."

"I'd never do anything to hurt you, Emmy."

"You might if we drink too much beer, and I'm not going to let that happen."

"We don't have to drink anything. We could just hang out together," Rory said as he touched her cheek. "Call me if you change your mind."

"I better not. I trust you, but not some of the other guys who go to those parties."

"Suit yourself. You're gonna end up like your sister," Rory shouted as he started the mower.

"No, I'm not!" Emmy muttered as she walked away. *I'm never going to be like Diane.*

The rest of the summer passed quickly, and school started again. Most of the people at Roosevelt High who really knew her, regarded Emmy as a pretty girl, but quiet and modest—almost the exact opposite of her outgoing sister who made friends very easily. Emmy came across as being timid and bashful at times. Emmy had always been much harder to get to know, but once she knew and trusted someone, her loyalty never wavered.

One afternoon at Roosevelt, the crowd jostled Emmy as she hurried to her next class.

"Hey kid, get out of the way. You're gonna get run over."

A boy bumped into her from behind, knocking her to her knees. Her books flew out of her hands. She banged into the lockers as someone else pushed her.

"Hey, freshman, this hall is for upperclassmen. Go back to your part of school."

Emmy retrieved her books, ducked into her classroom and took her seat. She put her elbows on her desk and rested her head in her hands. *I'm sixteen now. Why does everyone still think I'm a kid? When Diane was sixteen, she had dates every week. Not a*

112

single boy has even talked to me this year. She bit her lip as she watched three seniors enter the room. They were laughing and slapping each other on the back.

She sighed. *Those guys are never gonna notice me. I might as well be invisible. I wish Kenny was home.* The sound of a book being dropped on the floor next to her interrupted her reverie.

"Hey, kid, wake up. Class is about to start."

Emmy heard Dawn Matuzak. "Leave her alone, zombie-breath. She's too young for you."

"Then how about you and me getting together?"

"Name the time!" Dawn responded. She looked at Emmy. "You're Diane's little sister, right?"

Emmy nodded. Then she turned to look out the window. *I wish I had the confidence to talk to boys the way she does.*

"Yo, Colasanti, I might let you hang out with me since your sister and Glenda were friends," Dawn said.

Dawn appointed herself the leader of the cool clique of popular girls from Mayfield, a neighborhood not too far away from Raynor Park, where Emmy and Diane lived. Dawn kept her straight, dark hair cut short to frame her round face. She worked hard to keep her weight down with some measure of success. Dawn and the other girls in the clique wore too much makeup, and most of them smoked, just to be cool. Dawn actually didn't like herself very much, so she bossed the other girls in the clique and fooled around with boys to make herself feel more confident.

"Emmy, I did a huge favor for you." Dawn shouted as she walked over to Emmy's locker a few days later.

Emmy slammed her locker closed before Dawn could see the pictures of Kenny taped on the inside. "What are you talking about? I didn't ask you for any favor."

"Everyone knows you've never been on a date and never been kissed," Dawn said loud enough for the other kids to hear.

Emmy's jaw dropped. She and Kenny had been alone on many occasions at Darby's and other places, but they never thought of them as dates.

"So I've been asking around, and I finally found a guy

113

willing to take you on a date."

"But..." Emmy stammered.

"Don't worry. You can thank me later. Us Mayfield girls stick together, and we look out for our friends."

"But..."

"I know you want to be part of our group. Our sisters were like the leaders."

"But..." Emmy kept trying to interject with no success.

"Anyway, his name is Jayson Mathias, and he's hot."

Dawn finally paused and allowed Emmy to speak.

"I didn't ask you to find a date for me. Why did you do that?"

"If you want to be friends with us, you have to go out."

"I don't want to go out with a guy I don't know simply to please you and your friends, Dawn."

"Well, I already set it up for this Friday, so you're going. We're going to Kerry Lynn's Pizza and Pasta. Don't worry. It's a double date. Martin and I will be with you."

Emmy thought about it for a few seconds. "All right. I'll go out with him just this once because I love the pizza at Kerry Lynn's."

"Did I mention that Jason can play the guitar?"

"Oh, really?"

"Yeah. He's really cool, and if you want, we could always go over to Swallow Cliff. You guys can use the backseat to make out."

"Gee, thanks, Dawn," Emmy said facetiously.

"If you don't want to go out with him more than once, that's your choice, but you'll be sorry. I'm pretty sure you're gonna hit it off."

Emmy looked in the mirror on Friday as she got ready. *At least Mom and Dad aren't home yet. They would be pestering me to meet Jayson. Mom got all excited just because I'm going out.*

Emmy waited in the living room and kept looking out the window. She saw a car stop and heard the horn. "Well, at least I like the pizza there."

114

Jayson reminded Emmy of a six foot tall beanpole with long, stringy hair that always looked dirty. Traces of acne dotted his face. Emmy could just about count the hairs on his wannabe goatee. They sat in a booth, and he tried to impress Emmy with his ability to play guitar.

"I've learned all the chords that I need. I can play a couple of Tom Petty tunes. Now I'm learning to play solos like the guy in this band I saw on MTV. If you want, I'll show you how good I can play sometime."

Emmy asked Jayson, "How long have you been playing guitar?"

"I bought a used Gibson in the summer, and I started messing around with it. I'm getting pretty good."

"What model?" Emmy asked.

Jayson stared at her. "What do you mean? It's a real Gibson. It says so on the end of the guitar."

Emmy stared back. *I bet you don't know more than three chords. I bet I know more chords than you. You probably can't even read music.*

He leaned close and tried to kiss her, but Emmy put her hand on his chest and didn't let him.

Dawn whispered, "What are you doing? If you want to be friends with us, you will let Jayson kiss you. Got it?"

Emmy wanted to be popular, but she couldn't force herself to kiss Jayson. "I'm not going to kiss him." She crossed her arms over her chest.

Jayson tried to kiss her again. She hit him hard in his side and didn't let him get close to her.

"I'm sorry, Emmy. I won't try anything more if you kiss me just once," Jayson promised as he rubbed his side.

"Hell will freeze over, and cows will fly before I kiss you."

Dawn frowned at Emmy.

"What classes do you have?" Emmy asked to start a conversation.

Jayson didn't answer, but asked. "Want a smoke?"

'No, thanks. I don't smoke."

"Wanna try one for fun?"

"No, thanks, I can do without the fun," Emmy replied sarcastically.

Jayson scooted closer to Emmy, but she gasped from the overpowering smell of cigarettes on his breath.

"Hell is still as hot as ever."

He moved even closer to her, but she backed away.

"I will punch you in your nuts if you don't back off, bucko."

"Yeah, whatever." Jayson instinctively covered his family jewels as he slid away. *I just asked to kiss you. I didn't say I wanted to have sex.*

They finished the pizza and hung out for a while. Eventually, Dawn wanted to go home because her parents were out of town, so they went back to the car and headed for home. Martin dropped Emmy off first.

"You don't need to walk me to the door, Jayson," Emmy held out a hand as he started to get out of the car.

"See ya around school, Emmy."

"Oh, God, I really hope not," Emmy muttered as she walked up the sidewalk. She didn't want to go inside because her mother would grill her about the date. She turned around and decided to walk over to the Colwells even though she knew Kenny wouldn't be home.

Just then the front door opened. "Emmy, come inside and tell me about your date. I want to hear all about it."

"Mom, I don't want to talk about it. I'm gonna go for a walk."

"But I want to hear about your first date, honey. Did you have a good time with your new boyfriend? Where did you go? Did he kiss you?"

"Mom! I'm not going to discuss this outside where the entire neighborhood can hear." Emmy waved her arms. "I'll be back later."

"All right, but don't stay out too late," Mom hollered as she went back inside.

Emmy rolled her eyes, because she saw the neighbor lady across the street waving at her. *Great! The biggest gossip on the block knows about my crappy date with Jayson.*

At school the following Monday morning, Dawn met Emmy by her locker. "Did you kiss Jayson or not?"

Emmy closed her locker and held the textbooks she needed that morning in her arms. "No, I didn't kiss him. I don't like the smell of cigarettes and would prefer not to kiss a boy who smokes if I have to kiss one at all." *Besides that, he has BO.*

"Oh, you prefer not to kiss a boy who smokes," Dawn mocked Emmy. "Do you know how much trouble I went through trying to find a cool guy to go out with you, huh, do you?"

Emmy turned to face Dawn. "I didn't ask you to find me a date in the first place. I don't care how much effort you spent. Jayson is a jerk, and I'm not going out with him again." Emmy saw three football players standing by their lockers on the opposite side of the hallway. *Why did I ever think I wanted to be friends with you?*

Dawn looked at her scornfully. "Jayson is cool. Who the hell do you think you are? You think you're hot stuff because you know Kenny Colwell." Dawn's face turned red. "Let me tell you something, little miss prissy... Hey, come back here. I'm not through talking to you," she shouted as she chased after Emmy, who had walked away. The football players followed.

"Diane doesn't smoke or drink, and she is popular."

Dawn grabbed Emmy's arm. "Maybe you don't know your sister as well as you think you do."

"Leave me alone. I've got to get to class." Emmy broke loose from Dawn's grasp.

As Dawn turned around to leave, Emmy stuck out her tongue and made a face at her.

"Don't worry about her. Matuzak is a bitch like her sister," the biggest football player told her.

"Yeah, and Mathias is a real wuss. I don't blame you for not wanting to kiss him."

"None of us smoke. You wanna kiss us?" the third player teased.

Emmy took off running for class as the jocks laughed.

Chapter Twelve

"Don't let Daddy see you in that dress, he'll get mad," Diane warned Emmy while braiding her hair. "And sit still."

Emmy squirmed in a kitchen chair. She hummed a tune as she got ready for her first high school dance—the senior class Sweetheart Ball. Her overprotective parents finally gave their permission.

"I've seen you wear shorter ones, and he didn't say anything," Emmy said.

Emmy wore her favorite dress. One of two that had not belonged to Diane. The dark maroon one made of a soft velvety material with a white collar. A bow tied in back accented her slim waist.

"Yeah, but he's given up on making me dress the way he wants. You're still his innocent baby." Diane tugged on Emmy's long, curly hair as the doorbell rang. "Mom! Could you get that? I'm almost done with Emmy's hair."

Mom answered the front door, and Amy Porter entered.

"Hi, Mrs. Colasanti. Thanks for giving us a ride."

"Not a problem." Mom stared at Amy's Goth-like appearance. Everything Amy wore was black. Her clothes, her eye make up, even her hair was jet-black, even darker than Emmy's. She wore white make up on her pale face, but she did have on dark red lipstick. Lots of lipstick.

"I'm ready to go, Mom," Emmy said.

As Mom dropped Emmy and Amy off at school, she disclosed some last-minute instructions. "Be polite." Mom pointed a finger at Emmy. "No smoking or drinking and no kissing any boys."

"Mom!" Emmy sputtered turning red. "I just wanna dance."

"You will call home if you need a ride, right? I don't want you to walk home alone."

"We should be able to get a ride with my brother, Mrs. Colasanti," Amy said. "I'll keep an eye on her for you."

After they got out of the car, Amy asked, "Is your mom always so weird, or is tonight an exception? I can't believe the way

118

she treated you. I would never take that crap from my mother."

"Mom can be a little overbearing, but she only wants to make sure I don't get into any trouble."

"I stole some cigarettes from my mom's purse. I'll share with you later if you want."

"No thanks," Emmy replied as she thought about her grandfather who died of lung cancer. "Is Rory going to be here or not?"

Amy shrugged. "Who knows?"

They could hear the band as they flashed their student IDs and entered the multipurpose room. Emmy looked at the red and white streamers hanging from the ceiling. *Wow! There must be 500 kids here.* She shouldered her way through the kids standing in small groups and reached the dance floor. She moved her body in time with the music. *This is going to be so much fun.*

Amy Porter's appearance immediately fascinated many of the older boys. Emmy watched as boy after boy walked past her to ask Amy for a dance. *Geez! Am I invisible?*

When Amy sat down next to Emmy to take a break from dancing, Emmy asked, "See those two boys over there? Do you think they're cute?"

"Those two by the pop machine? They're hot, but I think they are with those two girls."

"Oh, well, do you know their names at least?"

"I'm not sure, Emmy. I think maybe one of them is Todd something. Should I go ask, since you are afraid to by yourself?"

"I'm not afraid, Amy." Emmy poked Amy in the side.

"Are you gonna sit here all night? It's not a crime to ask a boy to dance with you. Most of them need a little encouragement."

Emmy noticed a girl with wavy golden hair that hung gracefully to her shoulders. *I think I've seen her in the hallway, and I heard someone call her name, but I can't remember it.*

The girl caught Emmy looking at her once and smiled. Emmy smiled back and walked over to where the girl stood, but by the time she got there, the girl had disappeared.

She saw Grady Harris and Maris Miller, a slightly overweight couple she knew from math class who were always together. "There was a girl here a minute ago, Maris. Do you know where she went?"

"I'm not sure who you mean, Emmy. What did she look like?"

"She's wearing a yellow dress with some white trim that fits like it was designed for her and has blonde hair." Emmy held her own hair.

Maris asked, "Do you mean Kristen Keasling? I saw her a minute ago, but I didn't see where she went. Sorry, Em."

Now Emmy remembered her name.

Grady asked, "Emmy, would you dance with me?"

Emmy looked at Maris.

"Go ahead, Emmy. He's not the worst dancer in the world, but close," Maris whispered.

As Emmy and Grady danced, he whispered in her ear, "I think I'm in love with Maris."

Emmy whispered back, "I am pretty sure that Maris loves you, too."

After the song faded out, Grady thanked her for the dance.

"Thank you for asking me, Grady. You're a better dancer than Maris thinks."

"Yeah, sorry about your foot. I'll see you around." Grady left and rejoined Maris.

Emmy sat down and rubbed her foot. *I hope another boy asks me to dance.* She spotted someone dancing across the room. *He looks interesting. I like his black jeans and that sports coat. Not many of the guys are dressed up. I bet he never steps on his partner's foot.* Finding Amy again, she leaned in to be heard over the music. "Amy, who's that guy with the girl in the yellow dress?"

Amy looked around the room for another dance partner. "His name is Darren, Derrick or Eric Keasling, or something like that. I think he's in Rory's class. They're rich kids, Emmy. They don't hang out with kids like us." Amy dashed away to dance with another boy.

After awhile some of the girls from Emmy's gym class went outside with boys to get away from the chaperones. They came back inside to tell Emmy and Amy all the details.

120

"You aren't supposed to go outside," Emmy said. "That's against the rules."

"Hey, you guys know our rules. If you want to be part of the cool kids, you will find a boy, go outside and let him kiss you. Otherwise, forget it," Dawn Matuzak informed Emmy and Amy.

Amy bragged, "No problem. I turned down several offers to go outside already. I can find someone willing to kiss me."

Emmy didn't want to kiss a boy she didn't know.

Emmy asked Dawn about a boy. "Who were you dancing with a few minutes ago? He's kinda good-looking."

"That's Bert Hodges. He's a senior, on the student council, and a star on the football team."

Emmy glanced at him again. He stood six feet tall with coal black hair that he kept cut short.

"He's one of the hottest hunks in school. Do you want me to introduce you?" Dawn asked.

"Okay," Emmy answered shyly.

Dawn took Emmy over. "Hey, Bert, this is a friend of mine. She thinks you're cute and wants to kiss you." Dawn intentionally embarrassed Emmy and then walked away.

"Hi, I'm Bert Hodges. Are you a freshman this year? I don't think I've seen you around."

Emmy answered, "No," but didn't elaborate.

"You're really supposed to be in high school to come to this dance."

"I am in high school. I'm sixteen and a junior."

"Get out of town!" Bert exclaimed. "I don't believe that for a second, but I won't rat you out." Bert tilted his head as he tried to guess her real age. *Oh, what the hell. She's here, and she is pretty. I might as well try to get something out of her.* He used a line that worked more often than it failed—at least with the younger girls. "I think you are much prettier than any of the girls here, and I would like to take you out sometime. I'm not busy Saturday, so what time should I pick you up? That is, if you really are sixteen."

"Do you want me to show you my birth certificate? I don't have a driver's license yet."

Bert laughed at her joke.

121

Emmy listened to him for a couple of minutes and then chuckled before thinking, *You must really think highly of yourself. I don't think I've ever met a person with such an inflated ego.*

"Do you want to go outside and get some fresh air or something?" Bert asked.

Emmy thought about it, but wondered what his intentions might be. "I don't think so, but thanks for the offer."

"No problem. It's your loss, not mine." Bert dismissed her with a wave of his hand.

Emmy walked away. *What a rude, ignorant, pompous ass. He never even asked me my name.* She wound her way through the crowd to Amy while Bert headed off to search for Dawn.

"Hey, Dawn, is she really sixteen years old?" Bert asked.

"Who?"

"The girl in the maroon dress over there with Amy Porter." He pointed at Emmy. "She looks like she's maybe twelve when you compare her body to Amy's, but she's claiming to be sixteen."

"It's possible, but I'm not sure. I do know she's a junior, but she's one of those really smart kids, so she might have skipped a grade or two. I fixed her up with Jayson Mathias because I don't think she's ever even kissed a boy before which is sorta strange because she's Diane Colasanti's little sister."

"Really? I remember Diane. She's got a body! I didn't know she had a sister. I wonder if her little sister is anything like Diane?" Bert remembered the stories about Diane's lack of morals.

Dawn walked over to talk to Emmy again and asked, "Did Bert ask you for a date? I went outside with him earlier, and he asked me for a date."

"Are you sure he didn't tell you what time he would be picking you up? That's the way he asked me for a date," Emmy responded sarcastically.

Dawn gave Emmy a funny look. "What's the difference? He wants to go out with me, and that's all I care about." It thrilled her that a cool senior wanted to go out with her. "After Bert goes out with me, he won't want to date any other girl. I can guarantee you that, so stay away from him." Dawn knew she was not as pretty as some of the other girls, but she would do whatever it took

122

to hang on to Bert.

Later, after watching Emmy talking to Dawn, Bert wandered over and asked, "Would you girls like to come outside with me and Todd and have a little fun?"

Dawn agreed right away, but Emmy shook her head. "No, thanks. I'm happy to stay inside." She looked up at Todd Delaney. *You're tall enough to be a basketball player, but you're too skinny.*

Dawn grabbed Emmy by the arm and dragged her along. "Delaney is a popular senior. You should be flattered that he wants to spend time with you. He usually only dates seniors, and I heard that he has been out with a couple of college girls. Don't blow your chance, or you will regret it."

"Let go of me, Dawn!" Emmy broke away. "I'm not going outside to smoke or whatever else you're doing. I don't want to get a detention."

"What a loser," Dawn said. "Who cares if you get a detention? Are you afraid of being grounded or something?"

"No, but I don't want to get in trouble. It took a lot of persuasion to even be allowed to come to the dance," Emmy said and then covered her mouth with her hand. *Crap! I shouldn't have said that.*

"Why? Aren't you old enough to be on your own?" Todd asked and then laughed. "I know who you are. You're Diane's sister, so I know you don't always follow the rules. Come on, let's go have a smoke." Todd tried to grab her hand.

"Leave me alone, Delaney." Emmy took a step back. "And you don't know anything about me. I'm not Diane."

Todd took a step toward Emmy, and she ended up with her back to the wall.

"If you let me kiss you, I'll make it worth your while."

"Dream on, Delaney." Emmy moved to her right.

Delaney grabbed her elbow and held her tight. "You aren't going anywhere, Colasanti. I'll get what I want from you."

Emmy froze and bit her lip.

"Are you coming outside or not?" Dawn asked as she and Bert headed toward the exit.

"Give me a minute," Todd said. "She's being stubborn."

123

Bert and Dawn paused. Todd leaned forward and tried to kiss Emmy.

"Back off, Bucko. I'm not interested." She gave him a hateful look.

"Yeah, right. I know you want me to kiss you." Delaney laughed and moved closer.

Todd's laugh and the smell of cigarette smoke on his breath made Emmy even more determined not to let him kiss her. He tried again, but she turned her head.

"Dawn, you shouldn't go outside with Bert."

"I think you should mind your own business, Colasanti. I'll do whatever I want."

"I'm going back to my friends now, and don't try to stop me!" Emmy yelled at Dawn and Todd.

Todd stopped trying to kiss her and grabbed the bow on the back of her dress.

"Let go of me, you ass." Emmy squirmed away and turned to face him. She slapped him and, for extra emphasis, punched him in the stomach.

Todd doubled over. "You little bitch! You're nothing but a tease." He turned to Bert and yelled. "I got the short end of this deal, Hodges. You swore she would be easy like her slutty sister."

Emmy was furious and crying as she blindly ran away from Delaney. She pushed two freshman nerds aside, turned her head to apologize and ran right into the back of the cute boy she saw earlier. He almost knocked her over without moving. She fled before he could turn and say anything to her. Emmy dashed to the girl's restroom and shoved the door with all her might. It banged against the wall as she bolted through and straight into Kristen Keasling.

Kristen's warm blue eyes opened wide as she reached out to fend off the petite girl in the worn, velvety maroon dress.

"Crap! I'm sorry," Emmy shouted as she felt the rich material of Kristen's dress. I wasn't looking where I was going." She looked up expecting to be scolded.

Instead, Kristen asked softly, "Are you all right? Are you hurt?"

124

Emmy realized she still had a hand on Kristen's dress and jerked it away. "I'll be okay. I needed to get away from a jerk named Todd Delaney."

"I know who you mean. He is a jerk." Kristen effortlessly opened her small black leather Burberry tote bag and handed Emmy a tissue. "My name is Kristen."

Emmy took the tissue and noticed Kristen's light pink nail polish at the same time she caught a whiff of her Tommy Girl perfume. She dried her eyes, blew her nose and looked at Kristen's purse. *I've never heard of that brand, but it looks expensive, and I love the smell of your perfume.* She looked at Kristen's dress as Kristen smoothed it out. *I wish I could buy a dress that fits like that.* Emmy gazed into Kristen's light blue eyes and smiled. "I'm Emmy... Emmy Colasanti."

"Did Todd try something?"

Emmy swished the tissue into the garbage from five feet away. "You could say that. He tried to kiss me, and I didn't let him. He got upset, and I slapped him and punched him in the gut." Emmy made a punching motion which caused Kristen to jump back.

Kristen laughed. "Good for you. I'm sure Todd deserved it. Would you like to come with me?"

Emmy nodded.

"Come on, I'll stay with you in case Todd is still around. I'll introduce you to my brother. Todd won't bother us if we're with Derrick." Kristen opened the bathroom door. *You are so tiny, but you must have some spunk to fight off Todd. We have that in common.*

Emmy followed Kristen back to the dance floor. Kristen looked for her brother. "There he is." Kristen pointed to where Derrick stood with a couple of his friends.

Emmy bit her lip. *He looks even better up close. He might be a little taller than Kenny, and more athletic. He's not as skinny. Those deep brown eyes look like they don't miss a thing.* Emmy glanced around to find Amy and spotted her dancing with Adam Wozniak. Kristen and Emmy cornered Derrick, and Kristen introduced her. "Emmy, this is my brother Derrick. Derrick, this is

125

Emmy Colasanti. Delaney hassled her."

Derrick understood what Kristen meant, but he didn't let on to Emmy. "Hi, Emmy. It's a pleasure to meet you. Are you enjoying the dance?" *You look familiar for some reason.*

Emmy smiled back at Derrick. *I bet you spend a lot of time at the dentist. I should be wearing shades when you smile, and I bet you've never had a pimple in your life.* She looked at Kristen. *Or you either. I don't know a lot about designer clothes, but enough to realize I could never afford what you guys are wearing.* "I'm doing all right now. I had a little trouble with Todd Dumbleberry."

Derrick laughed at her dissing Todd Delaney.

Kristen asked, "Are you a freshman, Emmy? I think I've seen you around school, but there are so many kids, it's almost impossible to get to know everyone."

"I'm a junior." Emmy didn't mind what Kristen assumed.

Derrick snapped his fingers. "Aren't you in my history class?" *Wow! Those eyes are amazing, and I love your tan.*

Emmy answered, "I've got history last period with Mr. Culbertson."

"So do I," Derrick said. "I had to switch my schedule around and just moved to that class yesterday."

"We've actually got a sub because Mr. Culbertson has been out. I miss him. He's my favorite teacher."

Emmy spent the rest of the dance talking to Kristen and Derrick. When the time arrived to announce the King and Queen, Emmy watched as Kristen held onto Derrick's arm. When Randy Braun, the senior class president, announced Derrick as the king, Kristen hugged him. Emmy shared the happiness of her new friends by hugging Kristen and didn't hear the announcement for the queen.

When the dance ended, Emmy looked around for Amy Porter. She saw Amy walking out the door with Adam Wozniak and realized Amy was leaving without her. *Thanks for nothing, Amy. Where's Rory? He might be a jerk at times, but he would at least make sure I got home safely. Who else can I catch a ride with?* She looked around. *Shoot! I don't see anyone else from the*

126

neighborhood. Mom and Dad are probably asleep now. She grabbed her faded army jacket and decided to walk home.

Kristen asked, "Do you need a ride home, Emmy? Derrick has his car if you need a lift."

"Thanks, but I can walk. I don't live too far away." She didn't want to impose.

"Don't be silly. We can give you a ride home. It's too late at night for you to be walking by yourself. Please let us take you home."

Emmy thought about it as she searched one last time for Rory. *Where are you, Rory?* Emmy looked at Kristen and answered, "Are you sure it won't be out of your way? I live in Raynor Park."

"That's where Kenny Colwell is from, right? Do you know him, by any chance?" Kristen asked.

Derrick gave his sister a funny look and nudged her elbow. She frowned at him.

"Yes, he lives a couple houses away," Emmy answered without giving away her relationship with Kenny.

"We can give you a ride, Emmy. I wouldn't feel right about letting you walk home."

"Thanks, Derrick. I appreciate it." *Mom would be pissed if I walk home.*

Emmy listened to Derrick and Kristen talking about the dance as she rode in the backseat of Derrick's Acura. She gave him directions when he asked, and he knew the general area.

Emmy pointed. "That's my house. The one with the little white fence."

Derrick parked the car in the street.

"Thanks for the ride, Derrick."

"You're welcome, Emmy. If you ever need a ride, let us know. I'll see you in history class."

"Good night, Kristen. I'm sorry I ran into you in the bathroom."

"I'm not sorry, Emmy. I mean I'm sorry about what Todd tried, but I'm not sorry that we ran into each other. I hope we see each other at school on Monday."

127

"Thanks again for the ride." Emmy got out and dashed up the sidewalk to her front door.

Derrick waited until she made it inside, and Kristen began to giggle.

"What's so funny? Care to share?"

"I have a picture in my mind of that little girl slapping Todd Delaney. She's barely five feet tall and Delaney is six feet or more. She probably had to jump to slap his face. I can see the expression on his smug face as he tried to kiss her, and then 'whap' as she slapped him."

"You don't realize who she is, do you?" Derrick asked.

"I know her name. Why? Who is she? Do you know her? History class, right?"

"She's Kenny Colwell's best friend. At least that's what I heard at the show we attended last year. Do you remember the girl he brought up on stage to sing?"

"Vaguely. Are you telling me...?" Kristen turned to look at the house, but Emmy had disappeared.

"Yep! That's her." Derrick pulled away from the curb.

"I never would have recognized her. She is so shy and quiet."

"Yeah, maybe around other people but not around Kenny, and she's got a beautiful voice."

Kristen turned and stared at her brother. "Are you interested in her? Are you forgetting about Clarissa? She would have been with us if she hadn't gotten sick."

"I'm just saying she has a good voice."

"And she's pretty, too." Kristen reached out and messed up Derrick's hair.

"Hey! Stop that." He pushed her hand away. "I paid thirty bucks for this style job."

"You got ripped off," Kristen teased. "Don't you think she's pretty?"

"I admit she is pretty, but she looks like she's ten."

Emmy sighed with relief as she walked into the living room. *Good! Mom and Dad must be in bed.* She tiptoed to her room. *Where are you, Diane? At Craig's again?* As she slipped into bed, she got goose bumps thinking about what happened at the dance. *I should never hang out with Dawn and those girls.* She pulled the sheet over her head. *It wouldn't surprise me if some of those girls are already having sex. I'm not ready for that.* Emmy tossed and turned and didn't fall asleep until three.

Diane snuck into the house at four, got ready for bed and saw Emmy sprawled sideways across the bed. *Give me some room, Em.* Diane pushed Emmy onto one side of the bed without waking her. *I hope you enjoyed the dance, Em. I always did.*

Chapter Thirteen

"I wish there was a way I could avoid coming back up this hill from school," Emmy muttered. She had just finished climbing the hill on Bridge Street when the gust of wind from a passing city bus nearly knocked her over. She saw Rory Porter sitting alone on a bus stop bench smoking a cigarette. She scurried past without speaking, but he saw her.

"Hey, Emmy. Hang on a second. Do you have time to help me with math today?" Rory asked though his intentions were something other than studying.

"Not really. I've got a lot of homework myself." She avoided the weeds growing up through the cracked sidewalk.

"Come on, Emmy. I won't try anything, but I need some help with my math homework. Can you please help me?" He smiled and turned on the charm that enabled him to get what he wanted from several other girls.

Emmy didn't fall for it. "I don't have a lot of time today." She kept walking.

He jumped up, took a final drag off his cigarette, tossed it aside and followed her. "Come on, Emmy. Give me a half hour, please. I swear I'll behave."

"You always say that, and then you try to get me to fool around."

"Oh, come on. I've never really tried to mess around with you. I like you better than that."

Emmy stared up at him and decided to be nice, even though he didn't deserve it. "Fine. A half hour. That's all."

They walked to Rory's house, and Amy and their mother were home.

"I've got to take Amy to the mall for a couple of hours. She's agreed to expand her wardrobe if I buy. You will have to get your own dinner, Rory. Think you can handle that?" Mrs. Porter asked sarcastically.

"I think I can make something."

He waited for his mother and Amy to leave and then grinned at Emmy. "Wanna come up to my room to study or maybe

130

something else?"

"No, Rory. I came over here to help you study. We can do that right here in the living room."

Resigned, Rory lead her to the couch in the living room.

"Where's your math book?" Emmy inquired impatiently as she glanced at the magazines on the coffee table.

"I'll get it in a minute, but first I want to kiss you."

"I'm outta here."

She stood up and started to walk away, but Rory grabbed her arm.

"I didn't mean it, Emmy. I'm teasing."

She frowned at him, and he let go of her arm. She sat back on the couch, ready to react if he tried anything.

"Since you won't let me kiss you, why don't we go upstairs and get into bed and..." he asked figuring he might as well try for a home run instead of a bunt.

"Will you stop quit wasting my time? Do you need help with math or not? If you don't, I'm outta here. I'm not putting up with that crap because it will never happen between us."

"What about Bert Hodges?"

Emmy stared blankly at Rory. "What about him?"

"Didn't you make out with him? That's what I heard at school."

"I did no such thing!" Emmy said indignantly. "Who told you that?"

"I heard some kids talking in the hallway. Dawn Matuzak told a couple kids that Hodges went outside with two different girls at a school dance. She mentioned your name."

"That is a lie. Dawn let Bert... forget it! I don't even want to talk about those two. None of that would have happened if you had been there. Why didn't you come?"

"I was kinda busy that night."

"Doing what?"

"You don't want to know, Emmy," Rory said. Then he looked away. "Don't ask."

She stared at him. *You were messing around. I hope you were careful.* "What did you hear about me?"

131

"Some of the kids are sure talking about you." He moved closer and put a hand on her jeans.

"Stop it! If you try anything, I will make sure you never have kids."

"Oh, come on. What's the big deal? If I really wanted to do anything, I would have those times we were with Grafton."

"I know better now."

"You were kinda innocent back them. Have you been fooling around with Kenny Colwell? I know you're always hanging out with him. Did you let him do you?"

She punched his hip. "I'm certainly not talking about my relationship with Kenny to you."

Rory laughed as he covered up. "You are such a tease, and someday someone will take advantage of you and not stop."

"It's not going to be today, and it's certainly not gonna be you." She slid away from him and then stood up.

"Why not? You might like it. I know you have a thing for guys like me."

"I do not! How can you say that?" She didn't move. "What do you mean about guys like you?"

"Troublemakers. Girls sometimes like certain guys even when they know they shouldn't."

"I'm not like that." She bit her lip. She had never been fearful of him, but was a little bit afraid now. "I don't know why you would think that. I do know you are a total jerk, Rory Porter, and I've been a fool to ever trust you."

He pounded on the couch. "Hey! Have I ever given you a reason not to trust me?"

She stared at him for a moment. "Not really."

"Just remember the times I've had your back. That's different than school. I hate school."

She shook her head. "You've proven that. You certainly aren't worth the little money your mom pays me. I'm done wasting my time. Tell your mom she needs to find another tutor."

"I don't care about school." He leaned against the back of the couch and closed his eyes.

"You should. You're not stupid, Rory. You could get good

132

grades if you try."

"It's a waste of time."

She sat on the edge of the couch and touched his knee. "You might think differently when you get older. Don't you want to have a career? Are you going to settle for crappy jobs your whole life?"

"I can get a job in construction and made a ton of money."

"Maybe, but you could do more."

He stood up. "Want a beer? I'm going to have one."

"No, thanks. I'm outta here. I really do have homework that I need to finish."

Emmy sat by herself in the cafeteria at lunchtime the next day. She read a paperback as she munched on a tuna sandwich.

Rory saw her and walked over. "Can I join you, Emmy?"

"I don't want to talk to you, Rory." She closed her book.

"What are you reading?" He sat across from her and grabbed the book. "Oooh! *Stacey and The Cheerleaders*. Is it about a guy who does the cheerleaders?" He saw the other book she had. "*Stacey and The Bad Girls*. I didn't know you liked to read porn."

She grabbed the books away from him. "They're about teenage girls who start a babysitters club. They're not dirty books like you're thinking."

"Yeah, whatever."

"I meant what I said yesterday. I don't care if you ever graduate or not."

He glanced around the cafeteria. "I thought about what you said. Will you give me another chance?"

"I've given you plenty of chances, and you've blown them all. Now leave me alone!" She raised her voice.

"Is this because of what I said about messing around with you? I didn't really mean it." He touched her hand.

She instantly pulled her hand away.

"Come on, Em. We should hang out together. I won't do anything you don't want me to."

"I never want to see you again," Emmy yelled.

That got the attention of the kids sitting nearby.

"Fine! I could care less. You're just a stuck-up snob."

"Just because I won't give in to you doesn't mean I'm a snob."

"You think you're so special. You're no different than the other sluts in this lame school." Rory made sure the other kids in the area could hear him. The fact that Diane always rejected his advances fueled his anger.

"What did you call me?" She kicked his shin.

"Sorry, I didn't mean it. I know you're not like that."

Emmy didn't notice three football players behind her listening to the argument, and hoping that Rory would try something to give them an excuse to beat the crap out of him.

Rory noticed the football players. *Maybe I should shut up and bug out of here.* For once in his life, he made a smart decision. He stood up and raised his hands as if surrendering. "I didn't touch her."

One of the football players jerked his thumb in the direction of the exit.

"I'm leaving. Don't lose your cool."

Rory left with his body intact, much to the chagrin of two of the football players.

"See you around, Emmy," he muttered under his breath. He turned his back to her as he walked away. *Out of all the girls in this school, I think you're the only one I will really miss. I know I acted like a jerk at times, but I think you know I would have never hurt you. I'm not a total ass like Owen.* He punched a locker, and then walked outside.

The other player, who happened to be wearing his number fifty-two jersey, stared at Emmy without her knowledge. He watched Emmy as she removed a purple barrette from her hair, and then replaced it. Although she tried to act as if nothing bothered her about the shouting match with Rory, her heart raced as she trembled. She stood up, glanced at the football players, and then walked away.

"What are you looking at, big guy? Come on. We gotta get to class."

"I think I know that girl. Her eyes are so pretty."

134

"Yeah, we noticed. She has two of them. How unique," they said and pulled him away to go back to class.

A few days later, as she got ready for bed, Diane mentioned to Emmy, "Hey, I heard you and Rory Porter got into an argument at school last week."

"How did you hear that?" Emmy sat up in bed.

"Dawn Matuzak told Glenda, and she told me. What's going on? Have you been doing more than tutoring him?"

"Of course not. He kinda made a pass at me, but I didn't do anything. He yelled at me in the cafeteria, but then he apologized."

"Well, Dawn was in the cafeteria when you guys argued, and she said it sounded like a lovers quarrel. Amy said that Rory moved out of the house over the weekend. He's dropping out of school, too."

"Am I suppose to care about that?" Emmy asked sarcastically. *He could be really nice when he tried.*

Diane stared at Emmy's face for several seconds to gauge her reaction. "No, I guess not. I say good riddance to him. He and Owen are both losers as far as I'm concerned."

Rory's not a loser. He's a lot smarter than people realize. "I'm never going back to the Porter house." Emmy plopped back down. "Amy is getting too weird if you ask me. She's gonna end up just like her brothers."

Diane laughed. "Her brothers won't get pregnant. At the rate Amy's going, she probably won't make it out of Roosevelt without having a baby."

"Are you sorry you and Owen... dated?"

"Hey, you know me. I don't worry about the past. What happened between us can't be changed. At least until someone invents a time machine."

Emmy tried to fall asleep, but she couldn't stop wishing that Kenny wasn't on another band tour. *I'll never go out with Bert Hodges or Todd Delaney. I don't care how popular they are!* She turned over in bed.

"Hey, let me have some room." Diane poked Emmy in the ribs. "Go to sleep already."

"I'm trying, but I've got stuff on my mind."

"Like what?"

"Not that I care, but did Amy say where Rory was living?"

Diane put a hand on Emmy's shoulder. "She didn't say, and I know you care about him."

"He's not a total jerk like Owen," Emmy whispered.

"I'll see if I can find out where he's staying. Right now you need to stay on your side of the bed. I'm trying to get to sleep."

"Every boy I know at school just wants to have sex. Is that all they think about?"

Diane turned on her side to face Emmy. "They're high school guys. They think about sex every ten seconds. They can't help it."

"There must be some guys who aren't like that. Kenny's not."

"He thinks about sex, too," Diane said. "Just because he doesn't try anything doesn't mean he doesn't think about it."

"Maybe I'm just hanging out with the wrong crowd."

"Then find some new friends." Diane rolled over. "I'm going to sleep, so be quiet."

Emmy moved over to the edge of the bed as she thought about the rich kids she met at the dance. *They went out of their way to make sure I got home safely. I'm gonna ask Barry Newton if he knows where they live or anything about them.*

Then Emmy remembered something Ronnie Rojas told the youth group one night at Kenny's church. She remembered how he talked about Jesus, and how Jesus loved them. She remembered how Ronnie talked openly and frankly about sex. He let them know that it was a good thing to wait until the proper time to become sexually active. It gave her confidence to know other girls, and even some guys, thought the way she did. She felt a desire in her heart, really a need in her heart, to learn more about Jesus. She wanted to go back to Kenny's church to talk to the youth minister again. She decided to wait until Kenny returned so he could go with her.

Chapter Fourteen

It was a chilly Thursday afternoon in early October as Emmy fought her way down the crowded first floor hallway at Roosevelt High. She stopped briefly at her locker, and then headed to her English class. She paused as she heard someone calling out her name.

"Emmy, Emmy. Wait up."

She turned around as she heard her name again. "Kristen, hi. I thought I heard someone calling me. How are you?"

"Great, I got an A on my science project. I stressed about it because it counts for a quarter of our grade. How have you been? I've been looking for you."

Emmy noticed Kristen's designer jeans. "I'm all right."

"Have you heard about Todd Delaney? He got caught with a copy of the Trig test and got suspended. His parents came to school with an attorney, but Principal O'Dell still suspended him."

"I heard something about him getting in trouble, but didn't know he got suspended. I think that's great. He's a real jerk."

"What are you doing after school?"

"Nothing really. Just gonna head home, I suppose. I don't have to work today," Emmy replied.

"Wanna come with Derrick and me to play some miniature golf over at Sandusky's? We're gonna hang out there, and then grab some food at La Cantina. Derrick will be happy to see you. If you can go, hang out with him after history class."

Emmy's eyes lit up at the mention of Sandusky's, so she answered immediately, "I'd love to go, but I need to stop at home first. Would that be okay?"

"Sure, no problem. It will be fun, and we can gang up on Derrick and pester him."

Later, as history class started, Derrick stopped by her desk. "Hi, Emmy, did Kristen find you? I know she wanted to talk to you."

"I saw her in the hall between classes. She told me about your plans after school. I said I could go, but I really have to stop at home first. I hope that's all right."

Derrick teased. "Well, I don't know... It's really out of the way and..."

Emmy looked crestfallen.

"Of course it's all right."

History class dragged on forever that day. To top it off, the substitute teacher, Mr. Hanna, needed to see her after class for a few minutes. Emmy wasn't sure why but hoped it wouldn't take long.

After the bell rang to end class, Emmy noticed that four other students needed to stay and talk to Mr. Hanna. Emmy looked for Derrick and saw him talking to Barry Newton at the back of the room. Emmy headed back to see Derrick.

"Hi, Derrick. Hey, Barry."

"Hey, Emmy," both boys responded.

"I've gotta talk to Mr. Hanna before I leave. Is that okay?"

"I've got to see him, too. I hope it doesn't take too long," Barry said.

Derrick leaned closer and whispered in Emmy's ear, "I asked Barry to go to Sandusky's with us. I hope you don't mind. He mentioned that you guys used to be good friends. I'll wait in the hall."

Emmy and Barry walked back to the front of the classroom to wait to see Mr. Hanna.

"How have you been, Emmy? I'm sorry I didn't talk to you the day you stopped by, but my acne was really bad that day, and I didn't want anyone to see me. Sorry."

"That's all right, Barry. You know I don't care how you look." Emmy waved her hands. "No wait, that didn't sound right. What I mean is that we've known each other for so long, and I want us to be good friends again. I know you get self-conscious about your skin, but I...how can I say this right? I'm your friend whether your face is looking like a pizza or perfectly clear. Does that make sense?"

Emmy hoped that Barry took this the right way. She wanted to be his friend, but not his girlfriend.

"I understand, Emmy. I know you only want to be friends. Can I tell you a secret?"

Emmy nodded. "Sure."

Barry smiled. "I have a girlfriend. Do you know Linda Bailey? She lives over on Republic Avenue by the library."

"I know her. Are you really going out with Linda Bailey? She's cute." Emmy decided to tease Barry a little. "I didn't know she was blind, though." She hoped he would not get upset.

He didn't and teased her right back. "Oh, that's a low blow even for you, Little Emmy."

She held out her hand to Barry. "Friends?"

"Yeah, friends." He shook her hand. "You should come over to the house sometime. I fixed up the attic and made it into my bedroom."

"Really? I didn't know you had any carpentry skills," Emmy teased. "I thought you only knew how to use a computer."

Emmy looked at her history book and noticed an envelope that wasn't there before. She started to open it, but Mr. Hanna called her name... Barry's, too. He handed them their Civil War reports.

"Mr. Culbertson needs you to rewrite some parts. The parts that you need to redo are highlighted. He needs the reports back in one week, okay?" Mr. Hanna looked at Emmy. "I'm sorry, Emily, but Mr. Culbertson asked me to tell you that he expects better work from you."

Barry and Emmy left the classroom to find Derrick. Barry looked at Emmy.

"Are you okay, Em? That sounded pretty harsh."

Emmy looked at Barry, trying not to cry. "I'm all right." She tried to smile, but couldn't. Barry put his arm around her shoulder.

Derrick saw them and hurried over. "What's wrong? What happened?"

"Mr. Hanna just ripped Emmy's report," Barry said. "He brutalized it."

"Harsh," Derrick replied. "Emmy, do you still want to go with us?"

"Oh yeah, I'm not gonna let Mr. Hanna ruin my fun."

Kristen joined them, and they headed out to Derrick's car.

"What were you guys talking about?"

Barry let Kristen know what happened. "Mr. Hanna ripped on Emmy's report. He laid it on her big-time harsh."

Kristen looked at Barry and Derrick. "Will you drop the *harsh* thing. You guys are so lame."

Emmy looked puzzled.

Kristen clued her in. "These two yahoos pick a new word to be the key word for a week and see how many kids pick up on it and start using the word, trying to be cool."

"Totally lame." Emmy grinned at Kristen, and they both laughed at the guys.

They piled into Derrick's car and headed to Emmy's house.

"Emmy, I'm sorry I didn't recognize you that night at the dance," Kristen said.

"It's okay. I remember seeing you at school, but I didn't know who you were."

Kristen touched Emmy's jacket. "What I mean is that I saw you before. Not in school."

"Where did you see me?"

"At a Fridays At Five show. Derrick and I both saw you, but I didn't recognize you. You are so quiet in person, but you sounded like a pro on the stage."

Emmy blushed. "Thanks, Kristen. I'm kinda surprised that you remembered me."

"Do you sing with the band all the time?"

"I used to sing with Kenny before the band even got together."

"I guess you can't now because they are on the road. Does everyone at school know you guys are friends?"

"Some kids do, but I don't usually mention it."

"Then I won't say anything about it if you're trying to keep it a secret."

"Thanks, Kristen." Emmy wondered if Kristen knew about her crush on Kenny.

Derrick stopped in front of the house.

"I'll be right back," Emmy said as she dashed up the sidewalk and disappeared inside.

"Anybody home? Mom, are you home?"

Emmy didn't get an answer, so she changed clothes, wrote a note for her mom and looked at her Civil War report. She tossed it on the dining room table and muttered, "I'll show Mr. Hanna how good a job I can do on this stupid report." She never settled for anything less than perfection in her schoolwork.

She ran out to the car and jumped in the back with Kristen. "Let's go. I'm ready to beat everybody at Sandusky's."

Sandusky's offered more than the indoor and outdoor miniature golf. They had batting cages, and in the summer they opened the go-cart track. An indoor concession stand stayed open all year round. They walked in, and Emmy looked around.

"We might have to wait a while. They look like they're real busy today."

"Anybody want a pop?" Derrick asked. "Kristen's buying."

"I am not. I didn't bring my purse, and I don't have any cash with me. Besides, it's your turn to pay."

"It's always my turn to pay. You never bring any money on purpose. I'm wise to you, little sister."

Emmy watched the interaction between Derrick and Kristen. She wondered out loud, "Are you guys twins?"

Derrick smiled as he pointed to Kristen. "No. Mom and Dad adopted her. Don't ask me why."

"Not true, Emmy. Mom told me she found *him* in a dumpster, and she's been sorry ever since that she didn't leave you there." Kristen poked Derrick in the chest as she teased him.

Kristen and Derrick pretended to bicker back and forth. Emmy listened and realized they really cared for each other.

"Actually, Emmy, he's only thirteen months older than me, so we're almost twins."

"All right, it's our turn to play. Boys against girls, or do you girls want to have a man on your team with you?" Derrick teased.

"I want a man on my team," Kristen said. "Do you boys know where there are any men who would be willing to play with a couple gorgeous women like us?" Kristen teased as she pretended to look around the building for a man.

"I'll take Emmy on my team so I can beat my sister's butt,"

141

Derrick said.

Kristen answered back, "Fine, Barry and I will beat you guys easy—no problem. Lowest combined score wins."

The game began, and the score stayed close for the first twelve holes. On the thirteenth hole, Barry ran into trouble. At the end of that hole, Derrick and Emmy were ahead by three strokes.

Kristen consoled Barry, "Don't worry. The water hole is coming up. Derrick always struggles there."

By the time they reached number eighteen (the water hole), Barry and Kristen trailed by only one shot. The water hole could be very tricky unless you played it safe. The safe way to required a person to go around the water, but there was a way to go over the water—a narrow bridge. Derrick went first, but he hit the ball into the water.

"Nice shot," Kristen smirked.

Barry and Kristen took their shots next. They played the safe way and ended up in perfect position. They tied the score for all practical purposes.

Emmy eyed her shot. "Why don't you guys go ahead and finish, and then I will play mine."

The other players finished, leaving it all up to Emmy. With a safe shot, Emmy could tie the score, but if she chose to go over the bridge, she and Derrick could win.

"Play it safe, Emmy. A tie is okay," Derrick recommended. "If you try the bridge, we could lose unless your shot is just perfect."

Barry and Kristen hollered, "Go for the win, Emmy, go for it."

Emmy calmly stepped up, stroked the ball across the bridge and into the cup for a hole-in-one. The other kids looked at her in awe.

"How on earth did you do that?" Barry asked.

"Piece of cake." Emmy twirled her putter like a baton. "My grandpa used to bring me here all the time. I've taken that shot a thousand times."

Barry grabbed the putter out of her hand. "That must have cost a fortune to play here that much."

"Not really." Emmy grinned. "My grandfather was Jim Sandusky."

"Sandusky?" Derrick asked. "You mean to tell us that your grandfather owns this place?"

"He used to own it, but he sold it a few years ago before he passed away," Emmy proudly informed them while taking the putter back from Barry.

"You're a ringer!' Kristen squealed.

"Okay, now it's boys against girls this time."

The girls beat the boys easily and gloated in the car all the way to La Cantina.

"Emmy, we should have taken pity on those losers. They are so pathetic." Kristen grinned as she leaned close to Emmy.

Emmy replied, "I tried to miss some shots to make it closer."

"Next time you should close your eyes."

"I did. A couple times."

"Really?" Kristen asked.

"Yeah, on the easier holes. I just line up the shot first."

It only took a few minutes to get to La Cantina. The hostess seated them immediately at a table by the windows overlooking the street. Emmy and Kristen sat together on one side of the table across from the guys.

"Emmy, does your family own this restaurant by any chance?" Derrick asked as they looked over the menus.

She laughed. "No, sorry. That might be better than owning a miniature golf business."

"You'd never go hungry, Em," Barry said.

Emmy glared. *Thanks, Barry. Did you have to bring up my family's economic status?*

"Order the most expensive thing on the menu, or at least the most expensive thing that you like. Derrick has a big allowance, and I like to make him spend it on me as much as I can." Kristen teased her brother while grinning at him.

"Don't listen to her, Emmy. I work hard for the little money I get from my parents. She, on the other hand, doesn't do a blessed thing to earn her riches," Derrick complained as he pointed at

143

Kristen.

She stuck her tongue out at him. "You're jealous because Daddy likes me better."

"You should see how she bats her eyes at Dad and begs for money for her clothes and stuff. It's disgusting." Derrick set his menu down. "I know what I want. Are you ready to order, Emmy?"

"Not quite, but I'll know in a minute. Go ahead and order if you're ready."

Emmy enjoyed listening to Derrick and Kristen tease each other. They were so much closer than she and Diane. The waiter came to take their orders. Emmy noticed that Kristen didn't order anything expensive, so she didn't, either. Actually nothing on the menu cost more than ten dollars.

"What are you going to do about your Civil War report?" Barry asked Emmy.

"I'm going to start on it when I get home tonight. I want to finish it and be able to hand it in to Mr. Hanna tomorrow."

"Will you help me revise mine?"

"Maybe. What's it worth to you if I do?" Emmy asked and then sipped her Coke. "I won't do it for free."

"Name your price," Barry said.

"A pizza."

Barry rubbed his chin. "Delivery or at the restaurant?"

"Delivery. I'm not going out with you."

"I didn't mean like a date." Barry laughed trying to save face.

"I'll help you over the weekend, but I'm not doing the whole thing for you. You have to do most of it."

True to her promise, as soon as Emmy got home, she began revising her report. She stayed up until one in the morning.

"Finally, that's it," Emmy whispered as she closed her book. "You better be satisfied with my effort now, Mr. Hanna."

Chapter Fifteen

"Get over it, Kristen. We let you win," Derrick claimed as they ate lunch in the school cafeteria.

"Oh, you let us win by twelve shots, huh? Anytime you want a rematch, let us know," Kristen teased right back at him. "Just because you might be one of the best tennis players in the state doesn't mean you are any good at golf."

Emmy ate lunch with Derrick, Barry, and Kristen, and the girls bragged about the miniature golf again.

"I didn't know you played tennis. Kenny and I play once in a while, but we're not all that good. I'm better at football. Maybe we could play doubles sometime." Emmy smiled as she remembered the one time she and Barry played tennis. "I talked Barry into playing once. He's such a klutz. He couldn't return a shot and tripped over his feet several times."

"I can't help it if I'm not as athletic as you, Em."

"You have other talents, Barry. I don't know anyone else who can do what you do on a computer."

Kristen proudly mentioned, "Derrick began playing tennis as soon as he could hold a racket. He played number one singles on Roosevelt's team and finished second in the state tournament last year."

"Oooh, impressive." Emmy high-fived Derrick. "Hey, did you know that today's Mr. Hanna's last day?"

"I heard someone mention that," Derrick said.

Barry added, "Mr. Culbertson is coming back on Monday. He's been gone for like three weeks because of some kind of surgery."

Emmy could hardly wait until her last period class. She fidgeted as she sat through Biology II and Physics. Finally, the last hour of the day arrived. She saw Derrick seconds before she walked into history class. "I can't wait to see the look on Mr. Hanna's face when I hand in my report."

Derrick smiled at her. "You're really serious about school."

She didn't have a chance to hand in her report before class and waited impatiently for class to be over. She couldn't sit still for

145

a moment and kept chewing on her pencil as she watched the clock. Finally, class ended, and Emmy hurried up to Mr. Hanna before he could leave.

"I revised my report last night, Mr. Hanna. Could you take a look at it and let me know if it is better?"

Mr. Hanna raised his eyebrows, scratched his beard and tilted his head as he looked up at Emmy. "You didn't have to turn it back in today. It wasn't due until next week."

"I know. I wanted to finish it as soon as I could before I forgot about what I wanted to write." Emmy smiled as Mr. Hanna began to read the revision she wrote.

"This is very good, Emily," he said.

"Nobody calls me Emily except my grandmother, Mr. Hanna. Everybody calls me Emmy."

"Okay, Emmy, this is very good work. I'm sure Mr. Culbertson will be very pleased."

"Thank you, Mr. Hanna." Emmy beamed with pride. "I hope you find a permanent teaching position soon, bye."

Emmy scurried out of the room and found Derrick and Barry waiting for her in the hall.

"Well, how did it go? Did he read your paper?" Barry asked.

"He read it, and I have to say he was very impressed."

"Good for you, Emmy. You're so smart. Will you rewrite my paper for me?" Barry asked, half seriously.

"No chance, buster. You have to do your own homework." Emmy walked in between the guys. "I said I'd help a bit."

"Just thought I'd ask."

"Is everybody going to the game tonight?" Derrick asked the group as Kristen joined them.

"I'm going, but Linda has to work," Barry said.

"Emmy, are you going?" Kristen asked.

"I'm not sure if my mom will let me go. I would need a ride because she doesn't want me to walk back to the school after dark." Emmy saw the looks on the other kids faces. "My mom still thinks I'm ten."

"Severe!" Barry replied and Kristen smacked his arm. "Ow,

146

Kristen. That hurt."

"No doubt, dorkbrain."

Emmy noticed that Kristen rubbed Barry's arm where she hit him.

"Come on, Kristen. I need to get home." Derrick pulled her along.

"We'll see you guys later." Kristen waved to Emmy as they walked to Derrick's car.

"I'll give you a ride to the game, Em," Barry volunteered as he and Emmy walked home. "Call me if you can go, and I'll pick you up."

"Barry, it'll only take me a minute at most to walk to your house. I'll call you as soon as I know I can go, but I'll walk over and meet you at your place. I can say hi to your mom."

Emmy loved watching football. During her first two years of high school, Emmy would ride with Diane to the football and basketball games. Even though Diane would not let Emmy hang out with her and her friends, it was a way for her to get to the games. She missed not being able to do that now that Diane had graduated. So far this year, Emmy missed all the games.

As soon as her mother got home from work, Emmy ran to meet her in the kitchen. "Is it all right if I go to the game tonight?"

"How do you plan to get there? I doubt if Diane will be going. Who are you going with? What time will you be home?"

Emmy rolled her eyes and shifted her weight from one foot to the other as her mom asked a hundred questions. "It's only a football game, Mom. I'm going with Barry Newton and Derrick and Kristen Keasling."

"Do we know the Keasling family? I better call Mrs. Newton later and talk to her."

Emmy ran to her bedroom. She knew that Diane would tell Mom her plans and not ask permission. She decided to get her homework done so she didn't have to think about it over the weekend. She sprawled out on her bed and began reading *Of Mice and Men* by John Steinbeck.

Mom knocked on the door. "I talked to Mrs. Newton. If your father agrees, you can go."

"Daddy won't get home till after seven. We're supposed to meet at six thirty. Please, can I go?" Emmy pleaded.

"Let me think about it. Maybe I will call your father at work."

Mom looked at Emmy and imagined her baby. Ten minutes later, Mom knocked on the door again. "You can go, honey."

Emmy looked up. "Yes!" She jumped off the bed and searched for the perfect outfit to wear. She found a clean pair of jeans and a Fridays At Five sweatshirt. She tossed them both on the bed as Mom announced, "Dinner is ready. You have to eat something before you go."

She immediately called Barry. "Hi, I can go. What time should I be at your house?"

"Quarter after six should give us enough time. See you then."

Emmy looked at the clock. It read 6:03. She ran into the kitchen and gulped down her food.

"Emmy, are you even chewing your dinner? I spent an hour making that casserole, and you are inhaling it in such a rush," Mom scolded.

"I've gotta hurry, Mom. I need to be at Barry's by quarter after."

She finished eating and ran into the bathroom. She quickly changed her clothes and headed for the door.

"Wait just a minute, young lady. Let me see you." Mom took a look at her. "What coat are you planning to wear? Do you have your gloves and a hat? It will get cold later."

"Yes, Mom, I have everything. I need to go. I'll be home after the game."

Mom watched as Emmy ran out the door and down the front sidewalk. She sprinted all the way to the Newton house, jumped up the steps and rang the bell. Mrs. Newton let her in.

"Hi, Mrs. Newton, is Barry ready?" Emmy asked as she caught her breath.

"Hi, Lit... Hi, Emmy. Barry will be ready in a minute."

Mrs. Newton remembered Barry telling her that Emmy didn't like to be called Little Emmy anymore. Barry came down the stairs.

"Ready to go, Em? See you later, Mom."

"Have fun," Mom yelled from the kitchen.

Emmy and Barry walked out to his car, which he parked on the street in front of the house.

"Does this thing run?" Emmy questioned as she took a good look at his pride and joy.

"Sometimes," Barry answered with a smile.

"What is it, anyway?" Emmy asked as she noticed the rusted body.

"It's a 1982 Ford Fairmont. I thought about trying to fix it up, but I might just get something newer someday."

It took several tries, but the car started and got them to school without any difficulty. They were supposed to meet Derrick and Kristen at the south end of the bleachers. They found a parking space and walked over to the football field.

"Emmy, Barry, over here," Kristen yelled as she frantically waved her arms.

"There's Kristen." Emmy grabbed Barry's arm and pulled him along.

"I'm glad you guys made it," Kristen said as she led them along the front of the bleachers. "Derrick is holding some seats for us, and you'll never believe who is here."

"Who?" Emmy looked at the crowd.

"Your favorite teacher, and he is sitting right in front of us," Kristen said.

Emmy saw Mr. Hanna. He looked so different without his jacket and tie. He could almost pass for one of the students.

"Hello, Mr. Hanna," Emmy said as she ran up the bleachers.

"Hi, Emmy. Hi, guys. Perfect night for a football game," Mr. Hanna replied.

The first game ended with Roosevelt winning by ten points. Between games, Derrick and Barry made a food run. Kristen ran to the bathroom. Emmy noticed Mr. Hanna sitting by himself and decided to talk to him.

"Do you mind if I sit with you for a moment?" Emmy

asked.

"Have a seat, Emily, I mean Emmy. Are you having a good time with your friends?"

"Yes, we blew them out that game, huh? Do you like football, Mr. Hanna?"

"Oh, yeah. I used to play on the team."

"What position did you play?"

"I played running back and wide receiver at times. Do you like football, Emmy?"

"Definitely. I used to play with the neighborhood boys all the time when I could get away from my mom. She always thought I would get hurt, but I never did."

Mr. Hanna looked at her and noticed that her blue eyes reminded him of his girlfriend Sherry. The boys and Kristen returned, so Emmy headed back to her seat.

During the varsity game, Emmy kept watching one of the players on defense because he played better than any of the other players. "Barry, who's number fifty-two? Do you know his name?"

Kristen heard Emmy ask Barry and answered for him, "His name is Tony Bertucci. He's pretty good, huh? And he's only a sophomore. Wait until he's a senior."

The crowd jumped up and yelled because number fifty-two hit the running back so hard that he fumbled.

"He's my favorite cousin," Kristen continued to talk to Emmy about number fifty-two, but because of the crowd noise she didn't hear.

"Did you say something, Kristen?" Emmy asked.

"Never mind. It's not important."

Emmy thought about the name. *Tony Bertucci. That sounds familiar, but I can't remember why.* She tried to think of why his name rang a bell during the rest of the game. Roosevelt won by twenty-eight points. As they were leaving, she saw Mr. Hanna.

"Good night, Mr. Hanna. Good game, huh?"

"Absolutely. Number fifty-two is really good. Have a good night, Emmy."

Barry mimicked. "Have a good night, Emmy."

"Stop it, Barry." Kristen pushed him off balance, and Barry

150

nearly fell as he got tangled up in his own feet.

Emmy watched as Barry regained his balance and popped back up.

"It's okay. I'm all right."

Emmy shook her head and said, "You've always been a klutz."

Derrick and Kristen said good night and headed to their car. Barry teased Emmy all the way to his car. They kept pushing each other on the shoulder until they got in the car. Barry turned the key, but nothing happened.

"Great. The battery is run down. Happens once in a while. I'll fix it." Barry opened the trunk and looked for his jumper cables. "I thought I put them back yesterday, but I guess I didn't. Hey, Derrick," Barry yelled as he spotted Derrick about to drive away.

Derrick saw Barry. He stopped and rolled down his window. "What's up? The old chariot broke down again?"

"I left my jumper cables at home. Can you run me back home to get them?"

"Sure, but I gotta stop at the gas station on the way," Derrick said.

Just then Mr. Hanna walked past. "Car trouble, Barry?"

"Again," Barry said and then sighed.

Emmy mentioned, "I told my mom I would come right home after the game, Barry. How long is this gonna take?"

Kristen jumped out of the car. "Derrick, I'll wait with Emmy until you guys get back."

"Do you need a lift, Emmy?" Mr. Hanna asked.

"Oh, that's all right, Mr. Hanna. I wouldn't want to be any trouble. I can wait for Barry. Kristen will be with me."

"I'll wait with you until Derrick and Barry return."

"That would be great, Mr. Hanna," Derrick said thankfully. "We'll hurry back."

Mr. Hanna parked his car next to Barry's and got out to wait with the girls. Emmy listened as some of the other kids surrounded him by the trunk of his car. Emmy and Kristen looked at each other trying to read each other's thoughts.

"Mr. Hanna is actually pretty charming, and handsome, too," Kristen said.

"I wonder how long he's had that beard?" Emmy wondered.

Mr. Hanna walked around Barry's car, chuckled as he noticed the rust and stood by Emmy and Kristen. "Good thing it's not too cold tonight."

"Where did you go to school?" Kristen asked.

"North Park College. I'm searching for a full-time teaching position, but right now I'm getting enough days as a sub to keep me busy."

Emmy and Kristen talked to Mr. Hanna until Barry and Derrick returned with the jumper cables. After a couple of tries, the car started.

"Maybe you can follow Barry home, or I will, to make sure he gets home all right," Mr. Hanna mentioned to Derrick. "Where do you live, Barry? Or where do you have to drop Emmy off, I guess is what I should ask. I assume you are taking her home."

Barry told Mr. Hanna where he and Emmy lived.

"I'm familiar with the area. It's just up the street from the Colwells. They're my aunt and uncle."

"You gotta be kidding me!" Emmy exclaimed. "You're really related to Kenny Colwell?"

"He's my cousin," Mr. Hanna explained. "Do you know Kenny?"

"He's been my friend since I was a little girl," Emmy declared with pride.

Mr. Hanna gazed at her for a moment. Then he slapped a hand to his forehead. "Oh, my God. You're the Emmy Frankie told me about. Frankie is Kenny's guitar tech, and he's also my brother."

"I know Frankie, but I never thought anything about you having the same last name. Then you're Tom. You never told us your first name in class, but I've heard Kenny talk about you and Frankie before. What a weird coincidence."

"Then you're the little girl who used to come over and play. Frankie and I would visit Kenny and you would come over. I remember one time we were playing with toy guns, and you got

152

your finger stuck. You couldn't get it out and started crying. You wouldn't let anyone help you except Kenny." Mr. Hanna smiled at her. "You've grown up since the first time I saw you."

"I kinda remember playing with Kenny's cousins, but you guys were so much older. I thought you looked kinda familiar, but the beard threw me off."

"I'll follow you and Barry home. Maybe I can drop in on my aunt and uncle." Mr. Hanna followed them to Emmy's house and parked right behind Barry.

Emmy hopped out of the car and hollered, "Thanks for the ride, Barry. I hope your car makes it the rest of the way home. I know it's a long way."

Barry turned and glared at her from inside the car.

"Where does Barry live?" Mr. Hanna asked. "Is it very far? Should I follow him?"

Emmy smiled and said, "He lives five houses away. I think he will make it home all right."

"Ah. You are being sarcastic." Mr. Hanna caught on to her sense of humor. "Do you want to go with me to see if they are home?" Mr. Hanna asked.

"Sure, but I don't think Kenny's home. Let me tell my mom where I'm going. Be back in a sec."

Emmy rushed up the sidewalk, took the steps two at a time, opened the door and saw her mother in her recliner. "Mom, I'm gonna be over at Kenny's. I'll be back later." She didn't give her mother a chance to object.

"Emmy!" Mom yelled but didn't bother to get up.

She and Mr. Hanna walked over to the Colwell house. The porch light was off, and the inside was dark. Emmy turned her back to the house about to walk away. She mentioned to Mr. Hanna, "Maybe it's too late to stop by."

"What do you think, Emmy? Should we leave?"

At that moment the porch light came on. She looked back to the porch as the door opened.

"Kenny!" she screamed.

"Emmy! Emmy, is that you?"

Kenny jumped down the steps and ran over to her. He

swept her off her feet, hugged her and twirled her around. She threw her arms around his neck and closed her eyes as he kissed her.

"I guess you really do know Kenny," Mr. Hanna said, but they weren't listening.

Kenny finally stopped kissing Emmy and set her down. "Tom, what are you doing here?"

Mr. Hanna explained how he happened to be there.

"Come on in and see the folks." Kenny took Emmy's hand and pulled her toward the house. "I called your house earlier and talked to your Mom."

"When did you get home? How long are you here for? How did last night's show go?" Emmy asked as fast as she could.

"Slow down, Emmy, and I'll tell you everything," Kenny implored her as they stepped inside.

"Mom, Dad, look who I found hanging out in the front yard."

"Emmy! Tom!" Mrs. Colwell exclaimed. "Come in and sit down. We were just talking about you, honey. I mean Kenny asked about you. We weren't talking about you behind your back."

"I think she knows that, Mom," Kenny said and then chuckled.

Emmy and Kenny caught up on everything as Mr. Hanna talked to his aunt and uncle. The time got away, and before Emmy realized, it was after midnight.

Emmy bit her lip. "Oh, no. I needed to be home a long time ago. My mom is gonna kill me."

"Don't worry, honey. Your mom called around eleven. I told her you were still here with us, and we would make sure you got home safely, but that it might be rather late. Your mom said she would leave the front door unlocked for you. You guys can talk all you want, but your father and I are heading to bed. Nice to see you again, Tom. I still don't like the beard. It makes you look older. Say hi to your mom for me. Kenny, you make sure Emmy gets home all right. Walk her right up to the front door and make sure she gets inside," Mrs. Colwell said.

"I will, Mom. Good night," Kenny said. "Come on guys.

Let's go out to the garage so we don't disturb my parents."

Kenny took them out to the old carriage house. Emmy noticed a change right away.

"You put in some different stairs."

"I thought I should before someone fell down the old ones."

Kenny turned on the lights, and Emmy noticed something else.

"You've still got the old couch. Aren't you ever going to get a new one?"

"No. I like this one just fine."

Kenny smiled at her, and Emmy smiled shyly back at him. She now knew the reason Kenny kept this couch. They talked for a couple of hours, and then Emmy looked at the clock.

"I really need to go home. I don't remember ever being out till two thirty in the morning before. I sure hope my mom isn't waiting up for me."

Kenny took her hand. "Come on, Em, we'll walk you home."

"I'm gonna head out." Mr. Hanna waved and walked toward his car as they paused in front of Emmy's house.

"See ya, Tom. Give me a call sometime."

Kenny walked Emmy home just as he promised his mother. They stood on her front steps for a moment, looking into each other's eyes. Emmy waited for Kenny to kiss her. Kenny wanted to kiss Emmy, but didn't know if he should.

"This has been quite a night. I still can't believe you're home. How long did you say you're home for?" Emmy yawned.

"I'll be home for a week, Emmy. I'll call you, and we can do something together. Go to bed and get some sleep."

"I think I'll sleep all day tomorrow."

Kenny put his arms around her and hugged her. Emmy rested her head against his chest for a moment, almost falling asleep before she opened the door and stepped inside. She dreamed about singing on stage with the band. She also dreamed about kissing Kenny.

155

What is that blasted noise? Emmy wondered. Finally it dawned on her, *Shoot, it's the phone.* She picked up the receiver and mumbled, "Hello."

"Emmy, it's me. I've called three times," Kenny said.

"What time is it?"

"It's noon. Are you still in bed?"

"Yeah, I guess I shouldn't have stayed out so late."

"You wanna do something this afternoon?"

"Sure. Give me some time to wake up and get dressed."

"I'll be over in a little bit. Don't fall back asleep. Tom called, and he's coming over. We'll call your friends and figure out something to do."

"I'll get ready."

Emmy crawled out of bed and headed to the bathroom.

"Mom... Diane... Daddy... Anybody home?" she called out as she wandered around the house. Finally she saw a note on the kitchen table.

Emmy,

Your father and I are going to Aurora Heights to visit Aunt Betty. We will be back later tonight. I put a five dollar bill on your dresser if you need some money today. Try not to spent it unless it's absolutely necessary. Diane is at work until six, I think. I let you sleep because I know you stayed out late. We will talk about that when we get back, young lady.

Mom

Emmy jumped in and out of the shower and dressed quickly. She grabbed a banana to eat and finished it as the doorbell rang. She ran to open it for Kenny banging her shin on the end table by her father's recliner.

"Ow! Crap, that hurts," she swore as she hopped to the door while rubbing her shin.

"I heard that!" Kenny hollered from outside the door.

She opened the door and smiled. "I hit my leg on that

156

blasted end table."

Kenny grinned, and she frowned at him. He kissed her cheek, making her smile.

"Hey, sleepyhead. You stayed awake. I was worried you would fall back asleep, and I would have to break in the house and drag you out of bed. What do you wanna do?"

"Anything. Whatever you want to do. Doesn't matter."

"Call your friends, and let's plan something. I don't want to waste any time while I'm home."

Emmy called Barry and Kristen, and they agreed to meet at Darby's in an hour. Mr. Hanna showed up fifteen minutes later. She opened the door, grinned and said. "Hi, Mr. Hanna."

Mr. Hanna replied with all the formality her could muster. "Good afternoon, Miss Colasanti. How are you? It is so good to see you."

"I guess you want me to call you Tom, huh? I'm not sure I can. I still think of you as my teacher more than Kenny's cousin."

"Okay, you can call me Mr. Hanna if you are more comfortable with that."

"Come in and have a seat in the kitchen with Kenny. He is emptying out the fridge. I don't know how he can stay so skinny and eat so much," she said.

"It's because I burn so many calories on stage. Hey, Tom. What's up?" Kenny said in between bites of an apple.

"Are you going to be able to eat anything at Darby's, or are we meeting there because it's close?" Mr. Hanna asked.

"I'm saving room for a chili cheese dog and onion rings. I still love going to Darby's every time I'm home. Tom, did you ever hear about the time Emmy went to Darby's with Barry when she was only a wee lass—couple months ago—and got grounded for a week?"

Emmy put her hands on her hips and tried to looked angry, but Kenny merely laughed at her.

"Anyway, she got in trouble because of Barry and couldn't ride her bike for a week. Oh, and the best part, after her week was up, she went right over to Barry's house and punched him out for getting her in trouble."

Mr. Hanna laughed. "I bet that would have been a sight to see."

"Are you guys through making fun of me now?" Emmy asked.

Kenny grinned and said, "No, we're just getting started teasing you, Em."

The doorbell rang again.

"That's probably Barry." She ran through the house and brought him back to the kitchen.

Kenny said, "I was telling Tom about the time Emmy punched you for getting her in trouble."

"I remember that. She walked up to me and let me have it in the belly without any warning. I couldn't hit her back because she's a *girl*." He poked her in the side. Emmy faked a punch at him. Barry covered his stomach as he laughed.

"Come on. Let's go over to Darby's. Derrick and Kristen are probably already there."

"Do you want me to drive?" Barry asked.

"No!" all three of them shouted at the same time.

"We're not taking your car, Barry. No way, no how," Emmy informed him sternly.

"All right. You don't have to be so severe," Barry replied.

Emmy gave him an evil look. *Don't be such a dork.*

Mr. Hanna drove to Darby's. When Derrick and Kristen arrived a few minutes later, Kenny was eating the last bite of two chili cheese dogs and onion rings. Emmy rushed over to Kristen.

"You aren't going to believe this. Mr. Hanna and Kenny are cousins."

"Get out of town! For real?" Kristen exclaimed.

"Swear," Emmy asserted as she crossed her heart.

"Just like Tony Bertucci is my cousin," Kristen said, but Emmy didn't hear because Kenny pulled her away.

"I can't eat another thing," Kenny confessed.

"Is that because Mr. Darby ran out of food, or is it because you are finally full?" Emmy asked with a grin.

Kenny grabbed Emmy around the waist and pulled her onto his lap as he sat down on the edge of a booth. "A real comedian,

158

aren't you?"

Emmy smiled and leaned back against him.

"See. I told you." Derrick nudged Kristen. "They're best friends."

Kristen wrinkled her nose at her brother. *It looks like they're more than friends.*

"Where are we going, and what are we gonna do this afternoon?" Kenny asked.

"The mall," Kristen and Emmy shouted together.

"Yes, the mall." Barry affirmed with a nod.

"We must go to the mall because we have to go shopping for clothes. I don't have a single thing to wear," Derrick answered back in a mocking manner as he looked at Kristen.

Kristen replied, "It's not my fault if Mom wants me to dress in the latest fashions."

Kenny and Mr. Hanna looked at them like they were nuts.

"Linda gets off at two, and I told her I would pick her up, so we gotta at least stop at the mall for a second," Barry said.

"Can we all fit in one car?" Emmy wondered.

"I brought the van in case we needed to fit everyone in one vehicle." Derrick pointed to his head. "Smart thinking, huh?"

"Yeah, you're a regular genius," Kristen said.

They agreed to leave Mr. Hanna's car at Kenny's house and used the van for transportation. When they got to the mall, everybody piled out as they talked to each other. Emmy touched some of the black and orange streamers that decorated the crowded mall. Fake cobwebs added to the effect. Soon Emmy noticed a bunch of teenage girls following them.

"Kenny, are you aware there are some girls following us?"

Kenny turned around, and the girls screamed. They recognized him even though he was wearing a baseball cap and sunglasses.

"Sorry, guys. I guess I've been spotted." Kenny shrugged his shoulders as he headed over to the group of teenage girls. He signed autographs and posed for pictures.

He returned and Emmy asked, "Does this happen often?"

"It's happening more often now, but I don't mind too much.

I guess it's the price I have to pay if we are going to be successful as a band."

"Must be rough," Barry said. "Got any openings in the band for a xylophone player?"

"You don't know how to play the xylophone, Barry," Emmy said.

"I took a couple lessons when I was a kid. So there."

"Yeah, we've been thinking about adding a xylophone player to the band," Kenny said with a straight face.

"For real?" Barry perked up.

"No!" the whole group shouted at him all at once.

Barry slunk away to get Linda. "It would be unique. Nobody else has a xylophone player," he said as he looked over his shoulder and bumped into an older lady. "Excuse me, ma'am."

"Why don't you kids ever look where you're going?" She swung her purse at Barry.

The other kids laughed, and Emmy shook her head. "Barry, you're a real dork, but a lovable one at least."

Barry teased her back, "Gee, thanks, Little Emmy."

They headed back to the van without Kenny being harassed for any more autographs.

"Let's go hiking," Emmy suggested.

"Where?"

"Windsor Park," Emmy answered. "There is that huge hill and the trail along the river."

"That huge hill is for sledding, and last time I looked there wasn't any snow on the ground," Barry said.

"We could hike along the river," Derrick suggested.

"Sounds like a plan to me." Mr. Hanna finally voiced an opinion. He thought perhaps hanging out with these younger kids all afternoon would be a waste of time, but a hike along the river would be refreshing.

Derrick drove, and Kenny grabbed shotgun. Barry, Linda and Kristen claimed the middle seat, and Emmy and Tom sat in the back.

Emmy asked, "Do you have a girlfriend, Mr. Hanna?"

"As a matter of fact, I do, and her name is Sherry Hastings.

She has eyes that look amazingly similar to yours, and she attends North Park. She has another year to go, and then we plan on getting married."

"Congratulations, Mr. Hanna."

They arrived at the park after a short drive.

"Let's head over to the waterfall," Kristen suggested.

"Yeah, and we can throw Emmy in the river and see if she can swim," Barry said.

Emmy chased Barry toward the river. They got close enough to feel the cool spray of water from the falls.

"My grandfather used to bring me here as a little girl," Emmy said. "I used to love the feel of the spray on my face."

Barry got behind Emmy and pushed her.

She squealed, "Stop that, Barry! I almost slipped."

"I wouldn't have let you fall, Emmy. I was holding onto you."

After watching the falls for a time, the group headed up the trail along the river. Emmy and Kristen talked about school and her Civil War report. Barry and Linda walked together. The three other guys tagged along behind everyone else.

Emmy whispered to Kristen, "I thought that Mr. Hanna was mean until I talked to him at the football game, but he's actually really nice. Did I tell you I knew him when I was younger?"

"No, how did you know him?" Kristen asked.

"He and his older brother would come over to Kenny's, and I would play with them. I didn't recognize him with a beard."

"Didn't you recognize the name?"

"I don't think I knew his name back then. I know Frankie because he works for the band."

"I heard him talking about his girlfriend. Too bad. I would go out with him in a heartbeat," Kristen said and then sighed.

"Well, he is pretty old," Emmy stated seriously.

"Emmy, he's only twenty-two. That's not that old. My dad is eighteen years older than my mom."

"Get out! Really?"

"Yeah. Quite an age difference, huh?"

That's so unreal. Daddy would totally freak out if I wanted to date a guy that much older. He and Mom think Kenny is too old for me. Emmy picked up a colorful rock and tossed it into the river.

After hiking throughout the afternoon, the group returned to the van.

"Anybody hungry?" Kenny turned around and asked.

"You can't possibly be hungry already," Emmy hollered from the backseat.

"How about some Mexican?" Kenny suggested. "La Cantina all right with everyone? My treat."

They headed to the restaurant, and the hostess led them to a table in the corner big enough for the whole group. While the others talked, Kenny pulled Emmy close.

"Will you sit by me, Emmy?"

"If you want me to, I will."

Kenny hadn't paid a lot of attention to Emmy since they left Darby's. He would smile at her once in a while when the other kids weren't watching, but he didn't hold her hand or do anything that might draw attention to them. He watched as Emmy slid onto the wooden bench first, and then he slipped in next to her. He squeezed her hand for a moment as they smiled at each other. The rest of the group slid onto the benches. Tom grabbed a chair and sat at the end of the table. Everybody quickly decided what they wanted to order, and the waitress strolled over with her order pad. She looked to be a college-age girl, and she recognized Kenny.

"Hi, Kenny. I don't know if you remember me, but we had a class together last semester."

Kenny thought for a moment. "Mathilda, right?" *I hope you're wearing your correct name tag.*

"Right! I'm surprised you remembered. I saw you guys play, and I love your music."

"Thanks. I appreciate it."

Mathilda took their orders and then smiled at Kenny. "I'll put a rush on your order." She walked away but looked back over her shoulder.

Emmy grinned as Mathilda bumped into the edge of a table. "Did you really remember her, or did you peek at her name tag?"

162

"Didn't have a clue," he confessed.

Emmy watched and listened to Kenny. He somehow treated everyone who recognized him with respect and not as a nuisance like some stars did. Mathilda returned with their drink orders, and the kids all talked at the same time. Emmy sat quietly in the corner as Kenny discreetly held her hand under the table. The food arrived quickly, and Emmy shook her head as she watched Kenny eat three tacos in the time it took her to eat one chicken enchilada. Kenny paid the bill, and everyone else chipped in for the tip.

"Where to now?" Barry asked.

"We could go to my house," Kenny offered.

Tom checked his watch. "I can hang out for a while, but then I need to see Sherry."

Emmy finished the last of her Coke. Kenny ate the last two tortilla chips, and they climbed back into the van and headed to the Colwell home. Kenny introduced everyone to his parents.

"Hey, you guys, I got something you gotta hear. Be right back." Kenny raced up the stairs to his room and came back with a CD. "These are rough mixes of some tracks we're considering for the new CD. It's not finished yet, but we're getting close. Listen to this and guess who it is." He played a track for them.

Emmy recognized the singer immediately. *Kenny, are you trying to embarrass me. I sound terrible.*

The other kids listened to the CD and tried to guess, but nobody knew for sure. Kenny pointed to Emmy.

"For real?" Kristen asked.

"Yeah, we recorded a show where I dragged her on stage to sing a solo and that's it." Kenny pulled on Emmy's ponytail. "Doesn't she have a beautiful voice?"

"She sounds better than a cat screeching in the alley," Barry said.

Emmy was close enough to smack his leg. "I hate you."

Derrick said, "Kristen and I saw the band over a year ago, and you brought Emmy on stage with you. We didn't know her at the time, but we met at a high school dance in September. Just think, we know two famous rock stars from SoHam."

Emmy blushed as everyone looked at her.

"Emmy, that sounds pretty good. Maybe you should consider a career in music," Mr. Hanna suggested as he looked through some of Kenny's CD collection.

"I know this place where we could hear this band if anybody's interested," Kenny suggested after hanging out and listening to CDs for an hour. "It's an all ages venue so everyone can get in. Even Emmy," he teased.

Barry said, "Yeah. That sounds like fun."

Derrick and Kristen nodded in agreement. Linda looked at her watch.

"I promised Sherry we would do something tonight. We might meet you guys at the club." Tom slapped Kenny on the back.

"You know which one I mean?" Kenny asked.

"Lights Out!, right?"

Kenny nodded, and Tom left to see if Sherry wanted to join them at the club. It was still too early to leave, so everybody chilled out at the Colwell home for a while longer.

"Hey, do you guys want to see the carriage house?" Kenny asked.

Derrick and Barry jumped up. "Sure. I heard that's where you started the band," Derrick said.

"It is!" Emmy grinned. "I've seen it lots of times. I think I'll just hang out here with the girls."

Kenny took Derrick and Barry out to the carriage house and showed them his set up.

"Nice couch. Ever think about getting a new one?" Barry jested as he sat with his arms stretched along the back of the couch.

Kenny smiled, and ten minutes later, the guys returned to the house. Kristen and Linda sat on the couch in the living room talking to Kenny's parents.

"Where's Emmy?" Kenny whispered in Kristen's ear as he stood behind the couch and leaned over.

"You just missed her. She ran home to check on Diane," Kristen said. "Is it all right if Emmy invites Diane along?"

"I don't mind," he replied.

Emmy bolted into the house and hollered loud enough to make sure Diane and the neighbors could hear. "Diane, are you

164

here?" She didn't want to ever walk into a surprise in the bedroom again.

"I'm in the bathroom. What do you want?" her sister responded.

"Do you wanna go with me and my friends to hear a band? Kenny knows this place and wants to go. We've got a whole group of people going. Are you interested?"

Diane came out of the bathroom. "Yeah, why not? Craig's working late tonight. Let me change clothes. Just gimme a couple minutes."

"Meet me over at Kenny's house." Emmy ran out of the house. She sprinted over to the Colwell house and took the front steps two at a time. She banged on the door.

Kenny grinned as he opened it. "Yes? May I help you?"

"Are you really a rock star? I heard that from some kids at school."

"I might be. I play in a band."

"You're not a rock star. You're a dork!" she teased. "Real rock stars don't drive Honda Civics. Are you gonna let me in?"

"Fine! Come in and join the party." He waved her into the room.

Diane arrived a few minutes later and rang the doorbell. Kenny looked at Emmy and whispered. "That's how you announce your presence."

Emmy stuck out her tongue.

Kenny greeted Diane at the door. "Hi, Diane. It's good to see you again. I'm glad you decided to join us."

"Thanks, it's good to see you, too. Em is always telling me where you guys are playing. She must be your biggest fan."

"I'm sure she is." Kenny winked at Emmy.

Diane sat on the couch next to Barry and Linda and watched as Kenny and Emmy talked to each other. Diane noticed that Kenny put his hands on Emmy's shoulders as she stood with her back to him. Emmy peered over her shoulder at Kenny with a look of admiration. Emmy smiled as she and Kenny talked and he held her hand. She hoped he would kiss her. Kenny thought about kissing her, but he noticed Diane staring at them, so he didn't.

165

"I guess everyone who's going is here. We can leave whenever you guys are ready," Kenny said.

All seven people piled into the van, and they headed downtown to Lights Out!. Kenny directed Derrick, and they parked at the lot reserved for VIPs. The parking attendant knew Kenny and promised the van would be handy when they needed to leave.

Inside the club, they grabbed a table close to the stage, but yet offered some privacy. Kenny made sure Emmy sat next to him. He even helped her slip off her jacket. Diane noticed how Emmy smiled and her eyes lit up whenever she talked to Kenny. None of the other kids paid any attention to the way Emmy behaved. Tom and Sherry joined them before the band came out to play their first set.

"What's the name of the band?" Emmy shouted into Kenny's ear over the noise of the club.

"The Notable Exceptions." He could still smell the strawberry shampoo she used earlier as he yelled into her ear.

"I like their set so far, Kenny. Would you dance with me?"

"Why don't you see if Kristen wants to dance?"

"You won't dance because people might recognize you, huh?"

"Yeah, I don't want to be a distraction."

"Oh, come on. You're in SoHam. Most people don't think of you as a celebrity here. Let's just try it for a couple tunes. Please?"

"All right, Em. I'll do it for you."

Emmy dragged Kenny onto the small dance floor in front of the stage as the band played some danceable tunes. Soon Barry and Linda joined them, and then Kristen convinced Derrick to dance with her. Diane sat at the table with Tom and Sherry.

"You taught Emmy, right?" Diane asked.

"I substituted for her regular history teacher for three weeks, but my time is over. Your sister is a very good student. She doesn't settle for anything less than perfect, as far as her schoolwork goes."

"Yeah, she's the smart one in the family. I never tried all that hard to get good grades. Emmy works her butt off at times."

"Are you going to college now?" Sherry asked.

"Not full-time, but I am taking a night class." Diane tilted her head. "You and Kenny are cousins, right?"

"We are."

"I kinda remember you from years ago. You would come over to the Colwell house."

"It's rather strange, but I didn't recognize Emmy at first." Tom watched Emmy dancing. "She's older, but she still looks young for her age."

"Yeah, she's lucky like that," Diane said. *I look ten years older than I really am.*

After a couple of songs, Emmy and Kristen were the only ones still dancing. Some of the other people at the club got up to dance, so Emmy and Kristen went back to their table. Emmy sat beside Kenny and held his hand. Emmy smiled every time she looked at Kenny, and he constantly hugged her and touched her face.

After finishing their set, the singer stopped at their table. Kenny pulled up a chair and introduced him. "Hey, guys, this is P.J."

"Hi, everyone. Did you enjoy the set?" P.J. asked.

Barry shook his hand. "Yeah! You guys are good. You should make a CD."

"That is our goal."

During the second set, P.J. invited Kenny up on stage to play guitar. Kenny sat in with the band for a few songs, and then P.J. asked him, "Wanna do a couple of your tunes?"

"Okay, I'll do a couple."

Kenny and the band played a couple of popular songs. Then Kenny asked P.J., "Would you mind if I play an old favorite of mine by myself?"

"Sure. Whatever you want. Go ahead." P.J. and the band took a break.

"Emmy, come here please," Kenny held out his hand.

She approached timidly, and he pulled her up on stage. "Remember the words to 'Storms'?"

"I think so," Emmy answered nervously.

167

Kenny handed her a microphone and started playing the intro. The sound guy brought up the level on her mic, and she started singing softly. She relaxed as Kenny smiled at her and finished the song to a loud ovation from the crowd—especially from a table close to the stage.

Kenny shook hands with P.J. "Thanks for letting me sit in with you guys and for letting me bring Emmy up. Maybe I can make it up to you sometime."

"Emmy, you sounded great!" Barry patted her arm.

All the kids gave Emmy a high-five for her performance and bravery. Tom and Sherry left around eleven, but the rest of the group hung around till after midnight.

"You looked tired, Em. Are you ready to go home?" Kenny asked as she yawned.

"I guess I should. It's been a hard day's night."

Kenny looked at her and broke out into the Beatles tune, "It's been a hard day's night, and I been workin' like a dog."

"Did you make that up?" Emmy asked.

"Are you kidding? You've never heard that before?"

"No, I've never heard it. You made it up, didn't you?"

"Girl, you've got a lot to learn. You gotta come over and let me play some tunes for you while I'm home."

On the way home, Emmy sat in the back of the van with Kenny, and he sang some old tunes for her. "Are you sure you've never heard that tune?"

"No, it doesn't sound familiar."

"Don't your parents have any records? Haven't you ever listened to an oldies station?"

"I've never seen any records around the house, and my parents never listen to the radio. They sit in front of the TV at night."

Kenny shook his head. *I can't imagine living in a house without music.*

"This has been an awesome day," Barry said.

Linda frowned at him. *You never take me out, and I'm supposed to be your girlfriend. I saw you staring at Emmy a few times. You better not be lying when you say she's just a friend.*

"I enjoyed it. We gotta do something else while I'm home," Kenny said as Derrick parked the van in front of the Colwell home.

After exchanging goodbyes with the group, Emmy and Kenny walked slowly over to her house. Diane trailed along right behind them.

"Do you want to sit on the back porch?" Emmy asked.

"Are you sure you can stay awake, Em?"

"I feel more awake now. Must be the fresh air."

"I'm going in the house," Diane said. "I'll try to make sure Mom leaves you guys alone."

I appreciate that. Emmy smiled. She took Kenny's hand and led him to the porch. They sat on the steps and talked quietly. The porch light came on, and Mom opened the door.

"Emmy, are you going to stay out here? Don't you want to come inside? Maybe Kenny wants something to drink, huh?" Mom asked with exaggerated politeness.

"No, thanks, Mrs. Colasanti. I'm fine."

Emmy looked at Mom and asked, "Would you please turn the light off when you close the door, Mom? Thanks. We'll be all right out here."

"How old are you now, Kenny?"

"I'll be twenty in January," he answered.

"And my little baby is only sixteen. That's quite a difference in age."

"I'm fully aware of that, Mrs. Colasanti." *Your point is coming across loud and clear.*

"Don't stay out too late. You need your sleep, especially since you were out so late last night. Believe me! I'm going to be keeping an eye on the clock, Emily."

"Mom! I'm not a baby. I know how much sleep I need." Emmy looked at Kenny to gauge his reaction to the way her mother treated her.

"Make sure you keep your coat on, honey. It's chilly out here."

Mom closed the door and, after twenty seconds, turned off the light. She watched from inside for a moment before heading back to the living room.

Emmy and Kenny sat close to each other.

"I'm getting chilly, Kenny. Would you put your arm around me to warm me up?"

Kenny held her closer with his arm around her shoulders. "I know you want to be kissed, Emmy, but maybe we shouldn't right now."

"I don't want you to kiss me. Why do you think I want you to kiss me?"

"Because I've known you a long time, and I can read your mind like a book."

"You can, huh? Well, what am I thinking now?"

Kenny looked at her and studied her face. He grinned at her and whispered in her ear, "You are thinking about the night we fell asleep together on the old couch."

Emmy smacked his thigh. "I was not. You are probably thinking about it and want me to stay with you again. You are such a Romeo now. You probably have your pick of girls every night on tour."

"You know that's not true. The guys all have girlfriends now, and Jeremy is married already. Jeff is engaged." He laughed then said, "The roadies are a different story."

They talked about life on the road for a while, and then fell silent. They sat quietly as they looked into each other's eyes. Kenny placed a hand on her cheek. "You are getting prettier every time I see you, Em. The boys must be lining up to ask you out."

"Hmmmph," she groaned. "I never get asked out for a date. Maybe I need to put an ad in the paper."

Kenny laughed. "Don't worry. The guys will be pestering you soon enough."

Emmy moved her face close to him, and he kissed her. They kissed again, and then the door opened.

"Mom!" Emmy yelled.

"It's not Mom."

"Diane, what are you doing out here?" Emmy frowned. "You promised to take care of Mom."

"Sorry, guys. Mom told me to come out here and keep an eye on you two. Don't be mad at me. You know how she is."

170

Diane sat on the step next to Kenny. "I'm really sorry, Kenny. I know you want to kiss her. I'll look the other way."

"It's okay, Diane. We were just talking, for the most part."

"Diane, do you have to stay here with us?" Emmy asked.

"I can close my eyes if you want," Diane teased.

Kenny kissed Emmy on the cheek. He stood up and pulled the girls to their feet.

"I need to get home. It was good to see you again, Diane."

"You, too, Kenny. I really do like your music."

"Thanks. I appreciate that."

Kenny smiled at Diane.

"All right. I can take a hint. I'm leaving."

Kenny turned to Emmy as Diane walked up the steps onto the porch.

"Kenny Colwell, if you try to kiss me on the cheek again, I will punch you in the stomach."

Kenny put his arms around Emmy's waist and pulled her close. With Emmy standing on the step, she was almost as tall as him. She closed her eyes and wrapped her arms around his neck. He gave her a long good night kiss as she held on tight.

Diane watched for a moment. *My baby sister is falling in love or maybe in lust. Good for her.* Diane smiled as she went into the house.

"Does that kiss meet your approval?"

"For the most part," Emmy answered dreamily.

"I gotta run, Em. I'll call you tomorrow."

"Night, Kenny. I had a great time today. Thanks."

"It was my pleasure, m'lady."

Kenny headed to the alley and waved goodbye as he disappeared behind the garage.

Emmy joined Diane in the bedroom and got ready for bed. They sat on the edge of the bed.

"Why are you looking at me like that?" Emmy bit her lip.

"You have a big-time crush on Kenny."

Emmy poked Diane in the side. "No, I don't. We're just friends."

"That's bull." Diane poked her back. "Don't try to deny it. I see the way you look at him. I can tell he likes you, too."

Emmy smiled shyly at Diane.

"Tell me you and Kenny wouldn't be dating if he wasn't on the road most of the time."

"But he is gone most of the time." Emmy plopped onto her back, but then sat up again. "That's why we like to spent time with each other when we can. We don't go on *dates* when he's home. We just hang out together."

Diane said, "Sorry, but I'm not buying that. How about the way he kissed you good night? That's not the way friends kiss."

Emmy sighed as she remembered Kenny's kiss.

"See what I mean? You are wishing he was kissing you right now."

"No, I'm not." Emmy slapped Diane's hand.

"Yes, you are. You want to kiss him. Has he ever tried anything with you? Tell me the truth." Diane grabbed Emmy's shoulders.

"No! He's never done anything like that." Emmy blushed, but Diane couldn't tell in the dark.

"You're holding out on me, Em. Have you guys made love? I bet you have."

"We have not. How can you think that?"

Emmy didn't sound convincing to Diane. "You have. I can tell. Tell me all about it, Em. When did it happen?"

"Diane! Kenny and I haven't made love. You should know better than that. I'm too young to be doing that."

Diane chuckled and then asked, "So if you were older, you would make love with him, right?"

Emmy didn't answer right away, so Diane answered for her.

"You would. You know he probably has girls on the road all the time."

"He does not."

"How do you know that, Em? Do you guys talk about sex when you're together?"

"I know because he told me. And no, we don't talk about sex."

"You said he told you about being with a couple girls.

172

Which is it? Do you talk about love and sex or not?"

"Maybe once in a while, but not all the time like you and Craig."

Diane grinned. "We don't talk about sex. We have sex."

"I really don't want to hear about that. Just because you and Craig started when you were sixteen, doesn't mean that I will."

"You better not be having sex with Craig," Diane teased.

"I meant with Kenny!"

"Aha! So you admit that you want to sleep with Kenny."

"You're putting words in my mouth." Emmy smacked Diane's leg. "I didn't mean to say that."

Emmy pushed Diane, and Diane pushed back, sending Emmy on her back. "Pretend I'm Kenny, and I'm about to kiss you." Diane moved close and pretended she was going to kiss Emmy.

"Stop it, Diane."

Diane moved closer and touched Emmy's side where she knew it would tickle. Emmy laughed and tried to make Diane stop. Soon they were both laughing and giggling.

"Be quiet, Diane. Mom will be mad if we wake her up. She will come in here and yell at us."

"Don't worry, Em. I won't tell Mom or Dad that you and Kenny are lovers."

Emmy groaned and stuck her head under her pillow.

Diane yanked the pillow away from Emmy. "I don't blame you for being his lover. He is pretty hot for someone from SoHam."

"It's no use trying to talk to you. You go ahead and believe what you want. I'm going to sleep now."

Emmy crawled under the covers and quickly fell asleep. She dreamed about singing on stage in front of a huge crowd with Kenny and the band.

173

Chapter Seventeen

"What are you arguing about?" Emmy stumbled into the kitchen still half-asleep the next morning only to discover Diane and Mom screaming at each other. "Please stop fighting," she implored them.

Mom turned toward Emmy and waved a finger at her. "What time did you get home last night, Emily Olivia?" Mom asked in a stern tone even though she knew the answer. Emmy knew it meant trouble when Mom called her by her full name.

"I think it was around one," Emmy answered softly.

"And the night before?" Mom asked.

"Even later," Emmy said meekly.

Mom started in on Diane again. "You didn't leave a note or anything. We had no idea what happened to your sister. She could have been in an accident or kidnapped. We were frantic and about ready to call the police."

"You didn't care about me, just her." Diane pointed to Emmy.

"You are old enough to take of yourself, but Emmy's not. She's still a child!" Mom screamed at Diane.

"She's not a child, mother. She's sixteen effing years old," Diane screamed back.

Mom slapped Diane's face. "DON'T YOU DARE TALK TO ME LIKE THAT!"

Emmy jumped back at the sound of the slap.

"Get out of here and don't come back," Mom screamed as she pointed to the door.

Emmy stood stone-still with tears flowing down her cheeks.

"Mommy, don't fight," she uttered timidly in a childlike whisper.

Diane grabbed Emmy by the hand and pulled her into the bedroom. She slammed the door as she shook with anger.

"We're leaving right now!" Diane said. Diane pulled her small suitcase from under the bed and started packing. "Emmy, stop bawling and get some clothes ready." Diane took her anger out on her sister, and then realized her mistake. "I'm sorry, baby."

Diane held her sister in her arms until she stopped crying. She took a Kleenex and tenderly wiped her tears away. "Get dressed. Find some other clothes to wear and put them in the suitcase. Enough for several days at least. We are leaving. I'm never coming back to this place as long as I live."

Mom, who had been listening at the door, entered the room. Diane screamed at her. "Get the hell out of here right now! Will you ever learn to knock before you enter our room?"

Mom seethed. Rushing down the hall, she snatched the phone from its cradle, knocking a family picture to the floor and shattering the glass. "I swear, Diane, if you take Emily with you, I'm going to call the police!" she yelled.

Emmy threw on some clothes. Diane finished packing the suitcase and pulled Emmy out of the room.

Emmy's lip quivered. "I don't want to go. Can't I stay here?"

"No, you have to come with me. If I leave you here, Mom will take out her anger on you. I'm afraid she might hurt you, Em. Who knows what Daddy will do if he ever comes home."

They grabbed their coats from the hooks by the back door as they heard their mother scream into the phone, "I don't care if you're busy. Get your lazy ass back here right now!"

Diane and Emmy left the house in a hurry without saying anything to their mother.

"Hello! Hello!" Mom yelled. "You are gonna pay for hanging up on me." She threw the phone against the wall. *I need a drink.* She walked into the kitchen and opened the fridge without realizing the girls were gone.

"I'm afraid of what Daddy will do when he finds out how you yelled at Mom," Emmy whimpered.

"I'm afraid, too, but we gotta get out of here. Get in the car, Em."

They drove to Darby's.

"It's not open yet, Diane." Emmy knew the hours by heart. "Mr. Darby's here though." She pointed to his cargo van.

"I'm not hungry. I'm too mad to eat anything." Diane said,

not caring whether or not Emmy might be hungry. "I want to get out of there so much, Emmy. I can't stand it anymore. I have to find somewhere else to live."

"But how would you pay rent? You don't make enough money to afford a place by yourself." Emmy turned to face Diane. "Daddy would never forgive you if you move in with Craig. You know that, right?"

"I know that, and besides, Craig doesn't want me to move in yet."

"Where are we going, Diane? What are we gonna do?"

"I don't know, Emmy. Just shut up and let me think."

Emmy sat back in her seat and waited a minute. "Can we see if Grandma is home?"

"She will call Mom and tell her where we are," Diane replied.

"Where else can we go?" Tears welled up in Emmy's eyes, and one escaped to roll down her cheek.

"Okay, Em, I'll take you to Grandma's for now."

Grandma Sandusky lived by herself a few miles away in a much nicer neighborhood than Raynor Park and spent her winters in Florida. She was still in SoHam but would be heading south in the middle of the week. Diane pulled into the driveway at Grandma's. Emmy jumped out before the car even stopped, ran up to the front door and rang the bell. Grandma answered after a minute.

"Hello, Emily. How are you?"

"I'm all right, Grandma."

"No, you're not, child. I can see you trembling. Come inside and tell me what's going on."

Grandma eyed the suitcase Diane was dragging up the sidewalk.

"Hi, Grandma. Mom kicked me out of the house. Can we stay here tonight?"

"Of course you can. Tell me what happened. Have you and Patricia been arguing again?"

They went inside and sat in the living room as first Diane, and then Emmy, told Grandma about what happened.

"You two are always going to be butting heads. You are a lot like your mother at this age." Grandma sighed as she remembered the fights she used to have with her daughter. "Are you hungry? It's too early for lunch, but I could make you some sandwiches."

"Thanks, Grandma, but I'm not hungry."

"Is it all right if I make myself a sandwich?" Emmy asked.

"Of course, dear. Help yourself to whatever you like." Grandma smiled at Emmy, and then turned to Diane and frowned. *You never think about anyone but yourself. Another trait you share with your mother.*

"I need to meet some friends. Can Emmy stay here with you? I'll be back later."

"Where are you going, Diane?" Emmy asked from the kitchen.

"Just out. I'll be back later."

Emmy stood in the doorway and shook her head. "I know you're going to Craig's apartment."

Craig Garrett lived in a cramped, two-bedroom, one-bath apartment on the first floor of an old three-story building in one of the poorer neighborhoods of South Hampshire. Diane cranked the volume of the *Appetite For Destruction* CD she always kept in the car. She parked in the street behind an old Plymouth Reliant. Diane barely glanced at the peeling paint on the front door of the building. She wrinkled her nose at the smell of stale beer and urine as she walked down the hallway to Craig's apartment. She knocked on the door, and after a minute, his roommate Gerry Marker let her in. Empty pizza boxes littered the coffee table along with cans of Budweiser.

"Hi, Diane. Craig is already at work, and I gotta head out in a minute. Make yourself at home if you wanna stay."

"Why is Craig working today?"

"Someone called in sick so he's covering for him. Are you gonna stay or not?"

"No, I'll call him later." *He should have called me. Wait till I see him.* Diane left and drove back to Grandma's.

Emmy let Diane in. "Wasn't Craig home?"

177

"No, he's working. I'm hungry, but I don't want to eat here. Grandma will be sticking her nose in my business, and I don't want to put up with it."

"No, she won't. Grandma is nice..."

"She's nice to you because you are the baby. Do you wanna come with me or not?"

"All right, but we're coming back here, right?"

"Yes, I won't make you stay at Craig's, if that's what you're worried about."

"Is it really as disgusting as you claim?"

"Pigs are cleaner than those slobs." Diane would have chuckled, but she meant what she said.

"Grandma, I'm going to go with Diane, but we'll be back later, okay?"

Grandma patted Emmy's hand but didn't get up from her chair. "Okay, sweetheart. I'm not cooking dinner, so if you girls want to order something later, I will pay for it."

"Thanks, Grandma. We'll talk to you later."

Emmy and Diane drove to the nearest fast food place and discovered a bunch of Diane's friends hanging out there. Diane had friends everywhere, it appeared. Emmy ordered some food for both of them as Diane found a table near her friends. Diane introduced Emmy to her girlfriends and also a couple of guys.

Diane explained, "I had a big blow-up with my mother, and she threw me out of the house. I need a place to stay because I'm never going back there. I hate my parents! You know what they're like."

"All parents are losers. I don't blame you for wanting to leave," one of the friends said.

Another friend added, "Yeah, if I could afford a place of my own, I would be gone like yesterday."

Emmy listened to all the negative comments. *Kenny loves his parents and never talks about them like that. Of course his parents treat him with respect and love.*

They ate their food and hung out for a couple of hours—just talking. Emmy didn't say much and wondered how long Diane would stay with her friends. One of the guys sat next to

178

her after a while.

"Hi, Emmy, I'm Robbie McCartney. Diane told me about the fight with your mom. If there's anything I can do to help, let me know."

"Thanks, Robbie. I appreciate your concern," Emmy said as she stared at his flaming red hair. *But what can you do? I don't even know you.*

Eventually, all the kids left except for Emmy, Diane, and Robbie.

Robbie sat close to Diane in the booth and kissed her.

What's up with that? Emmy's eyes opened wide as she sipped on her Coke opposite Diane and Robbie. *Who is this Robbie guy, and why did he kiss you?*

"I will call you soon," Robbie said. "Try to get along with your mom, Diane. She means well, I'm sure. You may not think so right now, but I'm sure she loves you both."

"You don't know our mom at all if you think that," Diane said with bitterness and sarcasm. "Have you ever met our mother or father?"

"No, I guess not."

"Then don't tell me everything will be all hunky-dory. You don't have a clue about what I have to put up with. She doesn't give a damn about me, and she treats Emmy like a precious little child."

Robbie shifted his attention to Emmy. *She does look a lot younger than you, but she's not a child.* "I find that hard to believe."

"I don't care if you believe it or not. It's the way she is."

Robbie checked the clock on the wall. "I better get going. Call me if I can help with anything. Nice to meet you, Emmy."

Robbie slid out of the booth and left. Emmy stared at Diane across the table. She wanted to ask Diane about Robbie, but she held her tongue.

"Are you finished with that Coke?" Diane asked. "What? Don't look at me like that."

"I'm sorry I got you in trouble with Mom. I didn't mean to."

"I know you didn't. Don't worry about it, Emmy. It's not your fault. Mom and I have been fighting so much lately. Mom

179

only used last night as an excuse to kick me out of the house. I don't think she loves me at all."

"That's not true, Diane. Mom loves you, but she is so afraid to let me grow up. I think Mom is really afraid of losing us after we grow up."

Diane slapped the table. "Too bad. She's lost me for good. I already planned on moving out as soon as I found a better job. This just means I will do it sooner than I expected."

"What will I do without you there?"

"You will have the whole bed to yourself," Diane said.

"Not funny, Diane."

"I'm sorry I made you come with me, but I was afraid to leave you alone with her. You don't have to stay with me. I'll take you home tomorrow."

They had never been really close as sisters during Diane's high school years. Emmy thought that might change now. Diane did her best to convince Emmy they shared a common enemy—their mother.

"I saw Robbie kiss you. How well do you know him?" Emmy asked.

"Not that it's any of your business, little sister, but Robbie's a very special friend of mine," Diane said.

"He's really handsome."

"Yes, and a good kisser, too."

The expression on Diane's face made Emmy wonder if he was more than a friend.

The manager of the restaurant stared at Diane.

"Let's get out of here, Em. That guy is giving me the creeps."

They returned to Grandma's house.

"We're back," Emmy announced as she rang the bell.

Grandma opened the door a moment later. "I should give you a key if you're going to be coming and going this much."

"Sorry, Grandma. I won't be going anywhere else today."

"I'm ready for my nap."

"You go ahead, Grandma. Emmy and I will be quiet," Diane said.

180

Grandma went to her bedroom on the first floor, and Diane turned to Emmy, "I'm going to crash, too. Will you be all right? You can watch TV or read a book if you want. It's Sunday. Why aren't you watching football?"

"I forgot it was Sunday. I'll be all right. Are you going to stay here tonight, or are you going to Craig's after he gets off work?"

"I'm not sure yet. Don't let me sleep past six, okay?"

"Okay," Emmy answered. She didn't want to turn on the TV, because she thought it would disturb Grandma. Instead she found a book that might be interesting: *Growing Up in a Small Town* by Lee Smith McGee. Emmy snuggled under a blanket on the couch and read. She finished the book in a couple of hours, and then fell asleep on the couch.

Diane woke up before Emmy and walked out to the living room. She saw Emmy on the couch. Emmy woke up as Diane fixed the blanket.

"Go back to sleep, Em."

"Where are you going?"

"I'm going to call Craig. He's on his dinner break. I'm not going anywhere."

Emmy closed her eyes but didn't fall back asleep. Diane went into the kitchen and called Craig. "Hi, I'm at Grandma Sandusky's. Mom kicked me out of the house and told me to never come back."

"Tell me about the fight with your mom." Craig rolled his eyes. *I've heard you complain about your mother a million times. I'm sick of hearing it.*

Diane explained what happened. Emmy threw back the blanket, jumped up and walked into the kitchen. She listened to Diane's side of the conversation.

"I can't believe your mom never wants you to come back. I'm sure she didn't mean it," Craig said.

"You don't know Mom like I do. She hates me and always has."

"That's not true and you know it, Diane," Emmy said. "You are just trying to make sure Craig feels sorry for you."

181

Diane looked at Emmy and knew she was telling the truth. "Do you mind if I talk to Craig? Go back to the living room, okay?"

"Who are you talking to, Diane?" Craig asked.

"Emmy heard what I told you."

"She's right, you know."

"Come on! Are you on my side or not? I want some sympathy from you. She's my sister, and I should love her, but sometimes I get so freakin' mad. Mom treats her like a infant, and I guess, in many ways, she still is a child. She lets Mom get away with it. I wish she would stand up to her more than she does. I never let Mom push me around like Emmy does."

"I gotta go, Diane. Call me tomorrow after five, and we can have dinner somewhere."

Grandma woke up from her nap shortly before five. She saw the girls in the living room. "Are you two hungry now?"

"Can we order a pizza, Grandma?"

"Sure, honey, you can order whatever you want."

Diane placed the order, and Grandma gave her enough money to cover the pizza and the tip. The pizza arrived, and Emmy and Diane finished most of it.

"There's some left, Grandma. Do you want it?" Emmy opened the pizza box.

"Not right now, dear. You can put it in the fridge. I'm going to watch my shows. If you want to watch something different you can use the TV in the basement."

Grandma never missed *60 Minutes,* or her other Sunday night shows. Emmy sat on the couch and watched with Grandma, but Diane went upstairs to the bedroom where she would be sleeping. She unpacked her suitcase, setting aside the clothes she would wear to work the next day. Yawning, she climbed into bed and fell asleep before eight o'clock. Emmy and Grandma watched TV until nine.

"I'm going to bed, Emily. You know where everything is, right?"

"Yes, Grandma. I'll be fine. You can go to bed."

Grandma went to her room for the night. Emmy locked the

182

doors and turned off the lights before she went upstairs. She used the other bedroom after she checked on Diane, who was already sound asleep. Emmy loved sleeping at Grandma's house because she slept in a bed by herself. She found another book to read, stretched out in the comfortable bed, pulled up the thick comforter and fluffed the pillows. She stayed up until midnight to finish the book. She turned off the light and didn't wake up until eight o'clock.

"Oh, no!" Emmy panicked realizing she was going to be late for school. She ran to the room where Diane had been sleeping, but she wasn't there. Emmy ran downstairs and saw Grandma in the kitchen.

"Good morning, Grandma. Where's Diane?"

"She left for work around seven. Do you want some breakfast, honey? I can make pancakes if you want. I know you like them."

"Thanks, Grandma, but I don't have time. I'm going to be late for school."

Emmy ran back upstairs and got ready in five minutes. Running downstairs and out the door, Emmy hollered to Grandma as she passed by, "Thanks for letting me stay. I'll see you after school."

Emmy saw a group of Roosevelt High students waiting for a bus. She dashed to the corner and made it there just as it arrived. When she got to school, Barry and Kristen were waiting by her locker.

"Where have you been? Your mom called my house a dozen times looking for you. You look like crap, by the way," Barry said.

"Thanks for noticing, Barry," Emmy replied sarcastically.

"She called my cell phone. How would she have that number?" Kristen asked.

"She probably got your number from my address book. I left it in my room. I'm sorry she bothered you."

"She didn't bother me, but I was worried about you."

"Me, too," Barry chimed in.

"I gotta run. I'll talk to you guys after school in the quad." Emmy left Barry and Kristen behind as she ran to her class.

Kristen turned to Barry. "What's going on with her?"

"Probably nothing," he said. *Probably just another family squabble.*

After school, Emmy met up with her friends again. They found an empty table in the quad where they could talk.

"What happened?" Barry asked.

"Oh, Barry, I got so scared. Mom and Diane were arguing and screaming at each other." Emmy explained everything to Barry, Kristen and Derrick.

"Our parents never scream at us," Kristen said.

Derrick nudged her in the side. "That might not be the right thing to say. We don't know anything about her home life."

Barry drove her back to Grandma's house. The door was unlocked, so Emmy and Barry walked right in.

"I'm home, Grandma. Where are you?"

"In the kitchen, Emily."

Emmy pulled Barry into the kitchen. "This is my friend, Barry Newton. He's going to give me a ride home."

"It's nice to meet you, Barry. Emily, I can't remember if I told you that I'm leaving Wednesday for Florida. Diane stopped by to get her clothes. She told me to tell you that she's going to stay with Craig. That's sure to please Patricia and your father to no end," Grandma said sarcastically while splitting a bagel in half.

"Thanks for letting me stay last night. You have a safe flight to Florida and enjoy the warm weather." Emmy hugged Grandma, and then dashed upstairs. She got her clothes, and Barry took her home.

Emmy and Barry walked in the back door, not knowing what to expect. She saw her mom sitting at the kitchen table peeling potatoes. Mom looked up and saw them.

"Emmy, where have you been? Your father and I have been so worried about you. I would have gone out of my mind if Kenny hadn't found out where you went and called us. Don't you ever do that again."

"I'm sorry, Mom. Thanks for the ride, Barry. I'll talk to you later." Emmy pushed him toward the door.

Barry shrugged his shoulders and headed home.

Emmy showered and asked her mom, "Is it okay if I go over to see Kenny for a while before dinner?"

"Go ahead, honey, but don't go anywhere else and be home by six for dinner. Your father will be home early and wants to talk to you."

Emmy flew out the back door and sprinted down the alley to Kenny's garage. She could hear him practicing his guitar and ran up the stairs two at a time.

He saw her and stopped playing. "You gave your Mom and Dad quite a scare, little one." Kenny called her by a nickname he used when they were much younger.

"How did you know where I went?" Emmy asked as she picked up a drumstick.

"I have ways of finding out things," Kenny said. "Now come over here and sit on the couch and listen to some old tunes with me."

She hit a cymbal, and then dropped the drumstick. "Really, how did you know?" She plopped down on the couch next to him.

"I called your grandmother. She told me you and Diane were staying there, but had gone out to eat."

"Diane is going to stay with Craig. Daddy will explode when he hears," Emmy said.

"How did your mother react when you got home?"

Emmy explained as she snuggled against him.

"So she didn't ask about Diane, huh?"

"Never said her name."

Emmy stayed until six, and then hurried home for dinner.

"Emily," Dad said sternly, "we need to talk. I'm concerned about the late hours you've been keeping. I know you were with friends, but that doesn't change the fact that you stayed out after your curfew. For the rest of the week, you are grounded."

"Daddy!"

"Let me finish. You are grounded to your room after nine o'clock at night. You can see your friends before that, but have to be home and in your room by nine. Understand?"

185

"Yes, sir. I understand." Emmy was not happy, but figured it could have been worse.

After school for the rest of the week, Emmy hurried home and hung out with Kenny at the carriage house. Some days her friends joined them. He gave them a history lesson about some music he liked. He sang songs by The Beatles, Herman's Hermits and other British groups of the early sixties.

"How do you know all this music?" Emmy asked.

"From radio, CDs, old TV clips—those sort of things."

"It's pretty good music, but not as good as your songs," Emmy said.

Emmy and Kenny hugged in the carriage house before he had to leave on Friday. Emmy kissed Kenny on the cheek.

"Is that the only kiss I get?" Kenny complained.

"If I give you a better kiss, will you promise to miss me?"

"Absolutely!"

Emmy wrapped her arms around his neck and pulled him close. She pressed against him and kissed him hungrily."

"How was that?"

"Amazing, Em."

"Just remember there's more where that came from, but you better behave and leave those groupies alone if you want me."

Kenny laughed and promised. "I'll try, Emmy, I'll try."

She looked up at him, and he hugged her again.

"Can I go with you?" Emmy asked.

"I really wish you could. It would be such a blast."

"Maybe you'll take me with you someday after I finish school." She lay her head on his chest. "Maybe I could go with you in the summer. That would be better than working at Darby's even if you don't pay me."

"You know your parents won't let you travel with me."

"I don't care. I'll sneak away."

"We can't do that, Em. You have to obey your parents."

"Maybe for now, but when I turn eighteen, I'm moving out."

"We'll worry about that when you get older. I've gotta go.

186

I'll call you."

Mom didn't mention Diane's name for a whole week. After several days of Emmy pleading Diane's case, Mom changed her mind and allowed Diane to move back home.

Emmy called Diane with the news. "Mom's willing to let you move back home. She told me that she never told Dad how you yelled at her, but if it happens again, she will. Please come home. I miss you."

"All right. I'll be back later tonight. It's kinda crowded here with three people trying to use one bathroom. But if Mom starts up on me again, I'm outta there." Diane didn't mention the nightly shouting matches with Craig.

Diane moved back home and shared the small bedroom with Emmy again.

"I'm glad you're back," Emmy said.

"It took me a whole day to clean up the apartment, and I never did get the smell out," Diane said as she unpacked. "My clothes are probably ruined."

Emmy sat on the bed with a pillow clutched to her chest and watched. "Those guys are slobs from the sound of it."

"Yeah, I suppose, but Craig is very romantic when he wants to be."

"Diane, I really don't want to hear about that right now, but I hope you were careful. I'm not ready to be an aunt yet."

"Don't worry, Em, I'm on the pill."

"That still doesn't make it right, you know," Emmy said.

"You'll understand someday, Emmy."

Chapter Eighteen

"I'm hungry, Emmy. Do you mind if we stop and grab a bite?" Kristen asked.

"I don't mind. I'm kinda hungry, too," Emmy answered.

In mid-October, Emmy and Kristen had stopped at the mall to shop for school clothes and look for part-time work for Emmy. She still worked a few hours per week at Darby's, but needed something more. They left the mall and drove past The Mole's Den, a local music store. Emmy glanced back at the store.

"Can we make a quick stop before we eat? I want to see if Kenny's CD is out yet. He said it was supposed to be released today."

"Sure, but I thought he was going to let you have a copy."

"He is, but I can't wait. I want to hear it today," Emmy answered excitedly.

They stopped, ran inside and immediately saw a large display of the debut disc of Fridays At Five. Emmy screamed like young girls used to scream for The Beatles.

"I'm going to buy two of them, Kristen. I will play one of them and save the other one. I won't ever open it."

Emmy grabbed two CDs, and Kristen bought three. They hurried out to Kristen's car, and Emmy ripped the annoying thin plastic wrap off and opened the CD.

"Why do they use this stuff? It's a pain in the butt." She popped it into the CD player, and they listened to the opening track. "Can you believe it? Kenny is going to be a rock star now."

"He already is," Kristen reminded her.

"I hope he remembers us."

I don't think you need to worry about that, Emmy."

When Emmy got home, she placed the unopened CD in the bottom of her music box. She sang along as she played the opened CD non-stop. Emmy soon knew all the lyrics by heart.

The next day at school, when Emmy pulled out her English book, an envelope fell out of her locker. She picked it up. *Shoot, I forgot all about this.* She opened it and read the short note from

Derrick Keasling.

"Emmy, would you like to go out sometime? Just the two of us."

The simple question surprised her. *Why would you want to go out with me? We're friends. With your looks and personality you could date any girl in school.* After history class that day, she saw Derrick and followed him outside as he walked with a couple of girls. They left, and Emmy caught up with him.

"Hi, Derrick."

"Hey, Emmy, how are things?"

They walked to the parking lot, and Derrick leaned against his car as Emmy faced him.

"I read your note today. I'm sorry, but I forgot about it, and it ended up buried in my locker. I didn't realize you wrote it."

"I wondered what happened to it. I thought maybe you never read it, or you did read it and didn't want to go out with me."

"I'm sorry I didn't read it sooner, Derrick. Are you still interested in going out?"

"I think it would be fun. Would you like to go out for dinner sometime?"

"Okay. Where do you want to go and when?" Emmy answered after recovering from the surprise of Derrick asking her for a date.

"How about dinner at La Cantina Friday night before the game? We can have dinner by ourselves, and then join everybody at the game."

"Sure, I can do that."

"Do you need a ride home?"

"I could use one if it's not too much trouble." Emmy grinned as she thought she would be alone with Derrick.

"I have to wait for Kristen. She's on her way."

Friday night arrived, and Emmy decided to wear jeans and a sweatshirt over her shirt until Diane got on her case.

"Emmy, you're not going out to play football with this guy. Wear something nicer." Diane pulled a sweater out of the dresser. "Try this. It's small on me now, so it might fit you."

189

"Are you sure? You never let me borrow any of your nice clothes."

"Yes, you can have the sweater if it fits."

Emmy tried on the sweater, and it fit. She used a purple ribbon to tie her dark, curly hair in a ponytail.

Diane checked her ponytail for her. "Oh, Emmy, you look so cute."

"Thanks, Diane."

"You also look about twelve years old."

Emmy smacked Diane's arm and then looked at herself in the mirror. She bit her lip as she realized that she did look very young.

"Diane, will you help me with some makeup? Maybe that will help me look my age."

"I will sometime. But really, Em, you don't need to wear any. You look so pretty without it. You have perfect skin."

Derrick arrived, and Emmy brought him inside to meet her parents. Her dad reminded her of her curfew, and her mom treated her like an infant about to leave the house for the first time.

"Do you have your coat, Emmy? You can always call us if you want to come home early."

"Mom! Please don't do this in front of Derrick." Emmy sighed as her mother went through her usual instructions. She didn't look at Derrick as they walked out to the car. She felt so embarrassed.

During dinner, Derrick shared some family background. "Kristen and I were both born at St. Bart's, and we lived in SoHam until I was in second grade. We moved to West Bartlett, and then back to this area when I was in junior high. I went to public school, but Kristen attended a private academy until this year."

"Why?" Emmy wondered.

"Grandma Dorothea wanted Kristen to attend The Barclay Academy. It's a school for girls only and costs a small fortune. Kristen finally convinced Grandma to let her go to public school after she pleaded and begged and finally cried so much that Grandma caved."

After dinner, Derrick drove to the stadium, where over five

190

thousand spectators would watch Roosevelt battle the St. Raymond's Crusaders, the local Catholic powerhouse. They met Barry and Linda and grabbed a couple of seats. Kristen arrived a few minutes later with her date.

"Hi, guys, this is Gabe McBride. He goes to North Park."

Gabe waved to everyone, and then sat next to Kristen. Emmy traded places with Derrick so she could sit by Kristen.

"Where did you guys meet?" Emmy asked.

"At the mall. Gabe works part-time at the Shoe Locker, and I just happened to bump into him. We talked for a few minutes, and he asked me out. So here we are."

Emmy glanced at Gabe and whispered, "He looks like the guy in that movie *Clerks.*"

"Which guy?"

"I don't know his name, but he wore glasses and never talked."

"I know who you mean, but I can't remember his name, either," Kristen said as she smiled at Gabe.

The Roosevelt Rough Riders lost in the last minute of a close game. Derrick took Emmy home and walked her to the front steps. She stood on the first step and faced him.

"Would you like to go out again?" Derrick asked as the front porch light came on.

She eagerly asked, "How do you mean? Just the two of us, or with all our friends?"

"I would like to spent some more time with you. We can hang out with friends, too, but I want to get to know you better."

Emmy thought that Derrick and Kristen didn't act like rich snobs, but like normal kids.

Derrick continued, "There is a dance at the country club next Friday. Do you like to dance? I guess I should have asked that first."

"I don't get much of a chance, but I'd love to go dancing." Emmy waited to see if Derrick wanted to kiss her good night, but he didn't.

On Friday evening, Derrick picked her up at seven. Emmy

191

wore a dress with a high neckline, like all the tops she favored, but it was not as short as the dress she wore to the high school dance.

"I need to clue you in about this dance, Emmy," Derrick said as he pulled away from the curb in front of her house.

"Why? Isn't it just a dance?"

"Sort of. Have you ever been to the Barclay Country Club?"

"Oh, sure. I go golfing there all the time," Emmy answered facetiously.

"The dance is a fundraiser for MS, and there will be a lot of older people there. Kristen and Gabe are riding with my parents."

"That's all right. There will be music, right?" Emmy asked.

"Of course," Derrick said. "I just didn't want you to be disappointed. The club members pay a ton of money to charity, and they write it off on their taxes."

Emmy smiled while watching the older couples as she and Derrick danced. "I've never seen so many tuxedos in my life." She glanced up at Derrick as another gray-haired couple waltzed past.

"The older crowd dresses more formally. An old habit, I suppose," Derrick said.

"Oh, Derrick, this is how I hoped it would be at the school dance where we met," Emmy mentioned later as they sipped on soft drinks. "I had such high hopes for that night, but it turned out to be a horrible night."

"Horrible, huh? If I recall correctly, that's the night you met Kristen and me."

"I'm sorry. I didn't mean it like that. Meeting you and Kristen was the only good thing that happened that night."

So far Derrick hadn't tried to kiss her. When they weren't dancing, Emmy sat next to Kristen and met Mr. and Mrs. Keasling. Later, as Emmy and Derrick danced to a slow song, Derrick looked into her blue eyes and touched her dark, curly hair. "Do you realize how pretty you are?"

She blushed and replied, "I don't think I'm all that pretty. Certainly not as pretty as Kristen, and I'm too small and look too young for my age."

"You look perfect for someone your size."

192

"Thank you, I guess." Emmy laughed at his attempt at a compliment and smiled at him. "Does Kristen really like Gabe?"

"I don't think Kristen is all that in to Gabe, but he likes her. She told me she wanted to see what it would be like to date a college guy. I don't think Mom is too thrilled about Gabe because of his age, but she can't say too much."

"Because of the difference in age between her and your father, right?"

"Yeah, Grandpa still talks about that sometimes."

They started talking about school, and Emmy wondered out loud, "Why didn't we know each other before this year?"

"I remember seeing you and Diane at a Christmas concert when I was in seventh grade. I didn't know your name, but I remember seeing you. It was shortly after we moved back to this area. You looked much younger than Diane, and it surprised me when I saw you in junior high the next year. I saw you a few times that year."

"I don't remember seeing you in junior high. How come?"

"I suppose because the seventh and eighth graders were in opposite sides of the building, and our paths didn't cross. I think I would have remembered a girl as pretty as you."

"Oh, stop it. We've been at Roosevelt for over two years. Why didn't we see each other before this year?"

"I've seen you before this year, but I thought you were shy and not interested in boys at all. Besides, you looked so young, I thought maybe you were one of those child geniuses that, you know, finishes college before they are fifteen or something."

"Oh, yes, that's me. I'm actually twelve and a genius at math. Did I ever tell you how I bumped into you at that dance earlier this year?"

"I remember a girl running into me, but I didn't see her face, only the back of her dress."

"Yep, I confess. I was trying to get away from Todd Delaney. I felt so embarrassed and wanted to hide, so I ran into the bathroom and right into Kristen."

"Kristen and I did see you a couple times about a year and a half ago."

193

"You did? Where? Did I see you?"

"You were kinda busy."

Emmy tilted her head. "I don't understand."

"You were on stage with this local band," Derrick said.

Emmy covered her mouth with her hand. "Are you kidding? Did you guys really come to some of the early gigs? Kristen said something about that once."

"I think they might have been the first gigs the band played. I recognized you at that dance where we met, but Kristen didn't. I had to clue her in."

"I was just a kid back then." Emmy looked at the time. "I need to get home before my curfew, or else I will be grounded."

Derrick immediately took her home and again walked her to the door.

"Thanks for tonight, Derrick. I'll see you in school Monday. Please ask Kristen to call me sometime."

Derrick kissed her quickly on the cheek. "I'll tell her. Night, Emmy."

Someone called on Sunday morning shortly after ten o'clock. Emmy quickly grabbed the phone in the kitchen because she didn't want the ringing to wake anyone else.

"Hello," she whispered.

"Hi, Emmy, it's Kristen. I'm sorry for calling so early on a Sunday."

"Hi, Kristen. What's up?"

"Derrick and I are going into the city to check out the new exhibit at the Sherman Aquarium. Wanna go with? We'll grab something to eat. Do some shopping. Might see a movie."

"Sure. Wait. Let me ask my mom and make sure it's all right. Can I call you right back?"

"Of course. Oh, we're taking the train into the city, if that matters."

Emmy hung up and timidly knocked on her parents' bedroom door.

"What is it?" Mom answered groggily. "You know I planned to sleep late today."

194

Emmy opened the door partway. "Mom, can I go into the city with Derrick and Kristen to see the Sherman Aquarium?"

Mom asked the usual questions and reluctantly gave her approval. Emmy called Kristen back. "I can go if somebody can pick me up."

"Good, we'll pick you up at eleven thirty, okay?"

They spent the afternoon visiting the Sherman Aquarium and the Macy Museum. They braved the brisk weather and strolled along the lakefront, and occasionally Derrick held Emmy's hand.

"I'm thirsty, Derrick. Would you be a saint and find something for Emmy and me to drink?" Kristen used her best smile to get Derrick to do as she wished. When he disappeared out of sight, Kristen smiled at Emmy and spilled a secret. "Don't say anything to Derrick, but he told me that he wishes he had known you better before. He is really sorry that he wasted time going out with Clarissa Morgan and wishes he hadn't asked her to the prom already. Don't tell Derrick I told you, okay?"

Emmy nodded her head and wondered how long Derrick dated Clarissa Morgan. *She is so stuck-up and possessive.*

Later, Derrick allowed Kristen and Emmy to do some window shopping along Michigan Avenue. "Please don't buy anything, Kristen. It's all so expensive, and I'll have to carry it anyway."

"We're only looking. We won't buy anything, unless I see a bargain I simply can't pass up."

Emmy was not about to spend any money. The twenty dollars in her pocket wouldn't go very far. She felt embarrassed that Derrick paid for everything.

The girls complained they were starving and needed something to eat.

"Where do you want to go, Kristen?" Derrick asked.

"Cicero's East isn't too far away." Kristen pointed. "They have absolutely the best stuffed pizza in the city. Have you ever eaten there, Emmy?"

"I've never really eaten anywhere in the city. I've been down here a couple times on field trips from school, but that's it."

They ate one of Cicero's East's famous stuffed pizzas and

then caught the train back to SoHam at eight o'clock. Derrick and Kristen brought Emmy home, and she brought them in the house, even though her parents were home.

"Let's sit at the dining room table to talk. Do you guys want anything to drink or something to munch on?" Emmy asked.

"We're fine, Emmy. We don't need anything." Kristen noticed the old buffet against the wall and wondered if it was a valuable antique.

Emmy felt relieved because she didn't know what she would have served—other than beer or wine. Her father always made sure he had stockpiles of that in the house. Diane came home and saw Kristen and Derrick.

Derrick smiled at Diane. "You probably don't remember me, but I saw you in junior high a few times. I even held the door open for you a couple of times."

"I'm sorry. I don't remember seeing you in junior high, but that was nice of you to hold the door open for me." *I saw you around Roosevelt over the years, but didn't pay any attention.*

"You were only interested in older boys back then," he said.

"Maybe I should have paid more attention to the younger kids." Diane smiled as she flirted.

"She still is," Emmy said and then clenched her teeth. "She has a boyfriend already."

After Derrick and Kristen left, Diane told Emmy, "Derrick is really handsome, and you guys look good as a couple."

"I'm not sure Derrick thinks of us as a couple, you know. I'm not sure if I even think of us that way."

"Do you like him more than Kenny? Has Derrick kissed you like Kenny?"

"I've known Kenny for a lot longer, and if you must know, Derrick hasn't kissed me except a little kiss on my cheek."

"Too bad. I wonder if he's a good kisser."

"Stay away from him, Diane," Emmy warned.

"Oooh, do I detect some jealousy or possessiveness?"

"No, but he's a good friend, and I know you aren't interested in being friends with any guy."

196

The following Friday night, Emmy and Derrick planned to stay at her house. Derrick brought over a pizza and his Scrabble game. They sat at the dining room table, devoured the pizza and played his game. Emmy worried that Mom would embarrass her by treating her like a child in front of Derrick, but she didn't. Mom did keep an eye on them from her recliner.

"Diane, your father and I are going to bed," Mom said after watching the news. "I would like for you to stay here with your sister until that boy leaves."

"Why, Mom? Derrick is not going to try anything with Emmy. They're just friends."

"Please, do as I ask."

"Fine, but I don't see why you are so concerned. He's not Kenny."

"What is that supposed to mean?" Mom watched Emmy and Derrick move to the couch.

"Nothing." Diane turned away.

"Do I need to have your father talk to Kenny's parents?"

"No, Mom, I didn't mean anything. Emmy and Kenny are just friends." Diane rolled her eyes. "Go to bed. I'll stay and chaperone your precious baby. It's not like I have plans of my own on a Friday night."

Mom chose to ignore Diane's sarcasm.

Diane sat on the couch with Derrick and Emmy, and Emmy looked at her sister with pleading eyes, because she wanted to be alone with Derrick. Diane stayed with them until she figured their parents were asleep.

"I'm gonna go out to see Craig. Will you be all right by yourself, Emmy?"

"I'm not by myself, and yes, I will be fine. Now go, okay?"

Emmy found herself alone with Derrick at last. "What do you want to do now?" Emmy asked.

Derrick smiled wickedly at her. She looked at him with an enchanting smile and informed him, "I am an innocent young maiden, and I don't have any idea why you are smiling so mischievously."

Derrick gazed at her as she held her finger to her mouth and gave him her best innocent little girl look.

"I don't know why you think I'm being mischievous. I thought we could do homework or tell ghost stories or something like that. You are the one thinking about other things."

"Okay, do you know a good ghost story to tell me?"

"Not really. I merely used that as an example," he said.

Emmy laughed as Derrick amused her with stories about Kristen. "There was one time when she slipped on the bank of the lake behind our house and fell in. She got really mad because I laughed at her. She chased me around and slipped and fell in the lake again."

Emmy glanced around the room. *I wish this house was bigger. There's no where I can take Derrick that my parents can't hear us talking.*

As much as she didn't want this night to end, Emmy looked at the clock on the wall above the TV and knew Derrick should leave. She didn't want to get in trouble. "It's almost midnight. You need to go home. If my mother wakes up and finds you still here, she will ground me. I don't want you to go, but I hope you understand."

"I'll call you when I get home, and we can talk on the phone." Derrick kissed her on the cheek and drove home.

Emmy got ready for bed and waited for him to call. Two months earlier Diane added a second phone line after fighting with her mother over her constant use of the family phone. Diane paid for it by herself and allowed Emmy to use it also. Derrick called Emmy twenty minutes later, and they talked on the phone for over an hour. When Diane got home, she found Emmy asleep in bed with the phone in her hand and a dreamy look on her face. Diane hung up the phone and brushed Emmy's hair out of her face. Emmy woke up and looked at her. She smiled, and Diane got ready for bed.

"Diane, what do you think about Derrick?"

"He's very charming, and he's certainly good-looking. Why?"

"I really like him as a friend, but I'm not sure how much he likes me. I like it that he doesn't try to kiss me all the time. Plus,

I'm not sure I want to be with him yet, but still, he is really nice."

"So, take advantage of him while he wants to take you out. Spend his money. You don't have to sleep with him," Diane said. *I just might take care of that.*

Emmy smacked Diane with her pillow. "You stay away from him," she warned. "I'm going to sleep." She turned her back to Diane and went back to sleep.

"Derrick, I need to talk to you," Emmy said at school on Monday.

"Good. I wanted to talk to you, too, Emmy. What do you need to talk to me about?"

"Can we talk in the quad?"

"Sure, Emmy. Are you all right? You have such a serious look on your face."

They sat at a table away from other kids, and Emmy stared at Derrick. She didn't know how to tactfully tell him what she needed, so she plowed straight ahead.

"Derrick, I have had so much fun going out with you. I really like you a lot."

"Uh-oh. That doesn't sound good."

Emmy looked down at her hands, which were in her lap. "Derrick, would you be upset if I told you that I think you should see other girls?" She lifted her head.

"Wow! This is amazing. You're a lot of fun to be with, Emmy, but I needed to tell you that I asked Clarissa out for dinner this weekend. I wanted to make sure I told you before you heard it from someone else. I hope you understand."

"I understand, and I'm not upset. In some ways, don't be mad, but you seem like a brother or cousin or something to me. It's probably because Kristen and I are such good friends, and we started out as simply friends. You are so handsome, and I love hanging out with you, but I'm not ready for a serious relationship." *Unless it's with Kenny.*

"I kinda feel the same way, Emmy. I think of you as Kristen's friend, and it's fun to do stuff together, but I want to date other girls, too. I wanted to tell you how I felt before things got too

199

serious between us. I would hate to lose you as a friend, and that would probably happen if we kept seeing each other. We would probably get romantic, and then eventually break up."

"We can be friends, and still see each other and maybe even grab dinner or something sometimes."

Derrick had no trouble getting dates since he looked so handsome—having money didn't hurt, either. Derrick Keasling and Clarissa Morgan became one of the most talked-about couples in school. Clarissa made sure of that. Even though Derrick did date other girls, Clarissa tried to make sure all her friends knew about her serious relationship with Derrick. Emmy didn't date anyone because none of the guys at school interested her. She would date Kenny Colwell when he came back from tour, if he asked.

Chapter Nineteen

Kenny arrived home on Friday, December twentieth, in the evening and called Emmy five minutes later. "What are you doing tonight, Em? Do you want to come over?"

"I'll be there before you can get to the front door," Emmy answered. "Mom, I'll be over at Kenny's if you're looking for me. I might be out late, so don't wait up." She ran out the door before Mom could object.

"Emmy, you need to wear a coat. It's winter." Mom took a deep breath, and then exhaled slowly. "You'll do anything for that boy. I just hope you're careful."

"Who are you talking to?" Dad asked as he slumped into his recliner.

"Your baby girl."

Emmy skipped through the falling snow, bounded up the wide wooden front steps at the Colwell home and slid across the slick porch. Kenny opened the door before she could ring the bell.

"Yes, may I help you with something, young lady?" Kenny teased as he noticed snowflakes on her face. He let her into the large entryway and wrapped his arms around her. He lifted her off her feet as he twirled around on the polished hardwood floor. "It's so good to see you, Emmy." He set her down, and they walked through the entrance to the large living room.

I love all this fancy wood and these old plaster walls. Emmy rubbed her hand on the woodwork. "It's about time you got home. Not that I miss you or anything." Emmy smiled at his parents, who sat in their chairs enjoying the fire in the brick fireplace. "Merry Christmas, Mr. and Mrs. Colwell. It's almost like Christmas because Kenny came home today."

"Merry Christmas, Emmy. We're content that he said hello before he called you," Mrs. Colwell said.

"What's in your hand?" Kenny asked as he tried to grab it from her. "And where's your coat?"

She put her right hand, with the present, behind her back and used her left hand to push his away. "It's your Christmas present. I suppose you can open it now if you want. You don't have

201

to wait until Christmas. I didn't think to grab a coat. I just wanted to get here as fast as I could."

"Come in and sit down. I'll open it after you open your gift. Unless you want to wait for..."

"No, I can't wait that long."

She sat on the edge of the couch and could feel the warmth from the fireplace to her left. Kenny retrieved her gift from under tree set in the front corner of the large living room. "You can go first, Emmy."

I love how you guys always have a real tree. I love the blinking lights and all those decorations. Emmy looked at the gift. "This is so much bigger than what I got you."

"How do you know it's not a gift card, and I put it in a big box to fool you?"

Emmy grinned. "If it's a gift card, it's the heaviest one in the world."

"Maybe I put a brick in there to make it heavier. Are you gonna just sit there, or are you gonna open it?"

She started tearing off the pretty paper very carefully.

"It's only paper. You don't have to save it for next year," Kenny teased.

She made a face at him, and Mr. Colwell laughed.

Finally, Emmy got all the paper off. She looked at the picture on the box. "Is this really what's inside?"

Kenny shrugged his shoulders.

She opened the box and discovered a new Bose radio and CD player.

"Kenny, these things are expensive. You shouldn't have spent all that money on me."

"Who said I spent anything. Maybe I stole it."

"I know you would never do that. Thank you so much."

"You're welcome, Emmy. I saw that old thing you use to listen to music, and I thought you needed a better player. Especially when you listen to this." He handed her an autographed copy of the new self-titled Fridays At Five CD. "There is a little note inside, Em."

She opened the CD and read the note from Kenny. Her eyes

got misty, and she hugged him. She didn't say anything for a moment as she hung onto him.

"I hope you like my present. It's not as big as yours."

Kenny could tell by the size and shape that Emmy had most likely bought a couple of CDs for him. He opened the gift, and his jaw dropped. Inside were two CDs he had been searching for without success. He held up *Speckled Bird* by The Lyricon in one hand and in the other he held *All Fall Down* by The 88s.

"Where did you find these? Do you know how long I've been looking for this 88s disc? And I love The Lyricon."

"I'm not telling you where I found them. If you want any more CDs by these guys, you will have to go through me."

"Thank you. Your gift means a lot to me." He leaned over and kissed her on the cheek. "Can we play them now?"

"Sure, I want to hear them."

They headed out to the carriage house and cranked up Kenny's stereo to listen.

"It's cold out here, Kenny. Can you turn up the heat?" She breathed into her hands to warm them.

Kenny adjusted the thermostat. "It won't take long to warm up. Come and sit on the couch next to me, and I'll warm you up for now."

Kenny said it innocently, but Emmy grinned and grabbed a blanket.

"Emmy, what are you doing?"

"Nothing. I thought we might need this."

She pushed Kenny onto his back and lay on her side next to him. She pulled the blanket over their heads. "Now tell me everything about the tour. I want all the details."

"Well, we sold 8,348 tickets for the first show in..."

"Not those kind of details. Tell me about the girls."

"I'm sorry to disappoint you, but I don't have any stories about *groupies*. Maybe I should have slept with a few of them so I would have juicy stories to tell you." He moved the blanket off of their heads.

"It's a good thing you didn't, or I would take back the CDs I gave you."

They stayed under the blanket on the old couch and cuddled as Emmy caught Kenny up on her life. "I bought books for Kristen and Derrick for Christmas. I had to give them to them already because I won't see them until school starts." She bit her lip. "Don't be mad, but Derrick and I went out a few times. He's a lot of fun to be with, and we had some good times together, but it felt a little weird."

"In what way?" Kenny asked.

"He's almost like a brother at times. I would think about Kristen and how close she and Derrick are. It's hard to explain."

"Did you kiss him and make out and get all mushy?" Kenny teased.

"No! He kissed me on the cheek like you do sometimes, but we didn't make out. Would you be jealous if I made out with Derrick?"

"Most certainly. I want you all to myself, Emmy Colasanti."

He kissed her, and then touched her side where he knew it would tickle.

Emmy started giggling. "Stop it!" She tried to get away and accidentally bumped her head against his chin.

"Ow!" Kenny yelled.

"Oh, I'm sorry, Kenny. Did I hurt you?"

Kenny stopped tickling her and smiled. He looked into her eyes and kissed her again. They held each other close, until Kenny suddenly got up.

Emmy sat up. "I know. I'm still too young."

"You are, but that's not why I stopped."

"Then why did you stop?" Emmy asked.

"I stopped because I didn't want to stop. Does that make any sense to you?"

"I think so."

"Let's just listen to the music."

They listened to the new CDs and then a few older ones from Kenny's collection as well. They danced as they listened to a variety of classic rock tunes.

"I should get home, Kenny. It's getting late."

He grabbed one of his coats. "Wear this. I don't want you to freeze."

He carried her Bose system, still in the box, as he walked her home around midnight. She stood on the first step, and he set the heavy box on the porch. He held her close as light fluffy snowflakes fell around them.

"Let me know if you need any help setting that up."

"I will, but I can probably follow the instructions. I do know how to read." She rolled her eyes and then giggled.

"You're a stinker! Maybe I should keep it for myself." He reached for the box.

"Don't you dare. It's mine now. You gave it to me."

"Will you share it with Diane?"

"No, it's mine."

"You sound like a spoiled little brat."

She removed the coat and handed it to him. "I'm teasing. Thank you so much."

"You're welcome, my sweet girl. Merry Christmas."

"Merry Christmas to you, Kenny. I can go to church with you Sunday if you want. Mom already agreed."

"I would like that very much, Em. Will you stay for dinner, too?"

"Sure, if you want me to."

Emmy spent the entire next day with Kenny. She helped him finish his Christmas shopping. He took her out for dinner, and, on Sunday, Emmy went to a special service where the children of the church sang Christmas songs and recited Bible verses.

Kenny and Emmy also spent time in his carriage house apartment. He played his guitar, and she sang and played his electric keyboard. They actually wrote some songs together. Kenny came up with the melodies, and Emmy wrote most of the lyrics. On Christmas Eve, she went with him to a special youth service at his church. Kenny took his guitar, and he and Emmy entertained the teens. They sang Christmas carols, and the kids sang along.

Ronnie Rojas approached Emmy and Kenny after they finished singing. "You guys sound awesome together. Your voices blend so well."

"Thanks, Ronnie. Emmy is amazing. She can pick up a song so quickly. We've been writing some tunes together."

"Would you do one of them for us?" Ronnie asked.

"I will if Emmy agrees. How about it, Em?"

Emmy shook her head and bit her lip, but Kenny convinced her. They chose a song with lyrics about the pressures teen girls faced in high school. The kids liked the song so much that they wanted to hear another one. Kenny mentioned a song to Emmy, and she agreed, even though the lyrics were rather personal.

"Why don't you tell everyone what this one's about, Em?" Kenny put her on the spot.

"Okay." Emmy gathered her thoughts. "My family is Catholic, but we don't go to mass very often. I came with Kenny to this church a couple times before Mom made me stop. She insisted I go to St. John's if I wanted to go to church. Anyway, I could tell there's something different about this church, and even though I wasn't sure what, it felt genuine. I guess the song's mainly about some questions I have. We call it 'What Is It All About,' and it goes like this."

Through my teary eyes, I see you.
In my wounded heart, I feel you.
There are a thousand voices screaming,
but You are all I hear.

Emmy sang the song to the teens, and the simple, yet profound words affected the kids. After she finished, Emmy noticed a couple of young girls crying with Ronnie and some of the other teens and gathered around them. Emmy looked at Kenny. "Didn't they like the song?"

"I think they liked it a lot, Em. I believe that God has used your song to reach those girls. You have a special gift, Emmy, even though you may not know it yet."

Ronnie came over to talk to Kenny and Emmy a few minutes later. "Thank you so much for that song. Chris told me that she has had those same thoughts and has struggled, but tonight

206

everything came into focus for her."

"I don't understand. Did I do something wrong?" Emmy asked.

"Not at all. You may not realize it, but God sometimes works in ways that we don't understand. His ways are higher than our human ways. Maybe you could read Isaiah 55."

"Thanks, Ronnie. I'll try to explain more to Emmy," Kenny said.

After the service concluded, Kenny took Emmy back to his place. "I know you don't understand everything, Emmy, but I believe God has a plan for your life."

"Could you show me what Ronnie meant in the Bible?"

"Sure, it's on my desk. Let me grab it." Kenny got his Bible and opened it. As he did, his bookmark fell out, and Emmy picked it up.

"Your bookmark has a Bible verse on it."

"Yeah, that's John 3:16."

Emmy read the verse on the bookmark.

"You can keep it if you want, Em. I've got several others."

He read several passages to Emmy.

"So you're saying that even though I'm not a member of your church or anything, God used our song somehow to do something good for those girls."

"Yeah! Doesn't that make you feel good?"

"To be honest, it kinda scares me. It freaks me out. I realize that I need to be careful, or else I might write a song that might hurt someone."

Although Kenny and Emmy were alone with the opportunity to do more than kiss, they didn't. They both realized that their relationship had changed in subtle ways. The love they shared for each other was maturing. Emmy didn't realize it, but a seed had been planted in her life.

Emmy woke up on Christmas morning and stretched out. Diane's side of the bed felt cold and empty. Emmy showered and dressed before her parents came out of their bedroom. She sat at the kitchen table drinking a small glass of eggnog.

"Morning, Emmy, did you make some coffee by any chance?" Mom asked as she walked in and reached for her coffee cup.

"I didn't, but I can if you want. Merry Christmas, Mommy."

"Yes, coffee quickly, and Merry Christmas to you, too." Mom noticed the glass of eggnog. "I hope there's some left for your father. He likes to have eggnog and rum for Christmas. You don't have any rum in yours, do you?"

Emmy giggled. "No, but I remember a few years ago when Daddy let me taste his. There's another carton in the fridge."

"Where is your sister? Is she still sleeping?"

"She's not here. I don't know where she is."

"I know where she probably is. We argued last night, and she threatened to spend Christmas with Craig. Oh, well. I suppose it's for the best."

Emmy started the coffee brewing in the Mr. Coffee machine. Dad walked into the kitchen five minutes later after smelling the coffee.

"Merry Christmas, Daddy." Emmy kissed his cheek with its two-day growth of gray whiskers. "The coffee should be ready."

"Did you add any rum?" He pointed to her glass. "It's all right if you did."

"Diane left already. She's with Craig," Mom said as she poured her second cup of coffee.

Dad tried to decide whether to have coffee or a glass of eggnog and rum. "She's eighteen. She can do whatever she wants." The coffee won—for the present time.

Emmy scrambled some eggs and made toast. By the time they sat down to eat, Dad had switched from coffee to his spiked eggnog. Emmy tried to start a conversation, but met with little success from her parents. She cleared the dishes after her parents moved to the living room and sat in their habitual places. Emmy brought out her gifts. She kept them hidden in her bedroom since her father had not brought home a real tree again this year.

Emmy handed out her presents. "I didn't buy much, but I got something for each of you."

Mom and Dad expressed thanks for the dish towels and flannel shirt.

"I thought you might like to go out for dinner sometime, so I bought a gift card for Ciao Bella." Emmy remembered Grandma and Grandpa Colasanti taking her and Diane to the fancy Italian restaurant in the Hill neighborhood of SoHam.

"You shouldn't have spent so much money on us, Emmy. You know we seldom go out for dinner."

"Maybe you should," Emmy responded as her voice cracked with emotion.

"Before I forget, there are two cards on the dining room table for you. One is from your grandmother, and the other is from us."

Emmy found the cards and brought them back to the living room. She sat on the couch and opened them. Grandma Isabel sent a check for fifty dollars. Mom and Dad gave her a twenty dollar bill.

"Thank you. I'll send a note to Grandma."

Dad held out his glass. "Emmy, would you fix me another glass of eggnog. You know how much rum to add."

An hour later, Emmy told her parents goodbye and trudged along the snow-covered backyard sidewalk to the alley. She needed to see Kenny. She turned in at his house and noticed the driveway and sidewalks had been cleared. She knocked on the back door, and Mrs. Colwell let her in.

"Merry Christmas, Emmy. Come on in before you freeze."

"Merry Christmas, Mrs. Colwell. Is Kenny in the house? I didn't see any lights on in the carriage house."

"We're all in the house."

Emmy followed Mrs. Colwell. She paused as she saw all the people gathered in the living room.

"Emmy! Come and sit by me," Kenny said as he got up and hurried to her side.

"I didn't know you had so many people over. Maybe I should leave."

"Don't be shy. My family won't bite."

Kenny introduced Emmy to his relatives. Grandparents,

uncles, aunts and assorted cousins filled the room with laughter and conversation. Emmy smiled at Mr. Hanna and Sherry and nodded at Frankie, Kenny's cousin and guitar tech. She didn't say much, but laughed often as people shared family stories.

An hour later, the women brought out the food. The older family members sat at the dining room table and everyone else sat wherever they found room. Emmy sat with Kenny and his cousins in the breakfast nook. Frankie, who normally never spoke a word, told stories about the early days of the band. Emmy giggled as Frankie embarrassed Kenny with tales of forgotten lyrics and other mishaps.

Three hours later, Kenny, Emmy and his parents sat in the living room. Tired, but happy. Kenny's family had said their goodbyes to him. His grandmothers had cried.

"This has been quite a day," Mr. Colwell said.

Kenny put an arm around Emmy's shoulder and pulled her close. "See, you survived. No one bit you."

"Your family is so... different than mine. My family would kill each other if they spent the whole day together." Emmy managed a weak laugh. "Why did your grandmothers get so upset?"

Kenny looked at Emmy, and then his parents.

"Kenneth Travis Robert, don't tell me you haven't told Emmy," Mrs. Colwell said with a stern look.

"Told me what?" Emmy sounded perplexed. "What's going on?"

"You should sit down, Em."

"I am sitting down. Do you have something to tell me?" she asked as she bit her lip.

Kenny sat next to her as he explained. "The band is leaving on Saturday, the twenty-eighth, for another tour. The longest one yet. We'll be gone for over a year."

"What? No!" She turned on the couch and pushed his shoulder. "You can't be gone for that long. I will miss you too much. You're teasing, right?"

"I'm sorry we're going to be gone for so long. We're going to be touring all across the U.S. and Canada, and then in Europe.

We're even going to Japan and down to Australia."

"But what about the other guys? Jeremy's married, and Jeff's engaged."

"Amanda's going to be traveling with Jeremy. At least for a while, and then she's going to run the office for us."

She jumped up from the couch. "Then I want to go, too."

Kenny stood up, faced her and put his hands on her arms. "Em, you're sixteen. You have to finish school."

"I can take classes while we travel. You could homeschool me." She put her hands on her hips and stared defiantly at him.

"You know that's not practical," Kenny said.

"Won't you be able to come home at all?" Emmy's tears flowed down her cheeks.

Kenny tenderly wiped them away with his hand. "When we do have breaks, we will be in the studio in LA, or New York. It's possible I might make it home for a day or two once in a while, but I can't be sure. Andy is keeping us busy while we are hot. No one knows how long this might last."

"You will be able to keep in contact, dear." Mrs. Colwell squeezed her shoulders to assure her. "You can write letters to each other."

"I can't hug a letter."

"Come on, Em. This is my career. I have to go."

"When do you have to leave?"

"This Saturday, Em."

"Then I'm gonna spend every hour with you until then, and I mean every hour."

Kenny looked at his mother.

"He will be rather busy packing for the next couple of days, sweetie. Why don't you plan to come over for breakfast on Saturday?" Mrs. Colwell had a feeling Emmy might not stay away until Saturday.

She didn't.

On Thursday evening Emmy saw a light in the carriage house. She bounded up the stairs.

"Hi, Kenny. I couldn't stay away."

211

Jeff stepped out from behind a stack of equipment. "Hello, Emmy."

"Oh, hi, Jeff. I didn't know you were here."

"We have to go over a few details," Jeff said as he coiled a guitar cable. "Tour details."

"That's all right. I'll wait until you guys are finished." She sat on the old couch and crossed her arms over her chest. *I can be more stubborn and defiant than you realize, Mr. Rawlings.*

Kenny sat next to her. "Em, Jeff is taking me over to Jeremy's house. I won't be back until really late."

She frowned. "I'll wait. I'll wait all night if I have to."

"I'll be in the car." Jeff left the room. *I sure don't want to get in the middle of this.*

"Emmy..."

She pulled him closer. "You will forget about me if I don't make sure..."

Kenny put an arm around her waist. "I'm never going to forget about you, and you aren't going to spend the night."

"Are you going to sleep with anyone while you're away?"

He grinned. "I'm sure I'll have plenty of chances, but I won't."

"You better not."

Kenny stood up. "You need to go home, Em. I'll see you on Saturday."

"What about tomorrow? I don't have to work or anything."

"I'm sorry, Em, but we are going to be in Chicago for most of the day. Band stuff."

"I'll wait until Saturday if I have to, but I won't like it."

Emmy came over to the house on Saturday and ate breakfast with Kenny and his parents. As she helped Mrs. Colwell clean up, Kenny brought his last two suitcases downstairs.

"Is that all you're taking?" Emmy asked as she walked into the living room.

"The rest is already on the bus." Kenny kissed her. "I'm so happy you came over,"

"I am, too." She bit her lip. "This hasn't turned out to really be a merry Christmas after all."

He held her shoulders and gazed into her eyes. "Don't say that."

"I don't mean it."

"I know, Em."

They stood in front of the fireplace and stared at each other.

"Do you promise to stay in touch?"

"I will, Emmy. I'm going to miss you so much." *I love the sparkle in your eyes. Especially when you get fired up about something.*

"I will miss you even more."

They kept looking into each other's eyes for a moment without saying a word.

"I'm sure God has something special in mind for you, Em."

"I don't know what God could do with me. I'm not anything special."

"I think God uses ordinary people sometimes to do extraordinary things. There are many examples of that in the Bible. You just have to be willing to do what He asks."

Emmy looked at Kenny and started to cry. It started to sink in that she wouldn't see him for what she considered an eternity. He held her in his arms. She rested her head on his chest. When she stopped crying, Kenny smiled at her and kissed her tenderly.

"Can I go with you? Maybe I could finish school somehow. I don't think I will survive you being gone for so long." Her voice quavered as she looked up at him.

"You will be all right, Em. I'll write you letters and send postcards when I can. We are always going to be best friends."

"I don't want to be just best friends."

Kenny closed his eyes for a moment. "Right now that's all we can be. Will you promise not to sit at home and mope? Will you go out with friends and have fun?"

Emmy bit her lip. "I guess so."

"You might even meet someone and start dating."

She crossed her arms over her chest. "Are you going to be looking for a girlfriend? Is that why you want me to see other guys?"

"Neither one of us can know for sure what will happen over the next year. I do know I will miss you. Will you promise me you will think about dating? You're old enough now. You never know, you might meet the perfect guy." Kenny chuckled and then put his hands on her shoulders.

"I already have." She wrapped her arms around him and held on tight. "Nobody could be more perfect than you."

"Oh, Emmy." Kenny fought against the tears filling his eyes. "You will meet lots of guys over the next few years. You have to finish high school, and I know you want to go to college. So much will change in the future."

"I can't think that far ahead. All I know is that I will die if you forget about me."

He ran a hand through her long hair and could smell her strawberry shampoo as he whispered in her ear. "I swear to never forget you. You know that, right?"

"I know, but I will still miss you."

"I've gotta go, Em. The guys are here." He had to pry her arms from around his waist.

They looked out the front windows as the new Prevost Royal Coach touring bus the band purchased pulled up in front of the house. Kenny said his goodbyes to his parents, and then Emmy walked outside with him. Even though snow fell and a cold wind blew right through her, Emmy felt warm inside. She stood by the bus door with Kenny, and he hugged her one more time. He whispered in her ear, "Just remember that I love you, and you have my heart. Always and forever."

Emmy smiled through her tears as Kenny turned away. He hummed a tune that she didn't recognize.

Chapter Twenty

A hundred lockers slammed shut. The loud voices of as many students competed to be heard as Emmy glanced at the red streamers and pictures of roses that decorated the hallway. She caught a brief glimpse of Derrick Keasling and Clarissa Morgan holding hands and stopped for a moment in the middle of the traffic.

Someone pushed her in the back. "Hey! Watch it, kid. You want to get run over?"

I'm getting tired of this. Emmy felt like screaming. She moved out of the way and leaned back against a locker as she thought about Derrick and Clarissa. *I just can't picture you guys as an old married couple.*

A heavyset girl frowned at her and said, "You're blocking my locker."

"Sorry." Emmy scooted out of the way.

Though Valentine's Day fell on Wednesday this year, the Valentine's Day dance would be in the large multipurpose room after the basketball game on Friday night. Emmy, who didn't have a date, caught a ride with Barry and Linda. Emmy walked in with Barry, and they both laughed at the cheesy red and white decorations.

"They should never let freshmen be in charge of a dance," Barry said.

I wonder if our class did a better job? Emmy thought as she looked around. She saw Kristen dancing. "Hey, Barry, do you know that guy?"

"Who?"

Emmy pointed. "The guy with the ponytail and those faded jeans dancing with Kristen. He must be from North Park because she's only dating college guys now."

"I don't know." Barry shrugged.

Emmy poked Barry's arm. "You're no help at all."

"Hey, Emmy!" Kristen hollered a few minutes later as Emmy danced with two freshman boys.

Emmy waved, and Kristen joined her as the DJ played a

215

fast song. One of the freshman tried to dance with Kristen.

Kristen stopped dancing and stared at his wild gyrations. "Who are these kids, Emmy?"

"I don't have a clue, but they're certainly having fun." Emmy laughed but kept dancing.

The two freshman bumped into each other and nearly fell to the floor.

"Come on, Em." Kristen tugged her away from the two energetic, but clumsy, boys. "I think Derrick wants to dance with you. I'll keep Clarissa busy."

"Are you sure?"

"I'm positive. Don't worry about Clarissa."

"All right. Who is that guy with you?"

"Dexter McGlinchey. He's a friend of Gabe's. No one special." Kristen waved at Dexter. "Just a date for tonight."

Emmy danced with Derrick while Clarissa glared at them from the side of the dance floor.

"Thanks for the dance, Derrick, but I think you better get back to Clarissa. She looks pissed," Emmy said between songs.

Derrick looked over his shoulder and sighed. "Yeah, I'll get the cold shoulder for the rest of the night."

The two freshman tracked Emmy down and danced with her most of the night. She never did catch their names.

In April, Derrick and Clarissa argued and broke up. The news about the breakup spread rapidly through Roosevelt High. Derrick called Emmy after school that day. "Will you go over to Darby's with me, Emmy? I want to talk to you."

Emmy closed her book and sat up in her bed. "We can talk now."

"I want to see you, too."

"All right. Is it about Clarissa?"

"Partly, but I want to talk about us, too."

Derrick picked Emmy up, and they went over to Darby's. They ordered fries and pop and sat on opposite sides of a booth. Emmy looked up at a photo of herself on stage with Fridays At Five. *Why did I pick this one?* She looked around and realized there were photos of the band above most of the booths.

"Did you hear the rumors?" Derrick asked.

"Did you guys really break up? I heard kids talking about it all day."

"Yes. Clarissa is too possessive and clingy. She wanted to know what I was doing every second of the day. I like her, but I don't need that. I want to be able to see other girls if I want. Clarissa can be so serious at times."

Emmy stopped slurping her pop. "I kinda got that impression."

"Sometimes she acts like she's thirty years old. I'm eighteen. I want to have fun and enjoy life. We had fun together, didn't we?"

"We did, but we were never a couple. Not the way you and Clarissa are, or were."

"Could we hang out and have fun like before, Em?"

"I would like that." Emmy dipped a fry into the paper cup of ketchup and took a bite. "But I should tell you about Kenny."

"You don't have to say anything, Emmy. I know how you feel about him, and it's okay. We are only going to have fun together—not get all serious or anything."

She waved a fry at him. "You're trying to tell me we won't be exclusive, aren't you?"

"Would it bother you if I occasionally dated another girl?"

"Why would it? We're just friends who enjoy each other's company."

"I won't ever do anything to hurt you, Em. I think we should kinda keep it to ourselves that we're hanging out with each other. That way the kids at school won't be gossiping about us."

"That's all right with me. I know how much they talked about you and Clarissa. If only some of the rumors were true, you've been a naughty boy."

"Don't believe everything you hear."

Emmy grinned. "But I should believe some of it, huh?"

He shrugged. "Hey, I'm human, and she is really pretty."

Emmy knew Derrick and Clarissa had been intimate. She couldn't help wonder how that would be like with Kenny. Her eyes filled with tears.

"What's wrong, Em?" *Shoot! I shouldn't have mentioned Clarissa.*

"Nothing." She bit her lip.

"I know better," Derrick whispered. "You can tell me."

Emmy didn't say anything for a moment but then blurted out. "Kenny's going to be gone for over a year. He might not remember me when he gets back."

"Wow! That's a really long time to be away."

Emmy's tears fell down her cheeks.

Crap! I shouldn't have said that. Derrick tried to make her feel better. "I don't think he will ever forget you, Emmy. You guys have been friends for too long for that to happen."

"He meets so many people when he's away."

"You mean girls, right? There's probably a lot of fans who follow them around."

Emmy wiped her tears with a napkin, and then threw it at Derrick. "If you're trying to help, it's not working."

"Sorry, Em. I didn't think about how that sounded." He took a drink of pop as he thought how it might be for Kenny. *I'm not sure I could resist having a bunch of pretty girls throwing themselves at me night after night. I take that back. I'm positive I wouldn't be able to refuse.*

Emmy stopped her sniffling. "It's all right. He's used to it, and he knows how to avoid the... temptations."

"Do you guys talk or communicate at all when he's gone?" Derrick took the last fry. "Should we order something else to eat? Are you still hungry?"

"I'm okay, but go ahead if you want something."

He ordered another large fry and refilled his pop while Emmy gazed at the photos on the wall. Derrick slipped into the booth a couple of minutes later.

"So, do you guys stay in touch?"

"He writes me letters and sends postcards," Emmy said as she grabbed a fry. "These are really hot."

"How do you answer back? He's always on the move."

"His parents have a way of getting letters to him. I write

218

something every week."

"Love letters, huh?"

She grinned. "I hope his parents never open them."

Derrick smiled at her. "Do you ever talk on the phone?"

"Not yet." She waved a fry around. "He calls his parents, and they have seen him. They flew to New York."

"But you didn't go?"

"It was during the week so I couldn't. Maybe I'll have a chance to see him in the summer. Be right back." She scooted out of the booth and refilled her pop.

Derrick looked around and spotted a few kids from Roosevelt. He waved as Emmy slipped back into the booth. "Maybe you could take a vacation and spend some time together."

"No way. My parents would never let me go by myself."

"Yeah, I suppose not."

Derrick and Emmy started seeing each other again, but just as friends. They doubled with Kristen and her date du jour. Emmy knew Derrick went out with other girls, but he didn't talk about them. She started wondering if he intended to ask her to the upcoming prom.

Diane cornered Emmy in the bedroom one afternoon. "Has Derrick asked you to the prom? It's getting pretty close. I know you turned down a couple of offers."

"I turned them down because those guys are dorks. It had nothing to do with Derrick."

"So," Diane said slowly.

"We haven't talked about the prom. We're just friends."

"Is he coming over tonight?" Diane pushed Emmy onto the bed. "Or is he seeing one of his other friends?"

"He's coming over, but you better not..."

"I'm going to ask him what he plans to do."

When he arrived, Diane wasted no time. "Derrick, are you going to ask Emmy to the prom or not?" Diane stood with her hands on her hips and tried to look intimidating.

"I've been having a dilemma about the prom. Before I started going out with Emmy again, I dated this girl, Clarissa

219

Morgan..."

"I know about her," Diane interrupted.

"Well, before we broke up, I sorta asked her to the prom. She has already bought her dress and..."

"What difference does that make? You broke up with her and now you should ask Emmy to go. Just tell Clarissa that you are going with Emmy, and that's that."

"It's not as easy as that," Derrick said. "The Morgans are good friends with my parents, and they still expect us to go to the prom together."

Diane stomped her foot. "Just tell her to find someone else. It's as simple as that."

"I hinted vaguely at that very thing, and Clarissa broke down into tears."

Diane rolled her eyes. "What a manipulating drama queen."

Just then Emmy walked into the room and heard them talking. "Derrick, I don't want you to break the date since she already has her dress. I can find another date for the prom, and we can see each other there."

"I'm really sorry, Emmy."

Emmy waved a hand dismissively. "No problem. I'll be all right."

The next day Emmy called one of the boys who asked her to go earlier.

"Sorry, Emmy, but I'm going with someone else."

She called the other boy and got the same answer. Diane tried to help Emmy find a date, but with no luck. Diane asked her about Jayson Mathias, but Emmy stuck her finger down her throat and pretended to gag. "I'd rather become a nun than go with Jayson."

Emmy talked to Kristen. "Did you decide who is taking you to the prom?"

"I'm going with one of my cousins. I had to practically beg him to go with me because he is so shy." Emmy didn't know who she meant, and Kristen didn't elaborate. "I turned down a dozen guys who asked because I know what they will want to do after the prom, and I'm not gonna do that just because they spent some money on a corsage and tux. Some of them actually made that a condition to go with me."

"That sucks."

"No kidding! Who are you going with, Emmy? I know you were hoping Derrick would ask you. Have any other guys asked you to go?"

"I turned down two boys, and no one else has asked."

"You could come by yourself, and I will keep you company. My cousin will probably hang out with the football players anyway."

"I'll think about it, but it would be too weird to go to the prom by myself."

In the end, Emmy stayed home from the prom, and Derrick promised to make it up to her.

During the last week of school before the summer break, Derrick tried to think of somewhere special to take Emmy on the weekend. He would be leaving shortly after graduation for a trip to Europe with his parents and Kristen. When Derrick returned, he would be headed to school at the University of Arizona in Tucson. Emmy knew she would not see him often after he left and wanted to enjoy the last couple of days with him.

On Friday, Derrick asked her, "Wanna go hiking tomorrow at Morriston State Park along the Kinmundy River?"

"That could be fun. I've never been there, but I hear it's really nice."

Although the weather in early June could sometimes be unpredictable, this Saturday brought clear skies and warm temperatures. Emmy woke up around nine. She showered and dressed before Diane got out of bed. She wore a pair of baby blue shorts and a white top. She knew Diane would be mad at her, but she borrowed Diane's light blue camisole and wore that under her shirt. Derrick picked her up at ten thirty wearing shorts and a t-shirt.

"It looks like it will be a beautiful day, Emmy. We should

221

have a great day for hiking."

"Do you think it will take long to get there?"

"About an hour. Do you have to be home by any certain time?"

"I told Mom I would be home before ten." Emmy paused and watched out the car window for a moment before she turned back to look at Derrick. "I never asked you about prom. Kristen told me you and Clarissa were runners-up for prom king and queen. Everyone knew Damon Barclay and Diana Ahronson would be king and queen. Did you have a good time with Clarissa?"

"Actually, I did. She behaved differently. She didn't act all possessive and even allowed me to dance with other girls." He looked at Emmy and knew she had something else on her mind. "What else do you want to know?"

"Did you guys do anything afterward?"

"I know you're talking about sex, Emmy." He tapped her thigh and grinned. "No, I took her home around two and left right away."

"What about on Sunday?"

"We didn't do anything sexual the next day, either. We met some other kids at Elaine Novicki's house and hung around there for the afternoon." He smiled and decided to tease her. "Would you be jealous if I had done something with her?"

She smacked his arm. "Why would I be jealous? I'm not your girlfriend. She is."

"Not anymore. We are now officially broken up." He smiled. "Prom is over, and so is our relationship. We probably aren't even friends now."

They arrived at the park and hiked the trail on the bluff along the river. The sun shone brightly in the cloudless sky, and the temperature soon climbed into the mid-eighties. At first they did not see many other people their age at the park, but later they saw a group of about twenty high school and college kids. They saw a sign for a scenic spot called Lover's Leap.

"Oooh, should we check it out, Em?" Derrick asked.

"Yeah, I want to see it. Maybe I'll toss you off," Emmy said as she followed the path.

They sat on the bench that afforded them a great view of the river. After a couple of minutes, Derrick leaned over and kissed her on the mouth for the first time.

She inhaled and held her breath expecting another kiss. She exhaled with relief when he didn't try to kiss her again. His kiss had felt kind of weird and awkward.

Derrick stared out at the river, dismayed that kissing Emmy felt about as arousing as kissing his sister.

Neither one mentioned the kiss.

"Are we still planning on staying for dinner?" Emmy asked a moment later. "I would like to. I hear the food at the lodge is pretty good."

"Yeah, we can stay, Emmy. I've never eaten here, but my parents have, and they liked it."

They started hiking back to the lodge with a couple hours to kill before dinnertime. Emmy spotted a tree with some low branches she thought would be perfect for climbing. The tomboy in her surfaced as she ran to the tree, "I bet I can climb to the top."

"Emmy, you shouldn't," Derrick said, but he was too late.

She grabbed the lowest branch, pulled herself up and sat on it. Derrick put his hands on her knees and looked at her. "Please don't climb any higher, Emmy. I don't want to have to explain to your father how you broke your neck falling out of a tree."

Emmy, of course, started to do that very thing; she climbed higher. Soon she was twenty feet up in the tree as Derrick watched her.

He shook his head. "Hey! Can you hear me up there?"

"Yeah. Why?"

"I like watching you, but I am kinda worried about you falling. Could you please come back down?"

She didn't go any higher and started climbing down. She stood on the last branch and jumped down to the ground and into Derrick. They tumbled to the ground, with Emmy landing on top of him.

"Are you all right?" she asked.

"No, my lip is cut, and it hurts," Derrick responded.

Emmy looked. "Where? I don't see anything."

223

"It's on the inside of my mouth, and you need to give me emergency mouth-to-mouth."

Emmy started to put her mouth on his, and then stopped. "You just want me to kiss you again. I'm not that naïve."

"How about one kiss?"

"Okay, one kiss, but that's all." She kissed his cheek, and then grinned.

"That's not exactly what I had in mind, but it's better than no kiss at all."

"Do you feel better now?"

"I guess so, but I'm still seriously injured."

She smacked his arm. "I think you'll survive."

He soon recovered from his *serious injuries*. They explored some different trails and chased each other through an area of huge boulders. Emmy climbed on top of the boulders and onto a ledge— as sure-footed and fearless as a mountain goat. They returned to the Lover's Leap lookout and sat and talked for a while, but Derrick didn't try to kiss her again.

They followed the trail back to the lodge and saw some of the other kids again. One of the girls asked, "Are you guys staying for dinner? If you are, you can join us. We have one whole end of the dining room to ourselves, and you're more than welcome to join our group."

Derrick answered, "We are staying, and thank you for asking, but I think we will get a table by ourselves. Is that all right, Emmy?"

Emmy grabbed his arm. "Derrick, would you mind if we joined the other kids?"

"If you'd rather do that, it's okay with me. I just thought... never mind."

Derrick turned back to the girl. "Thank you. We would be happy to have dinner with you guys."

A huge stone fireplace dominated the center of the dining room. Emmy craned her neck as she looked up at the high vaulted ceiling, which stretched to the sky. A few older couples sat at tables at the opposite end of the room. Derrick and Emmy joined another couple, and Emmy learned that the girl's father paid for everyone's dinner. She thought it must be nice to be that rich. She didn't know that Derrick's family was even wealthier. They enjoyed a pleasant dinner and talked to the other young couples. Afterward, everybody moved from table to table as they socialized. Eventually someone turned on some music, and couples started dancing. Emmy danced with Derrick and two other boys.

"Are you still having a good time, Emmy?" Derrick asked later as they danced close together.

"Yes, I am. I think it's been a perfectly lovely day."

Emmy looked at the large clock above the fireplace, and Derrick noticed the time.

"I should take you home, Em. I don't want you to get grounded for being out too late."

Even as he said it, it sounded so childish. He couldn't understand why she needed to be home by ten on a Saturday night. They said goodbye to the other kids and left. He felt as though his car would turn into a pumpkin if he didn't return Emmy home before her curfew. He looked down at her feet. *At least she's not wearing glass slippers.*

She sat next to Derrick and held onto his arm for a moment. "I had a lot of fun today, Derrick. More fun than going to the prom."

"Really? Why is that, Emmy?"

"Because I didn't have to wear one of those silly dresses and pretend to be all grown up."

Derrick laughed and agreed. "Emmy, my mouth hurts again. I think I need some emergency medical treatment."

Emmy smacked him playfully on his arm. "I think you will survive without any more mouth-to-mouth. If you recover from your serious injury, maybe we can spend the whole day together tomorrow."

"The whole day?"

"Not like that!" Emmy poked his side. "I'm not Clarissa."

Derrick took her home and kissed her good night on the cheek. He called her again when he got home, and they talked about plans for the next day. They couldn't make up their minds where to go.

225

"Let's just wait and see what happens, Em."

"Yeah, who knows what the weather will be like."

Emmy tossed and turned as she tried to fall asleep. Diane came home around midnight, but couldn't fall asleep because Emmy kept flipping over and disturbing her.

Diane sat up. "What's wrong, Emmy? You're keeping me awake."

"I keep thinking about Derrick. We're gonna do something tomorrow, but I don't know what yet. I have just as much fun with Derrick when Kristen is along."

"So ask her to go with you. Maybe I'll join you and take Derrick off your hands. He's really sexy."

"You better not try anything with him," Emmy warned Diane again.

"I'm just kidding. Now go to sleep so I can get some rest. I have to work tomorrow afternoon."

"Diane."

"What, Em?"

"I borrowed your blue camisole today. Please don't be mad at me."

"If I wasn't so tired, I would smack you. You know I don't like it when you borrow my clothes."

"I'm sorry, but I wanted to look nice for Derrick."

Diane sat up. "Tell me your wore something over the camisole. Did you?"

"Of course, and I wore a bra underneath it."

"So he never knew you even had it on, right?"

"He could see part of it because I didn't button my top all the way. It got really hot."

"Go to sleep, and I'll smack you in the morning."

Chapter Twenty-One

The sun was already shining into the bedroom when Emmy stretched her arms above her head and slowly opened her eyes the next morning. She looked at Diane—still sound asleep and dead to the world after not getting home until after midnight. Diane blatantly ignored any attempt by her mother to set a curfew.

Emmy slipped quietly out of the room hoping not to wake Diane. She froze for a few seconds as Diane rolled over and groaned. *Crap! If I wake you up, you might remember that I borrowed your camisole.* Diane didn't open her eyes. Emmy went to check if her parents were still home. She peeked around the open door into their bedroom. The room was thankfully empty. She knew her father was working, but didn't remember if her mother has any plans for the day. *I'm glad they aren't home. Now I don't have to explain where I'm going.*

Back in her room, Emmy picked out some clothes and took a chance on showering without waking up Diane. As she washed her long hair with her strawberry scented shampoo, she realized this would probably be her last date with Derrick. *What should I do if he tries to kiss me again? He's really handsome, but kissing him is sure not like kissing Kenny.*

Derrick picked her up right before lunch, and they drove off without a destination in mind until Derrick remembered something at home that he needed to do.

"Shoot, Emmy, I just remembered I have to send off some info to Arizona. Do you mind if we run back to my house for a minute?"

"I don't mind." Emmy thought she could ask Kristen to come with them.

Emmy caught a quick glimpse of the front of the house as Derrick pulled onto the large concrete driveway on the right side. He stopped in front of the four car garage, pressed a remote to open the door and they stepped out of the car. Emmy looked at the size of their house in awe. *Oh my God! This place looks even bigger than Kenny's house.* She went inside to talk to Kristen while Derrick took care of his business.

"Hi, Emmy, I didn't know you guys were coming back here."

Emmy explained why.

"Do you want me to show you around the place?" Kristen asked.

"Maybe when we get back. I think we're coming back here for lunch or dinner."

They ended up in the family room, and Kristen introduced her to her parents, Daniel and Karla.

"We met Emmy at the country club dance, Kristen. How are you, Emmy?" Karla asked.

"I'm fine, Mrs. Keasling. Thank you for asking."

Kristen asked, "Where are you guys going? Got any ideas?"

"We're not sure yet. We did a lot of hiking yesterday at the park in Morriston by the river. I liked that."

Kristen suggested, "You guys should go to the park on the far west side of town. I can't remember the name, but Derrick knows where it is. It's a lot closer and usually isn't very crowded since it's south of the river."

"It's Forbes Bend. That sounds like fun. Do you want to go with us?" Emmy asked. "I would like for you to come with us."

Kristen smiled and said, "I'd love to," as Derrick entered the room.

Derrick asked Kristen, "What would you 'love to'?"

"Can Kristen go with us?" Emmy asked.

"I guess it's all right with me."

Kristen thought about it as Derrick frowned at her. She thought Derrick really didn't want her to go. "Maybe I should stay home. I've got stuff to do. I should decide what I want to take to Europe."

Emmy looked at Derrick. "Please convince Kristen that we really want her to come with us." She pouted in such a way that Derrick agreed to let Kristen come along.

He whispered into Kristen's ear, "When you get a chance, make up some excuse so Emmy and I can have a chance to be alone for a while."

She understood. "Don't worry. I will make sure you and Emmy will have some time to yourselves, but you better not try anything."

Derrick grinned as he said, "I'm not going to do anything like what you and your dirty mind are imagining."

"Look who's talking!" Kristen said. "You're the one with all the experience, creep."

"I want to have some time to talk to her alone."

"Make sure all you do is talk." Kristen poked Derrick in the chest. "She's not Clarissa."

Sunday's weather promised to be a carbon copy of Saturday's—sunny and possibly even warmer. Emmy wanted to spend the time outside and liked Kristen's idea. They drove to Forbes Bend.

Emmy pointed to a wooden display. "There's a trail map over there."

They checked for the best hiking trails and set off on foot. Emmy walked in between Derrick and Kristen along the crushed limestone trail.

Emmy watched a large hawk soaring in circles overhead. "How long are you guys going to be in Europe?"

"Two months. It's a graduation present for Derrick from Grandpa Keasling. Daddy is only going to be there for a month, but Mom will be with us the whole time," Kristen said.

They walked along the tree-lined trail and could feel a light breeze on their faces. Today Emmy wore a red t-shirt with a Darby's Dogs logo on the front and a pair of denim shorts. They hiked through open meadows and groves of tightly-packed trees for thirty minutes and didn't see another soul after they left the pavilion area. They climbed a short hill and came upon a bench.

"Hey, you guys. I want to stop." Kristen sat down. "I'm going to rest here. You guys can go on ahead."

"What's the matter, Kristen? Are you wimping out?" Derrick asked even though he knew her reason for stopping.

"I'm bored. You guys go ahead, and I'll wait here or else go back to the car. Can I have the keys, please?" Kristen held out her hand.

"Okay, Kristen, we'll look for you here on our way back," Emmy replied.

Emmy and Derrick continued along the trail. They hadn't noticed the clouds and now overcast sky. The rain started less than five minutes later. At first it was only a light sprinkle that actually felt good as it cooled them, but Derrick noticed the darkening sky.

"We should get back to the car, Emmy, or else we're gonna get soaked."

"I'll race you back, Derrick." She dashed away.

They quickly passed the empty bench where Kristen was supposed to wait.

"She probably headed back to the car," Derrick said.

Emmy looked around. "You're probably right. She's too smart to sit here and wait in the rain."

They sprinted back to the car as the sky opened and the rain fell in heavy drops. They were thoroughly soaked by the time they reached the car. Kristen waited in the car, but she had also been caught in the rain. Derrick tried to open the door, but couldn't.

"Kristen, open the door. It's locked. We're getting soaked."

Kristen grinned at her brother. "What? I can't hear you."

"Open the door or else I'm going to let Mom know you borrowed her new silk blouse and spilled wine on it and ruined it," he yelled over the booming thunder.

"You promised you would never tell." Kristen sounded betrayed as she unlocked the car.

"I might still tell Mom just because you made us wait in the rain," Derrick said.

Kristen stuck out her tongue at Derrick.

"That was fun," Emmy said from the backseat.

Derrick and Kristen turned around to look at her.

"You seriously enjoyed getting soaked?" Kristen asked.

"At least we got cooled off," Emmy said.

It poured for another five minutes before slowing momentarily. Kristen needed to use the bathroom. She got out and ran to the pavilion as the rain started coming down even harder.

Now alone with Derrick in the car, Emmy asked. "You didn't really want Kristen to come with us today, did you?"

230

"Honestly, no, I really wanted some time for us to be alone today, but it's all right that she came along. I really don't mind. Look on the bright side—Kristen is getting as wet as we did," he answered as he saw his sister running toward the car. Derrick laughed as he watched his sister jumping over the puddles of water in the asphalt parking lot. *What difference does it make, Kristen? You are already soaking wet.*

Kristen returned to the car and tried to open the door. Derrick smiled at her.

"Very funny, Derrick. Now open the blasted door!" Kristen screamed.

Derrick opened the door, and Kristen jumped in the backseat with Emmy. Emmy now realized that Kristen used an excuse to give Derrick and her some time alone. Emmy liked Kristen even more now.

"Great! The seats are getting soaked. You're going to have to dry my car, Kristen."

"It's not her fault we didn't realize it was going to rain." Emmy squeezed some water out of her t-shirt. "It's no use. I'm never going to get dry."

"I'm hungry. Can we stop and get something to eat?" Kristen asked as they headed home.

"We can if you're buying," Derrick answered.

"Fine! I'll buy. Stop at the Wendy's by the mall."

"Emmy, it's a miracle! Kristen is going to spend some of her own money. I need to call CNN with the news. They will want to have a special newscast about this."

"Aren't you the funny one." Kristen made a face at Derrick as they looked at each other in the rearview mirror.

They went through the drive-thru at Wendy's, and then parked in the mall lot away from other cars to eat. Derrick kept the car running with the heater on to dry their clothes. Soon they were all sweating and couldn't stand the heat.

"Turn off the heater," Kristen begged Derrick. "I don't know which is worse—being soaking wet or sweating like a pig."

"Do pigs really sweat or is that merely an expression?" Emmy asked naively.

231

"It's a scientific fact that pigs cannot sweat because they have no sweat glands," Derrick said with a straight face.

"Is he making fun of me, Kristen?"

"I think so, but he might be right. I really don't care if pigs sweat or not, but I sure love bacon."

Emmy and Kristen laughed, and Derrick smiled at them. He opened the windows and turned off the car. Their clothes would have to dry on their own.

They finished eating and started for home, but Kristen needed to stop again. Derrick stopped, and Kristen ran inside the Casey Jones convenience store.

Emmy looked at him. "Hey, Derrick," she said but then paused.

"Yeah, what's up?"

She wanted to tell him something about how she felt about him. *How can I say this without him thinking I'm a total dweeb?* She was almost too shy to tell him and afraid that if she just blurted it out, it wouldn't come out the right way. She felt so awkward.

"Is something wrong, Emmy?"

"I need to use the bathroom, too. I'll be right back."

Emmy thought she really blew her chance to tell Derrick how she felt and left him the impression she was immature and stupid. Emmy went inside to find Kristen and to use the bathroom. She started to cry, and Kristen comforted her. Emmy stopped crying after a moment and looked at Kristen.

"Do you think I'm a big baby for being so emotional?"

"It's okay. We're girls. We can be emotional sometimes."

"If Derrick wasn't going to Europe and away to school, I might fall in love with him." Emmy covered her mouth with her hand. "Maybe. I don't know for sure. I'm so confused right now, Kristen. I never dreamed I would have so much fun with him. Before he asked me out, and we used to hang out with everybody, he never showed any interest in me at all. I thought of him as your brother and never gave a second thought about dating him."

"It's okay, Emmy. Derrick really likes you, but he told me that he didn't want to get too serious because he wants to be able to concentrate on school in the fall and not be thinking of someone two thousand miles away. I know that sounds harsh, but Derrick is very serious about school. He wants to be an attorney. Can you imagine. I always thought of Derrick as being honest."

"Harsh, huh? Is that the word of the week again?" Emmy laughed and felt better now.

Emmy and Kristen returned to the car, and Derrick took Emmy back to their house for dinner.

"I guess we can't take a tour of the outside," Kristen lamented.

"Why not?" Derrick asked.

Kristen poked him in the shoulder. "Because it's raining, you creep."

"What does it matter? We're all still soaked."

Emmy giggled. *I love the way they treat each other. I wish Diane and I were as close.*

Kristen shook her head. "I don't want Mom and Dad to think I'm not smart enough to come in out of the rain."

They pulled into the garage, and Kristen jumped out of the car. "I'm gonna run up to my room and change clothes."

"Kristen, would you mind if I borrowed something to wear while my clothes dry?" Emmy didn't have any other clothes with her.

"Of course not. Let's go up to my room, and I'll see what I've got that will fit you."

Kristen took Emmy upstairs to her room and found some clothes for her. Kristen let Emmy change behind a three-panel Japanese screen while she also changed. Emmy couldn't believe the size of Kristen's bedroom. *This is bigger than our whole house.* Emmy exaggerated. *I love the white furniture and whatever shade of pink is on the walls.*

Kristen wanted to ask her what happened after she left them alone, but didn't. Finally, she couldn't take not knowing. "Did Derrick try anything with you after I stayed behind?"

Emmy blushed as she thought about it. Kristen noticed her shyness.

"I'll never tell anyone, Emmy." They sat on the edge of Kristen's king-size bed.

233

"We just talked. We've never done anything, really. We've only kissed once or twice. It's weird—when Derrick kissed me, I thought about you, and how he's your brother. I almost feel like Derrick is my brother, too. Strange, huh? You know how I told you I could maybe fall in love with Derrick?"

"Yeah." Kristen scooted farther back onto the bed and waited for Emmy to continue.

"The more I think about it, the more I'm convinced that I really just love Derrick as a friend. I don't think that will change."

Kristen replied, "I think I know how you feel. I thought I was in love with my cousin when I was younger. Now that I'm older and wiser..."

Emmy smirked, "Oh yeah, you're so old now."

Kristen continued, "I realize that I love him as a friend and almost like a brother—almost as much as I love Derrick. I know we are always teasing each other and bicker sometimes, but I really love Derrick, and I know he loves me, too. Don't you dare ever tell him what I said."

"I won't, Kristen. I promise." *Maybe I should meet your cousin sometime. He sounds like a good guy.*

After a quick, simple, but very tasty meal of tacos, burritos, rice and beans, Derrick took Emmy to the English-pub-themed downstairs family room, and they sat on the leather couch.

"Are these your pajama pants, or do they belong to Kristen?" Derrick teased her and tried to tickle her side.

"Stop it, Derrick!" Emmy giggled as she fought to keep his hands away. "You know they're not mine." She pulled her knees up to her chest.

Derrick's parents and Kristen came in to watch a movie on the new sixty-five-inch TV. With the air conditioning running the room was cool. Kristen grabbed a blanket to avoid a chill.

"Wimp!" Derrick teased as Kristen covered her and Emmy's legs. Derrick tried to hold hands with Emmy under the cover of the blanket, but she wouldn't let him. The movie, *Happy Gilmore*, kept them laughing for most of its ninety minutes.

"Come on, Emmy. Your clothes should be dry by now." Kristen led the way back up two flights of stairs and down the

234

wide hall to her bedroom. Emmy changed into her own clothes.

Kristen grinned at her. "I could tell you guys were holding hands under the blanket."

"No, we weren't. Derrick tried to hold my hand, but I wouldn't let him. Then he tried to tickle me. Do you think your parents noticed?" Emmy wondered.

"I doubt it. They weren't really paying any attention to you guys and wouldn't care anyway."

"I suppose I should have Derrick take me home. Say goodbye to your parents for me."

"I will," Kristen said as she hugged Emmy. "Hanging out with you is never boring, Emmy."

Derrick took Emmy home a few minutes later.

"It's not even raining in this part of town," Derrick said as he pointed out the obvious.

He parked in front of her house, and Emmy jumped out of the car before he had a chance to open her door. She started up the cracked sidewalk. *I wonder what he must think about our house? The whole thing would fit in their garage, and it looks like a dump.*

"Slow down, Emmy." He ran to catch up with her.

"I had a good time today, Derrick," Emmy said as they walked up the sidewalk. "Are you mad that I invited Kristen along?"

"Not really." He stopped and held her hand. *How can I say this without hurting her feelings?*

She pulled him to the concrete front steps, stood on the first one and faced him. "You're a lot of fun to be with, but..."

"Yeah, I know. You think I'm your brother or cousin. It's all right. I'll get over being rejected by you. It might take years, but it will happen." Derrick lowered his eyes.

"You're being silly. We're just not meant to be romantically involved. Not with each other, I mean," she said and then giggled.

A couple of minutes later, he kissed her on the cheek.

"I'll see you at my graduation party, Emmy. You will be there, right?"

"I wouldn't miss it for the world."

235

Chapter Twenty-Two

"I can't decide what to wear to Derrick's graduation party." Emmy pulled another outfit out of the bedroom closet and held it up. "How does this one look, Diane?"

"I liked the last dress better, Em. This one is a bit out of style, but I like this material." Diane sat on the bed and rubbed a hand over the soft fabric. "Did you ask Mom if you could get a new dress?"

"Yeah, but she said no. She told me that you have a closet full of clothes, and I should borrow one of yours."

"That sounds like Mom. She'll never understand that we aren't the same size. My dresses just don't fit you right."

"That's cause you're bigger than me." Emmy put her hands in front of her chest and laughed.

"Stop that." Diane laughed then said, "You could spend your own money. I'd take you shopping."

"I need the money for college. Can't I wear my comfy jeans and a nice shirt?" Emmy asked once more.

"I doubt very much if many of the other girls will be dressed so casually. It's not like you're going to be playing football, Em. It won't hurt you to dress like a young lady for once."

"I could wear my new jeans."

"No." Diane shook her head.

Emmy ended up wearing her favorite dress. Diane dropped her off at the Keasling home.

Diane gawked at the Keasling house. "Holy crap, Em. You didn't say they lived in a mansion."

"Thanks for the ride. I'll get a lift home." Emmy got out, waved to Diane and followed the signs directing party guests to the back of the house.

"Emmy!" Kristen hollered.

"Hi, Kristen." Emmy gazed at the crowd. "There's a lot of people here already."

"Come with me. We can help Mom in the kitchen for a while and keep away from the crowd."

The Keaslings lived in a huge house set on nearly ten acres

236

in the very exclusive Barclay Estates neighborhood. The deck off the back of the house covered over a thousand square feet. Past the deck was an in-ground pool with a pool house, a tennis court and a beautifully landscaped flower garden.

"Kristen, you guys live in a mansion. I've never dreamed about living in a place so... so... fantastic."

"Come on, Emmy. I'll show you around the place. It was raining the first time you were here. What are you planning to do this summer?" Kristen asked.

"I don't really have any plans other than working as many hours as I can at Darby's. I might try to find another part-time job, but it would have to be close to home since I don't have a car."

"Are you going anywhere special on vacation?" Kristen found a tennis ball in the yard, picked it up and tossed it towards the courts. It fell well short of the fence.

Emmy laughed. "You throw like a girl. I don't think I'll be going anywhere on vacation because everybody will be working all summer... my parents and Diane, too. Where does that trail lead?"

"It winds through the woods, and there is a small lake back there. I'll show you sometime."

"Will your cousin, the one you went to the prom with, be here today?"

"No, he couldn't be here because he's in South Bend with his mother."

"Did he ignore you at the prom?"

"No, he even danced with me. He's a really good dancer."

Emmy and Kristen returned to the party and found Derrick surrounded by a group of the popular kids from school. Emmy saw Bert Hodges there with Dawn Matuzak. Dawn waved at Emmy, but Emmy didn't respond.

Derrick broke away and joined Kristen and Emmy. He saw Emmy looking at Bert and Dawn. "Bert's parents are friends with my parents and belong to the same country club. That's why he's here."

Kristen scrunched up her face as she offered her opinion of Bert. "He's an egotistical, pompous ass, and those are his good qualities."

"Bert made a few passes at Kristen before she convinced him to leave her alone. She threatened to tell Uncle Carmen if Bert didn't stop bothering her," Derrick said while munching on some chips.

Kristen smiled and grabbed a few chips from Derrick. "He left me alone after that."

"Kristen, do you mind if I take Emmy for a walk?" Derrick asked. "I want to have some time alone with her."

"Go ahead, I'll cover for you."

"Thanks. We won't be gone too long."

Derrick took Emmy for a walk along the trail at the back of the property. On their way back, they met Annie O'Dell and Matt Sullivan, two other kids from Roosevelt High. Annie was the granddaughter of Principal Liam O'Dell.

"Hi, guys."

"Hi, Derrick. Hi, Emmy. You know Matt, right?" Annie asked.

"Sure, we've talked a few times. Good to see you, Matt. This is my friend Emmy Colasanti."

Matt smiled at Emmy and noticed her pretty blue eyes. He knew her from school but didn't remember ever talking to her.

"Emmy, our dresses are almost the same," Annie noticed. "A bit of difference in the color."

"Yours looks much nicer. Mine is getting old." *I hope no one sees us together. They'll think my dress is so faded.*

"It still looks very pretty on you."

"Thanks, Annie."

"We were heading back to the house," Derrick explained. "We'll see you guys later."

Emmy stayed with Derrick and Kristen as much as she could, but she found herself alone at times.

Later, Derrick saw Emmy sitting by herself and walked over to join her. "Em, I'm sorry, but I've got to mingle with my parent's friends and relatives again. Do you want to meet some of the relatives? Almost all of my aunts and uncles are here, and you can meet them if you're interested. I know my uncles are kinda

238

intimidating, but they're really teddy bears once you get to know them. Kristen is going to be busy helping Mom and the caterers in the kitchen for some time."

"I'll be all right by myself for a while." Emmy begged off meeting his rich relatives. "Go ahead and do what you have to do."

Emmy walked past the pool house and saw Derrick's so-called friends hanging out at the fire pit and drinking beer. She saw Barry Newton. "When did you get here? I didn't see you before."

"I just got here a few minutes ago, Emmy. Are you still going out with Derrick? I assume you are since you're here today."

"I think yesterday was our last date because he's going to be in Europe for most of the summer, and then... well, you know as much as I do about his plans for school. Kristen went with us yesterday, so I don't know if you would call it a date. We're really more like friends. He sees other girls besides me. They're the ones he really dates. Are you still going out with Linda Bailey?"

"Still am."

"Unbelievable! I would have thought she would dump you for a... taller boy." Emmy started to say "more handsome boy," but she remembered Barry was self-conscious about his looks and decided not to tease him so much. "Where is Linda?"

"She's at work. She couldn't get the day off because her boss is a real jerk." Barry raised his voice because the other kids were getting rather loud.

A couple of the older guests heard the kids getting rather loud and stood at the corner of the pool house.

Emmy saw them and grabbed Barry's arm. "Look! I think those men are kinda upset."

"You're right, Em. I wondered why these kids were hiding back here to do their drinking. I bet Mr. Keasling will be pissed that they brought beer."

Seeing all the beer cans, the men left to find Derrick's father.

Emmy wondered about Derrick and Kristen. "Where are you guys? I wish you were with me," she whispered as she looked around.

"Did you say something, Emmy?" Barry asked.

239

"Oh, nothing. Have you seen Derrick and Kristen lately?"

"Can't say that I have," he answered.

Bert and Dawn approached with two cans of beer. Emmy saw them and turned toward Barry. "I don't want to talk to those two."

"Me, neither," Barry whispered.

But it could not be avoided.

Dawn popped open the beer and handed it to Emmy. "Here, have a beer." Emmy took the beer. Bert handed Barry a beer also.

Emmy tried to hand the beer back to Dawn. "I don't want this, Dawn!"

"Go on. It's just a beer. Hasn't your father ever let you taste his?" Dawn waited for Emmy to take a sip. "Or does he hog it all?"

At that moment Mr. Keasling and Uncle Carmen walked around the pool house and saw Barry and Emmy holding a beer. They also saw all the rest of the beer. Dawn smiled thinking Emmy would be in deep trouble now.

"I told you I didn't want a beer!" Emmy shouted at Dawn before she saw Mr. Keasling.

"What's going on back here?" Uncle Carmen bellowed and everyone shut up.

He startled Emmy, and she dropped the beer can, splashing her dress in the process.

"Crap! Mom will ground me for life if she smells beer on my dress."

"You're busted now, Colasanti," Dawn jeered.

"I know you kids aren't twenty-one," Mr. Keasling hollered. "Barry Newton, give me that beer." Mr. Keasling held out his hand.

Barry handed the beer to Mr. Keasling. "Emmy and I weren't drinking."

"I know." Mr. Keasling rested a hand on Barry's shoulder as he and Uncle Carmen turned to face Bert and Dawn.

"You can stay if you want, but there will be no more underage drinking on my property," Mr. Keasling warned as Uncle Carmen scowled menacingly.

For years the kids heard rumors that Carmen Lombardi

240

might actually be the boss of the local organized crime family; Uncle Carmen used the rumor to his advantage. Dawn Matuzak and Bert Hodges left along with several of the other kids, while Mr. Keasling and Uncle Carmen went back to join the rest of the adults.

"Thanks, Barry," Emmy said as she checked her dress. "Did you see the look on Dawn's face when Mr. Keasling understood we hadn't been drinking? She looked so pissed."

"She's nothing but a tramp and a troublemaker."

"Do you know where there's a restroom out here, Barry? I really need to find one. I need to take care of something."

"I'm not sure, but there's probably one in the pool house. Come on. I'll go with you, and we can check."

Barry led her away from the other kids, and they headed for the pool house. They walked around the corner and saw some of the older guests from the party watching them.

"Why are those people staring at us, Barry?" Emmy asked.

"I don't know. Maybe they think we were causing the trouble by the fire pit."

She and Barry stepped inside the pool house.

"I see why now." Barry picked up an empty beer can." Those kids must have been drinking in here, too."

"There's a bunch of beer cans." Emmy saw them scattered on the floor. "They couldn't even bother to throw them in the trashcan. Will you throw that away before you get caught again?" She took the can from Barry and tossed it in the trash. "I think this is a bathroom."

Barry looked into the room. "I do believe you are right. That appears to be a toilet," Barry said.

Emmy smacked his arm. "Wait for me, Barry. I don't want to be in the pool house by myself."

"I'll be right outside, Emmy. I won't leave you."

She locked the door and made Barry wait. Emmy did what she needed to and then turned on the faucet to wash her hands. *Darn it! That's all I need. First I get beer on my dress and now this water splashes me.* Emmy opened the door holding her dress, not knowing what to do.

241

Barry looked at her dress. "What happened?"

"What do you think happened?" she said sarcastically. "When I turned on the faucet, the water came out so fast."

"Let me try to wipe it up for you, Em."

Barry closed the door and locked it. He took some paper towels and wiped her dress for her.

"Be careful where you're drying it." Emmy held her dress away from herself as Barry dried it as best he could.

"Sorry. I didn't mean to touch you. That's about all I can do, Emmy. The sun will dry it off soon enough if we go back outside."

"Thanks, Barry. I'm sorry I snapped at you."

Barry took Emmy by the hand. They hurried out the side door and nearly ran over an elderly couple talking to each other. For some reason Emmy stopped as she heard the elderly lady's voice; she thought she recognized it. Emmy noticed they both wore white panama hats.

"I'm sorry. I didn't mean to run into you. Are you all right?" Emmy asked.

"We're fine, child."

They stopped for a few seconds, and the old man, wearing sunglasses, gazed right at her. Emmy looked at the lady and thought she knew her somehow.

Barry grabbed Emmy's hand again and pulled her away. "Come on, Em. Let's stand in the sun."

Emmy let Barry lead her away. She still didn't know what to do about her dress. A thought popped into Barry's head. He grabbed a bottle of water, which he intentionally spilled on her dress.

Emmy stared at him. "Barry! Why did you do that?"

"I don't know. I'm sorry. I guess it seemed like a good idea at the time."

"Well, it wasn't! Now my dress is even wetter." Emmy pushed Barry in the shoulder. "Such a dork."

"I'm sorry, Em."

"It's all right. I didn't mean to yell at you."

They returned to the other kids, and Barry spilled more water on her dress. This time accidentally. Emmy gave him a dirty look and said, "Will you stop doing that?"

Barry apologized, "I'm sorry, Emmy. I'm so clumsy."

At that moment, they both remembered an incident from their past and laughed.

"Remember when you spilled water on me at Darby's?"

"I remember. We were just kids."

"You were a dork then, Barry, and you're still one now. But you're still my friend regardless."

Randy Braun, the senior class president and valedictorian, staggered over to talk to Emmy. "How did your dress get all wet, Emmy? Did you fall in the pool?"

"I spilled a bottle of water on her dress because I'm such a klutz," Barry said as he touched the front of her dress.

Randy mentioned very seriously, "I've got a secret to tell you, Emmy."

"What is it, Randy?"

Randy waved his hand for Emmy to come closer. Randy told her his secret with the utmost sincerity. "I've never had a beer before today. I drank two or three cans, and now I don't feel so good. I think I might be getting drunk."

Emmy knew from experience he was already wasted. She smiled at Randy, took his hand and pulled him over to a lawn chair. "Sit here for a while, Randy, and be a good boy."

"Okay, I will. You are so pretty, Emmy."

Randy smiled at Emmy and promptly puked. Emmy jumped back just in time to avoid getting nailed. Her foot caught on a coiled garden hose, and she landed with a thud on her butt.

Barry saw her fall and hurried over. "Are you all right, Emmy?" He offered a hand to help her up.

She grabbed his hand. "Nothing is hurt other than my pride. Did anyone else see me fall?"

Barry looked around. "I don't think so. Why?"

"Because I fell like a klutz, and I'm wearing a dress." Emmy tried to check the back of her dress. "Barry, do I have anything on my dress?" She turned her back to him.

"You've got some dirt and grass stains right here." He wiped away the dirt, and then, pouring water on the stain, he tried

243

to rub it off.

"Barry! What the hell are you doing?" Emmy yelled.

Derrick returned and eyed Barry's hand on Emmy's dress. *I'd move your hand before she smacks you.* "I'm back. I heard there was some excitement."

Emmy pushed Barry's hand away and explained. "Barry came to my rescue when I had a little problem."

Derrick grinned then said, "Dad explained about the beer."

"I really didn't drink any, but it spilled on my dress."

"I know."

Derrick looked at Randy, as he vomited again, and shook his head. He turned back to Barry, "Are you all right? How many beers did you have?"

"I drank one when I first got here, but I'm not going to have any more."

"Are you all right?" Derrick asked Emmy.

"I'm okay. I had to jump out of the way..." She pointed at Randy. "and I tripped on that hose and fell on my butt. I think I ruined my dress."

Kristen rejoined them, and Emmy showed Kristen her problem.

"Don't worry, Em. Come with me, and we'll take care of everything."

Kristen took Emmy up to her bedroom and found a pair of shorts and a t-shirt that might fit Emmy. Kristen hugged her tightly when she started to get emotional and wiped her face with a Kleenex. "It's okay, Emmy. It's okay. Please don't cry. Try these on. I'll toss your dress in the dryer, and it will be dry in a few minutes."

Emmy removed her dress, put on Kristen's clothes and checked the dress. "I should be able to get the grass stains out when I wash it."

They returned to the party fifteen minutes later.

"Is everything okay now, Em?" Derrick asked.

"Everything is all right now. Thanks to Kristen."

The DJ finally arrived and set up his gear. He started his show with "Blood On The Dance Floor" by Michael Jackson.

Emmy, Derrick, Kristen and Barry started dancing in a group as they listened to the music. Emmy felt much better now that her dress was dry again and didn't smell of beer. She and Kristen sang along with the music, and they sounded pretty good. Later, Barry danced with her as the song "Don't Speak" by No Doubt played.

"I'm so happy we are good friends again. I missed being your friend."

"I was always your friend, Em. We just didn't hang out together," Barry said.

Later, Emmy asked, "Kristen, could I use a phone to call my mom? She's expecting me home soon, and I'd really like to stay later."

"Sure, there's one in the kitchen. Follow me." Kristen took Emmy into the house. "It's right there."

"Thanks." Emmy dialed home. "Mom, would it be all right if I stay out a little later tonight? Derrick will bring me home."

"What time do you think you'll be back?"

"Maybe ten or a little later."

"Okay, but make sure Derrick and Kristen bring you home. I don't think your father feels well, and he's already in bed. I don't want to have to wake him up to go pick you up. You know I can't drive at night, or else I would come and get you."

"Okay, Mom. Don't wait up for me. I've got my key."

As soon as the sun set, Derrick lit a bunch of candles.

"What are those for?" Emmy asked.

"They're citronella candles. They're supposed to keep the mosquitoes away."

Barry slapped his arm. "They're not working."

"Give them time." Derrick laughed.

Emmy and Barry stayed until the end—the last guests to leave the party. They hung out with Derrick and Kristen on the deck until after ten.

"Derrick, I can give Emmy a ride home. It's no trouble. Then you don't have to make the trip."

"Thanks, Barry, but Emmy promised her mom that I would bring her home, and I really want to be able to say goodbye to her."

"Oh, yeah. I guess you don't want me along when you kiss her," Barry teased.

"Barry! We're just friends." Emmy protested by poking Barry in the ribs.

"If you say so, Em."

"You're a creep."

Derrick gave Emmy a ride home and walked her up the front steps. He held her in his arms, and she wrapped her arms around Derrick's waist. Neither one wanted to let go, so they held each other without saying a word.

Finally, Derrick broke the spell. "Emmy, you are the sweetest girl I know, and I'm gonna miss you when I leave. I'm jealous of Barry."

"Why would you be jealous of Barry? He's only a friend. We've known each other for a long time."

"That's why. He has known you so much longer than I have."

"Derrick, that's so sweet of you. I gotta go in. Have fun on your trip to Europe and send me postcards from everywhere you visit, all right?"

Derrick kissed her cheek once very tenderly before he said good night. Emmy ran to her room, changed her clothes, fell on the bed and hugged her pillow to her chest as she daydreamed about Derrick until she fell asleep.

Ten days later, Emmy and Diane dropped in at The Mole's Den. Emmy screamed as she discovered a brand new release by her favorite band, Fridays At Five.

"What is it, Emmy?" Diane asked.

Emmy held out the CD. "Kenny didn't tell me this was ready to be released. It's called *Transitions*, and I'm going to buy ten copies."

Diane took the CD from Emmy and smiled. "Maybe you could buy two copies, but you don't need ten."

Emmy took it home and listened to it over and over as she wrote another letter to Kenny. Track number eight "Sweet Girl" became her favorite song. She already knew all the words by heart, but this version was more of an uptempo rock song than the ballad Kenny first sang to her. Emmy read the liner notes and found Kenny mentioned her as the inspiration for the song. Emmy held the CD to her chest, and tears filled her eyes. It still surprised her that Kenny, already a big star, would remember her that way.

Diane walked into the bedroom and sat on the edge of the bed. "Are you going to keep playing that CD all day?"

Emmy hid the letter behind her back. "I'm going to play it until I memorize all the lyrics. Then I'll play his first CD."

Diane put a hand on Emmy's knee. "Have you seen him or talked to him since he left?"

Emmy shook her head. "We write letters."

"I ran into Owen Porter yesterday," Diane said. "I could ask him about Rory."

"I haven't seen Rory since he dropped out of school."

"Would you like to see him, Em? I know you had a crush on him," Diane said as she tickled Emmy's knee. "And don't deny it. I know you guys did some stuff together."

Emmy pushed Diane's hand away. "We never did..."

"Maybe you didn't... you know, but I know you can't keep moping around waiting for Kenny to come home. Should I ask Owen if he knows where Rory's living?"

Emmy thought about it for a moment. "No, if he wants to see me, he knows where we live."

"Let me know if you change your mind, Em," Diane said and then left the room.

Emmy lay on her back and stared at the ceiling as she thought about Rory. *I can't think about him. Kenny will get home sooner or later.* She sat up and finished her letters to Kenny.

Emmy grabbed her letters and dashed into the kitchen. "Mom, I'm going to run over and see if Mrs. Colwell is home. I won't be gone too long."

"All right, but your father will be home by six. I made dinner, and I expect you to be here." Mom sounded upset because Diane ran out of the house a few minutes earlier without saying a word.

Emmy ran over to the Colwell house, bounded up the front

247

steps and rang the bell.

"Emmy, how are you? Come on in."

"Hi, Mrs. Colwell. Mr. Colwell. I'm sorry to bother you, but I saw the new CD. I have more letters, too." She held them up.

"Nonsense," Mr. Colwell said. "You are always welcome here. You were the band's first fan, remember? Have a seat on the couch and talk to us."

"I'll make sure he gets your letters, dear." Mrs. Colwell placed them on the coffee table. "Kenny always asks about you whenever he talks to us, honey."

"I'm surprised he still remembers me. We haven't talked since he left, and I miss him," Emmy replied. "I should get back home."

"Oh, don't leave yet, Emmy. Kenny sent something for you. I'll be right back."

Emmy stood up as Mrs. Colwell left the room and returned in a minute with an autographed copy of the CD.

"He mailed this from Japan."

Emmy opened the jewel case and a folded piece of paper fell on the floor. Emmy picked it up, opened it and read it. Kenny had written a short note to her and placed it on the back of the front cover.

She bit her lip as she looked up at Kenny's mom. "Oh, Mrs. Colwell, he still remembers me. I miss him so much. My heart just aches whenever I think of him."

"He still cares for you, Emmy." Mrs. Colwell took a tissue and wiped Emmy's tears away. "He won't ever forget you."

"I hope not," Emmy said as she hugged Mrs. Colwell.

When she got home, Emmy placed the CD in the bottom of her music box where she kept her most cherished mementos.

Chapter Twenty-Three

Hey, Derrick and Kristen,

I miss you guys so much. There's nothing to do here and I am so bored. I'm working over at Darby's to earn some spending money. I haven't seen Kenny since Christmas, and I really, really miss him. He won't be home until next year. He won't even be home for Christmas. He writes to me, but I can't really write back because he's always on the move. I get postcards from different places. We did finally talk on the phone on my birthday, but that's not the same as being together in person. I guess he wants to see other girls because he told me that I need to date other boys, but I don't really know anyone that I want to go out with. Maybe I will meet someone when school starts.

I got your postcard from Venice. Did you go on one of those gondolas? That looks like fun. I know we haven't known each other for too long, but I feel as if I've known you forever. I miss you. Oh, I guess I already wrote that, but I do miss you, Kristen, and I guess I miss Derrick, too. Keep the letters and postcards coming. They give me something to look forward to. Bye for now.

Love, Emmy

It was mid-July of 1997, the summer before her last year of high school. Emmy's seventeenth birthday came and went without much fanfare. Grandma Sandusky took Emmy and Diane to La Cantina to celebrate, but her parents only gave her a card. Although Emmy had seen Derrick and Kristen in June, it seemed longer. At least Kristen gave her an address in Milan, Italy, where the Keaslings would be staying whenever they were not traveling. Emmy knew that sooner or later, Kristen would read her letters.

Emmy gave serious thought to graduating after the first semester ended in January. She kept this idea from her parents because she thought they would forbid her from doing so. She also checked into the possibility of going to college. She couldn't think of anyone in her family who had graduated from college. She knew Diane did not plan on seeking a college degree though she had been taking a course at the local junior college.

"Hey, Mom." Emmy stood in front of her mother's recliner.

"What is it? Are the dishes done?"

"Yes, I finished the dishes and the kitchen is clean."

"Thank you. I'm glad that one of my daughters is willing to help out around here. I don't even see Diane much," Mom said.

"I need to talk to you and Daddy about something important. Do you have the time?"

Her father turned down the volume of the TV. "Will you bring me a beer, Emmy? Then I'll listen to you."

Emmy grabbed a beer from the fridge.

"Now what's on your mind?"

Emmy sat on the couch, faced her parents and took a deep breath. "I want to go to college."

"Pfffft!" Mom waved a hand dismissively. "Don't be ridiculous."

"Now hear her out, Patricia." Dad frowned at his wife. "Why do you want to go, Emmy?"

"I would like to earn a degree that would allow me to have a career and support myself."

"Why don't you look for a full-time job and start earning money. You will probably get married someday. Your husband should be the one with a college degree." Mom looked at her husband for confirmation.

"But I enjoy school." Emmy slapped her thighs.

Dad sat in his recliner drinking his beer. "Diane is taking a class, but I'm not sure she even goes. I know you've always been more serious about school."

"If you want to waste your time on college, you will have to pay for it yourself." Mom pointed a finger. "Your father and I can't afford to send you to a fancy college just so you can meet boys and party like Diane and her friends."

"I'm not like Diane. It's not my intention to go to college to party and meet boys. I want to get a college education, and if I have to pay for it myself, I will." Her eyes filled with tears as she stood up and put her hands on her hips. "And I'll do it without any assistance from you, or Grandma, or anyone else. I'll get a job and

250

pay my own way through college. I don't care if it takes me twenty years. I will earn my degree." She stopped crying and left the room.

"This is just a phase. Once she graduates from high school and gets a job, she will get over this foolish idea of going to college," Mom said and then turned her attention back to the TV.

Dad finished his beer. "I think you are underestimating her, Patricia. She can be very stubborn, and she's smart. If anyone in this family could get a college education, my money would be on Emily."

Friday, as Emmy was leaving Darby's after her shift, Sophia Hidalgo and Chloe Andersen stopped her in the parking lot. Sophia rolled down the window of her Ford Escort. "Hey, Emmy, whatcha doin' tonight?"

"Nothing that I know of. Why?"

"Chloe and I are gonna go to a party in Crest Ridge. You wanna tag along?"

"What kind of party. Where's it gonna be?" Emmy asked.

"There's a group of kids who meet at the O'Brien house. They let us hang out there and tonight the guys are having a party. Nothing fancy," Sophia said.

Chloe removed the rubberband holding her dishwater-blonde hair in a ponytail and added from the passenger seat. "The O'Brien's have three sons and the youngest one in probably close to your age. There will probably be twenty kids at the party."

"I would have to let my mom know I'm going," Emmy said. She didn't want to tell Sophia and Chloe that she really needed to ask for permission.

"The party is supposed to start at seven. Let us know if you can go, and I'll pick you up."

"Okay, I will. Thanks, Sophia," Emmy said as she watched her coworkers drive away. *Pigs will fly before Mom lets me go to a party in Crest Ridge but thanks for the invite.*

Emmy asked her mother about the party. Mom agreed to let Emmy go after talking to Mrs. Hidalgo who vouched for the O'Brien family. "I'm only agreeing to this because it's Friday."

"Thanks, Mom." Emmy hugged her mother and then called Sophia. "I can go if you pick me up and bring me home."

"We can do that. Your house is only three blocks away."

Emmy got ready, sat on the couch and stared out the window. "They're here! I'm going."

"Have a good time, Emmy," Mom said without taking her eyes off of the TV.

Emmy ran out the front door, and climbed into the back seat. "Thanks for picking me up."

"No problem, Emmy." Sophia pulled away from the curb.

Chloe turned her tall, skinny frame around enough to talk to Emmy. "Have you seen any good movies lately? Sophia and I saw *Jerry Maguire* the other day."

"I saw that, too. I loved it. I love movies about sports."

Twenty minutes later, Sophia parked on the street, and they jumped out. Emmy could hear some kids talking as she looked at the two-story stone house. Her eyes were drawn higher and higher. *That's a really steep roof.*

"Come on, Emmy. We usually hang out in back by the garage. There's a large driveway patio kinda area."

Emmy followed Sophia and Chloe around the side of the house. Sophia introduced Emmy to some of the other kids. Emmy smiled, but didn't say much. She glanced around and spotted a guy standing in front of a flower bed with a group of people. *Holy crap!* She thought. *He looks like a taller version of Tommy Cruz.*

"Hey, Emmy, are you still with us?" Chloe nudged Emmy.

"Oh, sorry. I was looking at that guy over there."

Sophia laughed. "Yeah, I know why. He does look like him, but obviously it's not him. Want me to introduce you?"

"Oh, I don't know. He's hanging out with those guys."

"Those are the O'Brien brothers. Ronan, Patrick and Sean. This is their house," Sophia said. "Their parents are Irish, and they have this accent."

"It's called an Irish brogue, Sophia," Chloe said. "I love Ronan's and Patrick's red hair and freckles. I would go out with either of them in a heartbeat."

"Whatever. Anyway, it's kinda hard for me to understand

252

because I'm from Mexico, obviously," Sophia said as she glared at Chloe. "Come on, Emmy. You have to meet them, at least, since this is their place."

Sophia brought a reluctant Emmy over to meet the brothers. Emmy smiled as Sophia introduced everyone, but she kept stealing glances at the Tommy Cruz lookalike. He ended his conversation with the three girls who surrounded him.

"Hey, Scott, this is Emily Colasanti. We met at Darby's. She's going to be going to school at Roosevelt this year," Sophia said.

Scott Simmons looked in her eyes and smiled. "Hello, Emily. It's good to meet you. I went to Lincoln High, but I've been to basketball games at Roosevelt. Are you friends of the O'Briens?"

"No, I don't know them. I'm here with Sophia and Chloe." Emmy looked up at Scott, who stood about a foot taller than her. *You really do look like him. Except your nose isn't as big.* She couldn't help but giggle.

Scott wondered why she giggled, but didn't for a second think she was laughing at him. "I'm glad you could make it tonight. Mr. O'Brien is going to grill some burgers and stuff and Mrs. O'Brien makes a mean potato salad."

Emmy stared into his dark brown eyes, and then stammered, "I... I like potato salad." She took a step back, caught her foot on an ornamental brick at the edge of the flower bed and landed with a thud on her butt. She muttered a curse under her breath. *What a great first impression I've made. Someone just shoot me.*

Emmy heard some of the other guys laughing, but not Scott. He reached out a hand and helped her up. "Are you okay?"

"I'll be all right. I think I just bruised my pride." Emmy wiped the back of her jeans. *Why did I have to giggle like a little girl. He's gonna think I'm such a dorky kid. And 'I like potato salad.' Come on. He's not Tommy Cruz. I never act like this around Kenny, and he actually is a celebrity.*

"I'll introduce you to some of the other kids if you want," Scott said as he looked around for some younger kids. *Thanks a lot, Sophia. All I need is some klutzy young kid trying to hang out with me.*

"Thanks, but you don't have to. I'll stay by Sophia," Emmy answered shyly. She bit her lip and looked around for a place to hide. *At least no one really knows me here.* She saw Sophia and Chloe standing with the other girls. They were all grinning and trying to stifle their laughter.

"I'm sorry, Emmy," Sophia apologized. "We shouldn't be laughing at you."

"It's okay. I would be laughing, too, if I had seen me trip and land on my butt."

Scott didn't ask, but assumed Emmy was much younger than the other kids. The way Sophia introduced Emmy made him think she would be a freshman when school started.

Emmy listened to him talking to the other kids. *Crap! He must think I'm a clumsy child because I could barely talk to him. Somehow I'm gonna prove to him that I'm an intelligent young lady.*

Emmy looked around and counted over twenty kids. Nobody drank any alcohol or smoked, and very few of the kids paired up as couples. Four kids played Bean Bag Toss, and several others played croquet in the large lawn at the side of the house. The O'Brien brothers and three other guys played basketball on the concrete court next to the large garage. Emmy watched the guys play and wished she could join them, but they were shoving each other around. She didn't want to get hurt.

"Is there an apartment up there?" Emmy pointed to the second story of the garage.

Sophia nodded and said, "Never been up there, but I know it's an apartment."

Later, Scott gathered the kids around. "Why don't we meet at the ballpark over on Frontage Road and 59th tomorrow afternoon? We could catch a game, and then meet back here. I'm sure the O'Briens wouldn't mind. I'll buy a case of pop if someone else could buy some ice..." Scott mentioned some other things they might need.

"That sounds like a plan. Emmy, do you want to join us?"

254

Sophia bunched her long, straight, jet-black hair into a ponytail.

"I'd like to, but I don't know if I can get there. I don't have a driver's license or a car."

"I'll pick you up and bring you home. It's not too far out of my way."

Saturday afternoon after the game, the kids gathered at the O'Brien home to socialize. Emmy saw a basketball under the basket and started shooting around. Sean, the youngest O'Brien brother and the only one of the brothers with blonde hair, joined her after a time.

"Hey, nice shot." He passed the ball back to Emmy after she swished a shot from the corner. "Think you can make two in a row?"

She grinned at him. "Do I get a prize if I do?"

"Maybe. I'm Sean, by the way."

"I'm Emmy. I came over here yesterday with some friends." Emmy shot again, but the ball bounced off the rim.

"I saw you watching us play ball. Where do you go to school? Crest Ridge Central?"

"No, I go to Roosevelt. How about you?"

"I graduated from Central, and now I'm working for the park district at the golf course."

"Don't your parents get tired of having so many kids hanging around? I know my parents would freak."

"They like having the kids around. Almost everyone is from the church we attend."

Sean's brothers and Scott interrupted his conversation with Emmy before she could ask about his church.

"Hey, Sean, are you up for a game? Who's your little friend?" Ronan asked as he grabbed the ball.

Emmy walked away as two more guys joined in. The guys picked teams and started playing.

Emmy watched Scott as he interacted with the other kids. *He is so confident, but he doesn't act like he's full of himself like Bert Hodges or Todd Delaney. He really has a way of making people feel like they matter. Hmmm. Plus, he's a fox.*

255

Scott noticed Emmy. *She's really cute for a freshman in high school. I should introduce her to some of the younger guys.*

A week later, Emmy joined the Crest Ridge group, as she came to think of them, for a baseball game on Friday evening. Halfway through the game her thoughts turned to the kids she knew at Roosevelt High. She nearly gagged as she thought of some of the guys she knew.

"Are you all right?" the girl sitting next to Emmy asked. "You sounded like you were choking."

"I'm fine. Do you know these kids?"

""Yeah. I go to church with most of them. I'm Serena."

"Emmy. I'm new to the group."

"You'll like them. They are different. They have fun without smoking and getting wasted on beer to be cool."

"I've noticed that," Emmy said.

"They don't try to force anyone to conform to certain social standards to be cool, but accept people for who they are."

Emmy glanced over her shoulder at Scott as he sat three rows behind her. *He seems like a friend already, even though I've really just met him. I can't think of him as a possible boyfriend. After all, he could choose from any of the older girls in the group.*

Just then the batter hit a foul ball which sailed high in the air toward them. Emmy stood up thinking she might catch it. She heard the girls sitting in front of Scott scream as the ball started coming down. She turned around as the ball was definitely behind her. Scott and Ronan O'Brien reached for the ball, and it bounced off their hands and popped into the air in front of them. Emmy kept her eye on the ball and grabbed it.

"Hey, nice catch... kid," Scott said as he smiled at her. He nudged Ronan, "Hey, do you remember that girl's name?"

"The one who caught the ball?"

"Yeah." Scott kept his eyes on Emmy.

Ronan shrugged. "I can't remember. Is it important? You could just ask her."

"Doesn't matter. She's just a freshman in high school."

Emmy threw the ball back onto the field, and then turned

256

back to look at Scott.

"Oh, Scott, thanks for saving us. I thought that ball was going to land on my head," Mitzi Singleton squeaked.

Emmy listened to the girl sitting in front of Scott, rolled her eyes and thought. *Can you make it any more obvious that you like him. Geez, you just have to use your hands and catch it.*

Scott listened to Mitzi as he grinned at Emmy. He tuned out Mitzi as he thought about Emmy. "Hmmm. Too bad you're so young. I like a girl who can stand up for herself."

"Did you say something?" Ronan asked.

"I was just thinking out loud."

Ronan said, "Mitzi still has a crush on you."

"Hush! Mitzi may be an airhead, but she still has ears."

Emmy caught Scott smiling at her. She felt her face turn red as her heart began to race. She turned around and bit her lip.

Emmy rode home with Sophia. She sat in front and looked out the window without really seeing anything as she thought about Scott. *Why do I always react this way when he smiles at me? What would I do if he ever really flirted with me? I should see if Diane will talk to me about him. She'll know what to do.*

Sophia poked Emmy in the side, interrupting her thoughts. "Are you all right? You've been staring out the window and haven't answered me."

"Sorry, my mind was somewhere else. What did you ask?"

"Doesn't matter now. It wasn't anything important."

Sophia pulled into the alley and dropped off Emmy.

"Thanks again for the ride. See you later."

Emmy dashed through the yard, up the back steps and into the kitchen. "Diane, can I talk to you for a minute? I want to tell you about this guy I met. I'm not sure how I feel about him, but he kinda gets me all flustered."

"Sure, Emmy. Give me a second to finish these dishes or Mom will get after me."

Emmy helped Diane finish the dishes, and then they went to their bedroom. Diane sat on the edge of the bed as Emmy plopped down in the middle. Diane looked at Emmy. "All right, tell me about this guy."

"His name is Scott Simmons, and he's part of the group that I've been hanging out with. He's twenty-one and in his last year of college."

"Twenty-one! Geez, Em, he's pretty old for you. He's almost as old as Craig. Go ahead. Sorry I interrupted. Scoot over." Diane moved Emmy over and laid down next to her.

"He's really good-looking, like movie star good-looking, and outgoing, and the girls all like him. Some of them are pretty obvious that they are into him in a big way. I asked Sophia about him, and he doesn't have a steady girlfriend, but he takes some of the girls from the group out. The other day I saw him kissing one of the other girls..."

"Has he kissed you at all?"

"No, and I'm sure he has never thought of me like that. I don't think I would let him. I'm pretty sure he thinks I'm way too young for him."

"You want me to find out if he's a good kisser? I'm a pretty good judge of that," Diane teased.

"Don't you dare." Emmy poked Diane in the ribs.

"He might be a real hunk from what you've told me, but it also sounds like he's not very loyal to any one girl. I know I'm never sharing a boyfriend again, and I can't see you sharing a boyfriend with other girls, if that's what you wondered about."

"Yeah, I think you're right. Thanks for listening, Diane. I wanted to get your opinion."

"Anytime, Em." She paused and looked at Emmy. "I know you miss Kenny."

"I miss him so much, but he wants me to date other guys because he will be gone for so long."

"Do these new friends know about your relationship with Kenny?"

"I haven't told them, but Sophia and Chloe might know because Mr. Darby asked about him the other day."

"Has anyone from that new group of friends asked you for a date? Are there other guys? Maybe some younger guys?"

"I think there are a few guys still in high school, but they look like nerds. Most of them are in college."

"Some college guys are nerds, too, Em."

"That's for real."

They giggled as they thought about some of the dorky kids they knew.

"No one has asked me for a date, but I haven't met anyone I would even consider dating."

"Are you sure?"

"Well, the youngest O'Brien brother is kinda cool... then there's Scott."

"I know you like a challenge, and I kinda think you're thinking of this guy in that way."

"No, I'm not," Emmy said emphatically and then bit her lip. *Maybe I am. Maybe I want to see if he will notice me again. God, I wish I could erase that first impression from his mind.*

The phone rang, and Emmy grabbed it before Diane could.

"Hey, Emmy, it's Lynette Rosas. We were at the game together today."

"Oh, right. How's college going?" Emmy didn't know what to say and shrugged her shoulders as she wondered why Lynette would call her.

Diane whispered, "Is that him? Is it Scott?"

Emmy shook her head and mouthed the words. "Go away and let me talk in private."

Diane grinned and tried to grab the phone away so she could talk to who she thought was Scott.

"I finished college in May, and I'm looking for a job." Lynette could hear Diane in the background. "Is this a bad time to call? Are you busy?"

Emmy frowned at Diane. "Nah, I'm not busy."

"I've noticed that you're kinda shy, but I think you're enjoying hanging out with our group. I don't know if any of the other kids have invited you, but would you be interested in going to church with me on Sunday?"

"Maybe, where do you go? What parish?" Emmy asked.

Lynette answered, "It's Crest Ridge United Nazarene. It's on Canton Lane here in Crest Ridge."

"I've been raised Catholic, but we don't go to mass much

anymore. I went with my friend to his church youth group for a while, but Mom made me stop. I went back to church with him when he came home last Christmas, but I stopped when he left... for his job." Emmy still kept her relationship with Kenny a secret.

"That's all right. Several of the kids were brought up as Catholics. Please think about it. I think you'd like it."

"Okay, Lynette. I promise I'll think about it."

Early on Sunday morning the phone rang. "Hi, Emmy, it's Lynette. Have you thought about checking out my church?"

"Yes, I did, and if you're willing to give me a ride, I'd like to go with you."

Lynette picked Emmy up, and, twenty minutes later, they turned off of Canton Lane and into the church's parking lot.

"I appreciate the ride, Lynette."

"You're welcome."

Lynette parked in a lot on the side of the building.

Emmy got out and waited for Lynette. "This place has a huge parking lot. It's like a Walmart or something."

"Yeah, it's pretty big. There's another lot in back, too." Lynette explained as she grabbed her Bible from the backseat.

Emmy glanced up and noticed a cross at the top of the roof as they approached the square-shaped building. *I wonder how big that is?*

Lynette led the way through the foyer and into the large sanctuary.

Emmy looked around and smiled when she saw the padded chairs, sure they'd be more comfortable than hard wooden pews. She guessed there must room for close to a thousand people in the auditorium. She checked out the stage. *Cool! Guitars, keyboard and a drum kit.* The stage was set up for a full band. A grand piano sat off to the side. The service hadn't started so Lynette introduced Emmy to some of her friends. She sat with Lynette in the middle of the large group of teens and college-age kids. Emmy noticed some of the same kids who hung out at the O'Brien house—including Scott Simmons. She bit her lip as she spotted Scott. He noticed Lynette and came over to talk.

260

"Good morning, we missed you in class."

"Sorry, I didn't make it, but I wanted to pick up Emmy."

Scott smiled and said, "It's good to see you again. Nice catch, by the way. I know you were at the game on Friday, but I don't remember if you made it to the party afterward."

"No, I had to leave right after the game." Emmy blushed. She didn't want Scott to know her mother wouldn't let her go because she had to be home by nine.

Scott left and Emmy watched as he sat with a group of guys.

Maybe he doesn't have a real girlfriend.

Emmy looked around and did a quick head count. She realized there must be close to a hundred kids in the group. The service started, and she was pleased to see a full band get up on stage to play.

When the band paused between songs, Emmy asked Lynette, "Is this the way you normally have mass?"

"It is, but we don't call it mass. We call it a worship service. Do you like it?"

"I really like the music. It sounds exactly like a real band."

Lynette showed Emmy the large screens with the words. She sang along with the other teens. Lynette smiled at Emmy as she sang. "You should be a singer. You have a beautiful voice."

"Thanks, Lynette. I do like to sing."

"I can introduce you to the guys in the teen band. They can always use another singer."

"I don't know. Some of the kids might not like it."

"Think about it, Emmy. The kids won't mind. They would love to hear you sing."

Emmy didn't mention singing on stage with Fridays At Five. She thought it might come across as bragging.

After the band finished, a young man walked out on the platform and prayed. Some people passed baskets around for an offering while a college-age girl sang. Emmy cringed as the singer struggled to stay on key. Then the young man came back to the platform to talk to them. Emmy listened to what he said.

He sounds really sincere. Emmy glanced at the other kids.

These kids are sure paying attention.

She didn't understand everything he talked about, but he brought up some points that made her feel as if he spoke directly to her. He read from the Bible and made some suggestions that she understood. She noticed Lynette writing notes on the bulletin, so she did the same thing. The band came back out to play a couple more songs as some people gathered at the front to pray. Emmy watched and though she knew what was happening, she didn't feel the need to join them.

After the service, Lynette introduced Emmy to some of the younger girls.

"Where do you go to school?"

"I go to Roosevelt," Emmy answered.

None of the other kids she talked to went there. They attended either Lincoln High or Crest Ridge Central. A couple of them came from West Bartlett.

That's a long way to go just to attend a church. Emmy stared at Scott for a moment.

The man who gave the talk walked over to talk to Lynette; she introduced Emmy to Pastor Brian Riley.

"Hello, Emmy. It's nice to meet you. Are you a friend of Lynette's?"

"Yes, we are becoming good friends. It's nice to meet you, Father Brian. I really enjoyed your mass... I mean, worship service."

He chuckled before saying, "Thanks, Emmy. I'm glad you enjoyed it. You can call me Brian, or Pastor Brian, if you're more comfortable with that. I'm not a priest, just a youth minister. Pastor Ausland is on vacation, so I filled in today. Boy, I had butterflies all morning. This was the first time I preached in front of the whole church. I was sweating like a big ol' sow."

Emmy giggled because of his honest and down-to-earth personality.

"Come back whenever you can. You'll always be welcome." Brian shook her hand and thanked her again for coming.

"I'd like to come back if I can get a ride."

Brian looked at Lynette. "Lynette, do you think you could help Emmy out with a ride?"

Lynette answered, "I think I can arrange that without too much trouble."

Emmy mentioned to Lynette one Wednesday evening, "I really like the more laid back Wednesday service."

"It's geared for teens. We can't do that on Sunday morning," Lynette explained. "How do you like the teen band?"

"They're actually pretty good," Emmy answered. *I know they're not pros like Kenny and the guys, but they are talented. I wonder if I should mention Kenny to Lynette? Maybe I shouldn't.*

Singing songs took up most of the service. Then Pastor Brian gave a short devotional message for the kids.

Lynette usually sat by Emmy and listened to her sing. "You really should sing with the band. You have the best voice out of anyone here."

"Thanks, Lynette. I do like to sing, but I'm not sure I could." Emmy bit her lip. *If Kenny was here, I would have more confidence. One thing I know is that this church makes a difference in the lives of these kids.*

When school started in late August, Emmy stopped going to church. Lynette called to talk on Saturday evening.

"Hi, Emmy. It's Lynette. I just wanted to see if you are all right, and to let you know that I can still give you a ride to church if you're interested."

"Thanks, Lynette. I've been meaning to call you. I started a new part-time job at the Timbers Nursing Home, and I have to work on Sunday mornings. I really need the money if I want to go to college."

"Oh, that's too bad, Emmy. The teen group still meets on Wednesday nights. You're always welcome anytime you can make it. Let me know if you need a ride."

"Thanks, Lynette. I will."

"I will remember you in my prayers, Emmy. Take care, and I hope to see you again sometime."

Chapter Twenty-Four

"Kristen, I'm so happy we are sharing some classes." Emmy lay on her bed reading through her English assignment.

"It's our last chance since we're both seniors." Kristen used her new Motorola StarTAC cell phone to talk to Emmy. "I'm going out this weekend with Christopher Braun. I could set you up with Randy. He's always liked you. How about it?"

"I know you're just trying to help me, but I don't want to go out with Randy. He's a good guy and all, but... he's not my type."

"Give me a few ideas about who might fit your type."

Emmy flipped over onto her stomach and wrapped her hair around a finger. "Okay, someone who likes music, is handsome and..."

"Kenny isn't here. What else?"

"He needs to like sports."

"If Christopher finds someone, will you at least go to dinner. You can even ride with me."

Emmy thought about it for several seconds. "Fine, but we need to have a secret word to use if I want to bail."

"You've been watching too many TV shows."

"I never watch TV. You know that."

"All right. What's the word?"

Emmy bit her lip as she thought. "How about? Um... let's use 'Jayson.' If I say 'Jayson,' it means I want to leave."

Kristen picked Emmy up, and they met Christopher and Dean Rogen at Beggar's Pizza.

"Why aren't we going to Kerry Lynn's Pizza? That's our favorite." Emmy jumped out as Kristen parked in the strip mall.

"Christopher said Beggar's is just as good, and it's closer to campus. They can walk over here."

"Hey, there's a Wok Wok next door," Emmy said.

The evening started off okay. Dean did like sports and music. He looked all right. He made her laugh. They spent an hour and a half at Beggar's and Emmy and Dean talked about football.

"I've got something I have to show you. It's a football that Walter Payton signed," Dean said.

264

"I'd love to see that!" Emmy's eyes sparkled.

"It's in my room. I could show you that and some other things. My roommate's not there."

Emmy nodded enthusiastically, but as they left, everything fell apart. Dean kissed Emmy.

She pushed him away. "Stop it, Dean. I'm not interested in kissing you."

"Oh, come on, Emmy. I know you're interested. You've been smiling at me and laughing at my jokes all night. Why don't we go back to my place for a while. I can show you the football. I can give you a ride home in the morning."

Emmy turned around, looked at Kristen, frowned and whispered, "Jayson." Then she turned to Christopher and poked him in the chest. "What did you tell him about me?"

"I swear I didn't say anything other than how pretty you are. His social skills are a bit lacking."

"No kidding! Come on, Kristen. We're out of here." Emmy began walking toward Kristen's car.

Dean and Christopher watched them leave and then walked back to campus. "I thought you told me she was Diane Colasanti's little sister."

Christopher frowned as he said, "She is, but she's not like Diane. I told you that."

"I guess I just assumed she would be easy like Diane. I really blew it, huh?"

"Ya think!" Christopher punched Dean's shoulder. "Now Kristen's gonna be mad at me."

In the car on the way back to Emmy's house, Kristen apologized over and over.

"It's not your fault. I guess I'm not ready to date college guys. All they have on their minds is sex. You better be careful, Kristen."

A week later, minutes after her last class of the day, Emmy closed her locker and saw Kristen talking with a boy Emmy didn't know. *Oooh, he's got to be a football player. He's wearing one of those letter jackets.*

Kristen held onto his arm and suddenly reached up and kissed his cheek. Emmy grinned. *Way to go, Kristen! He looks almost as handsome as your brother. He's got to be over six feet, and he looks like a tank.* She couldn't hear what Kristen told him.

"Her name is Emmy. Just talk to her. She won't bite you," Kristen said. "Look at how tiny she is. She couldn't hurt you if she tried. Now get over there and say something."

"What should I say to her?" he asked.

"For starters, try saying 'hi.' Think you can remember that? Now go." Kristen turned and headed the other way without talking to Emmy.

The boy stopped when he got to Emmy. "Hi, I… uh... uh... that barrette is very pretty."

"Thanks, I love the color purple," Emmy answered almost as shyly as the boy.

The boy hung his head and shifted his weight from one foot to the other. "I need to get to practice... uh... see you, bye." He turned to leave and almost ran to get away. Emmy didn't know his name but felt that she should for some reason.

Despite his suspension and ultimate expulsion near the end of the previous school year, Todd Delaney's parents exerted enough influence to allow him to return to school on a probationary status. Upon his return he started pestering Emmy and spreading rumors about her.

"Tell the other guys what I told you about her. She is easy like her sister. She will do almost anything on a date," Todd said.

"Tell me her name again."

"Emmy, Emmy... some Italian name. Just do it, okay."

Emmy tried to ignore him, but Todd kept bothering her, along with a couple of other boys she didn't know. Emmy heard some kids talking about her in the hallway one day and felt despondent because of what she heard around school. She overheard one boy tell another that she would go to bed with anyone who took her on a date.

Two days later, Emmy saw the shy boy after school again, and they smiled at each other. She bit her lip and hoped he would come over and talk to her. *You have got to be a football player. Look at those biceps!* She waited expectantly. When he didn't make a move toward her, Emmy gathered her courage and walked to him.

"Hi, I'm Emmy. We talked for a little bit the other day."

"Hello, I remember you," Tony Bertucci shyly answered Emmy as he stood up against the lockers, almost as if he were trying to disappear into them.

Todd Delaney's voice suddenly rang through the hall, "Hey, slut. I want to talk to you."

Todd's friends hung back, but he marched up to Emmy, put his hand on her arm and tried to pull her toward him.

"Ohhhh crap," Todd muttered as the young man picked him up and held him against the lockers.

"I think you should apologize to Emmy right now," Tony said without raising his voice.

Holy crap! You lifted him up like he doesn't weigh more than a feather. Emmy stared in amazement as her heart raced.

Todd's buddies turned and sprinted away as soon as they saw what happened. Todd mumbled an apology to Emmy."

"I'm sorry, but I didn't hear you. What did you say?" Tony asked.

"I'm sorry I called you a name, Emmy."

"I don't think you should call any girls by that name any more," Tony said.

Todd nodded his head and promised. "I won't, I swear it."

Tony set him down. Todd ran for his life.

Emmy looked up at Tony as tears began to form. "Thank you for doing that. That jerk and his friends have been bothering me ever since school started."

Emmy was so grateful for what he did that she stood on her tiptoes, reached up, pulled him down to her, and felt his heavy stubble on her lips as she kissed him on the cheek. She experienced a very brief memory flash of a little boy. "You didn't tell me your name the other day. What is it?" She bit her lip as she looked up at him trying to fight back the tears.

"I'm sorry, I forgot."

Emmy giggled, and then smiled at him.

"I mean, I remember my name. I forgot to tell it to you the other day. It's Tony, Tony Bertucci."

Emmy looked at him and thought that she knew that somehow. She looked at his brown eyes eyes and thought of Derrick Keasling. "You're the linebacker, aren't you?" she asked.

"Yeah, number fifty-two." He was surprised that such a pretty girl would kiss him—and a senior at that. "I'm sorry Todd and his friends have been bothering you. I don't think he will anymore, but if he does, let me or one of the other football players know, okay? Do you know his friends' names?"

"No, I don't know, but I might recognize them if I see them again. I only saw them from the back because they took off running as soon as they saw you."

"Sorry, I didn't see them. Did I tell you that I play football? Oh yeah, you already know that. I start at linebacker on the varsity, and I'm a junior." Tony looked at Emmy bashfully. "I've always been kinda shy with girls, but Kristen told me you were nice and kinda quiet, too."

Tony kept talking to Emmy, and she realized that despite his shyness, he possessed an intelligence and maturity that exceeded his age. She meant to ask him how he knew Kristen, but it slipped her mind as they talked.

He certainly is so much more muscular than any other guy I know. She checked his arms.

He concentrated on her eyes. *She has the prettiest eyes I have ever seen and when she smiles... Oh, man.*

She remembered seeing him play football now. "You're number fifty-two." She mentioned again as if that number should mean something to her.

He stared into her eyes. "Yes, that's always been my favorite number."

Emmy decided to take a chance and be brave. "If you ask me, I will go out on a date with you." The prior thought that he might be Kristen's new boyfriend faded into the deep recesses of her mind. She remembered that Kristen only dated guys in college now. She used her best smile and flashed her blue eyes.

Tony looked at her eyes—totally enthralled. "Emmy, would you like to go out with me sometime?" He managed to ask without shyness. She was the first girl he ever asked for a date.

"I would like that very much. I'll be happy to go out with you, even if you are a shy junior." She thought he looked very handsome in a rugged way. He kept his straight dark hair neatly-trimmed. His heavy five-o'clock-shadow made him look older than a high school student, and, at over six feet tall, he towered over Emmy. She noticed a small scar on his chin and thought it must be from playing football. His dark brown eyes danced with youthful excitement. His arms looked bigger than her legs. She also knew he excelled at football—her favorite sport.

He had to get to practice, so Emmy walked along with him. He waved goodbye as he entered the locker room. Emmy walked home and called Kristen.

"Kristen, you'll never guess who asked me out."

"Let me guess, who could it have been? Could it have been... Tony Bertucci?"

"Yeah! How did you know?"

"Just a lucky guess."

"We were talking in the hallway, and Todd Delaney started bothering me, and Tony stopped him and scared the crap out of him. I think he peed his pants right there in the hallway. Todd, not Tony!" she said and then giggled. "I don't think I'll have any more trouble with Delaney."

"I'm so happy for you, Emmy. I really am."

A few days later, Tony picked Emmy up at her house. He opened the passenger door for her and then ran around the car and got in. "I made reservations at Ciao Bella. I hope that's all right."

"Oh, I love that place," she answered. Emmy thought about the family-owned restaurant in The Hill neighborhood. *That's such a cool area.*

"I like the center of the neighborhood with all the restaurants and other shops," Tony said. *Actually I've never been in any of the other businesses, but I've walked past them on my way to Ciao Bella.*

269

"That little area used to be like a downtown business district. Grandpa told me. I love the way the brick buildings are all right up against each other." She glanced over at Tony. *I hope I didn't sound like a kid talking about Grandpa like that.*

"I hope you don't mind walking."

"I know it's not easy to find parking. I don't mind if we have to walk a few blocks." Emmy remembered holding Grandpa's hand as they would walk through the neighborhoods of SoHam.

"I usually drop my mother off, and then go find a parking spot," Tony said.

"So you're like her own valet service, huh?" Emmy said as she grinned.

"I suppose so. Would you like me to drop you off?"

"No, I'd rather walk with you, but thanks for asking."

They drove along without talking for a time.

I wonder if the radio works? Maybe he doesn't like music. Emmy kept her eyes away from Tony.

They arrived in The Hill, and within five minutes Tony found a parking spot.

"We're just three blocks from the restaurant." He pointed to the south. "The river is over there."

Emmy glanced at the lovely old homes along Baltimore Street, admiring a particularly nice one with a wrought iron fence *Some of these look like they're older than Kenny's house. I'd bet they're the original ones.*

They turned the corner onto Fell's Point.

"Ciao Bella is down at the end." Tony motioned.

"I love this street." Emmy glanced at the different businesses. "I've been in that dress shop and that old book store."

Tony said, "It's amazing that cars can even get past each other. The street is so narrow, and I read that it was originally paved with bricks."

They reached the end of the block and climbed the three worn marble stairs to Ciao Bella. Tony opened the door and immediately heard a familiar voice.

"That's Mr. Sabatino," Tony told Emmy.

Mr. Sabatino, the owner, seated them at a table along the

270

wall.

"It's good to see you again, Tony. How is your mother?"

"She's doing great. This is Emmy Colasanti, Mr. Sabatino."

Mr. Sabatino bowed. "It's a pleasure to meet you, Miss Colasanti." He tilted his head as he gazed at her. "Excuse me for asking, but would you happen to be related to the late Joseph Colasanti?"

Emmy grinned and said, "He was my grandfather. My grandparents brought Diane and me here when I was a little girl."

"Joseph and I were good friends. By the way, I highly recommend the special tonight—Chicken and spinach manicotti. It is one of my wife's greatest creations." He waved his arm.

Emmy giggled as she remembered how Mr. Sabatino liked to be theatrical.

"What would you like to drink, Miss Colasanti?"

"Could I have a Coke, please?"

"Certainly."

"A Coke would be all right with me, sir."

Mr. Sabatino snapped his fingers at a waiter and made a simple hand gesture. Two Cokes appeared within seconds.

"Would you like an appetizer, Emmy?" Tony asked as he sipped his Coke.

Emmy touched the rich burgundy tablecloth, lay the white cloth napkin on her lap and then picked up the leather bound menu.

"They have breaded mozzarella sticks and stuffed mushrooms. Do you like either of those?" Emmy asked.

"I do. Let's order both."

They ordered the appetizers and decided to try the special.

Emmy glanced around the room. It appeared exactly as she remembered. She loved the vineyard mural on the wall. She stole a few peeks at Tony as he munched on the appetizers. *His shoulders are so broad, and his arms are so muscular. I must look like a little girl compared to him.*

Later, Tony took a large bite of his entree. "This is really good. It tastes a lot like my mother's."

"Is your mother a good cook?" Emmy smiled as she smelled the special, and then took a much smaller bite.

"I think she's an excellent cook, but I might be kinda prejudiced."

Emmy finished her entire entree. "Look, Tony, I cleaned my plate. I usually can't finish everything, but it was so good. I don't know if I can eat another bite."

"Would you like to split dessert? They have ice cream."

"You might have to eat most of it, but I'll have a few bites."

As they ate the ice cream, Tony noticed Emmy's small hands. *I bet my hands are twice as big. She looks so young, but I know she's in Kristen's class. Maybe she's actually younger and just skipped a year or two.*

After dinner, they went for a walk in the park along the river. They walked next to each other without the need to fill the air with trivial conversation. They stopped for a moment, and Tony looked down into her eyes.

"Emmy, you are so pretty. You have great eyes, and your hair looks so nice. I love the way you smile and the way you bite your lip at times. You're not stuck up like most of the other popular girls."

"I'm not really one of the popular girls," Emmy replied.

She could tell that he was sheepish and bashful about giving her compliments. He didn't really know what to say or how to say it. She felt as shy and bashful now as Tony. Yet, somehow he restored her self-esteem on that one single date.

Could this someone I could actually date? She contemplated this as she stared up at him.

She gave him a good night kiss on the cheek at the end of the date. "I had a great time tonight, Tony. If you want, I would like to go out again sometime."

Tony answered quickly, "I would like that very much, Emmy. I'm kinda busy with football right now, but I would like to see you again."

She whispered, "I don't think you should be so shy with me, and I'll be your friend... forever."

Chapter Twenty-Five

"I saw Tony in the hallway on the second floor, but I didn't have a chance to talk to him," Emmy said as she and Kristen walked through the cafeteria carrying their food trays. "I don't know if he saw me or not. I thought we both enjoyed going out, but now I'm not sure if he's interested in a second date. Do you ever see him or talk to him?"

"Sure, why wouldn't I?" Kristen turned her head to smile at Mr. Hallecki, the first-year science teacher. "Maybe you should cut him some slack because of football season. He practices every day and lifts weights. If he wanted to take you out it would have to be on a Saturday, and I know you sometimes have to work on Saturday nights."

"I suppose I should be patient. I really did have fun the night we went out."

"Has he ever called you?" Kristen asked.

"He did a couple times, but I was at work." Emmy pointed to a table with several empty seats. "Let's sit over there."

"Maybe I'll rattle his cage a little and remind him that he needs to call you."

Emmy and Kristen went to the football games together, and they usually stayed for the dance afterward. Kristen occasionally brought her college guys to the games and dances. Emmy felt a little envious of Kristen because of her self-confidence and popularity with the college crowd. Emmy felt more comfortable with the freshman boys.

One Friday night as she and Kristen left the dance floor to sit down to take a break Emmy looked around the multipurpose room and asked, "Doesn't Tony ever come to the dances?"

"Not usually during football season. He heads home after the games to let his mother know he's all right. She worries about him."

Emmy mumbled, "I wonder if his mother treats him like mine does."

"What did you say?"

Emmy turned her head as two guys started shoving and yelling at each other.

Kristen continued, "Everyone calls his mother 'Mama' except my mom. She's the only one Mama lets call her by her real name. I think it's because Mama helped Grandma raise Mom." Kristen looked at the two guys who were now moving closer to where she and Emmy sat. "Hey, are you listening to me, Emmy?"

"Did you say something, Kristen. I'm sorry. I've been watching these two jerks and didn't hear a word you said."

"Forget it. I'll tell you later when you're listening."

"Did you see that? That guy punched the other one, and now they're coming this way. Look out!"

Emmy didn't have time to get out of the way as the two brawlers crashed into her and knocked her to the floor. One of them landed on top of her.

"What the hell do you think you're doing? Get off of me, you sorry excuse of a bastard!" Kristen's jaw fell as Emmy let loose with a string of expletives.

Three teachers ran over and pulled the two guys apart. As they did, Emmy punched the guy, who had fallen on her, in the belly.

"Emmy! Are you all right?" Kristen asked as she helped her to her feet.

"I think so, but that guy landed right on my chest," Emmy replied as she rubbed the spot where he landed.

Once Kristen knew Emmy wasn't hurt, she started to giggle.

"And just what is so funny about me almost getting smashed by that jerk?"

"I don't mean to laugh, but do you realize what you called him? I've never heard you use such language before."

Emmy blushed, "I'm sorry. I kinda lost my temper and used some words I learned from my parents. I've heard them swearing at each other all my life. I try not to talk like that, but sometimes it just comes out."

"I would get grounded for life if Daddy heard me use that

274

word."

"Did I use the *f* word?"

"Yeah, you did! Several times, in fact."

Emmy bit her lip, "Do you hate me now?"

"No, of course not," Kristen said, and then added, "Uh-oh, here comes Mr. Kemmerick, and he looks upset." Kristen referred to the school vice-principal.

"Emily Colasanti, I need to have a word with you."

"I'm sorry for swearing, Mr. Kemmerick. I didn't mean to. I got mad, and the word just popped out."

He tilted his head and then chuckled as he looked around. "Don't worry about that. Those guys probably deserved it. Would you tell me what happened?"

"Kristen and I were sitting here, and I noticed that guy in the black shirt push the other guy..." Emmy explained everything as Mr. Kemmerick kept nodding his head. "And that's why I said what I did."

"Did you punch him?"

"I might have. I can't remember."

"Let me rephrase the question. Did you punch him on purpose?" He asked slowly as he shook his head.

Kristen caught on. "I didn't see Emmy hit him, Mr. Kemmerick."

"Good. I didn't think a girl as sweet as Miss Colasanti would do such a thing. The jerk... I mean student... in the black shirt told me you punched him. Obviously, that's not the case."

Emmy bit her lip. "Am I in trouble?"

"No, but maybe you should have that hand looked at. It might swell up on you," Mr. Kemmerick said as he walked away grinning.

Some of the freshman and sophomores asked Emmy to dance; they didn't realize she was a senior. Emmy didn't mind dancing with the younger kids; she felt safer with them. The seniors were more likely to hit on her. Diane's reputation still haunted her.

"Have you talked to Tony lately?" Kristen asked a few days

275

later as she and Emmy walked into the English class. "I told him to call you."

"I haven't talked to him, but I've seen him. I don't think he saw me though," Emmy said.

"I'll have another talk with him. He can be kinda shy at times, and he's really busy with football now."

"Oh, Kristen, did I tell you the news?" Emmy asked as she sat down.

"What news?"

"I'm taking driver's ed now. I'll be able to get my driver's license." Emmy raised her hand for a high-five, but Kristen didn't respond.

"That's so cool, Emmy. I already have my license. Derrick gave me his '96 Acura CL when he left for the University Of Arizona. That's in Tucson, so I get to drive it now."

"He just gave it to you?"

"Well, yeah. He bought a different car, so Daddy suggested he give me the old one. Are you going to buy a car?"

"I doubt it." Emmy shook her head. "I can't afford to on the money I make at Darby's. I use the SoHam Metro to get around."

"I've never ridden the bus. I'd be afraid." Kristen wrinkled her nose. *I've heard they smell awful.*

"The buses aren't that bad. I'm used to riding them."

"That's all right. I'll drive us around."

Emmy sometimes met Barry Newton and Linda Bailey after school to grab a bite to eat. They usually went to Darby's since it was convenient, and Emmy still worked there part-time. One day in mid-October, Barry asked Emmy to go to Darby's without Linda along.

"So what's up?" Emmy asked as they slipped into a booth.

"Do you think I'm too young to get married?" Barry asked.

Emmy took a sip of her root beer, tilted her head and stared at Barry for several seconds.

"Well, do you?" Barry asked.

Emmy shrugged. "I guess it would be better if you had a full-time job, but, okay, I'll marry you."

276

"Very funny, Em. I'm serious."

Emmy stared at Barry again as she continued to sip her drink. "You're serious, aren't you? You really want to marry Linda." Emmy paused, and then realized something. "Oh, my God! Is she pregnant? Have you guys been doing it? Don't you know how to use a condom?" She smacked him on the arm.

He gently smacked her back on her arm. "She's not pregnant and, no, we haven't been doing it. I want to ask Linda to marry me after we graduate."

"Do you mean after you graduate this year, or after you graduate from college?"

"I don't think I could wait until we graduate from college. I want to get married sooner than that. Maybe even in the summer, if I can find a decent job."

"You just want to have sex," Emmy teased and made Barry blush. "I think you should ask Linda to marry you, but wait to get married until you've been in college a couple years at least."

"Linda's not going to college. She's gonna take classes to become a beautician."

"How long will that take?"

"A couple of years, I think. Linda knows more about it than I do."

"It would be better if you wait till you graduate, but I know some couples get married while they're still in school. Are you sure she's not..."

"Positive!"

"Okay, you don't have to yell at me."

Later that afternoon, Emmy sprawled across the bed as she read her history book. Diane's phone rang, and Emmy reached over to the nightstand to grab it. "Hello." She answered as she continued to read.

"Hi, Emmy, it's Robbie."

"Who?"

"Robbie, Diane's friend. We met a while back."

"Oh, yeah, I remember. How are you, Robbie? Diane's not here right now. Can I take a message?"

"Actually, Emmy, I wanted to talk to you. I was wondering,

is Diane still hooked up with Craig Garrett? I thought maybe if they had split up, I would see if she would want to have dinner, but if they are still together, I won't bother her."

Emmy wasn't sure she should give Robbie any information about Diane and Craig, because they fought again last night, and Diane swore she never wanted to see him again.

"I should let you talk to her when she gets home, Robbie. I'll tell her you called. Does she have your number?"

"Thanks, Emmy, she's got my number. Talk to ya later."

Emmy left a note for Diane on the dresser and headed to the library where she met Kristen to work on a school project.

"I got a call from one of Diane's friends today," Emmy said. "He asked about Diane and Craig, and sounded like he wanted to take Diane out on a date. I'm not sure, but I think maybe they've gone out before."

"Isn't Diane still together with Craig?" Kristen asked absentmindedly as she looked through a book.

"They had a major fight last night, and Diane came home really pissed off at him. All they do lately is fight, break up, and then get back together. I wish they would make up their minds."

"How does this picture look?"

Emmy and Kristen worked on their project for almost two hours. When Emmy got home, Diane was on the phone with Robbie.

"I'll be ready at eight. See you then, bye." Diane hung up and looked at Emmy.

"Are you meeting Robbie?"

"He wants to grab a late dinner. He's got something important he wants to tell me, but he won't do it over the phone." Diane wondered what could be so important or secretive.

Robbie stopped by the house shortly before eight. Emmy let him in.

"Have a seat, Robbie. Diane is late as usual. How are you? Want something to drink?" Emmy tried to be a good host, but her curiosity about what Robbie wanted to tell Diane nearly got the better of her.

"I'm ready," Diane announced as she entered the living

278

room. Emmy wondered why Diane had dressed up so much. She wore a short, sexy dress and fixed her hair differently. Emmy thought Diane looked rather slutty because of all the makeup she wore.

Robbie took Diane out for dinner, and they made small talk until Diane couldn't stand the suspense. "Okay, Robbie, what is it that you wanted to tell me?"

"I got called to active duty. I have to report to my unit in two weeks. We will be shipped overseas in a month. I wanted to make sure I saw you alone before I left."

Diane stared at him with her mouth open.

"Can't you say anything?"

"I knew you were still in the National Guard, but I never dreamed you would get called to active duty. You have to leave before Thanksgiving, too. That sucks. Do you know where you will end up?"

"We are going to the Middle East somewhere but they won't, or can't, tell us where yet."

Robbie brought Diane home, and they talked on the couch until midnight. Diane came to bed, and found Emmy still awake.

"What's the news? Tell me, or else I will be up all night wondering."

"Robbie is being called to active duty and will be shipping out in a month. He has to leave in two weeks, and he has no idea how long he will be gone."

Diane started to cry. Emmy sat up in bed and put her arm around Diane to comfort her.

"It will be all right. I'm here if you want to talk about anything."

"Thanks, I appreciate that, but I can't talk about it right now."

Chapter Twenty-Six

"Kristen, are you busy?" Emmy asked as she lay on her bed on Saturday morning.

"Not really, Em. I just finished my homework and turned on the TV. What's up?"

"I have to talk to you right away."

Kristen shook her head. "We are talking, you goof." *You sound excited. I wonder why.*

"I meant in person. This is way too important and sensitive to talk about on the phone."

"Oooh, is it like classified material. Are you a spy, or a detective like Annie O'Dell?"

"This is serious!" Emmy sat up, kicked the comforter off and got out of bed.

"Fine. Should I come and get you?"

"No, I'll take the bus and meet you at the mall."

"I'm hungry. It's almost lunchtime. Let's meet at Darby's. That way you don't have to ride the bus. I'll be there in about thirty minutes. This better be good."

Emmy walked over to Darby's. She waved to Mr. Darby as she walked up to him. "I'm supposed to meet Kristen here. We'll order something then."

Mr. Darby knew Emmy well enough to see she was troubled by something. "You don't have to order something if you're not hungry. You can use a booth as long as you want."

"Thanks, Mr. Darby. I appreciate that." *You try to be all gruff with everyone, but you are always so nice to me.*

Kristen walked in only a few minutes later than she promised. She looked around, spotted Emmy and joined her in the booth. "Traffic was bad. Did you order anything?"

"No, I can't eat a thing."

"Well, I'm gonna get a hot dog." Kristen stood up and walked toward the counter.

"Can we split some fries, please?" Emmy asked.

Kristen turned to look back. "Sure, Em." Kristen waited a couple of seconds.

"Can I have a Dr Pepper, too?"

Kristen grinned. "Yes, I actually have some money with me." Kristen walked up to the counter. "Hi, Mr. Darby. I would like..."

"I heard. What would you like to drink? Root beer or Dr Pepper?"

Kristen giggled and then asked, "Do you remember what all your customers usually order?"

"No, just the ones I really like. Let's see. Two hot dogs. I know Emmy will want one when she smells yours. A large fry to share and two Dr. Peppers. Correct?"

"Could I have a root beer instead?"

"Certainly." He looked at Emmy, who was biting her lip and staring out the window. "I can tell something is bothering her. I hope it's nothing serious."

"Me, too," Kristen whispered.

"She still misses Kenny something fierce. I can tell."

Kristen brought the order back to the booth. She pulled the two dogs and the fries out of the paper bag. "Mr. Darby knew you would want a hot dog, too."

Emmy sniffed the food. "He knows me pretty well."

"Can we eat first before we talk about this important info?"

Emmy answered as soon as she swallowed her bite of the hot dog. "Yes, it can wait."

"You have mustard on your mouth."

Emmy used her hand to wipe off the mustard.

Kristen pointed to a stack of napkins. "We have these. You don't have to use your hand."

"At least I didn't use my sleeve," Emmy teased.

"You're a goof."

They chatted as they ate, but Emmy did not reveal her important information. After they finished, Emmy dumped the trash and took their tray back to the counter.

"Thank you, Mr. Darby."

"You're welcome, sweetie."

She walked back to the booth and slid in across from Kristen. "Now I'll tell you." She paused for a moment, and then

281

began. "I just happened to be coming home from the library the other day, and the bus got stopped at the light at Millner and Reed St. I happened to glance over to my right and guess what I saw."

Kristen slumped her shoulders. "How am I supposed to guess what you saw? Tell me!"

"I saw Craig kissing some woman, and it most certainly was not Diane. They kissed, and then he followed her into the apartment building."

"Maybe it was his sister or a cousin," Kristen said.

Emmy shook her head emphatically. "No one would kiss a sister or a cousin the way he kissed this woman."

"Are you absolutely sure it..."

"Positive! I know what my sister looks like, and this woman didn't look anything like Diane. What should I do? I don't know if I should tell Diane, or not. Should I confront Craig over the phone? Should I just forget about it? What would you do?"

"I'm not sure. If I saw Tony kissing somebody, I would go over and slug him, but I couldn't do that if I saw Kenny kissing another woman."

"There's something else you should know. Diane knows this guy Robbie, and he just got sent overseas on active duty. Diane spent a lot of time with him the last couple weeks. I think she might be involved with him."

Kristen raised her eyebrows. "You mean?"

Emmy nodded her head. "Yeah, exactly."

"So they're both cheating. That's so messed up."

"Ain't it though."

They looked at each other for a moment without speaking.

"Should we ask my mom?" Kristen asked.

"No, Kristen, I don't want anyone else to know. I have to figure this out on my own."

Kristen dropped Emmy off at home.

Mom saw the sad look on Emmy's face. "Emmy, is there anything you want for dinner? I could make pasta or maybe a casserole of some kind."

Emmy hung up her coat. "It doesn't make any difference. Whatever you and Daddy want is fine with me. Do you know when Diane is coming home?"

Mom laughed. "And how would I know that? She never tells me anything anymore. Why?"

"No reason. I just wanted to know."

Emmy went to her bedroom, fell into bed and sprawled out on her back. She looked up at the ceiling and followed a crack from one side of the room to the other.

An hour later Mom poked her head into the room. "Dinner's ready if you're hungry."

Emmy joined her parents at the kitchen table. Mom passed the pot of spaghetti around. Emmy took some, and then passed it to her father. He piled his plate high, and then tore off a hunk from the loaf of French bread.

Emmy put some salad in a small bowl. "Do you want some salad, Daddy?"

He popped the top on his beer. "No, the spaghetti is enough for me."

Mom poured herself a glass of wine. "I heard that the city might have to cut back on the bus lines. Not enough riders."

Emmy looked up at this. She depended on the bus for transportation around the city. No one spoke for the rest of the meal. Her father didn't like a lot of chatter at the table. Mom would sometimes ramble on, but Emmy didn't have anything to say tonight. She kept trying to decide what to do about the situation.

After cleaning up the kitchen, Emmy walked out to the living room. "I think I'm going to read in my room. I'll see you tomorrow."

Mom looked up from her *People* magazine. "Is the kitchen finished?"

"Yes, Mom, and I put the leftover spaghetti away, too."

Dad laughed at the stupidity of one of the criminals as he watched *Cops*. "While you're still up, could you grab me a beer and the can of Planters peanuts?"

Emmy did what he asked before she headed to her room. She still didn't know whether she would tell Diane what she saw.

Diane came home around eleven. Just after her parents went to bed.

283

"Where have you been?" Emmy asked.

"I had to work a late shift at Larry's, and then I went over to see Craig. Why? Did Mom complain about me not being home?"

Emmy sat up in the bed. "Not really. How did things go at Craig's?"

Diane stripped off her clothes and slipped into a long t-shirt. "Are you interested in my sex life all of a sudden?"

"No! I just wondered if things are all right between you two. I don't want to hear details about what you did."

Diane waved a hand. "Things are so-so between us. Are you gonna keep reading for long? I want to get some sleep. I've got an early morning shift."

"I won't be up much longer. I've got to work tomorrow, too."

Emmy worked four hours at the Timbers Nursing Home before heading over to Darby's for a six hour shift. She dragged herself home after that and collapsed on her bed.

Diane came home around eight. "Hey, Emmy, how did your day go?"

"Typical shift at the home. Then..."

"How can you stand working around all those old people?"

"It's not that bad. I read to them, or just listen to them talk about their families. After that I went straight to Darby's."

"Did you eat there? I know Mom doesn't cook on Sunday night."

"Yeah, I grabbed something at Darby's. There is a little bit of leftover spaghetti in the fridge if you're hungry. Would you like me to heat it up for you?"

"That's all right. I can do it myself."

Emmy joined Diane in the kitchen, but still didn't say anything about Craig. By ten they were both in bed, but Emmy couldn't fall asleep. Finally, she poked Diane in her side.

"Diane, I really need to talk to you. You're not gonna like it, and you might hate me, but I have to tell you something."

Diane turned over on her side to face Emmy. "What is it? You're not pregnant, are you?"

284

"No, of course not! How would I get pregnant?"

Diane laughed and Emmy poked her in the side. "I know how. I'm not stupid, but it's not possible."

"Only because Kenny hasn't been home," Diane said. "Go ahead and tell me, Emmy, so I can go back to sleep."

"All right. The other day I saw Craig kissing a woman and saw him go into an apartment building with her."

Diane sat up in bed. "Where? What time did this happen?"

Emmy explained.

"Are you absolutely positive it was Craig?"

Emmy crossed her heart. "Swear."

Diane collapsed back onto the bed and covered her eyes with her hands. "I suspected something like this. He's been a little... disinterested... lately. Crap! He lied to me."

"There's more."

"What else? Did you see something else?"

"No, but I know you and Robbie spent a lot of time together before he left."

"That's none of your business, Emily!"

"How can you get all mad at Craig if you were doing the same thing with Robbie? That's so hypocritical."

Diane turned onto her side and faced away from Emmy. "You don't understand. You're still a child."

Emmy put a hand on Diane's shoulder. "I'm old enough to know what you guys are doing is wrong, and you're gonna screw up your relationship. Isn't it important to you? You always say how much you love him, and now you do this. Maybe it's you who needs to grow up."

Diane slapped Emmy's hand away. "Leave me alone and stay out of my business. Either shut up and go to sleep, or go sleep on the couch. I'm through talking to you."

Emmy turned away from Diane as tears filled her eyes. "I'm just trying to be a good sister."

Emmy kept looking in the direction she knew Kristen would be coming from. She shifted her weight from foot to foot as she waited at Kristen's locker the next morning. Finally, she saw

285

Kristen coming and waved.

"Where have you been? The first bell is about to ring, and I've got to talk to you."

"Okay, let me put my coat and purse in my locker, and we can talk on the way to English class."

Emmy leaned back against the locker next to Kristen's. Kristen opened her locker, placed her purse on the top shelf, hung up her coat and grabbed the two books she needed. She closed the locker without slamming it. "I'm ready." Kristen turned to look at Emmy. "Are you gonna keep wearing that army jacket all the time?"

Emmy glanced down at her clothes, and then at Kristen's. "It's comfortable like my jeans and sweatshirt. I do have a shirt on, too. I'm sorry if I don't have the latest fashions like you." Emmy walked away.

Kristen walked with her. "I'm sorry. I'm not putting you down. I wish I could wear what you do, but Mom won't let me."

"It's okay. Even if I could afford nice clothes like you, I think I'd still prefer my worn jeans and stuff."

"Now tell me your news."

"I told Diane what I saw. Then I kinda confronted her about Robbie, and she got pissed at me. This morning she wouldn't even talk to me."

Kristen waved to a couple girlfriends as they kept walking. "She'll get over it."

"I suppose so. Maybe I shouldn't have said anything, but I feel better that I did."

That night as they ate dinner at the kitchen table, Diane glanced at Emmy from time to time. She would look away if Emmy made eye contact, though. Mom repeated the gossip she heard at work, but otherwise they ate in silence.

"Thanks for dinner, Mom. I'll help Emmy with the dishes."

Even Dad looked up. Diane never volunteered to help with cleaning up.

Emmy stood up and took her plate to the sink. "Thanks, Diane. I appreciate the help."

Mom and Dad moved to the living room and assumed their

customary positions in their recliners. Emmy filled the sink with hot, soapy water and began washing the dishes. Diane stood next to her, waiting to start drying. Neither one spoke.

Diane dried the last plate, placed it back in the cabinet and looked at Emmy. "I'm sorry I got so mad at you, Emmy. I guess the situation upset me, and I had a 'kill the messenger' reaction."

"All day long at school I thought I should have kept my mouth shut, but that wouldn't have been right. I'm sorry I called you a hypocrite."

"You were right, though. That's exactly how I acted. I saw Craig today for lunch, and we had a long talk."

"Did you tell him I saw him with that woman?"

"I told him someone told me, but I didn't say who. He doesn't need to know it was you, Em."

"Did you guys make up?"

Diane chuckled as she hung the wet dish towel on the front of the stove. "We didn't break up."

"That's good. Did you... never mind. I don't want to know."

"None of your business, little sister." Diane looked as Emmy bent over to place the leftover mostaccioli in the fridge. "When are you gonna get some new jeans? Those are getting kinda worn in the seat. Soon you'll have a hole there."

Emmy looked over her shoulder and tried to see what Diane meant. "I like these jeans. Is there really a hole?"

"Almost. They are kinda tight in the butt, too. The guys must like that," Diane said.

"Great! Now I'll have to buy a new pair. And, FYI, there's only one boy at school I let look at my butt."

Diane took Emmy's hand, pulled her into the bedroom and closed the door. "Kenny's not there, Em. Rory's gone. Who are you talking about? Do you have a crush on someone else? Tell me all about this boy. I want to hear everything."

"His name is Tony Bertucci, and he plays football. That's all I'm telling you for now."

Chapter Twenty-Seven

On Friday after school, Emmy saw Tony Bertucci talking to some other football players. She waited across the hall from him for a moment. *Should I stand here until he sees me, or should I be brave and walk up to him?* She decided to be brave and walked up to him.

"Hi, Tony, I'm sorry you guys lost last Saturday. I watched the game on TV."

"Thanks, Emmy. I guess finishing in second place isn't the end of the world. Maybe next year we will win the championship." Tony noticed the purple ribbon Emmy used to hold her long hair in a ponytail.

She looked up at him. "I really enjoyed going out. Do you think maybe we will go out again sometime?" She put her hands together behind her back and twisted back and forth.

"Ask her out, you dumb slug," one of the other players teased Tony.

"What are you waiting for? She's obviously available."

"Maybe I will if you guys back off and leave us alone," Tony said.

Tony was hooked—totally smitten by her charms. The other players left, and he asked, "Emmy, would you like to go out again?"

"Well, let me think about it... well... I suppose I will go out with you again," she teased.

"How would you like to go sledding over at Windsor Park?"

"I'd love to do that. I used to go there with my friend Kenny when we were kids, but is there enough snow?"

"We're supposed to get more snow tonight and tomorrow. How about we do breakfast first, and then go sledding?" Tony asked.

"Yes! What time can you pick me up?"

"Would nine be all right?"

"I'll be ready and waiting at nine. Do you remember where I live?"

288

"I remember." Tony smiled as he watched her walk away. *She has to be the cutest girl in school. Except maybe for Kristen.*

Emmy hurried home, took the back steps two at a time and walked into the kitchen. She took off her coat and hung it on her hook along with her backpack. She opened the fridge and grabbed an apple. She held the apple in her mouth as she walked into her bedroom and untied the ribbon in her hair. She shook her hair out, grabbed the phone, plopped onto the bed and called Kristen.

"Guess who I'm going out with tomorrow."

"Well, let me think... Could it be Brad Pitney, or is it Jayson Mathias?"

"Yuck! I would never go out with him again. I might consider Brad Pitney if he wasn't so old."

"Who on earth could it be?" Kristen laughed.

"Tony asked me out again. Isn't that great?"

"That's perfect, Emmy," Kristen said. "He must really like you if he asked for a second date."

Emmy stuck out her tongue at the phone. "You're the worst best friend in the world."

"So, what are you guys gonna do?"

Emmy talked to Kristen for an hour.

Tony picked Emmy up on Saturday morning and took her to breakfast at The Hungry Lion. She wore her favorite faded jeans and a sweater over her top. She took her heavy winter coat, gloves and a stocking cap, because of the cold weather.

"Have you ever been here before, Emmy?" Tony asked as they got to the restaurant.

"No, I never have. Do you come here often?" Emmy opened her door and got out before Tony had a chance. She looked at the sign above the entrance. "That looks exactly like a hungry lion," she said and then giggled. She noticed the freshly painted green trim on the white building. "Is this like an Irish pub?"

Tony nodded. "It has an Irish theme inside, too. I wouldn't say I'm a regular, but we've been here a few times. The food is really good. There is a bar in the other part of the building."

"Have you ever been in there?" Emmy asked with a grin.

"No, but I did take a look the first time we came here. I was just a kid."

The hostess gave them a choice of a table or booth.

"Do you have a preference, Emmy?"

"I'd like a booth, please."

They followed the hostess, sat down and read the menu.

The waitress came over a couple of minutes later, "Hi, guys. Are you ready to order, or do you need more time?"

Emmy noticed something on the menu that interested her.

"I would like the blueberry pancakes and a Coke to drink."

"Okay, and for you, sir?"

"I would like the Irish skillet with scrambled eggs and wheat toast."

"Anything to drink?"

"A Coke would be fine." Tony smiled at Emmy.

The waitress took the coffee cups with her as she left.

Tony waited until the waitress disappeared and then smiled at Emmy. "We didn't talk about family and stuff on our first date. I'd like to hear about your family."

"I'm not sure I should tell you. My family is rather... uh... dysfunctional. If I tell you about them, you might not want to see me again."

"They can't be that bad."

"You have no idea," Emmy said as she rolled her eyes.

The waitress returned with their Cokes.

"I'd really like to hear more about you and your family," Tony said and then took a long drink of his Coke.

"Maybe," Emmy said. She then talked about school.

It didn't take long for their food to arrive. As they ate their breakfast, Emmy told Tony about her life.

"I was born here in South Hampshire at St. Bart's on July 8, 1980."

"Me, too. On October tenth. Wow. You are actually three months older than me. I never would have guessed that. I knew you were a grade ahead of me, but I thought maybe you skipped a grade or something like the kid on that TV show *Smart Guy*. Have you ever seen that show?"

"I don't think so. I watch *Buffy The Vampire Slayer* sometimes, but I don't watch much TV. My parents monopolize it. Have you seen that?"

"No, that's a chick show. You sure don't look like a senior, Emmy."

Normally, Emmy would be upset with a person telling her that, but this time she didn't mind.

"Where did you go to school before Roosevelt?" Tony asked.

"Well, I went to Robert T. Colwell for grade school, and then I went to Adolph Tockstein. Where did you go?"

"I went to St. Andrew's through sixth grade, and then to Jamie McGee Junior High. Six years was enough Catholic school for me," Tony said and then laughed. "That must be why you are a year ahead of me in school. At St. Andrew's you had to be five when school started in September. If I had gone to public school, we would be in the same grade. Heather went to St. Raymond's, like my mother, but I wanted to attend Roosevelt. My father graduated from there."

"So did my parents. Who is Heather, anyway?" Emmy asked as she added more syrup to her pancakes.

"Oh, sorry, I guess I should tell you. Heather is my older sister. She was born in... uh... seventy-five, so she's a little over five years older than me. She went to Notre Dame and is going to be a doctor. She's actually home this weekend. I have an older brother named Marco. He's two years older, and he went to Roosevelt until... never mind." Tony didn't want to talk about his brother. "Now you."

"I have one sister, Diane, and she's two and a half years older. She graduated from Roosevelt, and now she's working a couple jobs and taking a night class at the junior college. What about your parents?"

"My father passed away when I was three. I hardly remember him, but my mother is still alive. You'll meet her later today. If you want, that is. I thought we could go to my house for lunch or dinner depending on what time we get through sledding. How about your parents?"

291

"I'm sorry about your father," Emmy said as she squeezed his hand.

"It's all right. I don't remember as much about him as Heather and Marco."

I suppose I should get this over with. Emmy took a deep breath. "My parents are old. Really old. Mom was thirty-eight when she had me, and Daddy was over forty. He turned sixty this year. They were at work this morning otherwise you would have met them."

They were quiet for a time as they ate. Then Tony asked, "Did you have a favorite teacher in grade school?"

"I remember two that I really liked—Mrs. Prater for second grade, and Mrs. Saylor for third."

"I had nuns for teachers in grade school. Most of them were all right, but I remember one... oh, man... Sister Maria could be vicious with a ruler."

"What do you want to do when you grow up, Tony?"

"After high school, I want to play football at Notre Dame. That's my dream, anyway. I want to get a degree, probably in business. After college — please don't laugh — I want to play in the NFL for the Bears. That's my ultimate dream. How about you?"

"I want to go to college, too, but I'll probably start at the junior college. I'd like to get a degree in Computational Biology or maybe Neurobiology."

Tony looked at her with surprise. *Kristen told me you're smart, but you sound like a brainiac.*

"I'm kidding. I don't know for sure what I want to study."

Emmy told him things she never shared with anyone except Kenny about her feelings and emotions. Tony was not used to talking about such personal matters with a girl. His jaw dropped when she mentioned having a beer at age nine.

"It's customary for my parents to have wine at dinner. Daddy sometimes drinks beer instead, though. I guess he didn't think it was a big deal that I wanted to taste his beer."

"We would have wine once in a while, but I never had a beer until last summer. I've had champagne at weddings before. I didn't much care for it."

She felt comfortable and safe with him. She even opened up to him about her family.

"My father works for the electric company, and he has a problem with alcohol. He and Mom fight all the time. I'm kinda surprised they are still together, but I think Mom doesn't want to get divorced because of the stigma attached. Do you mind if I ask how your father died?"

"I don't know for sure, but it happened real quick, and my mother doesn't talk about it much anymore."

They finished breakfast, and Tony took her to Windsor Park. They spent two hours climbing up the hill and going down on his sled. He held her in his strong arms, and she had a blast. One time, as they flew down the hill, they crashed, and Emmy ended up in the snow on her back with Tony beside her.

"Are you all right, Emmy?"

"I'm all right."

Tony started to get up, but she stopped him. "Wait! Don't get up yet."

Emmy put her hands on his coat and drew him to her. They looked into each other's eyes for a moment without saying a word. She kissed Tony on the lips, and in that instant realized that she could fall in love with this guy.

They kissed softly and tenderly several more times. She didn't realize it at the time, but her life would never be the same. Tony raised his head, but didn't get up. He stayed on his hands and knees above her and looked at her.

She smiled up at him. *I don't want this moment to ever end.*

"You are the prettiest girl I have ever seen. You have the most lovely blue eyes... and a beautiful smile... and a perfect little nose." He stopped for a second.

"Anything else you want to tell me? What about my ears?" Emmy asked as she smiled at Tony.

He took her stocking cap off and looked at her ears. "Your ears are perfect, too."

"How about my chin?" She stuck her chin out toward him, and Tony touched her chin.

293

"It is perfect also."

"What about my neck?"

"Every part of you is perfect, Emmy." He laughed at her and asked, "What about me? Do I look handsome to you?"

She looked at him and pretended to judge his features. "Well, you're not the ugliest person I've ever seen."

"You're gonna get it."

She laughed and squirmed to get away as Tony tickled her behind her knees.

Emmy now noticed that there were other people around. She had been so intent on being with Tony that she blocked out everybody else. They stood up, climbed back up the hill and took one final run down the side of the hill.

"Tony, that was the most fun I have had in such a long time. I'm so glad you brought me here."

"I like coming here. Sometimes I bring some of the neighborhood kids, and I carry their sleds up the hill for them."

Emmy kept looking into his eyes and thinking about something that happened a long time ago, but couldn't quite remember the details.

"Would you like to stop at Culver's for hot chocolate?" Tony asked.

"I would love some hot chocolate."

They left Windsor Park, drove to Culver's and placed their order.

"This place has the best hot chocolate in the city. That's what my mother claims," Tony said.

"It's pretty good, but my grandmother used to make the best hot chocolate. She died when I was nine."

"I'm sorry."

She bit her lip. *Gee! Why did I bring that up? His father died when he was just a little boy. He probably doesn't want to hear about people dying.*

They spent an hour nursing their hot chocolate. Minutes would go by in complete silence. Both stole glances at the other, but then look away quickly if the other caught them staring.

Emmy grinned as she peered out the window and recalled

her disastrous dates with Jayson Mathias and Dean Rogen. *Tony isn't trying to impress me the way Jayson did, and he's more of a gentleman than Dean. He's kinda classy like Derrick.* She put her elbows on the table and rested her chin in one hand while keeping the other hand on her hot chocolate. She slowly spun the cup around in a circle as she studied Tony's face without trying to make it obvious. *Derrick is probably more handsome, and he's really probably better at kissing than Tony, but I still can't help thinking about Kristen when I think about Derrick. I liked how Tony kissed me. He will probably get better at it if we keep going out.*

Tony stretched his leg and accidentally bumped her foot. "Sorry, I didn't mean to kick you."

"It didn't hurt."

He rubbed his ear, and then clenched and unclenched his hands. He rubbed his chin and shifted his weight around trying to get comfortable. "Did I mention I've never dated any other girl?"

She giggled and then asked. "Have you dated other boys?"

He blushed. "No, of course not. Would you like something to eat?" *What if she really hated the way I kissed her. I wish I was as confident with girls as Derrick.*

Emmy finished her hot chocolate. "That was good." She wiped her mouth with a napkin instead of her hand.

Tony looked at his watch. "Is there a certain time you need to be home?"

"I have all day. What do you have in mind?" Emmy asked. *I hope he's not going to turn into a Dean.*

"I would like to show you where I live and introduce you to my mother and sister."

"I would like that," she said with relief.

Tony took Emmy to his home in the Hampshire Park neighborhood and pulled into the driveway. Emmy jumped out and looked up at the two-story brick house.

"This is nice. It looks homey. My friend Kristen lives in this big mansion. This isn't as big and it looks more like a real home. Have you ever been to Derrick and Kristen's place?"

"Yeah, I've been there once or twice." Tony grinned. *Duh!*

I've been there hundreds of times.

They played outside in the backyard as the snow kept falling down. The snow turned everything into a picture of pure white as if nature was starting over anew. Emmy made snow angels, and they built a snowman together. She felt like a child as she and Tony played innocently in the snow.

"There must be six inches of new snow, Emmy. Don't you love it?"

"It's perfect! Oh, shoot, the rubber band holding my ponytail broke. Do you think you might have one in the house? Wait, I guess for right now I can keep it under my stocking cap."

"I'll find you one when we get in the house."

Soon they got into a snowball fight after she threw one at Tony. She screamed childishly as she ran around the yard. Tony chased her, trying to hit her with a large snowball. She ducked behind a large tree as he pretended he couldn't catch her. She screamed with delight when he finally caught her and tackled her to the ground. Tony looked at her face, and she wanted him to kiss her again, but he didn't. He put some snow on her nose. "That looks much better now." She pouted so Tony said, "I'm sorry, Emmy. I shouldn't tease you so much."

Emmy laughed and threw some snow at him. "It's okay. You're easy to tease back."

They rubbed noses, and Tony lowered his face to kiss her when they heard, "Anthony Peter Bertucci, come inside to eat and bring your friend."

He smiled at Emmy and threw her over his shoulder as Mama Bertucci called for them to come in the house.

Emmy raised her head. *That sounded familiar, but I can't remember why.*

Tony carried her inside to the kitchen, where his sister Heather scolded him, "Tony, will you put your little friend down before you hurt him? Who are you playing with? Timmy Murphy from next door?"

Tony set Emmy down, and put his arms around his mother. "Something smells delicious."

"You have to wait." His mother shook a spatula at him.

296

"Take off your boots before you track up my kitchen."

"Yes, Mama," Tony said. He removed his boots and coat and gloves.

Emmy removed her shoes and stood with her back to Heather and watched the interaction between Tony and his mother. *You look like a perfect Italian mother. Kinda like Grandma Colasanti except you're taller than you are wide.*

Heather didn't pay her much attention until Emmy took off her coat and cap, let her hair fall down, and then turned to face Heather.

Heather looked at her in surprise. "Oh, I'm sorry. I guess you're not Timmy. I'm Heather, his sister." *Why is my brother playing with a junior high girl?*

Tony introduced Emmy to his mother and Heather. "Mama, Heather, this is Emmy Colasanti. We go to school together. This is my mother, Emmy. Everyone calls her Mama."

"Hello, Emmy, how are you doing? I hope you like lasagna. Would you be a dear and help Tony set the table? He needs help." Mama smothered Emmy with a hug and talked to her like a part of the family already.

"How do you like high school, Emmy?" Heather asked while handing four plates to Tony. "Take these to the dining room, Anthony." *You better have a good reason for playing with Emmy.*

"I like it all right, but I can't wait to be finished."

"Four years will pass quickly," Heather said.

Tony laughed and then said, "Emmy is a senior."

Heather looked at Emmy and couldn't believe it. "Very funny, Tony. Do you mind if I ask how old you are, Emmy? Fourteen, maybe?"

"I'm seventeen," Emmy said.

Yeah, I'm not buying that. You sound like a kid. Heather still thought they were kidding, but didn't say anything else about Emmy's age.

Emmy sat down to eat with the family at the dining room table. She admired the mahogany Duncan Phyfe table with matching buffet and China cabinet. She knew it was a Duncan Phyfe because Grandma Sandusky had a similar set. At first she

297

kept quiet but soon joined in the conversation as if she had always been a part of the family. After dinner, Tony disappeared for a minute. He came back holding a piece of purple ribbon.

"I couldn't find any rubber bands, but I found this piece of ribbon that should work. I'll help you fix your hair."

"Thanks, Tony. This will work fine."

Emmy bunched her hair into a ponytail, and Tony tied the purple ribbon to hold it in place. He even tied it into a bow for her. He loved the way her hair smelled and how soft it felt in his hands.

Emmy glanced in the mirror above the buffet table. "Thanks, that looks very nice."

It took nearly an hour for Tony to take Emmy home because of all the snow. Twice he got stuck and used a shovel to free the car. They finally arrived, and he opened the car door and held her hand as they walked up the recently shoveled sidewalk to the front steps. Emmy paused on the first step and turned to face Tony.

"I really enjoyed today. Your mother made me feel right at home," Emmy said, hoping he would ask her out again.

"Would you like to go to the basketball game on Friday? We can see if Kristen and some of your other friends are going, and maybe stay for the dance afterward."

"That sounds like a plan."

Emmy hesitated before going in the house, to see if Tony would kiss her, but he only told her good night and walked down the sidewalk to his car. He waved at Emmy and drove away. Emmy ran in the house.

"Hi, Daddy! Hi, Mommy!" she gaily hollered as she skipped to her room.

Mom and Dad looked at each other, surprised by her cheerfulness. Dad shrugged and turned his attention back to the TV.

Emmy was floating on a cloud and couldn't wait to see Tony again. She looked in her bedroom mirror and saw the purple ribbon in her hair. She carefully untied it and retrieved the key to her music box. She opened the secret compartment and placed the ribbon inside.

Chapter Twenty-Eight

"Hi, Emmy, how are you doing?" Tony shouted in the crowded hallway.

"Hey, Tony. Where's your next class?"

"It's up on the third floor. Math department. I better run, or else I'll be late. I'll talk to you later." He waved, and then took off at a fast pace.

"See ya, Tony." Emmy backed up against the lockers to avoid the stampede of kids hurrying to class.

All week long Emmy and Tony kept running into each other at school—not an easy thing to do in a building as large as Roosevelt High. The enormous building stood three stories tall and took up a whole city block.

Later, Emmy followed Kristen through the lunch line. "Hey, Kristen, I talked to Tony again. How is it that we never met until a short time ago, and now we see each other all the time?"

"Now he knows where your classes are, so he looks for you. You notice him because he is kinda hard to miss." Kristen grabbed a salad. "You probably saw him plenty of times before, but since you didn't know him, you didn't pay any attention." Kristen asked, "How did your second date go?"

Emmy smiled, sighed and said, "It was almost perfect."

Kristen knew Emmy was falling in love. Emmy's classmates noticed a big change in her. Emmy Colasanti could actually talk to people.

Tony took Emmy to a basketball game the next Friday—Roosevelt against Crest Ridge Central. Emmy wore her favorite jeans and her comfortable army jacket. She walked in and heard the sound of sneakers squeaking on the hardwood floor. She searched through the bleachers and saw Kristen sitting with some other Roosevelt girls.

"Tony, I see Kristen. Can we sit with her, please?"

"Sure, if you want."

"You don't mind sitting with her, do you?"

"No, I guess I can tolerate her presence."

Emmy led the way, and she and Tony squeezed in next to Kristen

"Are you here by yourself? No date for tonight?" Emmy asked.

"I didn't feel like putting up with anyone tonight."

Emmy understood the subtle message.

"Hey, Tony." Kristen leaned forward to acknowledge him.

"Hey, Kristen." He waved.

Every kid in school recognized Tony because of his ability on the football field, but he didn't have an inflated ego. He still acted shy and quiet around other girls. Emmy soon realized that Tony's apparent shyness stemmed from the fact he acted politely toward other people and didn't talk about himself. He listened to other people.

At halftime, Emmy, Kristen and Tony headed to the concession area outside the gym. Emmy watched Tony as the girls flocked around him.

Kristen asked, "Are you going to be jealous about all the attention Tony gets from these other girls?"

"No, I won't get jealous. I sorta got used to it with Kenny. He's always got fans vying for his attention."

"I'll be back. I need to take care of something," Kristen said and then headed to the restroom.

Emmy scanned the crowd and saw a familiar face. "Lynette, is that you?"

"Emmy!" Lynette Rosas cried out. "How have you been? It's so good to see you again."

"This is my friend, Tony Bertucci. Tony, this is Lynette Rosas."

"It's nice to meet you." Tony shook her hand.

"Lynette used to pick me up for church," Emmy explained before turning to Lynette. "What brings you to the game tonight?"

"My younger brother, Richie, is on the team. He's number twelve."

"That's the guy our team can't stop," Tony said. "He's really quick, and no one on our team can stay with him."

"You look like a pretty big guy, Tony. Do you play ball?"

300

Lynette asked.

Emmy answered with pride, "Tony plays football. He's a middle linebacker. He made first team all-state this season."

"That's pretty impressive." Lynette looked directly at Tony.

He nodded his head modestly.

"Emmy, I want you to know that you and Tony are welcome to join us at church any time you can make it. We still have our youth group on Wednesday evenings. I remember you used to like hearing the band. We have more kids and all kinds of activities. Do you still have the New Testament Pastor Brian gave you? I can give you another one if you need it."

"I still have the one you gave me, Lynette. Thanks." Emmy felt a twinge of guilt because she knew the New Testament had been gathering dust in her dresser drawer. She hadn't opened it in quite a while.

"Well, it's good to see you again, Emmy. Nice to meet you, Tony."

"It's nice to meet you, too. I hope we have an answer for your brother in the second half." Tony smiled and turned to Emmy. When Lynette left, he said, "She seems like a very nice person, Emmy."

"She is. I don't know how to explain it, but she is different from anyone else I know. She has an inner peace. I think it's because of her church. They are always talking about Jesus there. Lynette used to say these prayers like she was simply talking to her best friend. She didn't use a prayer book or anything."

"We should get back to our seats before the second half starts."

"I'm ready." Emmy realized she almost never mentioned Kenny to Tony. She wondered if he even knew Kenny, or that she and Kenny had a special relationship. She decided not to mention it for now.

Tony took Emmy's hand and led her back into the gym. Emmy thought about Lynette as something tugged at her heart.

"Can you stay for the dance, Emmy?" Tony asked as they sat down. "If you can't, we can go back to your house, but I hope you can stay."

"I can stay out later tonight," Emmy answered. She would much rather spend time with her friends at the dance than go home and subject Tony to her mom's interrogation.

After the game, a local band set up to play in the all-purpose room down the hall from the gym.

"Would you like to dance, Emmy?" Tony asked as the band played their version of "What I Like About You."

"Sure!" Emmy replied surprised. She had him pegged for a non-dancer type.

He pulled her onto the dance floor. They kept dancing as the band played two more fast songs.

"We're gonna play a slow one for all the lovers out there," the lead singer announced.

Tony held Emmy close as they danced. She smiled as she looked up at him.

"Where did you learn to dance so well? I thought you would step on my toes and crush them."

"Mama made me take dancing lessons as a kid. It's strange, but the lessons actually help with football. I have better balance and flexibility."

Tony talked to Emmy about football and school. He had opened up to her so much since they first met. Several of the other girls asked him to dance, and Emmy didn't mind. Later, Kristen danced with Tony and whispered in his ear, "Thanks for taking care of her problem with that Delaney jerk."

"No problem! Let me know if he or anybody else hassles her. I don't think Todd will ever bother her again, but keep an eye on her for me."

Emmy danced with Kristen and a couple of other boys from the football team.

This is how a dance should be. She felt almost giddy.

"Hey, Bertucci, are you here with Diane Colasanti's little sister?" Floyd Maison asked.

"Hello, Floyd," Tony replied impatiently.

"You're not still mad at me for missing that tackle and costing us the game, are you?"

"No, I'm over that game. Anyway, one play didn't cost us

302

the game."

"So, are you here with her or not?"

"Her name's Emmy and, yes, I'm here with her."

Floyd and one of his friends laughed. "Just be careful. You don't want to catch anything."

"What are you talking about?" Tony didn't appreciate what they were suggesting.

"Everyone knows she's like her sister. Just use protection," Floyd said.

Tony balled his hands into fists as Floyd and his friend laughed while walking away. He thought about what Floyd said. *You guys don't know Emmy at all if you think she's like that.* His heart raced as he remembered one other teammate telling him the same thing.

When Tony took Emmy home, she bit her lip as she debated whether or not to let him meet her parents. She didn't know for sure if her father was home. Even worse, she didn't know if he would be sober or not. She decided to take a chance. After all, Tony would have to meet them sooner or later if he was going to be her boyfriend.

"Do you have time to come in?" she asked.

"Are you going to introduce me to your parents?"

"Be ready for a shock."

"I'm ready, Emmy."

She held his hand as they walked into the house. Her parents sat in their recliners as they watched TV. Neither one got up.

"Mom, Dad, this is Tony Bertucci. We go to school together."

Mom looked at Tony and asked, "How tall are you?"

"I'm six-two, Mrs. Colasanti."

"How much do you weigh?"

"Mom! You shouldn't ask him that."

"I don't mean to be rude, Emily. It's just he's so tall compared to you." She craned her neck to look up at him.

Tony sat stiffly upright on the couch with Emmy and talked respectfully to her parents about school and football. He noticed

303

the saggy couch and worn carpeting. Emmy noticed that Dad appeared to be sober. He kept quiet as Mom grilled Tony about everything under the sun.

""Mom! You're worse than a police detective," Emmy complained.

"I don't mean to be, Emmy."

Emmy rolled her eyes and shook her head in exasperation. About the only thing Mom didn't ask about was Tony's father. Tony remained very patient, but finally needed to get home. As he drove, he thought about what he had heard at the dance. *I've got to learn more about Emmy. My heart tells me that she's not like that, but I have to be sure.*

Chapter Twenty-Nine

Friday the nineteenth was the last day of school before the Christmas holiday. Emmy sat in her classes and stared at the clocks. *Is this day ever going to end? I usually like school, but the teachers are just going through the motions today.* Finally, the bell sounded ending the last period, and Emmy ran to meet Kristen.

"What are you doing for the holidays, Emmy?"

"Working some extra hours at Darby's, but other than that, nothing special. How about you?"

"Christmas with the family. Derrick's home, by the way. After Christmas we'll probably spend time in Wisconsin. There's a cabin up there. We'll go skiing and stuff."

"Sounds like fun." Emmy glanced at a clock in the hall. "I should get going. Have a Merry Christmas. Call me sometime."

"Merry Christmas, Emmy. I'll see you later."

Later that night, the phone in the kitchen rang as Mom walked by. Answering it, she spoke for a few minutes before calling Emmy.

"Mrs. Colwell would like to talk to you."

Emmy took the phone from Mom. "Hello."

"How are you, Emmy?"

"I'm fine. Is everything all right with Kenny?"

"Yes, dear. He's fine. The band is in England right now. Mr. Colwell and I are going to fly over to see him. I talked to your mother and asked if it would be possible for you to go with us, but she informed me that you don't have a passport."

"I've never needed one." *Mom wouldn't let me go even if I had one.*

"I'm sorry you won't be able to travel with us. Kenny would love to see you."

"I really miss him." Emmy sat on a kitchen chair.

"I know you work at Darby's, but would you have a few minutes a day to do something for me?"

"Sure, Mrs. Colwell. What do you need?"

"Would you check the mail for us and keep an eye on the house? I'll pay you."

"Oh, you don't have to pay me. I'd be glad to help."

"We're leaving on Monday morning. Would you have time to stop by and pick up a key?"

"I can run over right now if you're gonna be home."

"We'll be here."

Emmy ran over to the Colwells.

"Come on in, dear. Are you happy to be on your break?"

"Oh, yeah. I like school, but I'm glad we get a couple weeks off."

Mrs. Colwell gave Emmy a key and showed her where to leave the mail.

"There are a more letters for you, Emmy. Do you have any letters for Kenny? We could take them with us."

"I do, but I didn't bring them with me. Could I bring them over tomorrow?"

"Of course, dear."

Emmy came back over the next morning with four letters for Kenny.

"Thanks for taking these."

"It's a shame you can't send them to him. He's always on the move."

Emmy smiled as she looked at Kenny's parents. "I read his letters last night. He said he misses me. I thought he would forget about me."

Mrs. Colwell hugged Emmy. "He will never forget you. He asks about you every time he calls."

"How's the tour going, Mr. Colwell?"

Kenny's father refilled his coffee cup and sat at the kitchen counter. "So far it's been great. They are selling out most of the shows. CD sales are still strong for both of them."

Emmy sat on a barstool next to Mr. Colwell. "Aren't the guys homesick at all?"

Mr. Colwell glanced at his wife. "They probably are, but Andy keeps them too busy for them to have a lot of time to dwell on home."

"I better go. I'll make sure I check the house twice a day.

Please tell Kenny I said hi and I miss him."

"We will, dear. Please wish your family merry Christmas for us."

Tony stopped over at the Keasling's house later that morning.

"Hey, what brings you here?" Kristen asked as she came downstairs. "Derrick's not here, yet."

"I need to talk to you and I couldn't wait."

"Let's go downstairs to talk. My room's a mess."

Kristen wondered what was bothering Tony as she led him down to the basement family room. Tony plopped down on the black leather couch, and Kristen sat next to him.

"What is it? I haven't seen you this serious since Grandma's funeral."

"How well and how long have you known Emmy?"

"Let's see," Kristen said. "I guess I've technically known her since September of last year. We met at the Sweetheart Ball."

"What do you mean by technically?"

"Well, Derrick and I saw her over a year before that, but we didn't meet her. I didn't even realize I had seen her until Derrick clued me in."

"You've lost me." Tony shook his head.

"We saw her singing on stage with Fridays At Five. You do know she and Kenny Colwell are best friends, right?"

Tony slapped his forehead. "Oh, my God! She's talked a little about her friend Kenny, but I never realized she meant him."

"You do know who he is, right?"

"I'm not totally stupid. I might have met him several years ago before he became famous."

"As to how well I know her, we became best friends almost immediately. I think I know her pretty well."

"Have you ever heard... stories... about her?" Tony tilted his head as he looked at Kristen.

Now Kristen knew why Tony was so serious. "I should beat you upside the head. Are you seriously telling me you believe those awful rumors about her?"

"So you have heard them. I've heard them from several

sources and now that I know she's best friends with a rock star, well..." He shrugged his shoulders.

"You seriously need to wear a helmet when you play football. Your brain is scrambled."

"She started drinking beer when she was nine."

Kristen held out her hands palms up. "That proves she sleeps around. Anyone who has ever had a drink certainly will sleep with half the guys in school."

"I didn't mean to imply that, Kristen," Tony said angrily.

"Have you met Diane?" Kristen asked.

"Sorta."

"Emmy told me that Diane started having sex at a rather young age. Diane's reputation has haunted Emmy throughout high school. If you ever tell Emmy, I told you this..." Kristen shook her fist at him.

"I get the picture."

"Emmy is as sweet as snow. I mean as pure as snow. And I don't mean yellow snow. It wouldn't surprise me to learn that she thinks babies come from the stork."

Tony laughed. *I know better than that. She knows how to kiss.*

"Either, she's the best actress in the world, and she has all of us fooled, or she's one of the few innocents at Roosevelt High. Which are you gonna believe?"

Tony hung his head. "I'm an idiot."

"True, but I still love you."

"Please, don't ever tell her I talked about this."

"I could use this to blackmail you, but I won't. It will be another one of our secrets." Kristen held out her pinky finger. Tony took it with his, and they swore.

After trying to connect on the phone for several days, Tony finally caught Emmy at home on Tuesday night.

"Hi, Tony, I guess we've been playing phone tag. I've been working a lot of hours at Darby's. How have you been?"

"Doing all right. I got all my Christmas shopping finished. Say, do you have plans for Christmas Eve and Day? I know you probably need to spend time with your family."

Emmy twisted her hair in her fingers. "We don't do much together. We'll probably have breakfast on Christmas Day and open gifts, but that won't take long. What are you doing?"

"Heather is coming home tomorrow, but Marco won't be here. We'll have dinner together tomorrow night. Mama told me to invite you if you didn't have other plans. Would you like to come over? I could pick you up."

Emmy bit her lip as she thought about his invitation. "Sure, I'd love to have dinner with you."

"This year on Christmas Day the whole family is going to Uncle Carmen's house. You could come with me if you want."

"I'll have to think about that, but I'll have dinner with you tomorrow."

"Just let me know what you decide. Talk to you later."

"Yeah, later." Emmy hung up the phone. She paused for a second. *Did he say Uncle Carmen? That's weird. Kristen has an Uncle Carmen, too. It's not a very common name.*

"Mom, did I tell you that I'm going over to Tony's house for dinner tonight?" Emmy asked later.

"I don't remember you saying anything. Did you check the house for Mrs. Colwell?"

"I took care of that around noon."

Mom put her hands on her hips. "What time is he picking you up, and what time will you be home?"

"He's coming over at five, but I'm not sure when I'll be home."

"Just because you're on break from school doesn't mean you can stay out all night. I expect you home at a decent hour."

Emmy sighed and rolled her eyes. "How late can I stay out?"

"You need to be home by ten."

Emmy clenched her jaw and muttered, "Fine. Keep treating me like a baby."

She watched out the front window, and Tony arrived on time. As soon as he stopped the car in front of the house, she grabbed her coat and a small package. "I'll be back later, Mom."

"You need to be home by ten thirty. You can have an extra half hour since it's Christmas Eve."

"All right. I'll try. Thanks, Mom." *Tony will think I'm a child if I tell him I have to be home so early.*

She picked her way through the snow and met Tony on the front sidewalk.

"I'm ready to go."

"I would have come to the door, Emmy."

"That's all right. You don't have to. You've already met my parents." Emmy looked at the car parked in the street. "Whose car is this? It's not the same one you drove before."

"This is Mama's car. It's a '96 Buick Century. She wanted me to use it today."

Tony opened the door for her and then slid around the car and got in. "What's in the package, Emmy?"

"You'll have to wait until we get to your house. It's kinda for the whole family."

Tony pulled into the cleared driveway and into the garage. Emmy noticed the entire driveway and all the sidewalks were clear of snow.

"Did you shovel all the snow yourself?"

"Yeah, and I even did the neighbors next door and across the street." He pointed and then explained as they walked to the back door. "The couple who live there are kinda old, so I do their driveway for them."

"What's their name?"

"It's Murphy. Gerry and Annette. Mama's friends with them. They try to pay me, but I don't take their money. They've been living there even longer than we've been here."

Mama turned and smiled warmly as Tony and Emmy walked into the kitchen. "Hello, Emmy. Merry Christmas. I'm pleased you could be here."

"Thanks, Mrs.... I mean... Mama. I brought this for the whole family. It's not much."

"Why, thank you, dear. Should we open it now or wait till later?"

"You can open it now, but you can't... well, you'll see."

310

Tony opened the package which turned out to be a box of chocolates. "Thanks, Emmy. Can I try one now?"

"You should ask Mama."

Tony turned to Mama. "Can I, please?"

"Oh, I suppose one piece will not spoil your appetite."

Tony took a piece and then held out the box to Mama and she chose one.

Mama took a bite and smiled. "Mint. My favorite. You better offer a piece to Emmy."

Emmy looked over the choices and took a piece of dark chocolate. She bit into it and made a face. "This one's coffee-flavored. I drink coffee, but I don't like coffee-flavored chocolate or ice cream."

"Take a different piece, Emmy. I know what you mean. Mama likes coffee ice cream, but I can't stand it."

"No, it's all right. These are for you guys." She finished the chocolate.

"Dinner will be ready in about thirty minutes. We have to wait for Heather to get back. She's visiting some friends from high school. Tony, I need some help, please."

While Tony helped Mama, Emmy wandered about the living room. She admired the decorations on the ceiling-high, fresh Christmas tree in the corner. She touched one ornament that looked homemade. She turned it over to look at the back and laughed. Tony made it when he was eight. She moved around the room looking at family pictures that adorned the walls and covered most of fireplace mantle. *We don't any family photos hanging up at our house. I wish we did.* She spied a picture of Tony as a little boy. She thought he looked very familiar. Just then Heather returned, and Tony walked out to the living room.

"Heather's home and dinner is about ready."

Emmy forgot about the picture.

After dinner, Emmy and Tony returned to the living room.

"I love the Christmas stockings and the red brick fireplace. Do you use it often?"

"Mama likes to have a fire." Tony looked at the dwindling stack of firewood. "I need to bring in some more wood."

311

They resumed looking at the pictures. Emmy asked him to identify the various people in the pictures, and he did. He showed her a picture of his grandpa, taken as a young man. He showed her a picture of his grandparents with all his aunts and uncles, but her attention was sidetracked because she spotted one of Tony as a young boy that interested her. Tony showed her other pictures of himself as a younger boy.

"You were just as handsome then as you are now," Emmy said.

"Right! I looked like a dork back then. Does that mean you think I still look like a dork?"

Emmy smiled. "Not a complete dork."

"Oh, like a half-dork or something, huh?"

She saw a picture of Derrick and Kristen and wondered why it was here. Tony distracted her from the photos by picking her up and holding her feet to the ceiling.

At that moment, Mama and Heather walked in and Mama yelled, "Tony! What on earth are you doing? Put Emmy down this instant before you drop her on her head."

Heather chuckled at the sight.

"It's okay, Mama. He won't drop me," Emmy answered as Tony set her down on the couch, and she forgot to ask Tony about the picture of Derrick and Kristen.

Mama sat in her brown leather recliner, and Tony plopped down in the other one.

Heather shook her head at Tony and then sat on the couch with Emmy. "How is school going?"

Emmy remembered the first time she met Heather and her eyes sparkled. "It's okay, but I'm still not used to high school. The kids are so much older."

Heather poked Emmy's leg. "I know you're teasing."

"And she's working two part-time jobs."

"Are you having any difficulty with time management?" Heather asked Emmy. "If you are, I know an easy solution."

"What's that?" Tony fell into Heather's trap.

"Simple. You stop spending time with my dorky brother."

Emmy laughed and then stuck out her tongue. "I suppose I

312

could put that time to better use. He treats me like Timmy from next door, anyway."

"I beg your pardon! I've never kissed Timmy or Brenden Murphy before."

Emmy blushed, and Heather tossed a small pillow at Tony. "I only kissed him once."

Emmy looked at Tony and then at Heather. "Who's Brenden Murphy?"

"Timmy's older brother. Heather dated him a few times."

"Mama, please remind me to never tell him anything about my personal life in the future."

Emmy stood up and walked over to the picture of Tony's grandparents and their children. She inspected it closely, and then brought it over to Mama. "Is this Kristen's mom and dad? It kinda looks like them."

Mama took the picture from Emmy and patted the arm of the recliner. Emmy sat down. "These are my parents and this is Carmen. That's Vincent and this is Karla." Mama looked at Emmy. "What is it, dear? You look confused."

"Are you telling me that you and Karla are sisters?"

Mama laughed as she hugged Emmy. "Didn't Tony ever tell you that he and Derrick and Kristen are cousins?"

Heather frowned at Tony. "Why didn't you tell her?"

"I figured Kristen told her. She knew her before I did." He shrugged. "Wait! I told her about Uncle Carmen."

Emmy smiled, got up and stood in front of Tony. "That's right. Silly me! I thought you were talking about a different person. You and Kristen were together the first time I saw you at school. I thought maybe you were her boyfriend at first. Now I know why you guys are so close."

"Well, I'm glad we cleared this up." Mama got up, went into the kitchen and brought out the box of chocolates. This time Emmy chose a piece with a cherry inside.

"Emmy, wanna go downstairs and watch TV?" Tony asked.

"Sure, I think there might be basketball on."

Heather shook her head. *Emmy seems more interested in sports than a chance to be alone with Tony.* Heather stood up and tapped Tony's knee as she walked out of the living room. "Make sure you behave."

Emmy grinned but then looked at Mama Bertucci and blushed. She followed Tony to the basement.

"You've got a pool table. Can we play?"

Tony removed the cover. "Sure. My father bought this."

"It looks brand new." She ran a hand along the polished wood.

Tony handed her a cue stick. "Are you any good?"

"I haven't played for years. Grandpa had a table, but I was too little to really play."

Tony won all three games.

"You cheated." She poked him in the arm. "Can we watch TV?"

He turned it on and they sat on the couch.

Why are you sitting so far away? I won't bite. She scooted closer and put her hand on his arm. "Why did Heather tell you to behave? I thought I was the first girl you ever asked for a date. Am I wrong?"

"Heather was giving me grief. I've never been down here with a girl other than Kristen."

By the time Tony took Emmy home, she agreed to go with him to Uncle Carmen's.

On Christmas morning Emmy ate breakfast with Diane, Mom and Dad. Afterward, they sat in the living room and exchanged gifts. Emmy looked to a spot in the corner. She couldn't remember the last year they bothered to put up a tree.

Diane stood up and went to the kitchen. She came back a couple of minutes later with a tray of glasses, a carton of eggnog and her father's bottle of Bacardi Gold rum.

"Let's have some eggnog before I leave. I'll pour the eggnog. Everyone can add their own rum."

Dad and Mom added rum to their glasses. Diane followed suite, and then everyone looked at Emmy. She looked at her father.

He nodded his head. "You can have some, Emmy. Not too much, though. I remember the first time you tried some of my eggnog. You made such a face."

"I think I'll skip it for now. Maybe next year."

Diane took off fifteen minutes later to be with Craig. Emmy went to her room to change clothes. Tony arrived thirty minutes later. He sat on the couch and noticed the eggnog and rum on the end table in the living room.

Mom knocked on the bedroom door. "Emmy, Tony is here."

"I'll be out in a minute."

Dad sat in his recliner and glanced at Tony, who swallowed nervously. Dad turned his attention back to his day-old newspaper. Tony sat upright with his hands on his lap as he looked around the room. *Why isn't there a tree in here. That spot in the corner would be perfect.*

"Where are you taking Emily?" Dad asked without making eye contact.

"To my house first, Mr. Colasanti. Then everyone is meeting at Uncle Carmen's place. Carmen Lombardi."

Dad lowered the newspaper at the mention of the name. "I went to school with a Carmen Lombardi. Is that who you mean?"

"Yes, my mother is his sister."

Emmy walked out to the living room, and Tony stood. "I'm ready to go," Emmy said.

Mom followed her and sat in her recliner. "You two could stay here for a while."

"We need to go, Mom."

"But this is Christmas, and your father and I will be all alone."

"Mom, you agreed I could go."

"Let them go, Patricia. We can think of something to do while we're alone."

Emmy looked at her father, who grinned wickedly at her mother. Her jaw dropped as she looked at her father then at Tony. She felt her face turn red.

Dad stood up and shook hands with Tony. "Have a good time. We'll see you later tonight."

On the way to his house, Tony grinned at Emmy.

315

She saw the grin. "I'm so embarrassed. I can't believe Daddy said that."

"It's all right, Emmy. They are married."

They spent a few minutes at Tony's house before leaving for Uncle Carmen's.

As they walked out to the car, Heather opened the rear door for Mama and motioned to Emmy. "You can sit in front."

As he drove, Tony patted Emmy's knee. "I should warn you about what to expect. The men will stay in the family room and talk about business while the women get dinner ready. There isn't enough room around the table, so everyone kinda eats wherever they can. The cousins might not all be there."

Mama tapped Tony's shoulder. "Karla told me that none of Carmen's or Vincent's kids are gonna be there. Carmen's sons left after opening gifts this morning, and who knows where Vincent's kids are. She is rather upset about it."

When they arrived, Emmy saw Derrick and Kristen and rushed over to them. "I didn't know you guys are cousins, and I love your dress. Should I have worn one?"

"Who?" Kristen asked. "You look fine. At least you're not wearing that army jacket."

"You and Tony, duh!"

Kristen looked at Emmy. "I've tried to tell you before, but you never paid any attention. I assumed Tony told you."

Emmy saw Mama and Karla talking. "They don't look like sisters at all."

Tony stood behind Emmy and helped her take off her coat. "Aunt Karla looks more like Grandma, and Mama looks like Grandpa. And there's a big difference in their ages. I think Mama is fourteen years older than Aunt Karla."

"I thought the construction business that your father and Kristen's father started was the only connection between you guys."

"Well, at least now you know everything," Tony said.

Emmy looked at everyone. *I wonder about that.*

316

Chapter Thirty

"There's a couple empty seats over there." Emmy pointed. "I need to talk to you about something important."

"Sure, what is it, Em."

Emmy and Tony ate lunch together on the first day back at school. She waited for him to pull out her chair, but he didn't. She sighed and then sat down as he waved to some friends.

"Tony, I have enough credits to graduate early, and that's been my plan, but now that I've met you, I'm not so sure I wanna go through with it."

"Are you going to go to college, Emmy?" Tony asked between bites of his burger.

"I'm going to take some classes at Paul Frank Junior College and I want to get a full-time job. Oh, there's Kristen." Emmy stood up and waved. "My parents can't afford to send me to a four-year college, so I thought I would take classes at Paul Frank. I'm saving up for an apartment that I can share with my sister, too."

"Hi, guys. I'm so happy that school has started again," Kristen said as she dropped into a chair.

"Yeah, it must have been rough in Wisconsin. You had to go skiing and..."

"And I had to put up with Derrick." Kristen laughed. "What are you guys talking about?"

Emmy explained her plan.

"I can understand why, but I'm gonna miss you." Kristen smacked Tony's hand as he reached for her fries.

"I haven't totally made up my mind." Emmy glanced back and forth at them.

"We will still see each other if you go ahead with your plans," Tony reassured her. "I can understand why you need to get a job. Have you checked into any scholarships?"

"Yes, but I haven't heard back yet," Emmy said.

"Are you gonna finish those fries?"

"No, you can have them."

"Thanks." Tony finished Emmy's fries and then returned their trays.

Emmy stuck to her original plan. She graduated early, got a full-time job with Coventry Shield Healthcare, signed up for two night classes at Paul Frank Junior College and continued saving for an apartment. However, Diane quashed Emmy's plan to share an apartment.

"No, Diane, you can't move in with him," Emmy pleaded as Diane packed her clothes. "I thought we were going to get an apartment together. I'm not sure I can afford one on my own."

"Emmy, I've shared a room with you all my life..."

"Don't you like me?" Emmy grabbed Diane's arm.

"That's not the point and let go of me." Diane waited until Emmy removed her hand and then emptied the dresser drawer. "You will have more room for your clothes now."

"I don't need any extra room." Emmy sniffled and then wiped her eyes.

"Crying is not gonna make me change my mind. I need to get away from this family. I want to be with Craig."

"So what am I gonna do? I don't know how much longer I can stay here, either." Emmy sat on the edge of the unmade bed.

"You could stay with Kenny," Diane said.

Emmy jumped to her feet, pushed Diane, and then glared at her. "You're so funny."

"Hey, what's the big deal? You've stayed over there before."

"I didn't tell you this before, but Mom is trying to make me give her my paycheck. She wants to deposit it in their bank and give me an allowance."

Diane grabbed Emmy's shoulders. "Don't you dare do that, Em. That is your money. Haven't you opened a checking account, yet?"

Emmy shook her head.

Diane's shoulders sagged as she sighed. "Geez, Em. How are you planning to get an apartment if you don't even have a bank account?"

"I know you've got one, and I thought we would get an apartment together." Emmy sat on the bed again.

"Go to my bank and open a checking account and don't put

318

Mom or Dad's name on the account. If my bank won't let you open up your own account, then find one that will."

"I was planning to do that already. I do know some things, you know."

"I'm sorry we can't get a place together, but you have to understand and don't you dare move in with Kenny. You're too young to start..."

"I'm older than you were, and, besides, I'm with Tony now. Not that it matters." Emmy plopped onto her back and stared at the ceiling. "We were alone in the basement on Christmas Eve, and he didn't even kiss me. He probably won't ever want to move out of his mother's house."

Emmy kept busy with work and her night classes. Even on the nights she didn't have a class, Emmy often spent her evening at the Paul Frank library simply to avoid going home. She habitually carried a change of clothes with her in her backpack. Many nights she would forget to eat, or grabbed something quick at Darby's. The bright spot of Emmy's week happened when Tony picked her up after work on Friday. He brought her home, and she quickly changed before her parents got home. Tony's idea of a fun date would be hanging out with his football teammates at the basketball games and the dances that followed. On Saturday, Tony would pick Emmy up around noon and take her to his house. They spent the afternoons studying and watching movies in the basement. On Sunday mornings, Tony and Emmy took Mama to mass. Emmy thought about Lynette and her church as she sat through the ritualistic masses. She still sensed something different about Lynette's church that she didn't experience at St. Andrew's.

One Sunday after mass Emmy asked Tony, "Would you ever consider going to a different church?"

"Why? St. Andrew's is close to home. Don't you like it?"

"It's okay. I've been thinking about the church where Lynette attends. I really enjoyed it there."

"I don't think I should go to a church that isn't Catholic, Emmy."

Tony seemed determined to keep attending St. Andrew's,

so Emmy dropped the matter.

Emmy didn't see Kristen for a few weeks and was too ashamed to tell her about the problems at home. Emmy kept it from Tony, too, by deflecting his questions about her relationship with her parents. However, Kenny had purchased a new IBM ThinkPad 380 that allowed him access to the internet even while on tour. Emmy emailed him from the computer at the library and confessed to him about her family problems. He was the only person she confided in totally.

Mom is treating me like I'm ten. It drives me up a wall. She gets on me about spending time with Tony like she used to about you. It's like she never wants me to have a life. She hurts my feelings and Daddy just ignores everything. To make matters worse, he's drinking more than ever. It wouldn't surprise me if they get a divorce soon. Sometimes I even hope they do. I don't know what they will do with the house if they split up. I suppose they would have to sell it. If that happens, who would I live with? Mom would probably want me to live with her, but I get along better with Daddy. I'm sorry for dumping on you like this. How's the tour going? I want to hear all about it.

Kenny replied,

Emmy, I'm sorry about what's happening at home. You know the carriage house is always available to you. Mom would let you sleep in one of the spare rooms upstairs if you'd prefer that.

The tour has been great, but I really, really miss home. It was good to see my parents, but I miss you. We've played in a lot of famous venues. We did Madison Square Garden in New York. I've got a surprise for you. We've added a show in Chicago. Tickets are going on sale this Saturday, but you can ask my parents for comps. I hope you can make it to the show, because I want to see you so bad. Just hang in there, Em. I'm praying for you, and I know things will get better.

Emmy stayed in the carriage house a few times, but didn't

want to take advantage of the generosity of Kenny's parents. She spent a couple of nights with casual friends, but that ended quickly when one of the guys made a pass at her. Diane let her crash on the couch at Craig's apartment, but that created friction with his new roommate, Jorge, who didn't want her around. Often Emmy did not see her parents for days at a time, which suited her fine. The fighting between her parents kept escalating, and Emmy didn't realize her father would stay away for days, also. The family had never been exactly perfect, but now it disintegrated rapidly. She would sneak into the house for clean clothes and raid the fridge for a bite to eat—sometimes while her parents shouted and argued in the living room without realizing she had been there. She spent some nights at Barry's house and slept in his room while he slept on the couch downstairs. She climbed up a tree outside of his window and sneaked in the house without his mother knowing. Barry told his girlfriend Linda everything, and surprisingly, she understood and did not feel threatened or jealous.

Emmy asked Barry, "Is there any room at Linda's house? I don't want your mom to catch me sleeping in your room."

"No. She has six brothers and sisters who are already sharing three small bedrooms. And, uh, Emmy, uh, you don't need to worry about Mom catching you sleeping in my room because, uh, well, I told her."

"What! Why did you tell her? What exactly did you tell her?"

"Don't worry. I told her that you have been fighting with your parents, and she understood. She promised not to tell anyone."

"If your mom knows, then why do I have to climb up the tree and sneak in?" Emmy stared at him with her hands on her hips as she waited for an answer.

Barry smiled at her. "I thought you liked climbing up the tree."

Emmy rolled her eyes at him. "Sometimes you are too weird, Barry Newton."

Early one morning, she awakened and found Barry on the bed with her, both in their clothes. Barry woke up and looked at

321

her.

"Oh, sorry, Emmy. I was so tired last night. You were already asleep with a book in your hands. I took the book and set it on the dresser. I took off my shoes and laid my head down for a second and must have fallen asleep."

Emmy pushed Barry, and he rolled off the bed onto the floor with a thunk.

"Barry, are you all right?" Emmy looked over the edge of the bed at Barry on the floor.

"I'm fine. I landed on my head," he said.

"Well, go downstairs and stay down there where you belong. This is my room now." Emmy smacked him with a pillow and then giggled.

After not being able to reach Emmy at home for several days, Kristen talked to Barry at school and discovered why. She finally reached Emmy at Barry's house.

"Why didn't you ask to stay with me? We have plenty of empty rooms, and you could have moved in with me and not be crashing with strangers."

"I haven't been staying with strangers. I was staying with Barry and..."

"Who could be stranger than Barry Newton?" Kristen interrupted.

"Barry isn't strange, he's just... different, that's all, and we are old friends." Emmy glared at Barry for eavesdropping on her conversation. She waved at him to go away.

"I'm still mad at you." Kristen huffed.

"I've got my driver's license now, but I don't have a car, and it would have been too hard to get to work from your house. There aren't any buses that go to Paul Frank from there," Emmy explained.

"I've got a car. I would have been happy to take you wherever you needed to be. Does Tony know what you've been doing?"

"No, and please don't tell him. I'd rather take care of things by myself and not rely on anybody else."

"But you're relying on everybody else now. Don't you see?

You're depending on your other friends to let you crash. How is that being self-reliant?"

Emmy was afraid to tell Kristen the real reason she avoided staying home—her parents fighting with each other. Kristen came up with a solution.

"How about this for a plan: promise me you will stay home during the school week, and on the weekends you can stay with me if you need to escape from your parents."

After much pleading by Kristen, Emmy agreed to the plan.

"Okay, I'll give it a try."

Emmy stayed at home for a week and a half before she couldn't take any more of the arguing between her parents. She emailed Kenny and stayed in the carriage house. Kristen found out and got upset with Emmy again.

"You promised to stay home during the week. What happened?" Kristen asked as she and Emmy met at Darby's.

"I tried to get along with my parents..."

"You need to try harder. They are your parents, and they do love you," Kristen said.

"You wouldn't understand. Your parents don't argue and fight. Your father isn't an alcoholic. They never have to worry about money." Emmy broke down in tears.

Kristen didn't really know what to say to comfort her friend. She slid onto the bench next to Emmy and put an arm around her shoulder.

"I'm sorry, Kristen. I didn't mean to yell at you, but we live in two different worlds. You have an allowance that's more than I earn by working all week. My parents... well, you know where we live. Sometimes I wish I could trade places with you."

"I don't live in a perfect world, Emmy. We have problems like everyone else."

Emmy looked at Kristen and understood that money did not solve every problem. "Okay, I'll go home and try again, but I'm still going to save for a place of my own."

Chapter Thirty-One

Diane stopped by her parents' house when she knew they would be at work. She held an envelope in her hand and waved it at Emmy. "I've got two extra tickets to see Fridays At Five and can't find anybody to go with us. You wouldn't by any chance know anyone who might be interested in going, would you, Em?"

Emmy slammed her English Lit book closed, jumped up from the dining room table, grabbed Diane's shoulders and shook her. "Do I want to go? Are you nuts? Of course I want to go!"

"It will give you a chance to see Kenny again."

"I've been afraid to tell him I didn't get tickets."

"Now you can tell him you'll be there."

Emmy bit her lip and then gave Diane a hug.

"Hang on, little sister. You don't have to go all emotional on me." Diane broke off the hug. "Who are you gonna take with you"

"Tony, of course."

"Are you sure you want to take him? Do you want him to see you and Kenny together? Think about it."

"Oh," Emmy said. "I didn't think about that." She sat down. "I'm sure I'll get emotional when I see Kenny again, and you don't think Tony will understand, huh?"

Diane laughed as she said, "It would kinda be like me taking Craig to see Robbie."

"Yeah, well, Tony and I have only been on a couple real dates."

"I thought you were seeing him all the time. Aren't you staying at his house all weekend?"

"Yeah, we spend time together, but if we go somewhere, it's to a game or somewhere with a lot of other people around. Most of the time we just hang out at his house."

"With his mother around?"

"Yeah."

"So you haven't...?"

Emmy smacked Diane's arm. "No, we haven't done anything, and I'm not staying overnight."

"Because you still love Kenny?"

"I'm not discussing this with you."

"Whatever. We need to figure out how we're gonna get to the show. Do you think Kenny's parents are going?" Diane asked.

"I know what you want. I'll talk to them."

Emmy sat on Tony's bed with her feet tucked under her as he put his clean laundry away. "Do you want to go see Fridays At Five with me?"

"Sure! I didn't know you got tickets. I thought that show sold out in like two minutes."

"Diane bought them. I don't have a credit card."

"It's in Chicago, right?"

"Yeah, the Spencer Auditorium."

Tony hung up his shirts in the closet and then sat on the edge of the bed next to her. "Kenny must like being a rock star, huh? He probably rides around in a limo and flies everywhere in a private jet."

"I know he loves being in the band and all, but he's not like most rock stars. You know what kind of car he drives?" she asked and then laughed.

"No, what?"

"An old Civic. He lives with his parents," Emmy said. "He's the dorkiest rock star ever."

Emmy had a strange look on her face. *Oh, Kenny, I hope you haven't changed too much in the last year.*

"What are you thinking, Em?"

"I've never told you much about Kenny, have I?"

"I know you guys have been friends for a long time."

"We've been closer than friends. He's the first boy I ever kissed, and the first one I ever...." Emmy threw herself on her back and looked up at the ceiling.

Tony turned to look at her. *I'm not sure I want to hear this if you're gonna tell me about your love life.*

"I don't know how much I should tell you."

Tony stood up. "You don't have to say anything."

"I haven't seen him for over a year. If you come to the

325

show, you might not like what you see because I will get all emotional and stuff. I'll probably hug him and kiss him. I'm sure I'll bawl like a baby."

Tony laughed. "I'm sure it won't be that bad."

Emmy bit her lip. *You have no idea!*

The next day Emmy went over to see Kenny's parents.

"Hello, Emmy. Come on in." Mrs. Colwell waved her into the room. Kenny's father was on a stepladder.

"Carter! Did you knock over this picture?" Mrs. Colwell straightened up a family photo on the fireplace mantel.

"Sorry, I guess I did."

"Hi, Mr. Colwell. What'cha doin'?"

"I'm fixing this crown molding. A piece of it fell off."

"I want to thank you for those nights you let me stay in the carriage house." Emmy sat on the couch with Mrs. Colwell. "I love that floral arrangement. It smells so good."

"It's just roses, baby's breath and carnations, and you're always welcome to stay with us." Mrs. Colwell turned the centerpiece on the low coffee table. "I was going to call you, dear. Kenny booked a limo to take us to the show, and he wanted to make sure you came with us."

"My sister bought four tickets, and I'm going with her."

"There's plenty of room in the limo. Your group could ride with us. Kenny is so anxious to see you again. He's always asking if you've changed or anything."

"I don't think I look any different," Emmy said but didn't tell Mrs. Colwell about Tony.

"You look even prettier than ever."

Emmy blushed.

"We'll get to see him before the show. The guys are ready for this tour to be over. It's been a lot harder than they imagined. Jeremy's wife, Amanda, traveled with them for a while. She's managing the office for the guys now. Frances and Jeff have struggled, too. She wants to start a family, but with Jeff gone." Mrs. Colwell shrugged her shoulders.

"I remember their wedding. It was so lovely."

326

"Dave broke up with the girl he was dating. I can't blame her."

"So Kenny and Dave are the only single guys left."

"Andy Walker isn't married, either. He's just as much a part of the band as the other guys."

"I can't wait to see him, but I'm afraid it won't be the same as before. He probably won't like me."

Mrs. Colwell patted Emmy's thigh. "You don't need to worry about that."

Several days later Tony sat on the Colasanti's living room couch and watched Craig pacing back and forth. Tony looked at the plain walls and noticed a crack in the corner.

"Diane, tell your sister to hurry up. I don't want to be here when your parents get home."

Diane knocked on the bedroom door. "Are you ready yet, Emmy? We need to be over at the Colwell's in five minutes."

"Just give me a minute."

"Craig is getting impatient."

"I'm hurrying. Is Tony all right?" Emmy hollered through the door.

"He's sitting on the couch like he's got a broom handle shoved up his butt."

"Diane! Be nice."

"Come on, hurry up."

Emmy opened the door. "How do I look?"

"Oh, my God, Em! I didn't know you were gonna wear a dress. You look amazing."

"I'm scared to death. I'm sure Tony will hate me when he sees my reaction to Kenny."

Diane smiled. "Try not to attack Kenny when you see him."

They arrived at the auditorium ninety minutes before the show. A security-staff member brought them backstage to a room with cream-colored walls, and another crew member took their coats. Emmy looked around. *My God! There must be two hundred people here. How am I ever gonna see Kenny?* She stood still as she looked around. *You could hold a concert in this room.*

"Where is he, Emmy?" Diane asked loudly enough to be heard above the noise of the crowd, as she raised up on her toes. "Can you see him anywhere?"

"Not yet."

Tony and Craig stood behind the girls. Craig smiled at a blonde who caught his eye. Tony used his height to see over the crowd, but he couldn't spot Kenny.

On the other side of the crowded room, Kenny talked to Andy Walker. A security guard escorted Kenny's parents over.

"Excuse me, Mr. Walker."

Kenny turned around and smiled. "All right! You guys are here. Did the limo ride go okay?" He hugged his mother and then shook hands with his father.

"It was so much better than driving ourselves."

"Don't I get a hug, too?"

"Sure, Dad." Kenny hugged his father and then looked around.

"She's waiting for you over there somewhere." Mom pointed. "I should warn you, though. She's with someone."

"That's okay, Mom. I know she's been seeing Tony Bertucci, but it didn't seem too serious in her emails."

The crowd parted in front of Andy. Kenny froze when he saw Emmy. She was talking to Tony.

"Emmy," he said softly.

Even in the noisy room she heard his voice. She turned to face him, and her heart raced. He held out his arms and smiled. Her lip quivered as she stood still for a moment.

"Go on, Em." Tony gave her a gentle nudge.

Emmy ran into Kenny's arms, and he hugged her tightly. He picked her up and twirled her around. She cried tears of joy at seeing Kenny again, but also tears of sorrow because of her family difficulties. Tony crossed his arms across his chest and watched as Kenny held her until she stopped crying.

Kenny's mind raced. *I want to kiss you so much, but I won't embarrass you in front of everyone.* He softly whispered in her ear, "Everything will work out, Emmy. You'll see. God is in control."

She regained her composure, and Kenny let her go.

"Emmy, it's so good to see you. Let me look at you. I see you're still as pretty as ever. Who's this guy with you?"

"This is my friend, Tony Bertucci. Tony, Kenny Colwell."

"Nice to see you again, Tony. I think we met a few years ago at some kind of social event."

Kenny offered his hand. Tony shook it without crushing it.

Diane pulled her camera from her purse. "Kenny, is it all right if I take some photos, or is that against band policy?"

"You can take all the pictures you want, Diane, as long as you make sure you get some of me with Emmy." Kenny smiled and then added, "Make sure you take some of her with Tony, too."

After Diane snapped enough photos, Kenny brought the group over to see the rest of the band.

Jeff spotted Emmy first. "Emmy! Come here and let me see you. You look all grown up and as pretty as could be."

The other guys treated her as a long lost member of the band.

Mr. Colwell moved next to Tony. "Are you all right? It must seem rather strange to watch her with the guys."

"Emmy warned me that it would be an emotional reunion. She told me that she and Kenny have been close friends for a long time. The other guys seem to be happy to see her, too."

Mr. Colwell and Tony watched as Emmy high-fived Jeff and laughed about something.

"We've known Emmy since she was a little girl. She and Kenny have always been close," Mr. Colwell said.

Kenny and Diane talked secretively to each other as Craig chatted up the blonde he noticed earlier.

"Please, don't say anything to her, Diane. I don't want her to get all nervous."

"I won't say anything, Kenny. She's gonna hate us, though."

Later, just before Diane and Craig left to find their seats, Kenny asked Emmy, "Would you and Tony like to stay onstage with my parents? It's a different way to see the show."

"I'd love to, Kenny!" She put her hands together. "You don't mind if Tony stays with me, do you?"

"No, of course not. It would be kinda rude to just abandon

329

him."

"You're right. I guess I've been so excited about seeing you that I kinda forgot about him." Her eyes lit up as she smiled at Kenny. "I should go tell him." She spotted Tony standing next to Kenny's father as Andy Walker talked to Mr. Colwell. "I'll be right back."

Emmy ran over to Tony as Kenny was pulled toward a cluster of fans by one of the band's crew.

"Tony, Kenny wants us to stay on stage for the show. Isn't that great?" Emmy bounced up and down on her toes.

"Sure. Are you gonna be all right? I've never seen you so excited."

"I'm just so happy to see him... and the other guys, too." Emmy spotted Diane and Craig. Diane poked him in the chest, and they appeared to be yelling at each other. "I need to go tell Diane. I'll be back." She zigzagged through the crowd. "Diane, are you guys fighting? What's going on?"

"Nothing, Em. We need to find our seats."

"You'll never guess what Kenny asked. He wants me to stay on stage with his parents, but Tony and I will join you for the last part of the show. Is that all right with you?"

Diane answered back, "Emmy, you should stay onstage for the whole show. Who knows if you'll ever get another chance to do that?"

Emmy didn't know about the plan Kenny and Diane hatched.

"Are you sure you don't mind?"

"We'll be fine. Go have fun with your... friend." Diane pointed at Tony, shook her head and said, "Don't ignore him."

Kenny pulled Emmy behind one of the buffet tables so they could avoid the swarm of people filling their plates.

"Did I tell you I have my driver's license now?"

"All right! It's about time."

"I don't have a car, so it's not much use."

"You can use my car if you need. It's just sitting in the carriage house gathering dust."

"Thanks, but I couldn't do that."

"Sure you can. Mom and Dad use it once in a while to keep it running."

Emmy pictured his little red car. "I'd be afraid I would wreck it."

"Em, it's just a Honda Civic."

Emmy bit her lip as she looked at Kenny. "I have missed you so much. I know when you left you told me to date other guys. I didn't know anyone who grabbed my interest, so Kristen set me up with some college guys."

"How did that work out, Em?" Kenny saw Tony still talking to his father. He looked around and spotted his mother talking to Sue Lysecki, a local TV news anchorwomen.

"Not so good. They were only interested in sex."

"I'm sorry, Em."

"Nothing happened, but then Kristen set me up with Tony."

"Does he make you happy, Em? He plays football, right?"

"We have fun together, and his mother makes me feel like part of their family. Just like with your parents. The only bad part is..." Emmy stared at the floor.

"What is it, Em?" Kenny put a finger on her chin and lifted her face.

"Sometimes I get the impression that he thinks I'm just one of his guy friends."

"One of the guys, huh? What's wrong with him?" Kenny shook his head. "Did I tell you that I will be home in May. We're taking a vacation. No touring, no recording, or anything. Let's get together and do something."

"Definitely. Call me as soon as you get home."

"I will, Em." Kenny spotted Andy Walker and Ralph Glissman, the tour manager, herding the other guys toward the dressing room area. Andy waved at Kenny. "Gotta go, Em. Talk to you after the show."

"I know you guys are leaving for LA tonight, so if I don't get to see you, have a good trip."

"I won't leave without talking to you and my parents," Kenny said.

"Good! You better not leave without saying goodbye."

331

The band headed to their dressing room, and Tony and Emmy joined Kenny's parents at the side of the stage as Frankie Hanna brought over two chairs.

"These are in case you want to sit down, Aunt Elly."

Mrs. Colwell smiled because for Frankie, that was a long speech. "Thank you, Frankie. Could you find chairs for Emmy and Tony, please?"

Emmy smiled at Frankie. "We don't need any. I'm gonna stand for the whole show."

He nodded his head and returned to work. He talked to Kenny's guitars more than he talked to people.

Tony peered out at the stage and glanced up. *That's sure a lot of lights.* He noticed a crew member making an adjustment to a mic over the drum kit.

Emmy checked out the backline, where all the amps were located. She spied an addition to Kenny's rig. *I wonder if Frankie put that rack together?* She saw his pedal board on the floor. *I see you've added some new toys to your collection.*

Finally, the house lights dimmed, the stage went dark and the opening music started. The crowd rose to their feet and a thunderous noise of hands clapping, feet stomping and people whistling filled the auditorium. The band moved into position.

Emmy tugged on Tony's arm. "Are you ready for this?" Emmy shouted into his ear as he leaned down.

"It's gonna be really loud, huh?"

"It will be loud, but at least we're behind the house speakers. It will be louder out there." She pointed to the first rows. "Get ready! Here it comes!"

Dave banged his sticks together and counted off the first song. The stage exploded with lights as Kenny hit the first chord. The light show and the special effects amazed her. She sang along with every song.

Halfway through the show, Kenny addressed the crowd. "You guys are great! It's good to be back in Chicago."

The crowd roared, as Kenny expected.

"We're gonna slow things down for a few minutes, so why don't you have a seat."

He waited a few seconds as the crowd settled down.

"Go SoHam!" Someone yelled from the balcony.

Kenny laughed. "I want to get serious now. I'd like to play a song called 'Sweet Girl,' and I'd like to dedicate it to a very special friend, Emmy Colasanti. If you have the *Transitions* CD, and have read the liner notes, and then you know she was the inspiration for this song. She's still my best friend in the world." He strummed his guitar as he continued, "This is the first song I ever wrote by myself, and I'd like to play it the way I wrote it. Just me and my acoustic guitar. The lyrics are simple, but heartfelt."

He glanced at Emmy several times while he sang. At the end of the song, he turned to Emmy, took a couple of steps toward her and blew her a kiss. The crowd screamed so loud that she could hardly hear a thing. Frankie brought him one of his Gibson electric guitars, and he moved to the center of the stage as the rest of the band returned.

"I'd like to do one of the first songs we ever learned to play as a band. It's an old song called 'Storms,' and, since it's not part of our regular set, I need some help from the band's first, and our best, fan."

Emmy didn't realize he was talking about her until Frankie Hanna walked over, handed her a mic and pulled her to the center of the stage. The stage lighting dimmed to almost total darkness, except for a spotlight on Kenny and Emmy. Emmy trembled as she looked at Kenny.

"What are you doing? Are you trying to make me wet myself?"

Kenny laughed and placed a hand on her back. "Just relax. Close your eyes and pretend we are back in the garage with nobody else around."

"What if I can't remember the words?"

He pointed out the teleprompters at the front of the stage. "Look at the screens if you need help, but I don't think you will."

The lights dimmed even more.

"Are you ready?"

"If I screw this up, I'm gonna hate you forever."

"I know, but you won't, and I'll always love you."

Kenny started playing the intro. The crowd hushed as the song began.

"You are so gonna get it, Kenny Colwell."

Emmy started to sing and somehow managed to block out the fact that five thousand people were listening to her. She closed her eyes and imagined herself in the garage with only her friend.

Emmy remembered the words perfectly. The rest of the band joined in, and the song built dynamically. The crowd started cheering. Emmy opened her eyes and turned to watch as Kenny played his guitar solo. He made his guitar sing. The crowd erupted as he moved next to her. She turned her back to him, and they leaned against each other as his hands and fingers flew over the strings—just as they had done the first time she ever sang the song on stage with him.

Tony crossed his arms over his chest as Emmy looked over her shoulder at Kenny. *They are more than just old friends. I may not know much about girls, but I'm not blind. It's obvious that she cares for him.*

Kenny finished the solo, and they moved apart. They smiled at each other as Emmy finished the last verse and chorus. When the song ended five thousand people stood and cheered for her. Kenny handed his guitar and her mic to Frankie. He smiled at Emmy and squeezed her tight.

"You sounded like an angel, Em."

"Do you mean that?"

"Absolutely!"

He waited until the spotlight went black. Then he kissed her. She literally ran off the stage, and Tony caught her before she ran into some equipment.

"Emmy, you're shaking. Are you all right?"

"I'm okay. My heart is just about to explode."

Tony put his hands on her shoulders. "You sounded great."

"Thank you, Tony. I'm sorry for what happened."

"It's okay that he hugged you."

Emmy realized Tony didn't see the kiss.

Backstage after the show, Emmy stayed close to Tony while Kenny talked to his parents. She bit her lip when Kenny smiled at her.

"Did I tell you how pretty you look tonight, Emmy?" Tony whispered to her.

"Thank you. I bought this dress just for tonight." Emmy saw Diane out of the corner of her eye. "I'll be back. I have to go yell at Diane." She marched over to her sister and saw a guilty look on her face.

"You knew he planned to do that, didn't you?" Emmy frowned.

Diane nodded. "I didn't tell you because I knew you would get nervous and worry and not be able to enjoy the show."

"That was probably smart. Thanks, Diane."

Emmy saw some people pointing and waving at her. She couldn't hear their conversation.

"That's her! I tell you. That's the little girl who sang that song," one lady said as she jabbed another in the side.

"It can't be. That girl is just a kid," the other lady asserted.

Later, Diane nudged Emmy to get her attention. "Craig went to get our coats. We'll meet you over there by Kenny."

"Okay. Tony got our coats, and Kenny's parents have theirs on already."

Emmy weaved her way through the crowd and stood next to Tony.

"I know you want to be able to say goodbye. It's all right," he said.

"I'm sorry if this night hasn't been all that great for you."

"Hey, it's been fantastic. How many guys ever get a chance to see their girlfriend sing with a famous rock star, huh?"

Emmy grinned. "So tonight I'm your girlfriend and not one of the guys. Does that mean you're gonna kiss me?"

"I can't kiss you in front of all these people, Em."

"You're such a goof."

Mr. Colwell answered his cell phone. "The limo is here. We should go."

"I'll see you in May." Kenny hugged his parents. "We'll be home for a month or so. Maybe we can go somewhere." He looked at Emmy.

"You should ask her soon if you want her to go with you. She's a teenager, and teenagers are always busy," Mrs. Colwell said.

"I know, but I don't want to cause any trouble between her and Tony."

Mrs. Colwell hugged her son. "You be safe."

"I will, Mom."

"You should walk her to the limo. We'll keep Tony with us."

"You're so bad," Kenny teased his mother and then walked over to Tony and Emmy. "Dad wants to get going."

Tony reached out his hand, and Kenny shook it. Tony surprised Emmy by helping her on with her coat. "I'll let you guys say goodbye."

She smiled at Tony, and then he walked toward Mr. and Mrs. Colwell.

"This has been a perfect night, Kenny."

"I'm so glad I got to see you." Kenny took her hand as they made their way through the still crowded backstage area. "I would really like to see you when I get back in May."

She smiled and said, "You better make time to see me."

By the time Kenny and Emmy got to the limo, everyone else was inside. The driver held the door open for Emmy.

"I'll email you, Em. Take care, and I'll see you soon." He kissed her cheek. She sat between Tony and Mr. Colwell facing everyone else. "See you all soon." Kenny closed the door and waved.

Emmy settled into the leather seat. She scooted as close as possible to Tony. "I'm kinda cold. Will you put your arm around me?"

"Sure, Em." He put his arm around her, and she snuggled up close to him.

The limo driver pulled out of the building and turned right. Mr. Colwell turned off the lights.

"Are you gonna kiss me?" she whispered. "It's almost dark enough in here that we could make out."

"Emmy, we can't do that in front of everyone."

"One little kiss?"

Tony looked at Diane and Craig and suppressed a chuckle. "I think they're mad at each other."

Craig stared out the window as the limo pulled onto the Stevenson Expressway. Diane and Mrs. Colwell were talking. "Hey! Look it's snowing."

"I'm glad I'm not driving," Mr. Colwell said.

"Maybe I should wait until we get back to your place," Tony whispered to Emmy. He could smell her strawberry shampoo.

"Fine! Be that way." Emmy poked him in the ribs.

"Ow! Emmy, that hurt."

Ten minutes later Emmy looked at Diane. She could tell that Diane and Craig were upset with each other.

Emmy rolled her eyes. *I wonder what Craig did now?* She looked up at Tony. "Will it be too late to go out for ice cream or something when we get back?"

"Everything will be closed, Em. I'll probably head home."

"Okay." Emmy didn't really want ice cream. She just wanted to see if Tony would kiss her.

The limo driver pulled into the Colwell's driveway. Diane and Craig jumped out first and took off without a word.

Tony helped Emmy get out. "Thanks for letting us ride with you, Mr. Colwell."

"You're welcome, Tony. I hope you enjoyed the show."

"I did. I've never been to a show like that. It was totally amazing."

Mrs. Colwell hugged Emmy. "You need to come over and see us more often. I know you're busy, but..."

"I promise I'll stop over soon. Thanks again. I'm sorry my sister is so rude. I think she and Craig had a fight tonight."

"It's all right. You girls are so different."

Kenny's parents watched as Tony and Emmy walked away.

"What are you thinking, Elly?" Mr. Colwell put an arm around his wife as the snow continued to fall.

"Nothing special."

"I know you better than that."

337

She smiled. "I wonder if Emmy knows how much Kenny loves her. He told her to see other boys while he was away, but I know he didn't really mean it."

"She's a smart girl. Let's go inside before we freeze."

Emmy held Tony's hand as they walked to his car.

"Do you have a scraper or a brush? Your car is covered."

He started the car and then opened the rear passenger side door. "I always keep one in the car, Em. You never know when it's gonna snow around here." He started brushing off his car.

Emmy made a snowball and threw it at Tony.

"Hey! What are you doing?"

"Just having some fun. Are you gonna throw snow at me?"

"I would if it wasn't so late. We would wake up the neighborhood."

Emmy gave up trying to have some fun with Tony. "Are you at least gonna kiss me good night?"

Tony set the brush down and kissed her cheek. "I had a great time tonight. Thanks for asking me to go with you."

"You're welcome," Emmy replied sarcastically. "I need to go in before I freeze."

Tony walked her to the front steps. She paused on the bottom step and faced him.

"Did you really like hearing me sing?"

"Emmy, you sounded great. Maybe you should think about a career in music."

"I could never do that for a career, but it would be fun to sing in front of people once in a while."

"Thanks again for inviting me to the show. I better get home."

She watched him walk back to his car. *I hope you still like me.*

He finished cleaning off his car, waved goodbye, got in the car and pulled away. *I like you a lot, Emmy, but after tonight I have doubts you will ever like me as much as Kenny.*

Chapter Thirty-Two

Emmy kept her promise to Kristen and stayed at home until the Easter break in early April of 1998. At times her parents frightened her with their loud arguing. Her father never became physical with her mother, but she did witness her mother hit her father. Her mother instantly apologized, and they made up. Emmy noticed that even though her parents argued and fought, they did love and need each other. The whole situation became very stressful to Emmy, and she lost her appetite. She lost weight, and since she weighed under a hundred pounds, she couldn't afford to lose many pounds. One evening Mom got on her case about staying out past ten o'clock. Finally, Emmy reached the end of her patience.

"Mom, you don't understand," Emmy cried. "You never understand. I'm not ten anymore. I'm grown up. Why do you always treat me like a child?"

"All right! If you want to be treated like an adult, you can start paying rent. In the real world everything costs something. You can begin paying rent right now." Mom pounded her hand on the kitchen table.

"I'm still not giving you my whole paycheck. I have a checking account of my own."

Mom shook her head. "You don't know how to handle your money."

"I can probably do a better job than you," Emmy yelled.

In the morning Emmy realized the time had come to leave the nest for good. She wanted to keep her music box and Bose system safe so she took them to Kenny's apartment above the Colwells' carriage house. When she came back, she and her mother started arguing again.

"Where were you, Emily?"

"I took a couple things over to Kenny's apartment."

"Why, and how did you get in?"

"I have a key."

"Why on earth do you have a key, young lady?"

"Kenny gave me a key so I could check on his gear once in a while. I use his keyboard sometimes."

Mom's face turned red with anger. "I forbid you to go over there again. I'll call the police if I learn you're staying there. I should have never let you get so involved with him. He's too old for you."

Emmy looked at her mother and managed to hold her tongue. She went to her bedroom, packed two suitcases and left her parents' house. She hoped she would be able to return for her few other possessions after she found a place to live. She dragged her suitcases along the alley as she walked over to the Colwell's house.

Emmy struggled to hold back her tears as she asked Mrs. Colwell, "Could I use your phone to make a couple calls, please?"

"Of course you can, dear. Why don't you use the one in Carter's office. You can have some privacy." Mrs. Colwell noticed the suitcases and realized what probably happened. "Do you want to stay in the carriage house again, Emmy?"

"Thanks, but I can't. My mother found out I was staying there and she... well, she threatened to cause trouble for you. I don't want that to happen."

Emmy tried calling Kristen, but she wasn't home. She couldn't stay with Grandma Sandusky. She was in Florida.

With nowhere to go, Emmy called Diane.

"There's no room for you here. We already have four people sharing one tiny bathroom. Why don't you stay at Kenny's place?"

"I can't because Mom threatened to call the cops."

"She would, too." Diane sighed. "Sorry, Em, but I don't know what to tell you. I gotta run."

Emmy didn't want to stay with Barry, because she didn't want to make him sleep on the couch again. Desperation set in until she thought of Tony. *Things haven't been the same between us since the concert, but who else can I call?* She called him from the Colwell home.

"...and that's why I moved out, and now I'm looking for a place to stay until I get my own place. I know we haven't been seeing each other as much lately."

"Yeah, I've been kinda busy," he said. "Let me ask Mama, and I'll call you right back."

Before Tony could even hang up the phone, Mama asked, "What did you need to ask me, son?"

"Emmy is looking for a place to stay until she can find her own place. Might be a few days at the most. Can she stay here?"

"Of course she can stay here. She can stay as long as she needs, but tell her, I will put her to work."

"Thanks, Mama. Emmy, did you hear that? Mama said you can stay, but she will make you do chores. Do you need me to pick you up or anything?"

"No, I'll catch the bus. I don't mind doing some chores. Thanks, Tony. See you in a bit."

Emmy walked out to the living room and sat on the couch. Mrs. Colwell sat in her recliner facing Emmy.

"I'm gonna stay with the Bertuccis for a couple days. I put some stuff in the carriage house. I hope that's all right."

"Of course it is, dear. You could stay in the house with us if you want. I'm sure your mother wouldn't mind if you did that."

"Mom wants me to pay rent, and I wouldn't mind that, but she wants my whole paycheck. I might as well get my own place."

"It's not right for her to expect your entire paycheck," Mrs. Colwell said. "But, forgive me, you are rather young to be on your own. I'd be less concerned if you stayed here."

"I just can't. Mom is serious about causing trouble. Do you think it's a mistake for me to stay at Tony's house?" Emmy hoped Mrs. Colwell would tell her it would be okay. "His mother is really nice, like you."

"We know Mrs. Bertucci, and we knew her husband, too. Are you sure you and Tony will... get along... all right?"

"I think so. Maybe I shouldn't go over there." Emmy looked at the ceiling. She knew there were three empty bedrooms upstairs, besides Kenny's room.

"You can think about it, Emmy. You don't need to rush right over there. You're always welcome to stay here, and I'm not worried one little bit about your mother trying to cause trouble."

"Thank you, Mrs. Colwell. Would it be all right if I put

341

some of my clothes in the room next to Kenny's? That way I won't have to carry both suitcases on the bus."

"That would be a good idea."

Later, Emmy caught a bus over to Tony's house. He waited for her at the corner and carried her suitcase into the house.

Mama held Emmy's shoulders and looked into her eyes. "Before I let you stay here I want you to call home and let your mother know where you are, so she won't be worrying about you."

Emmy did what Mama asked. "Hi, Mom. I wanted to let you know I'm okay."

"Where are you, Emmy?" Mom screamed into the phone. "Your father and I are worried about you. Where are you gonna live? How will you get to work and school?"

"I've only been gone for an hour, Mom. Since you threatened to make trouble if I stayed at Kenny's house, I'm going to be staying with my friend Tony and his mother."

"What? No way, young lady! You get your butt home this instant!" Mom yelled loud enough that Mama Bertucci could hear every word. "You're not living with him. I don't care if his mother is there!"

Emmy held the phone away from her ear until her mother stopped yelling. "Are you through yelling, Mom?" Emmy asked calmly.

Mom took a deep breath. "I'm just concerned about you, Emily. That's why I yelled."

"Relax, Mom. I'm going to be fine here." *And it's not like I'm living with Tony. I'm not Diane.*

Mom's voice returned to a more natural level. "Is that the boy you brought over to meet us? He's a nice young man. Are you sure you should be staying at his house, though?"

"Mom! Nothing is going to happen. Tony's mother is here, and sometimes his sister comes home from college. I need to go, Mom. I will talk to you later."

"That wasn't so bad, now, was it? I know your mother appreciates knowing you are safe." Mama smiled at Emmy. "Tony, take Emmy's suitcase upstairs to Heather's room and show her around. After that I need to talk to Emmy for a couple of minutes."

342

"Okay. Come on, Emmy. I'll show you my room," Tony said a little too loudly.

Emmy stared at Tony. *I've been in your room before. Doesn't Mama know that?* She followed Tony up the wide stairs and saw more family pictures on the wall.

"Sorry, Em, but Mama doesn't know you've been in my room."

"I've only been in there once, and I haven't seen the other bedrooms."

Tony opened the door directly across from the stairs. "This is Heather's room. She doesn't come home too often, but you already know that." He stashed her suitcase in the corner.

Emmy followed Tony into the room. She looked up and saw a ceiling fan directly above the queen-sized bed. She touched the bedposts and felt the thick comforter. She turned and checked out the titles of some of the medical books in the floor-to-ceiling bookcase.

"If you will follow me, I'll show you my room again." Tony stepped back into the hallway. "Oh, maybe I should show you the bathroom first. It's here on the right." Tony pointed to the bathroom and Emmy looked inside. She noticed the double sinks in the vanity and the bathtub on the right.

"Where's the toilet?"

Tony pointed toward the back. "Oh, it's in the corner behind that half-wall."

Emmy suppressed a giggle. *This is bigger than Grandma's bathroom and almost bigger than the one at Kenny's house.*

"Mama's room is at the end of the hall on the left. She has her own bathroom, so the other one is just for us. I mean my brother and sister. Not you and I, us..."

Emmy grinned at Tony's obvious discomfort. "I get the picture. I'm surprised the hallway is this narrow."

Tony squeezed past her and walked to the end of the hall. "Yeah, I guess that's how they built them back then. Plus, I'm kinda wide. This is Marco's room," Tony opened the door to let Emmy see. "He doesn't come home much anymore, so this is more like a guest room now. Mama's room is in here." He opened the

343

door to her bedroom. They retraced their steps down the hall, and Tony opened the last door and waved his hand. "And this is my room."

"I know that, you goof. But I've only been in here once and only for a few minutes. I didn't really see everything."

Emmy stepped inside and looked around. Posters of football players adorned the walls. A desk took up one corner and a dresser the other corner. His bed was located in the middle of the wall to the left. She giggled as she saw the Chicago Bears logo on the comforter. *That wasn't here before.* Two footballs sat on a shelf above the desk. The shelf above that displayed trophies of different sizes, but all obviously from football.

"Who is this?" Emmy asked as she pointed to a large poster.

"That's Dick Butkus. He played for the Bears and is my favorite player, even though I wasn't born when he played."

Emmy laughed, "How could he be your favorite player if you never saw him play?"

"I've seen film of him. He played like a ferocious madman. Do you know who this is?" Tony pointed to another poster.

"I know that's Mike Singletary. I watched him play. He was ferocious, too. Is that why you play middle linebacker because you are so *ferocious*?" Emmy teased.

Tony grabbed her around the waist and held her in the air as she giggled. Just then Mama walked into the room.

"What are you doing to her, Tony?"

"I was just..." Tony dropped her.

"I teased him about football, and he tried to tackle me." Emmy stood next to Mama and stuck her tongue out at Tony.

"Come downstairs and eat. I made some lunch," Mama said and then shook her head at Tony.

"She started it!" Tony whined like a kid.

Emmy ran down the stairs and jumped over the last few stairs to the floor. Mama watched and thought that Emmy acted like a kid—a tomboy.

Mama shook her head. *I wonder if Tony likes you because of your beauty, or because he thinks of you as someone to play football with.*

"I'll show you the rest of the house if you want. I know you've been in all the rooms on this floor before," Tony said as he followed Mama down the stairs.

Emmy peered into the living room. "It's kinda dark in here with the drapes closed."

"I guess Mama closed them. They're usually open."

"I just love that fireplace."

Tony led her down the hall toward the back of the house, "There's a small bathroom in there. That's a closet, I mean pantry, and the dining room is in here. You've seen it."

"What is that other room in front?" Emmy asked curiously. "I've never been in there."

"It's like a den. It was my father's office at one time. Now Mama uses it as her TV and sewing room. We weren't supposed to go in there when we were kids unless Mama or Papa were in there."

"This house is almost as big as where Kenny lives."

"I've never been inside, but I've seen it."

"It's kinda like an old plantation house."

After lunch Mama took Emmy into the living room while Tony occupied himself in the basement. Emmy sat on the front edge of the couch. She kept her hands together and bit her lip.

"I know you will be working all day, and you have some classes at Paul Frank, right?" Mama asked.

Emmy nodded her head.

"Since you're going to be staying here, I would appreciate it if you keep me informed if you're going to be out later than expected. Tony doesn't have a curfew. He's never needed one. He's usually too tired from football to stay out late. I'm not going to insist you are home by a certain time, but let me know if you think it's necessary."

"I won't be staying out late, Mama. I'll come right here after work, and I won't go anywhere after my classes. Sometimes people go out for pizza, but I usually don't go."

"You can go, but please let me know if you're going to be out late."

Over the next few days Mama treated Emmy like a member of the family, but more importantly to Emmy, Mama didn't treat her like a child. Mama assigned her chores, which Emmy did without complaining. She kept busy with her job and checked out the newspaper for an apartment.

"Hey, Tony, listen to this. There's a one-bedroom apartment over on Janet Street. That's just across the river from where I work."

"How much is the rent?"

"It just says it's negotiable. I want to check it out. Could you go with me on Saturday?"

"I suppose so."

On Saturday Tony drove Emmy to see two apartments. The first place was too expensive. She liked the second apartment, but the landlord refused to rent it to her after he learned she wasn't eighteen.

"I think he's worried that we're going to be living together, Emmy," Tony said.

"I told him we're not."

As they drove down Janet Street, Emmy saw a sign in the window of a house.

"Tony! Stop. I think I saw a sign for an apartment in that house."

They parked the car and walked back to the house.

"Look! It says that they have a furnished one-bedroom for rent. I want to check it out."

Emmy knocked on the door and the landlord's wife opened it after a moment.

"Hi, my name is Emmy Colasanti, and I'm interested in the apartment."

"What did you say your name is?"

Emmy repeated it for the lady who opened up the apartment for Emmy, and then went back downstairs. Emmy didn't realize the lady happened to be related to her mother. They were distant cousins but played bingo at the same church.

"Well, what do you think, Em?" Tony looked around at the

small living room and kitchen.

"It's small and kinda old-fashioned looking, but I don't need much space. It's really close to work and not that far away from your house. The building where I work is just down the hill and across the river. I'll be able to walk to work and there's a bus stop at the corner."

Emmy talked to the landlady while Tony waited by the car. Emmy was surprised by the terms of the rent, but decided to take the apartment.

She smiled as she walked toward the car. She turned to face the house and waved her hands in the air. "This is my new home. She said I can move in next Saturday."

"How much is the rent?"

Emmy explained everything as they drove back to his house.

"Are you sure you're willing to live under those conditions? It seems kinda shady if you ask me. Didn't the landlady ask for a cosigner since you're not eighteen?"

"No, she didn't." Emmy bit her lip. "She didn't make me sign a lease."

"Did you even tell her how old you are? Did she even ask?"

"She didn't bring it up, so I didn't volunteer the information." Emmy looked out the window.

"Maybe you should keep looking, Emmy," Tony said. *I wonder how Mama will react to this?*

"I think it will be all right." Emmy turned to face Tony. "If it doesn't work out, I can always move. It's not like I have a bunch of furniture or anything."

Emmy wondered about Tony's father, and one day got up the nerve to ask Mama, "Do you mind if I ask about Tony's father?"

Mama smiled at her, and they sat down together in the kitchen. "Papa Peter passed away when Tony was a small child—three, almost four, if I remember right. No one knew about his bad heart. Tony stayed with his grandmother for a short time. Everyone suffered. Fire destroyed my parents' house, and then

347

Peter died. My mother stayed in one of my brother Carmen's apartments for a couple weeks. She took care of Tony while I took care of Heather and Marco. They were sick, and I didn't want Tony to catch what they had. My father was in Italy taking care of family business and couldn't get home right away. Our family owns vineyards in the Lombardy region in northern Italy. I prayed so much, and we got through it somehow." Tears filled Mama's eyes as she told Emmy the story.

Emmy shyly asked Mama a question. "Why didn't you ever get remarried?"

Mama looked at Emmy. "I never thought about it, dear. After Peter I could never love another man."

"Wasn't it a struggle raising three kids by yourself?"

"My family provided lots of support, and money never really became a problem. Peter and Daniel Keasling were lifelong friends, and the company they formed prospered. We got by. Daniel really struggled with grief when Peter passed away, but he made sure we received Peter's half of the profits."

Tears flowed from their eyes as Emmy hugged Mama. Emmy realized something. "Mama, I feel silly, but I don't know your real name."

"Oh, dear, I'm sorry, I never thought to tell you. No one in the family calls me by my name anymore, except my sister sometimes. And my father, too. It's Maria Catarina Lombardi Bertucci, a good Italian Catholic name."

Emmy stayed with Tony and Mama until Saturday and then moved into her furnished apartment. The building, originally a single family home, had, at some point, been remodeled and turned into apartments. The landlord lived on the first floor, and Emmy's small apartment occupied the front half of the second floor.

"Did you get the keys, Emmy?" Tony opened the trunk and lifted out her suitcases.

She ran down the porch steps and dashed to the car holding up the keys. "I've got two sets."

"If you open the doors, I'll bring in your suitcases and come back for the rest of your stuff. That's a nice Bose system. Where did you get it?"

"Kenny gave it to me for Christmas." She opened the rear passenger door. "I'll carry my music box. It's... not heavy." *It's my most cherished possession.*

Within an hour, Emmy was settled into her very first apartment.

"Make sure you thank Mama for letting me borrow this kitchen stuff." Emmy closed the silverware drawer.

"I don't think she wants it back. She has tons of plates and pots and pans and stuff." Tony stretched out his arms. *I can almost touch both walls in here. I guess it's a one-person kitchen.*

"Still, it's very generous of her." Emmy turned around. "Where did you go?"

Tony hollered from the bathroom. "Are you aware there's no shower in here, Em?"

She walked to the bathroom, stood in the doorway and noticed the cracked linoleum. "I know. I'll get used to it. The furniture is old and the wallpaper in the living room is hideous."

Tony followed Emmy into the living room. "What? You don't like pheasants and hunting dogs?"

"It's too dark. There's not much color." She ran a hand along the wallpaper and then glanced at the floor. "The carpeting has to be a hundred years old."

"It looks like new carpeting in the bedroom."

"Yeah, I wonder how disgusting that carpeting must have been if they needed to replace it. Anyway, this is going to be home." She sat on the edge of the bed and patted the spot next to her.

"Better not." He shook his head.

"I'll return these blankets and pillows as soon as I buy some. I guess I should have thought of things like this before I moved out. I was in a hurry and didn't think things through."

"It will be a challenge to live on your own."

She plopped onto her back and spread her arms. "I'm seventeen and living on my own. I admit to being a little anxious, but I love challenges."

"I should go."

"If you must." She got up and walked with him out to his car. "Thanks for your help, Tony."

"No problem, Em. Make sure you call the phone company right away."

"Diane is going to help me with the utilities. I don't want to be without a phone for long."

After eating at Darby's the first weekend, she ate dinner at Tony's house the rest of the week, and Mama sent the leftovers home with her. Mama made Emmy promise to call home at least once a week and let her mother know she was all right. Her mother quickly adjusted to being an empty nester. Not once did she ask Emmy to come back home.

Mama faced Emmy and Tony in the dining room one evening after dinner. "Tell me how you are doing in your apartment, Emmy."

"Well, to be honest... I've never been afraid of the dark or anything, but now I keep a light on in the living room. Sometimes I hear noises from downstairs and the other apartment upstairs, and it spooks me. I can hear the people in the other apartment arguing. I suppose I have to get used to being alone."

"Are you eating enough, dear? You look even skinnier than ever."

"I don't do much cooking in the apartment. I eat a lot of soup. I suppose I should learn how to cook. Mom never taught us."

"Do you have enough money to pay your bills?"

"Mama! You shouldn't ask that." Tony waved his hands around.

"It's all right, Tony. I don't mind. I can pay the bills as long as I'm careful with my money."

"Why don't you get a roommate?" Mama asked. "She could pay part of the rent and keep you company."

"The apartment is too small for a roommate. There's only one bedroom. Where would a roommate sleep?" Emmy answered as she looked at Tony.

"I could stay over and sleep on the couch," Tony offered.

Mama shook her head and wagged a finger at him. "Not

350

while I'm alive, young man. Not unless you are married, and you are both way too young to even think about that. Why don't you have Kristen stay with you on the weekends?"

"I would because Kristen is like my best friend, but we had a little disagreement, and I think she is still mad at me."

"Nonsense! Tony, call Kristen and let her know I need to talk to her, please."

"Okay, Mama," Tony answered. He got up and went into the kitchen to call. "Hey, Kristen, it's your cousin Tony."

"I know who you are. I've only heard your voice all my life. What's up?"

"Mama wants to talk to you. She needs a favor from you."

Kristen knew that whenever Mama asked for a favor, she expected results right away. "What does Mama need?"

"I'll let her tell you, okay?" Tony handed the cordless phone to Mama.

"Kristen, honey, I would appreciate it if you would stay with Emmy on the weekend sometimes. She's a little spooked staying all alone and could use your company."

"What are you talking about? Why is Emmy alone?"

"Oh dear! Didn't you know she moved into an apartment?"

"No, I didn't know. I'm going to smack Tony when I see him. He didn't say anything about that at school."

Mama frowned at Tony as she explained everything to Kristen.

"I would be happy to stay with her, but I think Emmy is mad at me. I haven't talked to her for a while."

"She's not mad at you, Kristen. Emmy thinks you're mad at her. She's here now. Why don't you come over, and you guys can talk about things?"

"All right. I'll be there soon."

Tony heard the front doorbell thirty minutes later. "I'll get it. It's probably Kristen."

"Why would she ring the bell?" Mama wondered.

"The door's locked," Tony hollered. He let Kristen in. "Took you long enough."

"Hush. I got here as fast as I could. Where's Emmy? She's

351

got some explaining to do."

Tony pointed to the living room. "In there."

Mama tugged on Tony's arm. "Come and help me in the kitchen."

"But I wanna hear what they're talking about," he said.

"They need some privacy."

"But, Mama..." Tony reluctantly followed Mama into the kitchen.

Kristen entered the living room. Emmy stood in front of the fireplace and bit her lip as Kristen approached. They faced each other without speaking for a moment.

"I'm sorry!" They said at the same time.

Kristen reached out, and they hugged.

"I should have told you what was going on, but I just couldn't," Emmy whispered in Kristen's ear.

Kristen let go. "It's all right. I'm sorry for getting upset. I should have been there to support you. That's what best friends do."

"Are we still best friends?" Emmy asked as she wiped away a tear.

"Always and forever, Emmy! Always and forever."

Chapter Thirty-Three

A few days later Mama insisted Emmy come over for dinner. Afterward as Emmy helped Tony clear the dining room table, she mentioned, "Did I tell you that I saw Scott Simmons yesterday?"

Tony stacked all the plates. "Who's that?"

"He's this guy I met back in the summer. He's older." She gathered all the silverware.

"No, you didn't say anything about that. Did you talk to him?"

"No, he was with some friends, so I didn't bother him. He is rather handsome. He sorta looks like Tommy Cruz, but taller."

Tony responded dryly, "I don't think he's all that good looking."

"You would if you were a girl, like me. I am a girl in case you've forgotten."

"Maybe you should set Kristen up with him." Tony pointed to the end of the table. "You forgot that knife."

Emmy sighed and grabbed the knife. "I don't think she's ever met him. Besides, she doesn't have any problem getting enough dates as it is."

"Are you trying to tell me you want to go out with him?" Tony stood in the doorway, holding all the dirty plates and trapping Emmy in the dining room.

"Maybe. Would that bother you if I did?" She ducked under his arm and squeezed past.

"You can go out with other guys if you want, Emmy," Tony said rather casually as he followed her.

She stopped in the hall. "Really?"

"Sure."

They loaded the dishwasher and moved into the living room. She sat next to Tony on the couch and continued teasing him. "Scott has never kissed me before, but maybe I should let him to see if he's a better kisser than you."

"Go ahead if you want, Emmy. I'm not afraid of a little competition," Tony answered.

Emmy certainly didn't expect this answer. She looked over at Mama who sat in her recliner reading a book. Emmy moved closer to Tony and tried to kiss him.

He grabbed her shoulders and held her away. "Emmy, you shouldn't try to kiss me in front of Mama."

"Why not? Don't you think she ever kissed your father? Oh, Tony, I'm sorry if that brings up bad memories. I didn't mean to hurt your feelings."

"No, you didn't hurt my feelings, but we should behave properly when other people are around."

Mama closed her book. "You better be behaving properly when nobody is around. Just because you're alone does not mean you can get away with things. I would rather you kissed Emmy right here than try to sneak around and do something behind my back."

Emmy grinned at Tony, moved close and closed her eyes, expecting a kiss. Instead of a kiss, Tony poked her ribs with his finger.

"Uh! Stop that." She backed away.

Tony grabbed her ankles as she moved.

"Let go of me!"

"Should I tickle your feet?" He held both ankles with one hand. "Are these clean socks?"

Mama shook her head and reopened her book. *You'd think you kids were siblings at times.*

"Who are you going out with this weekend, Kristen?" Emmy asked as soon as Kristen stepped into the stairway leading up to her apartment.

"Good to see you, too, Emmy. Some people use a salutation like hello when greeting their best friend." Kristen scooted past Emmy, across the landing at the top of the stairs and through the open door. "Now give me a tour of the apartment."

"Sorry. Hello, Kristen." Emmy showed Kristen around.

Kristen didn't comment while inspecting Emmy's place.

"Well, what do you think?" Emmy plopped onto her couch and let her feet dangle over the end.

What can I say that won't hurt her feelings? Kristen gingerly sat in the recliner after checking that it would be safe. "It's nice and cozy, Em. It reminds me of a room in Grandma's old house."

"Thanks," Emmy said. "Now who is your date?"

"I'm going out with Christopher Braun again. He told me that Randy has been asking about you. I think he would like to ask you on a date."

"No, thanks. How old is Christopher?" Emmy asked. *He looks like one of those surfer dudes from California. I love his long blonde hair. I wonder if it's natural or if he has it done.*

"He's twenty-one. The same as when you asked me last week. Are you trying to tell me something, Em?"

"Well, he is kinda older than us." Emmy thought about Scott Simmons, who was a year older than Christopher.

"He's more mature than the guys our age. High school guys are so immature. It's a waste of time to date them."

Emmy sat up and glared at her. "So I'm wasting my time with Tony, huh?"

"I didn't mean him. He's more mature than most high school guys."

"And I'm less mature than other kids my age, huh? Is that what you're telling me?"

Kristen laughed. "You're not immature, Em. You just have different interests than other kids our age."

"You're so funny," Emmy said. "Just be careful, Kristen. College guys are more aggressive."

"I'm not going to sleep with him, Emmy. I'm not interested in a serious relationship, yet."

Emmy made a habit of visiting Mama whenever Heather came home from Notre Dame. Emmy admired Heather's goal of becoming a doctor. Emmy didn't meet Tony's brother Marco because he went to John Hopkins University in Baltimore and didn't plan to come home until the end of the school year, if even then. Tony appeared very reluctant to talk about Marco, and Emmy didn't want to pry. She asked Mama about Marco one day, and

355

even Mama didn't say much, other than the fact that she missed him and loved him as much as her other children. Emmy wondered why no one in the family would willingly to talk about the mysterious Marco.

"Tony, do you ever want to do anything more than kiss me?" Emmy asked one evening when Tony dropped by her apartment. "Sometimes I almost feel like you think of me as your little sister. Like just now. You walk in and kiss my cheek. What's up? Don't you feel attracted to me anymore?"

"Oh, yeah, you better believe I do, but I can wait until we are ready. I don't want to rush you into a relationship that might be more complicated than we are ready to handle. I respect your wish to wait until you're married to become sexually active. That doesn't mean it's easy. Far from it. I try not to think about it, but sometimes when I look at you... well, I guess that's why I don't kiss you as much as you or I want."

Emmy's mouth opened as she listened in disbelief. "Did Mama tell you to say that?"

"Not in those exact words, but she kinda talked to me."

Emmy looked surprised. "Are you telling me you had a *sex talk* with your mother?"

Tony blushed. "I guess you could say that."

"I have never talked about sex with my mother, other than her accusing me of having sex. I can't imagine ever talking about that with Daddy. Anything I know about sex, I learned from Diane. She's an expert."

Tony's eyes followed her around the room as she picked up her schoolwork. *Is this where I find out that you're more like Diane than anyone knows? I'm not prepared. I'm not like the guys who carry protection in their wallets.*

Emmy looked at him, amazed that a normal teenage boy would not let his hormones take control; she understood the difficulty from her perspective so she kissed him. "I love you very much, Mr. Bertucci."

Tony grinned at her. "I'm fond of you, I suppose, but I don't know if I 'love' you." He assumed she was joking around because

356

she had never said those words before.

Emmy stared at Tony dumbfounded. Tony finally realized she really meant what she said, so he hugged her. "Emmy, I love you more than anything... even more than football." Then he laughed.

Emmy could tell Tony still wasn't being serious and poked him in the side. "I'm joking. I'm fond of you, but that's all." She blushed and bit her lip as she realized they both felt a bit uncomfortable saying 'I love you' to each other.

On Saturday evening Tony picked Emmy up at her apartment for their regularly-scheduled date-night. "Where do you want to go tonight?"

"Have you eaten yet?" Emmy asked.

"Not really. I guess we should get that out of the way before we do anything else, huh?"

"It would be a wise move. You sometimes get cranky if you are hungry," she answered somewhat sarcastically.

"I can't help it. It's because I have such a high metabolism."

"Yeah, whatever. Where do you want to go? Somewhere cheap, I'm sure."

"I take you to nice restaurants, too."

"Yeah, you do, once in a blue moon."

"Fine, where do you want to go? I'll splurge tonight."

Emmy grinned and said, "I want to go to Darby's."

"You're goofy, Em," Tony picked her up and threw her over his shoulder. "Should I carry you out to the car like this?"

"No, put me down, you big ox."

"Do you still get free food at Darby's because you used to work there?"

"Sometimes Mr. Darby doesn't charge me, but he won't let you have your food for free. He would go broke if he did that."

"I don't eat that much, Em," Tony said.

"Yeah, right." Emmy replied as she made him set her down. "How many hot dogs did you eat the last time? Four, or maybe five?"

"I'm a growing boy. I need lots of nourishment."

"And hot dogs are *so* nutritious." Emmy's reply dripped with sarcasm.

After they placed their order and found an empty booth, Emmy watched the other couples. Darby's attracted a lot of kids because they could afford to hang out there. Mr. Darby didn't mind as long as they behaved. She waved to a couple she remembered from school and then stared at Tony.

"What? Did I do something wrong again?"

"Not yet, but it's early." Emmy ate a few fries, and then stopped and looked at Tony again. "Last year Derrick and I kinda dated at the end of the year. Do you remember that?"

"You've mentioned it before," Tony said between bites. "Derrick said he kissed you, and it felt like kissing Kristen." He set his hot dog down. "Sorry, Emmy, I guess I shouldn't have said that. I don't think kissing you is like kissing Kristen."

Emmy glared at him.

"That didn't come out right. I've never kissed Kristen like a girl."

Emmy's eyes widened in mock surprise. "You kissed her like a guy?"

"No! No! I know she's a girl."

Emmy suppressed a laugh.

"Can we change the subject?" Tony pleaded.

"No, I want to hear all about how you kissed Kristen. Come on, confess."

"She kissed me once when we were like twelve."

"Did you kiss her back?" Emmy laughed because she had never seen anyone turn as red with embarrassment.

"I suppose I might have. It never happened again. Please, don't say anything to her."

"I won't. At least for now." Emmy grinned. "Did I tell you I turned down a couple guys who asked me to the prom because I wanted to go with Derrick. He ended up going with that snob Clarissa Morgan."

Tony listened in silence. Emmy stared at him. Finally, he understood. "Are you telling me you want to go to the prom?"

"Duh! Have you really been hit in the helmet too many

358

times? Do you think I'm waiting for Kenny to ask me?"

"Isn't he on tour? And isn't he too old for a high school prom anyway?" Tony narrowed his eyes. *He better not take you to the prom.*

Emmy groaned as she covered her face with her hands. "If he was home, I would ask him to take me. He would do it, too."

"Really?" He crossed his massive arms over his chest and frowned.

"No, I guess not. But he just turned twenty-one in January, so, technically, he's not too old."

"Can you even go?" Tony asked. "You aren't 'technically' a student anymore."

"Did you just use air quotes? That is so lame." Emmy laughed and the tension evaporated.

Emmy finished her fries and said, "I checked with Principal O'Dell. He told me I could come to the prom if I promised to dance with him one time."

"Really?" Tony asked.

"No! Yes!" Emmy giggled for a moment. "He did say it was all right for me to attend, but he didn't make me promise to dance with him. You can be so gullible at times."

"I didn't think you would be interested in the prom. Derrick told me you said you enjoyed going hiking better than getting dressed up and going to the prom."

"That was different," Emmy said. "Derrick and I were friends, and I was still a tomboy."

"You're still a tomboy, Em. That's one of the reasons I like you so much. You're not like other girls who never do anything but worry about the latest fashions, or who's dating who. I like the fact you feel comfortable in old jeans and stuff."

"Fine, do I have to do this the hard way?"

Tony finally realized the seriousness of the situation. "Okay. Emmy, would you please go to the prom with me?"

"No way! I don't want to wear some fancy dress that I would feel half-naked in." She giggled when she saw the look on his face. "I'm kidding, you dork. I would love to go to the prom with you."

"Great!" Tony smiled as he reached across the table to take her hand and wondered if he could still find a decent tux.

They left Darby's, drove to the mall and watched *The Object Of My Affection* because Emmy wanted to see a romantic comedy. Tony wanted to see *Species 2*, but Emmy got her way by using her charms. She pouted. After the movie, Tony dropped Emmy off at her apartment and went straight home without coming inside. Emmy immediately called Kristen.

"What's up, Emmy? Did you guys go out on your own tonight?"

"We ran over to Darby's and grabbed some food. Then we saw a movie. Guess what?"

"Uh, Tony ate every hot dog in the place?"

"No, he only ate three. He asked me to go to the prom with him. Isn't that amazing?"

"Did he ask you, or did you ask him?" Kristen asked. "Tell me the truth."

"I kinda had to persuade him. He assumed I wouldn't want to go because I would have to wear a fancy dress."

"You do have to wear a formal dress, Em. You can't wear jeans and a sweatshirt," Kristen said.

"Says who? As far as I know there isn't any dress code. Why should I buy a dress I will only wear one time when I have some perfectly good jeans and sweatshirts already?"

"You are a dork. So, when do you want to go shopping for your dress?"

"How about this one?" Emmy held up the light blue gown for Kristen's inspection. "I like this one because I feel covered up and not half-naked." Emmy said as she pointed out the modest neckline.

"You do realize this is the section for children, right?" Kristen teased.

"You should be on TV because you are just so funny. Who are you going with anyway?"

"Christopher asked me if I wanted to go. I told him yes, but that he shouldn't expect me to... spend the night with him."

360

"Why not? I thought the prom was supposed to be an all-night affair."

"If you are talking about the games and stuff at the school, yeah, but lots of guys expect something different. You do know what I mean, don't you?"

Emmy put a finger to her mouth. "I have heard about sex, Kristen, but I'm not sure what it means exactly."

Kristen rolled her eyes.

Emmy frowned. "I'm not totally ignorant or naïve."

"Will it bother you if Randy and his date ride with us that night?" Kristen asked.

"I don't think so. Who is he taking?"

"Do you remember Gretchen Fitzgerald? She's the student council president."

"I think so. Isn't she the one who led that demonstration in the library?"

"Yeah, I think you're right. They were protesting about censorship or something because the library refused to carry some so-called controversial books."

"She will probably be a politician when she grows up."

"What do you think of this dress?" Kristen held up a strapless, sleeveless pink gown cut very low in the back. "It's your size."

Emmy grabbed the dress, held it up in front of her and gazed into the mirror. "It's a little short for me."

Kristen checked. "No it's not. It comes down to your knees."

Emmy giggled and then said, "I meant it's a little short on top. I don't want Tony to see everything."

"Then buy the blue one. Try it on so I can make sure it fits right," Kristen said. "It might have to be altered."

Chapter Thirty-Four

Emmy was jarred awake early by the telephone. Groaning, she reached for the phone, dropped it, picked it up and answered.

"Hey, Emmy, I'm sorry to call so early in the morning, but I thought maybe we could do breakfast or something."

She broke out into a huge smile and said, "Who is this? Do I know you? Your voice sounds kinda familiar, but..."

"Maybe I have the wrong number. I'm sorry to have bothered you."

"Well, maybe I recognize your voice." She couldn't help but giggle now as she rolled over on her stomach. She put her feet in the air and moved them back and forth. "Oh, Kenny, I'm so happy you're finally home. When did you get back?"

"Sometime in the middle of the night. I didn't think I should call then, so I waited until now."

"What time is it anyway?"

"A few minutes after eight."

"What day is it?"

Kenny laughed. "It's Sunday, May third, and Mom is going to make breakfast. I thought I would see if you want to come over and eat with us. Then we could go to church. How about it? I can come and get you."

"You don't have to do that. I'll take the bus."

"Are you sure? I haven't seen your apartment."

"That's a good thing. It's nothing to brag about. I'll take the bus."

"Okay. Breakfast should be ready around nine."

"I'll get there as soon as I can."

Emmy threw back the covers, jumped out of bed, took a bath—there was no shower in her bathroom—got dressed in record time and caught the bus. The bus stopped at the end of Fifth Street. She sprinted to the Colwell home, flew up the front steps and rang the bell. Kenny opened the door, and Emmy tried to calm her racing heart.

"That was quick. I didn't expect you to get here for another twenty seconds," Kenny teased.

362

"I got here as fast as I could because otherwise you would eat everything your mom made for breakfast. Is there any food left?"

"We haven't started eating yet. Come on back to the kitchen." He took her hand and led her through the living room and dining room.

"Hi, Mrs. Colwell. Do you need any help?"

"It's so good to see you, dear." Mrs. Colwell walked over and gave Emmy a hug. "Everything is about ready."

Mr. Colwell walked in through the back door and saw her. "Hello, Emmy. Do you remember this guy? He claims to be a musician and has been traveling all over the world."

She looked at Kenny and grinned. "I think I remember him now. Didn't you used to play guitar while I sang for a teen group at some church? I wondered whatever became of you."

Kenny took a step toward her and held out his arms. "Don't I get a hug or anything?"

She smiled as she wrapped her arms around him. She buried her face in his chest and whispered, "You've been gone for so long. I was afraid you would forget about me."

He raised her chin and looked into her sparkling blue eyes. "You know I will never ever let that happen." He kissed her as he held her close.

Kenny drove the Honda Odyssey to church, and Emmy sat next to him during the service. Afterward, Ronnie Rojas came over to talk to them. "It's good to see you again. It's seems like it's been years since you were here."

"It has been a long time, Pastor Ronnie. Do you remember Emmy?"

"Certainly, it's a pleasure to see you again, young lady. You look older."

Emmy's eyes lit up because no one ever said that to her before. Not that she could remember at least.

Emmy's bubble burst as Pastor Ronnie added, "You must be about a junior in high school now if I remember correctly."

After lunch, Emmy helped with the dishes while Kenny and his father looked at photos of the band. Emmy and Mrs. Colwell joined them while Kenny and Emmy sat side by side on the couch.

"Carter, I think we need to take our afternoon nap now."

"We do? Oh, right, Elly. It is good to see you again, Emmy. You know you can always come over to see us even if he's gone." Mr. and Mrs. Colwell headed upstairs to their bedroom.

Kenny ran his fingers through her hair. "The last time I saw you you were with Tony Bertucci. Are you guys still dating? You didn't say anything in your last email."

"Yes, are you seeing anyone special?"

Kenny got the impression that she didn't want to talk about Tony for some reason. He didn't press the subject. "I don't have time to start a relationship on the road. You know I see people all the time, but it's not like going on a date."

"I understand," she said. *Sometimes it doesn't feel like a date when I see Tony, either.*

"Mom and Dad are going out to Virginia to visit family for three weeks. Dad has two younger brothers, Thomas and Parker, who live on horse farms that have been in the family for generations. I kinda wanted to go with them."

"I've never been to Virginia," Emmy said—disappointed that Kenny would be leaving again.

Kenny held her hand and asked, "I'd really like it if you came with me? We could have some time to be alone."

She bit her lip as she thought about his suggestion. "I would really love to go, but I can't. I can't take any vacation time until I've been there for over a year. I've also got one more week of classes before final exams. I can't go anywhere."

"Oh, I guess I didn't think about that."

"There's something else, too." Emmy paused. She let go of his hand, and then continued, "Tony asked me to the prom. It's May sixteenth. I told him I would go. I even have a dress already."

"That should be fun. I didn't go to the prom my senior year because the only girl I wanted to take wasn't interested. She was only a freshman at the time and too much of a tomboy."

Emmy's eyes lit up. "You wanted to go to the prom with me? I never knew that."

"I never brought it up because I didn't think you would go."

364

Emmy thought about it. "My mother would have never let me go. She wouldn't let me go now if I still lived at home."

"Maybe I won't go on vacation with my parents. I've been traveling so much the last eighteen months. If I stay home, we can spend some time together."

Emmy looked at him. She wasn't sure how Tony would feel about her spending time with Kenny.

"You could bring Tony along... sometimes... not all the time though. I do want to have some time just for us."

"Can we go out to the carriage house?" Emmy asked as she bit her lip.

"Sure, Em. The couch is still there."

Later that evening they drove over to Darby's. Mr. Darby greeted them gruffly—like he treated all his favorite customers. "It's about time you two came to see me. I was beginning to believe your ego wouldn't fit through the door anymore. Now what do you guys want to eat?"

They placed their order, and Mr. Darby refused to take Kenny's money. They stayed at Darby's for over an hour before Emmy needed to get home. Kenny offered to take her, but she refused. "I'll catch the bus."

"Why? I can give you a ride."

"Please understand."

"Is there something you aren't telling me? Are you afraid to let me see your apartment?"

"You can't come over! You wouldn't like it. It's small and the furnishings are old."

"That doesn't matter to me. You haven't even told me the address. What would I do if I have to send you a letter or something?"

"Send it to your parents. I'll explain everything to you later. You just can't come over."

Emmy came over to see Kenny after work on Monday, but couldn't on Tuesday because of her night class. On Wednesday after dinner, they went out to the carriage house.

"My parents are leaving on Saturday morning, Em. They're

driving the Odyssey."

"Have you made up your mind about going with them?"

"I really should go, Em. I haven't seen my uncles for several years."

"I wish I could go with you, but I can't."

"I understand, Emmy. You have school and need to keep your job. There will be other opportunities."

"Can we go to Darby's after work on Friday? I might not have a chance to see you on Saturday."

"Sure, that will give us a chance to say goodbye until I get back from Virginia. Have you seen Tony at all this week?"

"No, but I talked to him after class yesterday."

"Would you like to bring him over tomorrow or Friday night?"

Emmy bit her lip. "No, I'll see him after you're gone."

"Are you afraid for the two of us to be together? Do you think we will get in a fight over you?" Kenny teased.

"No, but he might not understand... our relationship. I know he wouldn't appreciate what we did on the couch on Monday."

"We just kissed, Em."

"It was pretty intense kissing."

"I shouldn't have..."

"I let you touch me." She put her finger on his mouth to keep him from talking. "Can I come over after class tomorrow? We're getting out early."

"Of course you can. I could pick you up at school, so you don't have to take the bus."

"You don't have to. I don't mind taking the bus."

Emmy ended up staying at the library after class on Thursday. She needed time to study and also think about her relationship with Tony and Kenny.

After work on Friday, Emmy went directly to the Colwell house. She brought a change of clothes with her.

"Do you still want to go over to Darby's, Em? We could go somewhere else."

"Darby's is fine with me. It's still warm out. Let's walk."

366

They ate dinner and then went back to the carriage house.

"How long will you be home after you get back from vacation?"

"Just a couple of days. We will be gone until close to the holidays, but I will be home this Christmas."

"Are you all packed?"

"Yeah, the suitcases are in the house. Dad wants to hit the road by seven tomorrow. I'll call you before we leave. Unless you'd rather sleep..."

"I can go back to sleep after you call. I might stay in bed all day. It's been a busy week at work, but at least my classes are finished for the semester. I have my finals, and then I'm done until the second summer session starts in July."

She ended up staying with Kenny later than she planned.

"I really need to get home." She stood up and tucked her top into her jeans as Kenny lay on his back on the old couch.

"I'm not letting you take a bus home this late. I'm not even sure they are still running. It's after midnight." He jumped up and searched for his keys.

"Okay, you can give me a ride, but you have to drop me off at the corner by Cooper's Drugstore. I'll walk from there."

He drove to Cooper's and pulled into the parking lot.

"Thanks for the ride, Kenny." She opened the door but didn't get out right away.

He put a hand on her arm. "Em, why won't you let me take you to your apartment? What's going on?"

"Please, Kenny, just let me out here. I'll be all right, and don't you follow me down the street. Promise you won't follow me."

"All right. I won't follow you." He still didn't know why she wouldn't tell him the exact address of her apartment. *It must have something to do with Tony. Surely she's not letting him stay with her.* He sat in the car and watched until she disappeared from sight. *Maybe it's best that I'm going to Virginia. I could always stay a week and then fly home. I'll see what happens. I don't want to cause her any trouble if she's really serious about Tony.*

A few minutes before seven the next morning Kenny called. "We're going to leave in a few minutes. I'll call you when we get to Virginia, and I'll see you when I get back. Go back to sleep, Em."

"Have a safe trip, Kenny, and..." she paused.

"What is it, baby?"

"I'm sorry about last night."

"It's all right, Em. We didn't do anything too terrible."

"I didn't think it was all that terrible. I thought it was pretty great actually."

"You know what I mean, Em."

"I'll tell you about the apartment soon. I'm sorry for being so secretive. I've never kept anything a secret from you before. I feel terrible about it, but you have to trust me."

"I do, Em. I do."

Chapter Thirty-Five

"Knock, knock. Can I come in? Are you awake?" Mrs. Keasling asked early on the morning of May sixteenth—the day of the prom—as she pushed open Kristen's bedroom door. "You told me to make sure you got out of bed by eight."

Kristen groaned and rolled over onto her stomach. She covered her head with a pillow. "Can I sleep for another hour?"

Mom walked over to the bed and sat on the edge. "You made me promise not to let you sleep past eight. I've already given you an extra thirty minutes."

Kristen turned over and sat up. "Oh, all right. Emmy is supposed to call me when she wakes up. We have so many things to get done."

When Emmy hadn't called by eleven, Kristen called her.

"Hello."

"Hey! Are you still sleeping? It's time to get up. We have to get ready. We have to be at the hairdresser's in an hour. We have to get our nails done..."

They spent most of the afternoon with friends from school going through the same routine. They finally got back to Kristen's house shortly after four.

"We still have lots of things to do, Em. We have to eat and get dressed."

"What time are the guys supposed to be here? Is Gretchen going to meet us here or what?"

"I think Christopher and Randy are gonna pick her up. Tony is driving his car over here. The limo should be here at seven thirty."

"What else do we have to do except get dressed? How am I supposed to take a shower and not get my hair all wet?"

"Haven't you ever had your hair done in a salon before?"

"Not like this, and I've never had my nails done, either," Emmy said. "I'm a lousy tomboy, remember?"

"Oh, Emmy, I didn't mean to upset you. You may be a tomboy, but you're the prettiest one I know. Tony will be so surprised when he sees you. I love what they did with your hair.

Those braids are amazing."

Emmy made a fist. "If he says anything about my hair or my dress, I'm gonna punch him where it will hurt the most."

Three hours later the guys and Gretchen waited in the family room for Kristen and Emmy to make their grand entrance. Mrs. Keasling wanted pictures of all three couples. Finally, the two girls made it downstairs.

Tony looked at Emmy and grinned. "You look fantastic, Emmy. I really like..."

"Don't you dare say a word about how I look."

"Okay, but you look very pretty."

"Are you just saying that, or do you really mean it?"

"I really mean it. I know you don't really like dressing up, but you do look amazing."

"If you mess up my hair, I will hurt you. I spent an hour, and a small fortune, getting it done like this."

Tony looked at the back of her hair. "I like this braid and the curls. I figured you would wear it in a ponytail."

Mr. and Mrs. Keasling hustled the couples into the family room.

"Tony, you look so handsome in your tux. Did you let Maria take a picture before you left the house?"

"Yes, Aunt Karla, she took some pictures and made a big fuss about how I looked."

Emmy suddenly realized something. "Tony, you took Kristen to the prom last year, didn't you?"

"How did you know that? I don't remember seeing you there. Oh, of course, Kristen told you. "

"I didn't go because Derrick took Clarissa instead of me." She poked Tony in the side. "Kristen told me she needed to bribe you to take her."

"Yeah, I remember she kept after me to take her, and I didn't want to. Then she explained why she didn't want to go with the guys who asked her, so I agreed to be her date, if you wanna call it that."

"I think that was very considerate of you."

"Don't tell her, but I enjoyed it. Kristen is like a sister to

370

me. We've been close all our lives."

"The limo has arrived," Mr. Keasling said. "Thanks for arranging it, Kristen."

Roosevelt High became the last-minute location for the prom after a fire gutted the first floor of the Regency Hotel. Several of the students tried to organize a protest to boycott the prom unless school officials located a more suitable site. The protest fizzled out. With a senior class of over six hundred students, the gymnasium would be filled to capacity.

It was after eight by the time the three couples made it inside. As long as you didn't look too closely at the fake palm trees and amateurishly painted backdrops, the gym looked very much like a tropical paradise.

"Can you believe how crowded it is already?" Gretchen complained as they moved through the crowd. "I knew it was a mistake to have the prom here."

Tony pulled Emmy onto the dance floor. She always enjoyed dancing with him in spite of the large difference in their heights.

Just after ten o'clock, it was time to announce the king and queen. Alice Bromilow, the junior class president, took the mic. After thanking her fellow classmates, who sponsored the prom and did most of the work, she opened the envelope. "This year's Junior Class Prom King is... Luke Roberts!" Luke Roberts, a tall, good-looking African American star player on both the football and basketball teams, made his way up onto the stage and pumped his fist while pointing at his teammates. After the applause for him died down, Alice spoke again. "And now to present the crown to this year's prom queen please welcome last year's winner, Diana Ahronson." Alice waited for the applause for Diana to stop, opened the envelope and smiled. "This year's prom queen is... Kristen Keasling!"

Emmy screamed and hugged Kristen. "You won! I knew you would. Oh, Krissy, I'm so happy for you."

Tony smiled, kissed Kristen's cheek and said, "Way to go, Kristen."

Kristen made her way to the stage, and Diana placed the

crown on her head. She and Luke posed for pictures and shared a spotlight dance.

"Tony, doesn't Kristen look so beautiful? I can't wait to tell Derrick she won. He finished second last year."

"I know, Em. I was there."

Emmy poked him in the ribs. "I know that now, you dork."

Although the prom officially ended at midnight, the school stayed open until five in the morning. There were games and other activities for the students who stayed.

"Emmy, are we gonna stay all night, or what? I think Christopher and Kristen are going back to her house. I'm not sure what Randy and Gretchen have planned."

"I want to stay out all night. It doesn't matter where we go, but if we go back to Kristen's, I could change clothes."

Tony said, "You really don't like to wear formal dresses, huh?"

"Not any more than you like to wear that tuxedo. Did you bring a change of clothes?"

"We all did, even Gretchen."

"I'd rather go to Kristen's than stay here. I know! We can go for a hike in the woods. That will be fun."

Tony called the limo driver, and by twelve thirty they arrived back at the Keasling house. They changed out of their prom clothes and met in the downstairs family room.

Emmy raised her hand. "Who wants to go hiking?"

Kristen complained, but they all headed out to the trail that led into the woods.

"Isn't this spooky, Krissy? Do you think we might run into a bear or something?" Emmy looked into the shadows as she held onto Tony's arm.

"There aren't any bears in SoHam, goofy. Just because we are in the woods doesn't mean we are in the wilderness."

At that moment they heard something crashing through the brush.

"What was that?" Kristen hollered as she held onto Christopher.

A few seconds later they heard something else running

372

through the trees. Everyone stood still for a moment, and then Emmy giggled as two deer crossed the path a few yards ahead of them.

"Did you see those vicious creatures, Krissy. We're lucky we weren't eaten alive."

"You're gonna get it, Emmy. I hope a wolf comes by and gets you."

They kept walking and soon made it to the lake.

"I've never been past here. Where does the trail go from here?" Emmy asked.

"It keeps going and ends up back at the main entrance on Barclay Drive."

"Tony, lets keep going. I want to hike all the way around the trail."

Tony and Emmy kept hiking while everyone else returned to the house.

Emmy kept rather quiet as she and Tony walked along the trail.

"Emmy, are you disappointed that Kenny isn't here? I mean he was gone for so long, and then he took off again right after he got home."

"He asked me to go with him, but I couldn't. I've got my finals this coming week. I'm sorry I didn't see you last week."

"It's all right, Em. I assumed you wanted to spend some time with Kenny."

Emmy stopped walking. "You're not mad at me for that, are you?"

"No, do I have any reason to be mad?"

Emmy looked away and didn't answer. They started walking again and thirty minutes later arrived back at the house. They could hear the other couples talking as they walked around to the back.

"I think they're by the pool house, Em."

As they approached the pool area, Kristen saw them. "There you guys are. We were worried that a bear might have dismembered you."

"What are we gonna do for the rest of the night?"

Christopher asked. "It's too bad the pool isn't ready to use. We could all go swimming."

Emmy peeked under the pool cover. "I can't. I didn't bring a swimsuit."

Christopher and Randy grinned.

"I think you are missing the point," Gretchen responded with disgust as she frowned at Randy.

Emmy looked at Kristen, and then she understood. "You guys are creeps!"

Emmy and Kristen brought out some soft drinks, chips and other munchies. The guys scarfed everything down in a matter of minutes.

"Do you know of any pizza joints that might still be open?" Tony asked.

"You can't still be hungry?" Emmy asked.

"I could eat something else. We could go to Lenny's. It's open all night."

Gretchen said, "I'm not going anywhere else, unless it's home to my warm, comfy bed."

"Me, neither," Kristen added. "There are frozen pizzas if you guys want to make something."

Tony popped two Home Run Inn pizzas into the oven. The guys finished both pizzas as the girls talked about the different couples they saw at the prom. They stayed outside until around four. By then the girls were ready to call it a night.

"There is a bedroom upstairs you could use, Gretchen. I'll show you which one," Kristen said. She turned to the guys. "If you wanna stay here tonight, you can crash out here. There are those long lounge chairs with pads in the pool house. Or you could use the family room in the basement and crash wherever."

Randy asked Christopher, "Do you want to crash here, or head home?"

Tony said, "I'm staying here tonight."

Randy asked his brother, "Are we gonna go anywhere tomorrow afternoon? I know of several parties we could check out."

"I'm awake enough to drive. After all, we haven't been

374

drinking," Christopher said.

Randy asked Gretchen, "Are you going to stay here? We could give you a ride if you want to go home."

"I think I'll stay here tonight, but thanks for the offer, Randy. I enjoyed this night immensely."

"Yeah, right. Me, too," Randy replied without catching Gretchen's sarcasm.

"Yes, thanks for a pleasant evening, Christopher. Maybe I'll see you tomorrow." Kristen shook his hand. She tried to keep a straight face because she knew both guys wanted kisses, at the very least.

Kristen headed to the house, and Gretchen followed.

"That was cruel of us," Gretchen said.

Kristen grinned and then glanced over her shoulder at Christopher. "True, but anticipation can be a good thing."

The Braun brothers looked disappointed as they left. Emmy watched Kristen walk away and then looked at Tony.

"You better run, Em." He pointed to the house. "Otherwise you might be locked out and have to spend the night in the pool house with me."

"Are you really gonna sleep in the pool house?"

"I guess so. I don't think Kristen wants me in the house," he teased.

Emmy bit her lip. "Maybe I could crash out here, too. As long as you promise to behave."

"You can't stay out here with me. Kristen would kill me."

"Okay, I'll see you later. It's been fun." She took off running to catch up with Kristen and Gretchen.

"Wait, Em! I'm kidding. Kristen told me I could sleep in the downstairs family room."

Emmy kept busy at work during the week. On Tuesday and Thursday she took her final exams and was pleased to have them out of the way. She and Tony double-dated with Kristen and Travis Michaelson, another college guy Kristen knew, on Friday and Saturday. The next week was much the same, except that Emmy didn't have to be at Paul Frank for any reason. She did spend two evenings helping Tony study for his final exams.

Mama walked into the dining room where Tony and Emmy were studying. She stood with her hands on her hips and pointed at Emmy. "I am very upset with you, young lady."

"Why, Mama? What did I do?"

"It's what you didn't do." Mama walked up behind Emmy and squeezed her shoulders. "You haven't come over to see me."

Emmy smiled. *I guess things are back to normal.*

Shortly after noon on May thirtieth, Kenny and his parents returned home from their visit to Virginia. Kenny called Emmy right away. "We're back. Can you come over?" He assumed she still didn't want him to see her apartment.

"I can be there in two hours. I have to go over to Tony's. I'm helping him study for his exams."

"Are you sure you can leave him?" Kenny asked jealously.

"Yes, it's all right. I already told him you were coming home today. He understands that I want to spend some time with you before you have to leave."

"I don't want to cause any problems for you guys."

"Don't you want to see me?"

"Of course, I do."

"Then I'll be there when we finish. Could we order a pizza for tonight. I haven't had a good pizza in like forever."

"Sure, we can order whatever you want. I'll be out in the carriage house, so come on up when you get here." He paused, and then added, "You could bring Tony with you if you want."

Emmy shook her head. "No, I don't want to bring him over there."

Emmy caught a bus over to Tony's, and they studied in the dining room.

"Are you still going over to see Kenny today?" Tony asked as they took a break.

"I want to see him again before he leaves," she said. *This could turn into a problem. Both of these guys are acting jealous of each other.*

"It's all right if all you do is 'see' him, and I don't care if it's

376

lame to use air quotes." Tony grinned.

This time it didn't ease the tension.

Tony drove Emmy over to Kenny's after they finished studying.

"Thanks for the ride, Tony. I would invite you to stay, but..."

"It's all right, Em. I know you really don't want me to stay. You and Kenny need to have some time together. After all, he is your oldest friend."

She waited to see if he was going to add a smart aleck comment.

"Do you really mean that?"

He stared out the driver's window for a moment. "Yes, I mean it." He turned back to look at her. "As long as you aren't hiding anything from me."

"I'm not!" she said and then bit her lip. *Oh my God! I can't believe I just lied to him. Now I'm gonna feel like crap.*

She's hiding something. I know it. He moved closer to kiss her.

Emmy kissed him on the cheek before getting out of the car and running up the sidewalk. She stopped, waved at Tony and waited until he drove away. *I'm not going to do anything but give Kenny a kiss on the cheek like I did with Tony.* She ran around the house to the side entrance to the carriage house. She flew up the steep stairs and hustled over to where Kenny stood. She wrapped her arms around his waist and held on.

"Does this mean you missed me, Em?"

"Maybe a little." She let go and kissed his cheek. "You need a shave."

They ordered a pizza, and Emmy only stayed until nine. She wanted to make sure she could catch a bus home.

"I'll see you tomorrow. Gotta run." She kissed his cheek again.

He rubbed his cheek after she left. "A kiss on the cheek? What am I? A brother?"

After work on Monday evening, Emmy came straight to the

377

Colwell house without going home first. Mrs. Colwell prepared one of Kenny's favorite meals for dinner.

"The meat loaf and cheesy potatoes smell so good, Mrs. Colwell. Is there anything I can do to help?"

"Would you mind setting the table for me, dear." Mrs. Colwell knew Emmy needed to feel useful.

"Thanks for making this for me, Mom. You can't imagine how much I miss home-cooked meals when I'm gone."

"You're welcome, son."

Emmy asked for the recipes later as she helped with the cleanup.

"Okay, everything is finished," Mrs. Colwell said. "You and Kenny should go somewhere and have some fun."

Emmy grinned as she said, "Thanks, I think we will hang out in the carriage house."

He would be leaving the next morning while she was at work. She had to say her goodbyes tonight.

Kenny followed her up the stairs and into the carriage house. "Are you gonna tell me what's going on with your apartment? Why won't you tell me which one it is?"

"Okay, I'll tell you, but you have to promise not to get mad."

"All right, I promise."

"Let me explain some things. The only reason I was able to rent the apartment in the first place is because the landlord's wife is my mother's second or third cousin. Somehow Mom convinced her to rent me the place. The landlord didn't want to, but his wife convinced him. I found out their last name is Didirosi."

"Didn't you know that when you rented the place? Don't you have to give them a check for the rent?"

"No, I have to pay in cash, and she gives me a hand-written receipt. Anyway, my mother informed me that the landlord's wife would be keeping track of who comes to see me. Mom threatened me by saying she would have the landlord kick me out if I have any boys come over. Especially if you came over there." She paused to catch her breath. "I know that's true because Tony stopped over one night, and Mom called me the next day and got on my case."

"Emmy, she can't do that. I'm sure you have some rights as a tenant."

"Maybe so, but Mrs. Didirosi told me I would not get my deposit back if they booted me out. There's one more thing."

"What's that?" He raised his eyebrows.

She bit her lip. "I don't actually have a real lease."

He sighed then said, "Sorry, but they don't sound like very respectable people, Em. I think you should move out of there and stay with Mom and Dad. We can fix up the carriage house and make it into an apartment for you."

"You know I can't do that. My mother already threatened to cause problems for your parents."

"Really? Think about it." Kenny waved his hands. "What could she do, Em? She's just making empty threats."

"Maybe so, but I can't stay with you. She would be over here every day to harass me."

"This is what I think. You should stand up to your mother and your landlords. Tell them you are going to have whoever you want come over to visit. It doesn't matter if they are male or female. It's none of their business. It's your place. I don't think they will follow through on any threat."

"But what if they do?"

"Then you take them to court. If they are making you pay cash, they are probably not reporting it as income. I'm sure they won't want the IRS to get involved. If they do kick you out, then we find another place for you. Or else you move into the carriage house. That's the best option."

"But I'm not eighteen yet."

"I am. I could sign the lease."

"We can't live together," Emmy said and then bit her lip as she looked up at him. "Can we?"

Chapter Thirty-Six

"I thought the warm weather would never arrive." Emmy stared out a window as she complained to her coworker one afternoon. "Now that it's here, I'm stuck inside this stuffy office."

"You'll get used to it. Working is a fact of life," one of her coworkers said.

Emmy found the last file on her list and pulled it from the cabinet. "There must be other ways to earn a living."

"Certainly, but you need a college education to land the really good ones. Even a degree is not always a guarantee these days. I have a cousin who has a masters degree in chemical engineering and he's working as a sales clerk at the mall in one of those kiosks..."

Emmy listened as her coworker rambled on for another minute."

Kristen graduated in the top ten percent of her class from Roosevelt High and called Emmy the day before the graduation ceremony.

"What do you mean you're not going?" Kristen asked. "You have to. How else will you receive your diploma?"

"Principal O'Dell said they mail the diplomas," Emmy said as she checked her mail.

"Won't your parents be disappointed?"

Emmy laughed. "Ha! They haven't even mentioned it. They didn't go when Diane graduated because they were fighting." Emmy changed the subject. "Did I tell you I got an A in both my classes?"

"No, but I assumed you would. If you change your mind, you can still attend the ceremony. I can pick you up."

"I'm sorry, Kristen, but I'm not going."

"You can be so stubborn."

"I know. Are you still my best friend?"

"I suppose so, though I don't know why I should even like you. You are coming to the party if I have to kidnap you."

"Yes, I'll be there for your graduation party. Unless I have to work that day."

"It's a Saturday. You're off on the weekends. You didn't start working at Darby's again, did you?"

Emmy opened the last piece of mail. "No, but that's a thought. I could pick up some extra cash."

"I'm hanging up now. You will be there or else."

"Wait, Kristen! I see your mother bought some fancy invitations for your graduation party."

"Yeah, I tried to talk her out of it, but she insisted."

"I'm not sure I can make it. I might have to work that day."

"We've been over this before, you stinker. You gotta be there. It won't be as much fun if you're not with me."

"I don't know." Emmy stifled a laugh as she sat cross-legged on her couch.

"Please say you'll come. There won't be any beer like at Derrick's party. Derrick is home, by the way. He asked about you, and I told him you were still dating Tony. You are still dating Tony, right? I know you spent a lot of time with Kenny while he was home."

Emmy said, "I'll be there. Did you really think I'd miss your party?"

"No, because I would shoot you if you did," Kristen said.

"I'll call Tony and make sure he remembers the date."

Emmy called Tony as soon as she hung up with Kristen.

"Hi, Mama, it's Emmy. Is Tony home?"

"He's out back mowing the yard. Should I get him for you, or can he call you back?"

"It can wait. Would you please have him call me when he finishes?"

"Of course, dear. Oh, wait, he might be finished now. He just turned off the mower. Hang on a second." Mama hollered out the back door, and Tony came inside.

Emmy told him about the party.

"You know I can't be there that day, Emmy," Tony reminded her.

"Why not?"

"I'll be in South Bend the whole week at that football camp.

381

I won't get home until Sunday. I thought I told you about it."

"Crap! Yeah, I guess you did, but I didn't realize it was the week of Kristen's party. I really want to go."

"You can go to the party without me. I mean, you have to go. Kristen is your best friend."

"I don't want to go alone."

"You won't be alone, Emmy. Derrick and Kristen and a whole bunch of their friends will be there." Tony nodded his head as Mama placed dinner on the kitchen table.

Emmy didn't say anything for a moment.

"Are you still there, Em?"

"Yes, I'm here."

"You want to have a date for the party, don't you?"

"I guess so," she answered glumly. "I assumed we would be going together."

"I'm sorry, Em, but I can't cancel going to the football camp. Those kids have a pretty rough life. They don't have much going for them, and they really look forward to this camp."

"I know, and I'm not upset with you."

"It's all right with me if you ask someone to go with you. How about Linda Bailey? You could go with Linda and Barry," Tony suggested.

"Not exactly how I envisioned going to the party."

"I'm sorry, Em. Mama just put dinner on the table. I gotta run."

"Okay, I'll talk to you later. Call me if you want. I won't be doing anything tonight."

Emmy wanted to go with someone because most of the kids would be with dates, but she resigned herself to going alone.

"Hey, Em. I got your message and was going to call you later. How are things back home?" Kenny said into the phone, a finger pressed to his free ear so he could muffle the sound of the band's rehearsal.

"Good, but I always miss you when you're touring."

"I know. Me too, Em. What's up?"

"I confronted both my landlady and my mother."

"Good for you." He held up a finger to let Frankie Hanna

382

know he would be ready in a minute.

"It was just like you predicted. They backed down from their threats, and now I can have my friends visit. You will be able to see my apartment in December. Sooner if you can get away for a day or two."

"That's great, Em. Hey, I gotta run. Frankie is giving me an evil look."

"All right. Bye, Kenny. I'll talk to you later."

The landlord's wife still kept track of who came to see Emmy, but now Emmy didn't worry about losing her apartment.

Emmy took the bus to the mall one evening. She purchased a ticket to see *The Horse Whisperer* and a medium popcorn, She handed her ticket to the usher, rounded a corner and bumped into Scott Simmons.

He nearly spilled his popcorn. "Whoa! Hang on there."

"Hi, Scott. How are you?"

"Hi..." He tried to remember her name. Fortunately, it popped into his mind just in time. "Emily. I'm fine. How are things with you?"

"Good."

"Are you here by yourself?" Scott watched his friends continue down the hallway without him.

"Yes. I came by myself."

"I'm here with my friends," he said. "Are you enjoying your summer vacation? Must be good not to have to get up for school every morning."

Scott began walking after his friends. Emmy followed along as she checked the signs above the doors for her movie.

"I still have to get up to go to work."

"Oh, I didn't know you worked a summer job. I thought you were too young to get a job."

"How old do you think I am, Scott?" Emmy asked, a little agitated.

"Well, I know you've started high school, so I assume you are fourteen or maybe fifteen. Why?"

"I graduated from high school in December. I'm seventeen.

I'll be eighteen in July."

"Really?" Scott tilted his head as he looked down at her body. "I didn't know. I'm sorry if I offended you by thinking you were so young."

"I hear that from everyone, so I'm used to it, I guess. Is that why you have never asked me out? Because you thought I was too young for you?"

Scott lifted his eyebrows in surprise. "Emily, even at seventeen, you are too young for me. I don't mean to hurt your feelings, but I don't usually date high school girls. I've noticed you with the other kids, and I think you are really cute, but I never thought about asking you on a date."

Emmy's feelings were hurt. "I understand."

"You're not spending your whole summer working, are you? Do you work on the weekends?"

Emmy's countenance brightened. "I don't usually work weekends. In fact, I'm invited to a graduation party this Saturday, and I wanted to find someone to go with me. My boyfriend will be in South Bend and can't go. Would you happen to know anyone who might be interested. Not like a real date, but as a friend."

"Sorry, but no one pops into my head." *Geez! What do you think I am? A dating service.*

One of Scott's friends came back and overheard his conversation with Emmy.

She sighed with obvious disappointment. "That's all right. I expect everyone already has plans."

Emmy sounded so forlorn that Scott felt sorry for her. "When is the party, Emily?"

Scott looked at his friend, who shook his head and mouthed the words, "No way! Don't even ask. She's just a kid."

"It's this Saturday afternoon and evening. There will be food, and stuff to do all day, really." She tilted her head. "Why are you calling me Emily, anyway?"

Scott got embarrassed, thinking he called her the wrong name all together. "I thought that... I'm sorry. I'm not real good at remembering names—never have been."

"Oh, it is my real name all right, but everyone calls me

Emmy."

"That's right. I forgot, sorry." Scott tapped his temple for a moment. "What about Tim Riley? He's closer to your age."

"Is he a friend of yours?"

"Yeah, do you remember the guy with the red hair who always hung out with us at the O'Briens and at church? He's Pastor Brian's younger brother."

Emmy thought for a moment. "Not really."

"Well, how about..." Scott couldn't think of anyone else to go with Emmy. He really didn't want to waste his Saturday afternoon. "If you want me to, I will take you to your party and stay as long as I can, but I have to work Saturday night. Will that be all right?" He felt safe asking. *No way she is going to say yes after I practically told her she was a kid.*

"That would be great!" Emmy's voice jumped up an octave. "I'll call you with all the details later." Emmy took off without giving Scott a chance to change his mind.

"But... Oh, no. Darn it." He shook his head in disgust as he watched her disappear into one of the shows.

His friend heard the last part of his conversation and laughed. "Scott, are you robbing the cradle now? That girl looks much too young to be going out with you."

"Aw! Shut up. I'm only doing her a favor. I might ask around and see if someone wants to go with her. I'll get out of it one way or another."

Scott's friend punched him on the shoulder. "Yeah, well, remember that under eighteen is jailbait, old buddy."

When Tony called her later that night, Emmy told him about Scott. "I ran into Scott Simmons at the mall."

"He's the older guy from church, right?"

"Yeah. He was with some friends, and I talked to him." Emmy hesitated for a moment before continuing. "I told him about Kristen's party, and I kinda talked him into taking me. He didn't want to at first. He tried to set me up with one of the other guys. Are you upset that I'm going with him?"

"Not upset, but I'm not thrilled to death about it, either," Tony said. *Why can't you just go by yourself, Em?*

"He's a good guy, and I told him you were going to be out of town."

Tony paused for a second. "That's the guy you teased me about."

"When?"

"You were over and you said something about kissing him," Tony reminded her.

"Oh, I remember. I've never kissed him, and I'm not planning to let him kiss me at the party." She recalled the situation. *I was only teasing you about kissing him to get you to treat me more like your girlfriend.*

"I gotta go, Em. Have fun at the party—but not too much fun."

"Talk to you later." Emmy stared at her phone after ending the call. She sighed and sat down on the couch. She put her elbows on her knees and her chin in her hand. *Maybe I need to think about someone else. Tony is always busy with football. Kenny's main focus is his music. I have to think of myself a little.*

Chapter Thirty-Seven

On Saturday, the day of Kristen's party, Emmy got ready and decided to call Tony. She left a message, and he called back a few minutes later.

"Hey, Em, what's up? I'm on a break, so I can't talk long."

"Are you still upset about the Scott thing? If you are, I'll call him and cancel it."

"I'm not upset, but I don't totally understand why you feel such a need to have a date for the party."

"It's because of what happened in school after we met." She bit her lip. "You're gonna think it's silly."

"I promise I won't." *This should be good.*

"Some of Kristen's friends commented about me looking like a kid, and that's why I always hung out with the freshmen boys. You know, at dances and stuff. I guess I figured I could prove to them that I was just as mature as they are if Scott brought me to the party. Silly, huh?"

He laughed. "Maybe, but I kinda understand. You shouldn't worry about what other people think. Your real friends know you the best."

"Should I cancel or not?"

Tony hesitated.

"Well?"

"No. Have a good time, and tell Kristen I'm sorry for missing the party."

"All right. I will."

Emmy decided to wait for Scott on the front porch. He arrived a couple of minutes early and saw she was already outside. Emmy dashed to the car before Scott had a chance to get out. She wore a fairly new dress and braided her hair in two places. She looked fantastic, but so very young and innocent.

Emmy got in the car, buckled her seatbelt and smiled at Scott. "Thanks again for doing this, Scott. I really appreciate it."

"No problem. What could be better than free food and a party? You remember that I have to leave early for work, though, right?" Scott asked. He sounded bored already.

"Yes, that won't be a problem."

Scott took a good look at Emmy as she sat in the car. She looked even prettier than he remembered, but he still had trouble believing she was almost eighteen.

Emmy directed him to the Keasling home without getting lost. They parked on the street and walked up the driveway.

"Pretty fancy place, huh?" Emmy said.

"You can say that again. Must be nice to have money," Scott answered.

Kristen saw Emmy with Scott, grabbed her arm and pulled her away. "Who is that old guy you're with? He must be at least twenty-five, and he kinda reminds me of that movie guy. I can't remember his name."

"Tommy Cruz and he's not twenty-five," Emmy said as she looked over her shoulder at Scott. "His name is Scott Simmons. He's one of the guys that I know from the group of kids I met a while back. I talked to Tony this morning, and he said to say he's sorry about missing your party."

"He wasn't invited. I made sure I scheduled the party when he was gone," Kristen joked. "Does Tony know you are bringing Scott to the party?"

"Tony knows, but he wasn't real happy about it. I promised Tony that Scott didn't think of this as a real date, so he grudgingly gave his approval."

Kristen took another look at Scott. "He is very good-looking, and he does look like Tommy Cruz except his nose isn't as big. Anyway, I gotta go mingle with some relatives to keep Mom happy. I'll see you in a bit." Kristen ran into the house to help her mother and Mama in the kitchen. "Emmy's here with an older guy she knows. Did you know about it, Mama?"

"Tony mentioned something about it," Mama replied, but didn't appear too concerned.

"I'm never going to use this catering company again," Karla said. "They are thirty minutes late already."

"Relax, Karla. I'm sure they are on their way," Mama said.

Emmy saw Scott roll his eyes as they listened to some of Kristen's friends. "What's the matter, Scott? You look bored."

"Sorry. I'm not bored," he replied. *It's just that I have no interest in listening to these kids talk about their high school experiences.*

Emmy heard several kids commenting about how handsome Scott was. One girl even said, "Can you believe that guy is here with Emmy Colasanti? I've never seen her with an older guy. I thought she and Tony Bertucci were dating, but I could be wrong."

Mission accomplished!" Emmy pumped her fist. She saw Derrick with his new girlfriend and felt slightly envious of her. Scott excused himself to visit the food and drink tables on the deck at the back of the house.

Derrick came over to talk to Emmy. He gave her a big hug, lifted her off her feet and twirled her around. "Emmy, this is Amber Quinlan. Amber, this is Emmy Colasanti. She is Kristen's best friend, and we went out last year for a short time."

Amber looked at Emmy and wondered about her age.

Emmy looked Amber over. *You look like you're older than Derrick.* "Derrick and I dated a few times, if you want to call it that. Really, he is almost like my big brother."

After Emmy finished talking to Amber, Scott returned with a plate of food and a drink, all for himself—nothing for Emmy. Emmy saw Barry Newton and Linda Bailey and hurried over to talk to them leaving Scott to trail behind her. He took his time as he stole a couple of surreptitious glances at Amber.

"Who's the old guy with you?" Barry asked. "Where's Tony?"

Emmy sighed and explained again. "Tony is in South Bend at a football camp. Scott Simmons is here as my friend."

"He doesn't look at you like you're only a friend. He stared pretty intently when Derrick hugged you, and I don't think it was your shoes that he was admiring."

"He's only a friend, Barry, and I had to practically pay him to bring me here today."

"Why did you come with him? I know you said Tony is in South Bend, but why didn't you come by yourself?"

Emmy rolled her eyes. *Am I going to have to explain this to*

389

everyone. "I wanted to come with someone because I knew all Kristen's friends would have dates, and I didn't want to be the only girl by herself."

"Okay, but why such an old guy?" Barry asked again.

"I thought if I came with an older man, the other kids wouldn't think I looked so young."

Barry tilted his head and scrunched his forehead. "But you are still young, Emmy."

"You're a guy. You wouldn't understand." Emmy stomped her foot and then spun around and walked away.

This year the party stayed under control, and the kids weren't allowed to have any beer. Uncle Carmen and Uncle Vincent intentionally kept a high profile to intimidate the kids. Mrs. Keasling hired a DJ for music, and the kids danced along with the older crowd. Emmy danced with all of her old friends, and many of them asked her about Scott.

Should I just make an announcement? Emmy sighed.

Later, Barry asked, "Are you still a virgin?" Leave it to him to get right to the point.

She opened her eyes wide as she punched his arm. "Geez, Barry. Yes, I am, not that it's any of your business, and another thing—Scott doesn't know anything about my love life, or rather lack of one, so don't be telling him anything, okay?" She shook her head. "I can't believe you asked me if I'm a virgin. Can't a girl have any secrets?"

"Emmy, I have known you for so long. I know all your secrets. Does he know Tony?"

"He doesn't know Tony, but knows I have a boyfriend named Tony. Don't you tell him anything about me, Barry Newton."

"Maybe I will, and maybe I won't. What's it worth to you?"

"I'll let you live. How about that?"

Barry smiled at her. "Emmy, you look very pretty in that dress. I'm serious. You really look nice."

She waited for a punchline that never appeared. "Thank you, Barry. That's sweet of you to notice."

"Do you want me to get it wet for you, like last year?" He

390

laughed as he teased her.

"You better not if you want to survive the day." She shook a fist at him. "Linda is very lucky to have you. I mean, you are very lucky to have Linda. I still don't know what she sees in you. Since we're asking very personal questions today, are you still...?"

Barry grinned wickedly, but didn't answer her question. Emmy realized the truth. "You better be very careful, or else you'll end up being a daddy, and God knows the world doesn't need another Barry Newton."

Emmy used the bathroom in the pool house. As she came out, she saw an old man sitting alone on a bench. *I can't tell for sure because of the sunglasses and that Panama hat, but I think I should know you. You kinda look like Tony's grandpa, but a lot thinner.* She stared at him for a moment. "Hello. I think I recognize you from somewhere."

He heard her voice and turned in her direction. "And I remember you as well. I am the old man you ran into last year when you came flying out of the pool house. I imagine you were pretty frightened, but you don't need to be afraid of me. I'm rather harmless now. Why don't you sit by me for a moment?" He patted the empty spot beside him and Emmy sat down. "I am dying of cancer and will not be here too much longer, I hope."

"I'm sorry to hear that."

"No, no!" He shook his hand. "Please, don't pity me. My wife passed away almost a year ago, and I miss her very much. She was my guiding light."

Emmy listened attentively to his story. He opened his wallet and pulled out an old photograph. He held it up for her to see. "This is a picture of us on our wedding day from many years ago."

She looked at him and heard the love in his voice for his departed wife. Her eyes filled with tears, and her heart opened to him. The man remained silent for a moment as he raised his face to feel the warmth of the sun, and then he began to tell her more of his story. She listened to him as he reminisced about his late wife.

"I can't wait until the cancer takes me, and I can see my beautiful Dotty again."

Emmy closed her eyes as she let him talk. When Emmy opened her eyes, she noticed tears streaming down his cheeks.

"I hope you feel better soon." She kissed the old man on the cheek as she left to join Scott and her friends. Then she realized that he never told her his name.

Emmy saw Scott talking to Derrick. She joined them as they talked about sports. She stood in front of Scott, with her back to him, and he put his hands on her shoulders.

"How do you know Emmy? Did you go to the same school?" Scott asked Derrick.

Derrick answered, "Yes, we both went to Roosevelt. I graduated last year. Now I'm at the University of Arizona."

"Lincoln High and then North Park for me," Scott said.

Emmy appeared afraid Derrick would tell Scott something to embarrass her. She put her finger in her mouth, bit it and looked at Derrick so demurely. Derrick saw the hope in her eyes.

"I've known Emmy and Diane since junior high, and I've always thought of Emmy as being very pretty for a tom... young lady." Derrick looked at Emmy and saw a smile on the face of a very grateful girl.

"I'm gonna get something to drink. I'll be back." Scott turned to leave but then hesitated before turning back. "I'm sorry, Emmy. Where are my manners? Can I get you something?"

Emmy smiled. "Thank you. Could you bring me a bottle of water, please? I'm gonna talk Derrick into dancing with me."

Emmy put her hands on Derrick's shoulders as they danced, Emmy said, "Thank you for not telling Scott that I'm a total tomboy."

"Emmy, are you trying to impress an older man?"

"No, I just don't want Scott to think of me as just a kid. I want him to think of me as a woman."

Derrick laughed. "Emmy, you may be a woman, but you're still a tomboy. You'd rather play football than go shopping for clothes any day."

"Yeah, so what?"

"Should I tell Kristen you are trying to make sure Scott knows you are a femme fatale?" Derrick teased.

392

"You better not!"

"Why not? You guys share everything, don't you?"

"Because she'll tell Tony."

"I think you might have told me, but I forgot — where is Tony today, and why are you with Scott?"

I should wear a sign around my neck to explain this. "Tony is in South Bend at a football camp for under-privileged kids, and Scott is an old friend I met before I knew Tony. Yes, Tony knows I'm here with Scott, and he's not twenty-five, if that's what you're thinking. And, by the way, how old is Amber? She looks older than you."

"She's two years older, but you better not say anything about that."

"I'm not stupid. I'd never say that to a lady."

"I have some very fond memories of our time together, Emmy, even if we were not really in a romantic relationship."

"Is your relationship with Amber romantic?"

Derrick smiled. "You could say that."

"Are you sleeping with her?"

"A real gentleman never tells."

Emmy punched his arm. "You're a creep."

"You know what? I am glad that we weren't lovers because if we had been, and then broke up, we probably wouldn't be friends today. Although it would have been special to be your boyfriend."

"It would have been special, but like you said, it probably would have ruined our friendship, and I think our friendship is worth more than a few kisses, or whatever else you had in mind, you naughty boy."

"Emmy, you are the sweetest girl I know. How do you manage to look so sweet and yet so sexy at the same time?"

She blushed at his comment. "I don't feel sexy at all. Sweet and innocent, perhaps," she added as she smiled coquettishly at Derrick.

"You have such an innocent looking baby face, and you can still pass for a freshman." Derrick saw her perplexed look. "I meant that as a compliment, Emmy. You are very sexy. I like pretty girls who don't realize they are."

"They are what?" Emmy asked.

"Pretty." Derrick grinned. "See! You don't even realize how amazing you look."

"Get out of here. Amber is elegant. Not me."

Scott approached with a bottle of water for Emmy. The music stopped, and Derrick kissed her on the cheek and asked, "Is that a new dress? It looks almost as lovely as you, Miss Colasanti."

"Thank you, Mr. Keasling. How kind of you to notice."

"I'll talk to you later, Em. I need to find Amber."

"You better be good," Emmy warned.

Derrick eyes twinkled. "I'm always good, Em. You should know that."

Emmy turned bright red.

Scott looked at Emmy and then Derrick. *Maybe you're not as innocent as I think?*

"Thanks for the water, Scott."

Emmy and Scott were talking when she saw Barry approaching with a bottle of water and a mischievous grin on his face.

"You better not," Emmy warned, as she remembered the previous year.

"It's just a bottle of water, Emmy. Why are you afraid of it?" Barry asked. "I'm not going to get you wet."

Scott raised an eyebrow. *I may have totally underestimated you, Emmy.*

Barry grinned as he launched his water at Emmy getting her dress wet.

"I'm gonna kill you, Barry." Emmy splashed her bottle on Barry.

Barry took off running.

Scott shook his head. *What on earth are you doing, Emmy?* He watched with intrigue as Emmy chased Barry.

Barry ran back toward Scott with Emmy in pursuit. He tripped and collapsed next to Scott. Emmy emptied the rest of her bottle on Barry's head as he lay on the ground.

Barry looked at Scott as Emmy helped him get up. "It's an old story from last year."

394

Scott looked at his watch. "Emmy, it's almost six. I need to leave to get to work. Are you ready to go home?"

"Would you mind if I stayed, Scott? I'm sure I can get a ride with Barry or Derrick. You don't have to worry about me. Thanks for bringing me, though."

"You're welcome, Emmy. I'll talk to you later." Scott shook hands with Barry. "It was nice meeting you." But he sensed that Barry didn't trust him.

"I'll walk you to your car, Scott."

"You don't need to, Emmy."

"I don't mind."

Emmy leaned against his car as Scott stood in front of her.

"Thanks again for bringing me. I hope it wasn't too boring."

"I enjoyed being with you, Emmy. You kinda surprised me. When is your birthday?"

"July eighth."

Scott gazed into her eyes. He thought about calling in sick and taking Emmy away from the party. He leaned closer and kissed her quickly.

Emmy's heart raced. *Oh, no! I didn't know you were going to do that. I promised Tony I wouldn't kiss you.*

"I should get going, Emmy." *If I don't leave now, I'm gonna kiss you again. If I kiss you again, I won't want to stop.*

Emmy's chest rose and fell. *Oh, Scott, don't kiss me again. Maybe Tony will understand if I tell him you kissed me, but I didn't kiss you back.*

"I'm sorry if I surprised you." Scott stepped back. "Maybe we can do something special to celebrate your birthday." Scott looked at his watch. "I really have to go. I'll call you soon." He pulled his keys out of his pocket and got in the car.

Emmy watched him drive away while Barry covertly kept an eye on her.

Shortly after nine Barry asked, "Hey, Emmy, do you still need a ride home? Linda wants to leave."

"Yeah, I'll be right there. I need to say good night to Kristen and Derrick."

395

"Don't take too long."

"I won't. I see Kristen over there," Emmy said as she ran over to Kristen.

"Are you taking off, Em?"

"Yeah, Barry wants to go. Great party, by the way. I had a blast."

"Thanks. See you later. I gotta go help..."

Emmy didn't hear the rest as Kristen took off. Emmy let Derrick know she was leaving. "Amber is gorgeous, Derrick. I'm happy for you."

"Thanks, Emmy. I'm happy for you and Tony. Say hi for me when you see him again."

"I will. I wish he could have been here today." She saw the old man talking to Kristen. "Derrick, who is that man with Kristen? He looks so familiar. I assume he's family, but I don't know his name."

"That's Grandpa—Mom's Dad. Howard Lombardi."

"Really? He looks so much older and thinner than in the photograph at Tony's house."

"He's dying of cancer, Em."

"That's right. He did mention that earlier."

"The doctors don't think he has much time left. He really should be in the hospital, but he insisted on being here today because it's Kristen's party. He's always spoiled her. His wife died suddenly last year, only a few days after my graduation party, of a heart attack."

"You mean your grandmother, right?"

Derrick nodded his head.

"That is so sad."

Emmy hurried over to his grandfather. "I'm sure you will feel better soon, Mr. Lombardi." She kissed his cheek.

"Thank you, young lady."

Emmy whispered tenderly to him, "Your wife told me to kiss you, and she can't wait to see you again."

He smiled.

Chapter Thirty-Eight

Tony walked in the back door early Sunday afternoon and saw Mama pulling a pie out of the oven. "That smells good. Is it apple?'

"Yes, but it has to cool." Mama set the pie on the stove and turned to face Tony. "How was camp?"

He hugged his mother and sniffed the pie. "I think I enjoyed it more than the kids."

"Are you hungry?"

"Mama," he said as he smiled, "have you ever known me to turn down food?"

She laughed.

"How was Kristen's party?"

"Are you asking about the whole party, or just about Emmy?" She pulled a pan of lasagna from the warming oven.

"Mostly the whole party, but did Emmy have fun?"

"It was a good party. I saw Emmy dancing with everyone."

"With Scott?"

"I can't say I ever saw her dancing with him. I think he left early. What kind of vegetable would you like?"

"Do we have any of that broccoli cauliflower mix?"

"Yes, and I'll heat some garlic bread. Your grandfather made it to the party. He shouldn't have, but you know how he can be."

After dinner Tony called Emmy.

"Did you have fun?"

"Yeah, I really did." Emmy poured a can of Campbell's Tomato Soup into a pan and added milk. "I danced with lots of people and chased Barry."

"Did he try to pour water on you again?"

"Yeah, but I got him back. Scott left early, and I only danced with him once. He's not as graceful as you." She paused and bit her lip. *Should I tell you he kissed me? No, you don't need to know.*

"What did people say about him?"

Emmy laughed. "Everyone thought he was like twenty-five

397

or so."

"Are you happy he took you?"

"I guess I shouldn't have made a big deal about coming to the party with someone. I had just as much fun after he left." *But I did get a kick out of some of the comments about him.*

Emmy talked to Tony for over an hour.

"Mama said Grandpa made it."

"Oh, right! I talked to him. He told me about... his condition."

"He is a fighter, Em. He never complains."

"Maria, Carmen just called," Karla Keasling said over the phone several days later. "Daddy took a turn for the worse last night. It won't be long now."

Mama closed her book and jumped up from her rocking chair. "I'll be right there."

Howard Lombardi insisted on dying at home. He hated hospitals, so a room had been set up in Carmen's house for hospice to take care of him. The family gathered together, and over the next several hours, everyone had a chance to say goodbye.

"I know he's in a coma, but do you think he can still hear us?" Karla clung to Mama after sitting by her father.

"Some doctors believe that is possible."

"I thought he would have more time," Karla said. "I'm not ready to say goodbye."

Mama held Karla close. "None of us are, but his suffering will be over. I believe he will be together with Mother in heaven."

Emmy's phone rang early the next morning. "Hello," she answered sleepily.

"Emmy, it's me." Tony's voice cracked.

"Hi, Tony. You're up early."

"I've actually been up all night. My grandpa passed away last night.

"I'm so sorry. Do you want me to come over right now?"

"Yeah, if you can. I'd appreciate that."

Emmy jumped out of bed, ran into the bathroom, turned on

the hot water, and then dashed back to her bedroom. By the time she grabbed some clean clothes out of her dresser and tossed them on the bed, the water in the tub was hot. She took a quick bath, dressed, called work, grabbed a banana and sprinted out the door.

Emmy caught the bus which dropped her off at the end of Tony's street. She jumped off, turned to her right and began running. The strong morning breeze blew her long hair out of control. She cut across the driveway, jumped over Mama's flower bed and took the front steps three at a time. Tony opened the front door before she could even ring the bell.

"I got here as soon as I could."

"Let's sit out here, Emmy. I need some fresh air."

"All right. Are you okay, Tony?"

"I'll be all right. Would you be able to come to the wake and funeral with me?"

"Of course I will."

Emmy put her hand on his knee as Tony sat down on the front porch steps. Two blue jays squawked at each other and Tony looked up. He continued looking in the same spot even after the birds flew away. She didn't want to disturb his thoughts, so she remained respectfully quiet. Tony finally looked at her and put his arm around her shoulder.

"When I was a young kid, Grandpa intimidated me. He frightened me until one day when he took my hand and we went for a walk down this very street."

Emmy leaned her head against his shoulder.

"He told me stories about when he was a little boy. After that, he didn't scare me as much. I'm gonna miss him, Emmy."

"I remember when I lost my Grandma and Grandpa Colasanti. I was nine, and I cried so much."

"We didn't expect him to slip away so fast, but at least all his kids were with him at the end."

Three days later, Emmy rode to the wake with Tony, Mama and Heather.

"Could you please turn down the radio, son?" Mama asked.

Tony turned off the radio. Emmy listened to the hum of the

tires on the pavement as everyone was lost in their private thoughts. She squeezed his hand as they walked into the funeral home.

I wonder if this was someone's house at one time? Emmy wondered as she looked at the high-peaked brick funeral home. "Tony," Emmy whispered to get his attention.

"What is it, Em?"

"I don't know what to say to your mother. She's been really quiet the last few days."

"Yeah, I know."

"Like last night when I came over after work. She made dinner, but she didn't say hardly anything. I feel that I should say something to comfort her, but what?"

"You're a comfort to her by just being here, Em. I don't think anyone really knows what to say."

Emmy saw Kristen's parents, and she and Tony walked up to them. Tony tenderly embraced Mrs. Keasling.

She brushed some imaginary lint off of his lapel. "Tony, you look very handsome today. Is that a new suit?"

"Thank you, Aunt Karla, Mama made me buy a new one."

Mrs. Keasling looked at Emmy. She noticed Emmy's dress did not fit well. She hugged her, and then drew her aside and whispered, "Emmy, dear, where did you get that dress?"

"It's not mine. I borrowed it from my sister. I know it doesn't fit right, but..." Emmy bit her lip.

Mrs. Keasling realized that Emmy might not be in a position to buy a new dress. "Kristen has a couple of black dresses that are a bit small on her now. I'm sure she could find one that fits better if you need something for tomorrow."

"Thank you, Mrs. Keasling."

"Kristen will be here soon. She's riding with Derrick. She's taking this pretty hard. I think she cried most of the night."

The crowd started arriving at two and were soon lined up outside the door. Tony pointed to two guys in expensive looking suits. "That's the mayor and the chief of police, Em."

"Your grandpa must have been pretty important."

"I guess you could say that. He knew a lot of people. He

never liked being out in front, if you know what I mean. He stayed in the background, kinda behind the scene. He never wanted to draw attention to himself."

"You never told me what he did for a living."

"Hmmm, he did a lot of things during his life. There are the vineyards back in Italy. He owned Lombardi Distributors here in SoHam. That's a big liquor warehouse. He owned a bunch of other businesses."

"Mama told me a little about Bertucci and Keasling Construction. I checked out their website. How did they get started?"

"The stories I heard growing up is that my father and Uncle Daniel had been best friends all their lives. They roomed together in college and knew they wanted to start a business. They both worked construction, so they felt comfortable in that field."

Emmy watched as Mama talked to Karla. "I still don't see much of a family resemblance. They don't look like sisters at all."

"Yeah, I can see that, too. There's a big difference in their ages."

"It's kinda funny now that I never realized you guys were cousins."

"Now you understand why Kristen and I are so close."

Shortly after two thirty Emmy saw Derrick and Kristen enter the room. Kristen walked over and Tony embraced her. He rubbed her back as she cried. Tony released her and gave her a kiss on the cheek. He pulled his handkerchief out of his back pocket and dried her tears.

"Hi, Emmy. Do I look awful? I've been crying so much."

"Your eyes are red, but that's understandable." Emmy suddenly realized. "Kristen, except for Tony, you're the youngest grandchild."

"Yeah, Tony and I are the two youngest."

Derrick put an arm around his sister. "Kristen has always been Grandpa's favorite grandchild from the day she was born. He spoiled her rotten, and now we're stuck with the result."

"You love me anyway." She jabbed his side.

Emmy noticed that the two Lombardi brothers and their

401

sons congregated together in a group. The lack of interaction between the cousins surprised her, but she didn't feel comfortable mentioning it to Tony or Kristen.

Tony nudged Emmy and whispered, "Kenny's parents are here."

Emmy turned and saw them standing in line. "I should go talk to them." She walked over and Mrs. Colwell hugged her.

"How are you doing, Emmy?"

"I'm all right. Tony, Derrick and Kristen are taking it rather hard. Kristen especially. Did you guys know him?"

Mr. Colwell answered as his wife was distracted by three women. "We certainly knew of him, but we weren't friends. We knew Tony's father, of course. I graduated from Roosevelt a couple of years after Peter Bertucci and Dan Keasling. After college I used their company whenever I needed any work done on the house."

"How's Kenny?" Emmy asked.

"He's okay. He actually called yesterday from somewhere in Texas. I told him about the wake and all. He offered to fly home if you wanted."

"I hope you told him not to."

"I did. He really couldn't. I hope you understand."

"I do."

"You should join your friends, Emmy. We'll talk to you later."

Emmy saw Heather looking at some of the family photos. *No one has said a word about Marco. That's kinda weird. Maybe Heather will tell me.* She walked up and put a hand on Heather's arm. "Hey, Heather, I'm sorry we didn't talk in the car, but I'm happy to see you, even though this is such a sad occasion."

"It has been rather difficult for Mama to lose both parents almost within a single year."

"I can understand. My father's parents passed away within two months of each other." Emmy hesitated, and then plunged right in, "Is Marco coming?"

"No, I talked to him, but he still has classes and can't get away." Heather immediately changed the subject. "Tony told me you are living in an apartment now."

Emmy explained a little about her situation, and then rejoined Tony.

Tony reintroduced Emmy to Uncle Carmen. Uncle Carmen still looked very intimidating to her, even when he smiled. He looked at Emmy and began talking to Tony in Italian. Tony answered him back and Carmen walked away.

"I didn't know you could speak Italian. That was Italian, right?" Emmy asked.

Tony nodded. "Grandma and Grandpa used Italian between themselves all the time. I'm not super fluent, but I understand it enough. Uncle Carmen had to tell me something private. That's why he spoke in Italian."

"It's all right. I understand," Emmy said. "I mean I didn't understand. Daddy's parents spoke Italian, but I never learned it. Grandma Isabel is Italian, but she was born here. I don't think she understands it at all."

"What about your other grandfather?" Tony asked as he nodded to a cousin walking past.

"His name was Sandusky. I think he was Polish or something. Mom doesn't talk about him much. I don't think they got along."

"This is gonna be a long day," Tony said as he looked at the line of people. "We should go see if Mama needs anything."

Tony stood with Mama in the line. She shook hands and introduced him to everyone. "This is Tony, my youngest. He plays football."

Emmy hid behind Tony. She glanced at Mr. Lombardi's casket and at the floral arrangements. She bumped into Tony several times as she shifted her weight from foot to foot.

"Emmy, relax. No one is going to embarrass you."

"You know I don't like to talk to strangers."

"Is this your daughter, Mrs. Bertucci? I thought she was older." An elderly lady asked. "I'm sorry about your grandfather, child. How old are you?"

Emmy looked at Tony.

"This is Emmy Colasanti. She's my friend," Tony

403

explained.

"She looks a lot like your grandmother. I used to live next to Dorothea and Howard." The elderly lady looked around. "I haven't seen Dorothea for several weeks. I should talk to her and see if she needs anything."

Tony nodded his head. "Yes, ma'am."

Emmy looked at the lady then up at Tony.

"It's all right," Tony whispered. "She has Alzheimer's."

Tony and Emmy stayed by Mama's side for the next hour.

"Emmy, do you have to use the bathroom? You're fidgeting so much," Mama asked quietly.

"I'm all right." Emmy smiled because Kenny's parents were next in line.

"We're very sorry for your loss, Maria," Mrs. Colwell said as she embraced Mama.

"It's good to see you, Elly. Thank you for coming."

Emmy's hand flew to her mouth to stifle a laugh.

"Why are you grinning like that, Em?" Tony asked.

"Because Kenny's mom called Mama, Maria. A bunch of other people called her Mama even though they weren't family."

"How are you doing, dear?" Mrs. Colwell asked Emmy.

"I'm okay, Mrs. Colwell. If you talk to Kenny soon, will you tell him hi for me?"

"Of course. You do know he has a cell phone. It's okay for you to call him."

"I hate to bother him. I know he's busy."

"He's never too busy to talk to you. You know that."

Later, Tony, Derrick and Kristen showed Emmy some old photos of their grandfather and family set up on several display boards around the room.

She saw one that looked familiar. "I think I've seen this before."

Derrick removed the photo from the board. "This is a copy of the photo Grandpa always kept in his wallet. Mom said he held it in his hands the day he passed away. The original is in the casket."

"Yes, I remember now," Emmy mentioned. "He showed

404

the original to me at Kristen's party. He looked at the photo, and it brought tears to his eyes to see his young wife."

Tony gasped, and Kristen started to cry.

"I'm sorry. Did I say something wrong?" Emmy asked.

Derrick looked at Emmy with a puzzled expression on his face. "Emmy, Grandpa couldn't possibly have seen Grandma in that picture. His diabetes caused him to go almost totally blind. It got worse and worse until he couldn't see anything except for a little bit of light."

Derrick handed Emmy the photo, and she turned it over to see the back. The old faded writing on the back read, "Howard and Dorothea Lombardi on their wedding day. June 4, 1935." She started to cry, and Tony held her in his arms. Now Emmy realized she had always seen Grandpa Howard holding onto someone's arm.

"Tony, I am such a fool. How could I not have noticed that?"

"It's okay, Emmy. A lot of people didn't realize. He didn't want people to feel sorry for him, so he learned to get around on his own. He didn't go anywhere new or unfamiliar without Grandma, or one of his sons. He remained fiercely proud and very independent-minded, and didn't want anyone to ever feel sorry for him."

Are there any more secrets I need to learn about this family? she wondered.

Chapter Thirty-Nine

"Did you get any sleep last night, Maria?" Karla asked as she walked into Mama's kitchen.

"Not really. I kept thinking about Daddy's mass. I was too keyed up." Mama's eyes were still red from the previous day.

"I'm still mad at Marco for not coming to the funeral." Karla frowned. "Carmen's and Vincent's kids made it. Marco should have been there for you."

Mama started to say something, but Karla interrupted. "You can't keep making excuses for him. He needs to come home and clear the air."

"He will when he's ready."

"Carmen made an appointment to see the attorney about Daddy's will. I don't even want to think about that stuff yet."

The sisters paused for a moment as they thought about their parents.

Mama sighed. Then she checked her kitchen fridge. "I don't need to cook for a few days. Maybe you should take something home."

Karla answered, "We did yesterday, remember? Our fridge is full, too."

"I thought the luncheon after the funeral service turned out nice," Mama said as she closed the refrigerator door.

"These are so good." Karla grabbed a dinner roll from the scuffed, wooden breadbox on the counter. "Carmen told me that Mr. Barclay didn't charge him for the use of the country club."

"His father and our father were pretty close. Dennison Claymore Barclay. Such a formal sounding name."

"He was probably named for one of their Revolutionary War ancestors."

"It was very generous of Douglas to let us use the facilities."

"I still call him Mr. Barclay." Karla finished her roll and reached for another one.

"That's because you're so much younger. Mother always insisted we call older people Mr. and Mrs. I call him Douglas

406

because he's my age."

"And look at you. Everyone called you Mama at the wake," Karla teased.

"They did not. They called me Mrs. Bertucci. Most of them did, anyway." Mama looked out the window and shook her head as she saw Tony toss Emmy in the air and catch her. "I've never seen the cathedral so full, and I loved the mass."

"Except for the part when the bishop almost tripped and fell," Karla said and then chuckled. "I wonder how much wine he drank."

The back door flew open with a bang. Karla dropped her roll.

"Put me down, you dork!" Emmy shrieked.

Mama and Karla turned to look as Tony carried Emmy into the kitchen.

"Mama, did you see what he was doing?"

"Yes, dear, I did." Mama shook her finger at Tony. "You shouldn't do that."

Tony set Emmy down, and they both laughed.

"Hi, Aunt Karla, should I carry you around, too?" He moved toward her.

She put her hand to his chest. "Not if you want to be able to keep playing football."

Mama placed her arm around Emmy's waist and muttered, "Still too skinny."

Tony opened the fridge. "Is there anything to eat?"

"Take a look, Tony. You might find something," Karla replied sarcastically.

Emmy pushed some sweaty hair off of her face. "Mrs. Keasling, would you remember to thank Kristen for letting me borrow her dress."

"Of course, dear. You looked so charming yesterday." Karla looked at Emmy. "You look like yourself today—torn jeans and a t-shirt. So fitting for you, but every woman needs a simple black dress in her closet, and I loved how Kristen fixed your hair."

"Yeah, I like when you have braids in your hair, Em. You want some lasagna?" Tony asked.

"Is there any chicken left?" Emmy ducked under his arm and peeked into the fridge. She grabbed a chicken leg and took a bite. "I'll get the dress back to Kristen right away."

"Don't be silly. You can keep it. It doesn't fit Kristen anymore."

"Emmy, don't talk with food in your mouth," Mama scolded as she opened the silverware drawer.

"Thanks, Mrs. Keasling. I really appreciate it."

Karla patted Emmy's shoulder. "You're welcome. Oh, Maria, we need to sort through those photos today. Some of them belong to Carmen and Vincent, but most of them are yours."

"We can do that a little later. I want to organize this refrigerator." Mama pulled a dish from the fridge, lifted the lid, smelled it and held it out to Karla. "I don't even know what this is supposed to be."

"File it under 'g.'" Karla emptied the contents down the garbage disposal.

Tony and Emmy ate lunch, and then went outside. Tony sat on the front porch steps. He reached down, picked up his football and began tossing it from one hand to the other.

Emmy stood on the sidewalk in front of him. "Aren't you hot in that jersey?"

"Not really. It's thin."

She grabbed the football away from him. "Would you wear a jersey I bought you if it had... say... the number fifty-one on it?"

"Why would you do that? You know I've always worn fifty-two."

"I'm teasing. Come on. Let's play football."

Only a few photos remained to be sorted. Mama picked one up. She glanced at it briefly and was about to set it in her pile when she took a closer look.

"Oh, my." Mama sighed and put her hand over her heart. "Karla, look at this."

Karla scooted closer on the couch. Mama handed it to Karla.

"I've never seen this before. Where did you find it?"

"It must have been in that box I found at Dad's place. The

people at the funeral home must have displayed it, but I don't remember seeing it anywhere."

"Aw. The little girl is holding his hand. Too cute. She's looking up at him, and her eyes are sparkling." Karla paused. "I don't recognize the building behind them. Do you?"

"That's an apartment building Carmen owned. They tore it down to put up a strip mall."

"Do you know the little girl? Maybe she lived nearby."

Mama grinned.

"It can't be Kristen with that dark hair. I wonder who took the picture? It doesn't say anything on the back?" Karla handed the photo back. "Do you know?"

"I'm positive..." Mama paused as she heard a scream outside. "Come with me. I want you to see this."

"Where are we going?"

Mama gingerly held the photo in her hand as she led Karla out the front door and onto the wooden porch.

"Hey, Tony, I bet you can't catch me," Emmy yelled as she took off running with the football.

"I bet I can." He caught her and tackled her.

She squealed like a little girl. "Get off of me, you big goof."

"I thought we were playing tackle football," Tony said as he held Emmy on the ground by sitting on her.

Mama pointed to Emmy. "Karla, do you see that purple ribbon in her hair?"

"Yeah, she wore it yesterday, too."

"Take a close look at the photo." Mama handed the photo to Karla.

"What am I looking for?"

"Look at her hair. Part of it's in a ponytail, but the rest is kinda wild."

Karla looked closer. "Is that a piece of ribbon in her hair?"

"Yes, it's a piece of purple ribbon."

"Get the hell off of me this instant before I knock your block off. That tickles. I'm gonna tell Mama," Emmy yelled and punched Tony in the leg. Then she laughed as Tony kept tickling

409

the back of her knees.

Mama glanced at Emmy and Tony, and then smiled at Karla. "I remember when Carmen and Vincent used to play rough with you. Mother would shake a wooden spoon at them, but Daddy would laugh and encourage them."

"I remember some of that." Karla laughed and pointed a finger at Emmy. "She still acts like a little kid."

Tony stood up and Emmy threw the football as hard as she could at him. Tony caught it and turned to run away, so Emmy jumped on his back. He purposely fell to the ground. She punched the ball out of his hands. "You fumbled! My ball."

"Oh, my God!" Karla exclaimed.

"Do you get it now?" Mama nodded her head.

"Are you sure?" Karla handed the photo back to Mama.

"Positive. I don't know why I didn't remember this. Maybe the way they're playing in the yard now triggered something in my memory. Anyway, part of her hair is in a ponytail, but the rest of it is just hanging loose and free. When Tony stayed with his Grandma during that time..."

"I know when you mean."

"I came over to see him one day, and I remember him playing with a little girl from the upstairs apartment. He came running in the house saying something about kissing a girl, and they were going to get married."

"Get married?"

Mama grinned. "I think it was her idea. He was not quite four."

Tony threw the ball to Emmy. "Try to get past me and score a touchdown, Em. I bet you can't."

Emmy caught the ball and scrambled back and forth across the lush green lawn. Tony cornered her by the porch, so she ran up the steps. She stood with her back to Mama.

"Protect me, Mama! Tony's trying to tackle me again." Her heart raced, and her chest heaved.

Mama threw her arms around Emmy and held her protectively. "Will you hold still for a minute, Emmy. I want to show you a photo."

410

"Okay."

Mama let go, and Emmy threw a perfect spiral to Tony. He caught the ball and held it in the crook of his arm.

Emmy glanced at the photo, and then yelled at Tony. "Don't throw the ball at me. Mama wants me to look at this."

Emmy took the photo from Mama and stared at it for a few seconds. She looked at Tony. She noticed how he was standing. Then she noted his jersey again. "Number fifty-two," she whispered. She peered closely at the little boy in the photo. "He's wearing number fifty-two and holding a football." Her heart began to race even faster. She gazed intently at the little girl in the photo. She concentrated on the rag doll in the girl's small hand. "Doll Kitty," she whispered. "It's my Doll Kitty." She turned to face Mama as tears filled her eyes. "This is me and Tony, isn't it?"

"Yes, baby, it is. Do you remember much about it? Do you remember living in that apartment?"

"Not really, but I do sometimes have quick flashes of memory about him. He's always a little boy. I haven't thought of Doll Kitty for years." She turned and waved at Tony. "Come here."

"Hey, what's going on? You all right?" Tony walked up the steps and stood on the top one.

Emmy handed the photo to him. He tossed the football over his shoulder and looked at the picture. He tilted his head as he gazed at the little girl. No one spoke a word for what seemed an eternity. Finally, Tony whispered, "Emmy." He handed the photo to Mama and held out his arms. Emmy moved close and Tony hugged her.

She put her head on his chest and let the tears flow as she asked, "Where did you go? We were 'posed to get married."

Mama smiled. "Let's go inside, Karla."

"Do you really know who took the picture?" Karla asked.

Mama nodded emphatically.

Karla asked, "How can you be so positive?"

Mama Bertucci sighed contentedly and put her arm around Karla's waist as they turned and walked back into the house.

"I'm positive because I took the photo."

411